Sowing Dragon Teeth

A Novel of the Battle of Lexington and Concord

Dana R. Dillon

MILFORD
HOUSE

an imprint of Sunbury Press, Inc.
Mechanicsburg, PA USA

MILFORD HOUSE

an imprint of Sunbury Press, Inc.
Mechanicsburg, PA USA

For information about special discounts for bulk purchases, please contact Sunbury Press Orders Dept. at (855) 338-8359 or orders@sunburypress.com.

To request one of our authors for speaking engagements or book signings, please contact Sunbury Press Publicity Dept. at publicity@sunburypress.com.

FIRST MILFORD HOUSE PRESS EDITION: July 2024

Set in Adobe Garamond Pro | Interior design by Crystal Devine | Cover by Lawrence Knorr | Edited by Lawrence Knorr.

Publisher's Cataloging-in-Publication Data
Names: Dillon, Dana R., author.
Title: Sowing dragon teeth : a novel of the Battle of Lexington and Concord / Dana R. Dillon.
Description: First trade paperback edition. | Mechanicsburg, PA : Milford House Press, 2024.
Summary: On April 19, 1775, an enslaved African American and a tavern-owner turned reluctant-Patriot must battle the British regulars and an aristocrat hiding a carnal secret to stop the British raid to destroy Minutemen arms at Concord.
Identifiers: ISBN : 979-8-88819-211-5 (softcover).
Subjects: FICTION / Historical / Colonial America & Revolution | FICTION / African American & Black / Historical | FICTION / Literary.

Designed in the USA
0 1 1 2 3 5 8 13 21 34 55

For the Love of Books!

To my deeply loved and lovely wife, Kelly S Dillon,
my most kindhearted critic and fiercest defender.

———————

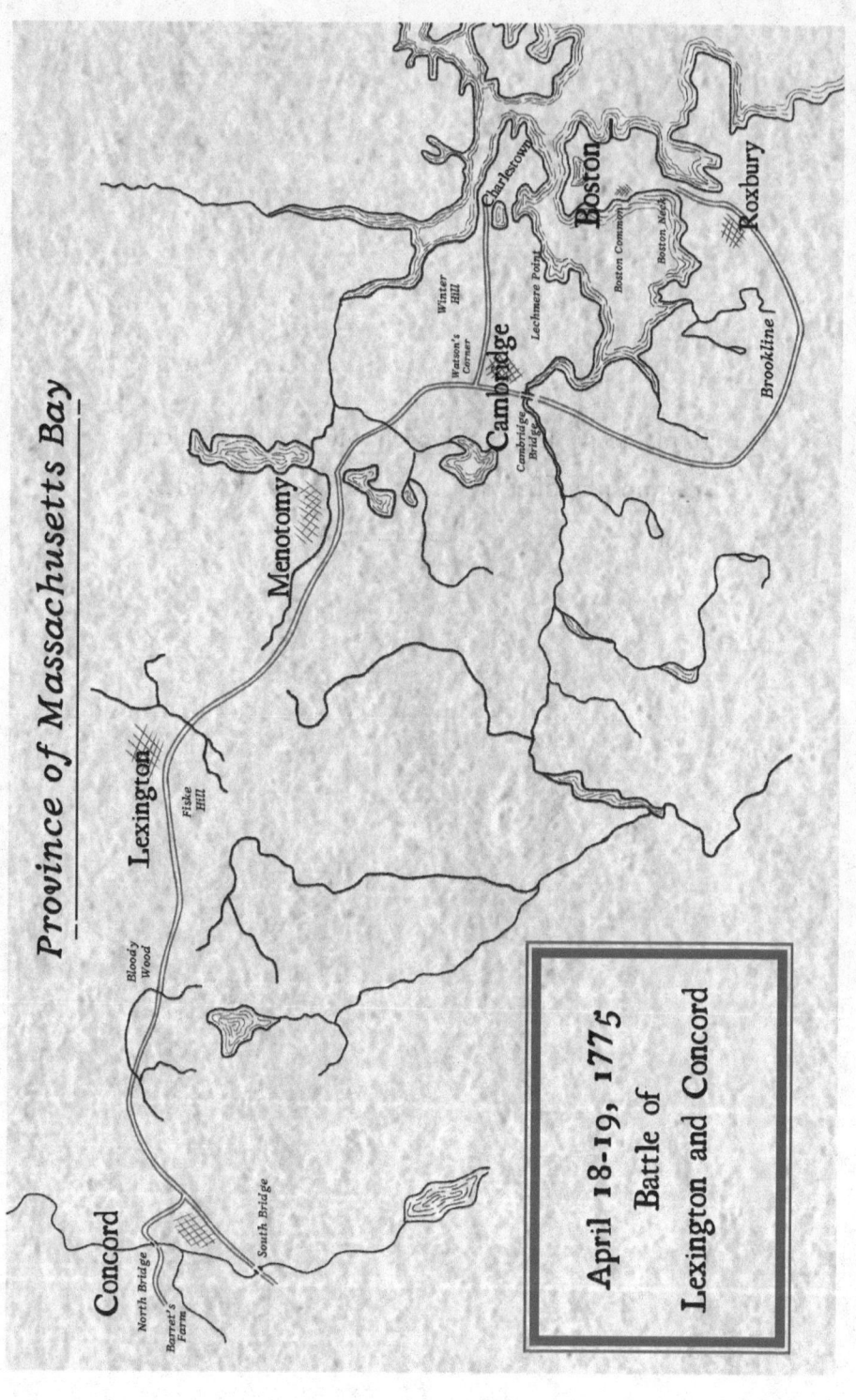

Province of Massachusetts Bay

Concord
North Bridge
Barret's Farm
South Bridge
Bloody Wood
Lexington
Fiske Hill
Menotomy
Watson's Corner
Winter Hill
Charlestown
Cambridge
Cambridge Bridge
Lechmere Point
Boston
Boston Common
Boston Neck
Brookline
Roxbury

April 18-19, 1775
Battle of
Lexington and Concord

Prologue

Wednesday's Child
July 4, 1764

Nine o'clock ante meridiem.

Tears rolled down Quock's cheeks onto his patched, threadbare shirt. Around him, people browsed the belongings of the dead Van family, picking some things up, carrying other things away. Through the gloom of his sorrow, Quock wondered if any of the people were the Creditors. Missus Isenberg said he was being sold to satisfy the Creditors.

A yellow butterfly fluttered by. Quock watched it dip and glide in the warm morning air. It was not sad or afraid. It sailed to Missus Isenberg and landed on a flower on her hat, slowly opening and closing its wings. A big man was talking to Missus Isenberg and nodding toward Quock.

"How old is he?"

"Six, and he's healthy," said Missus Isenberg.

"He's crying."

"He just lost his mother. The pox struck the whole Van family. His mother was their slave. My husband found him in her room holding her hand."

"The pox was bad here?"

"Not as bad as it could have been. Thank God for variolation. Doctor Warren inoculated Quock, but he was too late for the others." Missus Isenberg raised a bent finger to her mouth, "I don't normally engage in this kind of . . ." She rolled her hand, her eyebrows raised in a plea for understanding, ". . . trade, but we knew the family. We're hoping to find a good place for Quock."

"Anybody considering?"

"There's a supercargo who wants a cabin boy he can sell when he gets to Barbados." Missus Isenberg spoke softly, "Eli and I prefer something better." The big man grunted. Quock knew they were talking about him, but he didn't understand.

The big man asked Quock, "Are you in pain?" The big man smelled of sweat and new-mown hay. His face was weathered and brown; the dark brown hair under his straw hat was frosted with gray, but his blue eyes were clear.

"No, sir."

"Can you stand?" The big man took off his hat to wipe the sweat off his brow. Quock stared at his shiny baldness and wanted to touch it, but he was too timid.

"Yes sir," Quock stood. The big man made a circle with his finger. Quock walked in a small circle.

"Are you interested?" Missus Isenberg asked.

"I don't know how my church would feel about me bringing home a slave."

"There were slaves in the Bible."

"Yeah, just the same . . . He's kinda small."

"You're investing in a boy that will grow to help you."

The two adults continued to talk, but Quock's thoughts returned to his mother. He sat back down and put his head in his hands. Despite watching the Van family die one by one and enduring his mother's painful death, he wished she somehow might come back. A woman called his name; he looked up, hoping it was her.

"Quock, get your things," Missus Isenberg was talking to him. "Mister Nithercott has . . . You're going with Mister Nithercott." The big man was walking back from his wagon.

"Yes, ma'am." Quock tried to pick up his trunk, but it was too heavy. He started to drag it.

"Here," Nithercott picked up the trunk and carried it to the wagon. "I haven't owned you five minutes, and I'm already carrying for yuh."

"Yes, sir. It's all right, I can carry it," Quock ran beside him.

Mister Nithercott put the trunk on the flatbed of his hay wagon and lifted Quock in next.

"Goodbye, Quock," Missus Isenberg reached into the wagon and rubbed his head. "You are going to a good family."

"Goodbye." Quock waved to the only living person he knew.

Mister Nithercott climbed up onto the wagon seat, took the reins, and looked back, "Climb up here and sit next to me, Quock. This is Massachusetts, not Virginia."

Quock climbed up onto the plank seat next to him. Turning around, Quock watched his home recede in the distance. His heart swelled with grief and homesickness. He buried his head in Mister Nithercott's shoulder and cried.

"We're going to Lexington," said Mister Nithercott, letting Quock cry. "Our farm is just outside. It's about seven or eight hours on this old wagon." Mister Nithercott continued to speak in an unassuming tone as the cart rattled along the road. He spoke about the farm, his family, the church, and community, "It's not Eden, but as close as you'll get in New England."

While Mister Nithercott talked, Quock's misery drained away with his tears. He looked up to see the world passing by the cart. They had already left the built-up areas of Boston. The road ran on a narrow strip of land with water on both sides. "Boston Neck," said Mister Nithercott. The strip ended with high earthen walls and an open gate, "During the war, soldiers guarded it."

"Were you in the war?" asked Quock.

Mister Nithercott shook the reins as the horses pulled the wagon off the Neck, "I fought the King's enemies in both of 'em. King George's War, then the last one against the French and Injuns."

"Why?"

Mister Nithercott side-eyed Quock. "Missus Nithercott asks me the same question. I tell her it won't get done if I don't do it. I've been talking about myself; tell me about you."

"I'm six and a half years old."

"Yeah, what else?"

"My mamma died."

"We have that in common." Mister Nithercott's face was solemn. "When I was about your age, the pox killed my family, too. Mister and Missus Lee adopted me." Mister Nithercott wiped at something in his eyes.

"Do you have children?"

He smiled, "Yes, I do, three girls. Charity is the oldest, Hope, and the youngest is Faith. She's five, just a little younger than you. All of them pretty as their mother."

"No boys?"

"Daniel, but he passed away before his first birthday. Missus Nithercott hasn't gotten over it yet." Mister Nithercott cleared his throat. "He'd be about your age."

"I'm sorry for your loss." It was a saying he had heard often since his mother died.

The ride to his new home was sunny and fun. Quock asked lots of questions, and Mister Nithercott was never impatient with him. When he could no longer sit still, Mister Nithercott let Quock run and gambol beside the wagon. Mister Nithercott shared his dinner when they stopped for a picnic. Finally, they drove through Lexington and arrived at Mister Nithercott's farm near sunset. Three girls ran to the wagon. They stared at Quock as Mister Nithercott guided the wagon to the barn.

"Daddy, you said you were going to get a boy to work on the farm," whined the tallest one, eyeing Quock with a frown.

"Quock is a boy, Charity, and he will work on the farm," Mister Nithercott unhitched the wagon from the horses.

"Oh!" She stomped off to the house.

"Is he going to help with the chores?" asked the other older girl with raised eyebrows.

Mister Nithercott took the reins of the horses and led them to their stalls in the barn. "Yes, he is Hope. He is going to learn to help me." He loosened the buckles on the harnesses. "Your mother has three girls to help her." Hope rolled her eyes, and she left, too.

Signaling Quock to watch what he was doing, Mister Nithercott took the harness off the horses and hung them on pegs. He brushed the horses and made sure they had oats, hay, and water. The whole while, Faith, the youngest girl, watched Quock, silent, her eyes wide. When Quock edged closer to her to avoid the moving horses, Faith, with deep concentration, reached out and touched his hair. They smiled at each other. When Mister Nithercott finished caring for the horses, the three of them went into the house.

Inside, Missus Nithercott must have heard about Quock from the girls because she smiled and evinced no surprise as she served him and Mister Nithercott a supper of cheese, bread, and strawberry preserves. Afterward, she led Quock to a small room off the kitchen. Shelves loaded with jars, bottles, and pots lined the far wall. A rope bed was against the inside wall. The mattress had a linen tick stuffed with pea shucks, a plain linen blanket and a woolen rose blanket lay folded on top. Mister Nithercott put Quock's trunk at the foot.

"We'll do more for you tomorrow," said Missus Nithercott. Quock liked her. She smelled of baked bread, like his mother.

A bed of his own was a new experience, both luxurious and lonely. He lay on his new bed, listening to the girls move along the floor over his head. Quock had always slept with his mother. Laying in the dark, remembering her, tears seeped from his eyes. Quock wondered if Missus Nithercott would let him sleep with her. She was still in the kitchen talking in a low voice to Mister Nithercott, but he could tell she was vexed. He could hear only snatches of their conversation.

". . . Why a slave? . . . What will the neighbors say?" Mister Nithercott responded in patient tones. Quock fell asleep before they finished.

The next morning, Mister Nithercott woke Quock before sunrise. He had never been on a farm and stared in wonder while Mister Nithercott milked the cows. Quock helped shoo the cows out to the pasture, then scattered corn for chickens while the girls gathered eggs. Quock and Faith carried a bucket of well water between them into the kitchen. They all ate breakfast together at the kitchen table, red velvet hash with a fried egg on top and milk still warm from the cow. Not his Mama's cooking, but pretty good.

After breakfast, Mister Nithercott took him around the farm, showing him the fields, livestock, and buildings as they worked. After they ate their dinners, Mister Nithercott told Quock he was still too small for the other chores and let him go with Faith.

Faith showed him around the farm to the places interesting to kids. At the apple orchard, there was an old sailor's hammock strung between two trees. Faith's neighbor Isaac, who was also six and a half years old, was swinging in the hammock. They took turns crawling in and pushing each other, all three of them screaming with delight as they swayed wildly. Quock laughed for the first time since his mother died. They ate apples and played there until Missus Nithercott rang the dinner bell.

The next morning, Mister Nithercott was in the yard behind the house chopping kitchen wood and splitting it down to stove size. Quock was carrying the pieces to the wood box by the kitchen door. Missus Nithercott called to them through the window, "There's a cart coming down the road, and I think it's the parson and Blanche."

Bending over setting a small log, Mister Nithercott stood up straight. "You know why he's coming," and nodded toward Quock.

"Did you expect any different?" Her face was pinched with disapproval.

Quock felt a pang of fear in his stomach. Would he have to move again?

Mister Nithercott laid his ax against the stump. "Tuck in your shirt; you're going to meet the Reverend Jonas Clarke."

Quock brushed off his shirt and put on his hat. He wasn't wearing shoes or stockings, but hopping on one foot at a time, he buckled his breeches at the knee and followed Mister Nithercott around to the front of the house. Mister Nithercott, on the other hand, did nothing other than sweep the wood chips off his shirt, and he left his hat and coat on the log pile.

At the front of the house a one-horse dogcart rolled through the gate packed with the Clarke family. The kids were already jumping out of the moving cart. Mister Nithercott took the horse's head and tied it to the hitching post.

"How ya' Jonas," he touched his forehead politely to Missus Clarke, "To what do we owe the pleasure?"

"I wanted to meet the newest member of my flock," Reverend Clarke smiled at Quock. Further talk was interrupted as Mister Nithercott helped Missus Blanche Clarke down. The kids from both families were already running toward the apple orchard behind the house. Chastity Nithercott invited Blanche into the house for tea.

Quiet restored, Clarke reached out and held Quock's shoulder. "What's your name, lad?"

"Quock," said Mister Nithercott.

"Where are your parents?"

"He doesn't have a family," said Mister Nithercott.

"The boy can speak for himself, Ebenezer." Clarke asked, "Where is your family?"

"Mama died of pox," Quock's voice was just above a whisper. "Daddy lives in New Jersey."

"I'm sorry to hear about your mother, but be assured she walks with God."

"Thank you, sir." The Reverend seemed to be about the same age as Mister Nithercott. His coat was black, but he also wore a straw hat.

"Do you know your letters?"

"Yes sir, Mister Van taught me."

"His former master was a bookseller in Boston," said Nithercott. "I plan to send him to school, just like the girls."

"Very good. Christians should be able to read God's word. I hope we will see you in church this Sunday."

"Yes, sir." Quock looked into the faces of the two men, looking for direction.

"Come in for a dish of tea," Nithercott extended his right hand to the door.

Clarke patted Quock on the head, "You are fortunate to come into the service of the Nithercott family. They are pillars of the community."

"Thank you, sir." The tight grip of anxiety lessened its hold on Quock's heart. He was relieved that Clarke wasn't taking him away, but why was he here then?

"Quock, finish up the kitchen wood then you can play with the others."

"Yes sir," Quock bowed to Reverend Clarke and then ran around to the back of the house. He wanted to play with the other children, but he felt that Nithercott and Clarke still had more to say about him. He piled the finished wood into the box, then ran back to the front of the house. Ducking below the sill, he ran to the window nearest Mister Nithercott's chair. He was rewarded with the sound of Nithercott's voice. ". . . blessed with girls. I'm not getting any younger, and I need help with the farming."

"You know how we feel about slavery in this community, Eb."

"Jonas, I wasn't looking for a slave. I wanted an indentured servant or an orphan. I was leaving Boston empty-handed and stopped at an estate sale to get something to bring Chase. Quock was sitting on a trunk crying. It was pitiful." There was a pause, "If I hadn't bought him, he would've ended up cutting sugar cane in the Carib."

"You're a great humanitarian, Eb." No one spoke for several long seconds. Quock wished he could see their faces. The parson spoke, "Now, from what you tell me, this boy, through no fault other than the color of his skin, was born into slavery."

"I suppose."

Quock had never heard white folks talk about black folk like that. He kneeled up, getting his ear closer to the window.

"People aren't livestock, Eb. They have a divine spirit. It is not illegal to own a slave, but neither is it moral to keep a man in perpetual servitude."

"There's slavery in the Bible, Jonas. You marry and baptize slaves."

"You're right; I have seen the injury of slavery up close. Families torn apart—children snatched from their mother's arms."

Quock remembered his mama crying when they left Daddy in New Jersey.

"Jesus's promise to us was freedom. Slavery is an evil cargo we brought with us from the Old World, but it is a moral burden New England need not bear."

Another pause.

"He cost all the money I had with me."

"I am not disputing your need, Ebenezer. I have no authority to tell you what to do with Quock, but even Old Testament slaves could free themselves from their servitude."

"If he does right by me, I was planning to free him when he comes of age. By then, God willing, my girls will be married, and their husbands will help with the farm."

Quock's heart leaped. He slapped his hands over his mouth to keep from crying out. It could happen! His mother would be so happy. As she lay dying, she had told him about her dreams for him. Quock was to be more than a slave. She told him to live a life of consequence. He didn't understand what she meant, but it seemed that gaining his freedom was a step toward consequence.

"That is a moral solution. I wish all the problems of my parish could be solved so easily."

Quock heard the children laughing and snuck away to join their play. For the first time since his mother died, relief and joy filled his soul. Isaac and Faith saw Quock and waved, "Hurry! Join us!" As Quock ran toward them, he could see dark thunderheads forming on the eastern horizon.

Eleven years later . . .

Chapter One

Boston, Province of Massachusetts Bay
April 18, 1775

Half past six o'clock post meridiem.

Dressed in his best uniform coat, a silver gorget with "23rd" engraved on its polished surface hanging around his throat, and Welsh Fusilier's bearskin cap on his head, Lieutenant Colonel Llewellyn Caradoc hurried to his appointment, skipping over puddles in his rush.

He carried two letters in his pockets. The first was a list of officers whose interests he intended to advocate, good lieutenants and captains aging in place with no other prospect for advancement. The second letter was a mystery. Governor Gage's adjutant, Major Stephen Kemble, had summoned him at dinner and given Llewellyn the letter.

"When may I open it?"

"Later," Kemble said. "Keep it safe and tell no one you have it."

Just as he thought he may have missed it and was ready to turn back, Llewellyn found the green-painted wooden sign adorned with a carving of a Golden Fleece hanging above the tavern door—Green's Fleece. A chalkboard in the window read, "No Tories, No Whigs, Beer Drinkers Welcome."

Llewellyn pulled out his watch. He was not late. His shoes were not too muddy, considering the state of Boston's streets. He took off his bearskin cap, tucked it under his arm, straightened his shoulders, and pulled open the door.

The taproom was half-full. A woman lit candles, illuminating the room with a golden patina. He'd missed his dinner because of the secret business with Kemble, and the odors of cooking food made his mouth

1

water and stomach grumble. Near the window, with their backs to the setting sun, a string quartet was just finishing a ballad. "Seat yourself anywhere," said a man wearing a green apron. "I'll be right with you."

The nearest empty place was a typical battered tavern table, sturdy and worn smooth to his touch. He pulled out a chair and put his cap on it. An American side-eyed him, but Llewellyn didn't care; bearskin caps cost six quid.

The tavern appeared much the same as any tavern he'd visited in Wales or England, with just enough differences to make it exotically American. The string quartet included a Negro playing a banjo, and at a nearby table drinking with two white men sat the first Indian Llewellyn had ever seen. He wore a linen shirt and moccasins, and his head was shaved except for a small circle of standing hair on the crown. To keep from staring Llewellyn returned to examining the room. A framed print illustration of George III in its proper place behind the bar reassured him, but hanging next to it was a same size, nine red and white stripe embroidery—the flag of the Sons of Liberty—*bloody terrorists*.

They did not stare, but he could feel the eyes of the Americans on him, and silence descended on the room. Llewellyn wondered why Robert had asked to meet here. Boston was bursting with taverns; why this one? Just loud enough for Llewellyn's ears, someone behind him said to his companion, "And a military governor in time of peace. Lord knows what parliament is thinking." Llewellyn wished he were supping in the warm comradeship of the officer's mess.

Finished with the ballad, the quartet began playing *The White Cockade*, the tune of the Scottish rebellion. As if it were a secret signal to the American patrons, they stood up almost together and began settling their bills. They flowed out of the tavern smiling at each other; some threw smirks at Llewellyn, but they parted for a tall, scarlet-coated king's officer stepping through the open door. To Llewellyn's relief, it was Lord Robert Dandridge.

Robert was ten years younger than Llewellyn and seemed to have barely aged from their service together in the last war, but there were welcome signs of maturity. Robert wasn't wearing one of those ridiculous macaroni wigs that Llewellyn had so disliked. Instead, his blond hair was neatly pulled back and tied with a black ribbon. His coat was tailored from fine broadcloth but no foppish ribbon or lace. Just enough decoration to convey his rank and position. The effeminate adolescent he remembered from the last war had grown into the fullness of manhood.

"M'Lord . . . ," began Llewellyn, standing up and moving to attention.

"Robert, for God's sake, Llewellyn, call me Robert." Robert took Llewellyn's hand and shook it vigorously.

Robert's agelessness and bright scarlet coat made Llewellyn conscious of his own aged and impoverished appearance. His black hair was touched with grey, more so since Elizabeth had died. He had lost weight, too, more than a stone, and his coat hung on him like a scarecrow. Further, his coat was madder red, rather than Robert's scarlet; to Llewellyn, the difference in shades was glaring.

"Robert, I beg your pardon for missing you at dinner. I was drilling the regiment. I've been away for months, and I needed to knock off some rust." A white lie so he didn't have to explain his meeting with Kemble or the secret letter.

"Lord, I miss that Welsh accent of yours." Robert tossed his cocked hat on top of Llewellyn's grenadier's cap, knocking them both to the floor.

Llewellyn picked up the hats. The lush beaver felt of Robert's hat contrasted with the rough linen lining of his grenadier's cap. Llewellyn gently brushed the bearskin, "Elizabeth bought this for me for our twentieth anniversary."

"Forgive me, Llewellyn. I meant no disrespect," Putting a hand on Llewellyn's shoulder, "I was very sad to hear about Elizabeth. What a wonderful woman she was. I miss her dearly."

Llewellyn appreciated the many expressions of sympathy from his friends, but each new condolence was a fresh twist to the pain that would not go away. "I am deeply obliged to you, Robert, for allowing me to stay in Britain to attend to Elizabeth and the funeral."

"There are no obligations between us, brother. It was the very least I could do. How is your family?"

"It was a terrible blow for the children. I settled them in Ludlow with my sister. Don't know what I would have done without her." Trapped by the conventions of friendship, Llewellyn added, "I visited Lady Clara on my way through London."

Lowering his head, Robert gave a peculiar high-pitched laugh.

"She sends her love." Robert's wife had not sent her love but rather a litany of complaints, both great and petty. Llewellyn had been taken aback by her contempt for her husband.

"Ah! An ocean between us makes marriage easier to bear." Robert's response seemed practiced but still uneasy, and his smile feigned.

"But I forget myself," Llewellyn changed the subject. "Congratulations on your promotion and title." At one time, he had resented the younger man's inherited wealth and peerage. As a line officer with limited means and influence, Llewellyn endured near poverty and years of plodding up the ranks. Since their time in the German states, Robert had inherited more wealth, an earldom, and now Llewellyn's former lieutenant was a brigadier and his commander.

"Ha-ha! Yes, it was clever of me to have my uncle marry a barren woman and to depart his worldly troubles, leaving me his only heir, wasn't it?"

"Posh Robert, I give you joy," with maturity; however, Llewellyn learned to love his calling to Army service and to show proper deference to those of higher birth in order to leverage his connections for promotion and patronage.

"I don't mean to sneer at my good fortune, but I value more that I stood against the French on the Minden plain than acceded to an earldom."

"You have both!"

"Ah, Llewellyn! You missed the point entirely," Robert smiled, rapped the table, then waved his hand, "I was trying to be humble, but enough of that. Let's sup, drink, and reminisce on our brave youths."

"There's no better way to spend an evening."

"Tell me, how was your passage? You were on the *Nautilus*?" asked Robert.

"Passing safe. One of the passengers is the quartermaster for the Dragoons. Fine fellow, good conversation." Unlike himself. Llewellyn knew that he had been a sad companion, mourning his wife and spending most of his time staring out to sea.

"Was he carrying dispatches?"

Llewellyn was surprised that Robert knew about them, "Yes, all very hush-hush. When we landed, he went straight to Province House to deliver the pouch."

"I dread the content of those papers."

Llewellyn's eyes widened for a moment. He scanned the room to see if anyone had overheard and touched the pocket with Gage's secret letter. He thought about telling Robert about the letter but, seeing the pub keeper approach, instead cleared his throat and said, "During the passage, I read your pamphlet on cannon in maneuvers and much admired it. Very insightful. Changed the way I think on artillery."

"Ah, my efforts are undeserving of praise." Robert smiled with delight, "But your opinion means a great deal to me. When we were on the continent, I wanted so much to be like you. At Minden, the French cavalry broke on your company like waves against a cliff."

Llewellyn smiled. Now Robert had touched his pride.

"May I suggest a flip, gentlemen? To chase away the spring chill," asked the pub keeper standing at their elbows. "We serve the best in Boston."

"Brilliant, two glasses, and we'd like to sup," said Robert.

"We make the best clam chowder, and we have some squabs."

"Wild pigeon, is it? Passenger pigeon?"

"Of course."

"Excellent, make it so," said Robert.

"I was surprised the regiment was transferred here in my absence," said Llewellyn after the pub keeper left.

"We are still too few." Robert looked about the tavern, but it had emptied except for the pub keeper and his wife. "Parliament's acts to force the people of Boston to return to a state of obedience had the reverse effect. Rather than obedience, we have sedition, and the country people are arming against us."

"Will they rebel?" The Yanks' open animosity to the British troops had distressed Llewellyn.

"We are on razor's edge, I'm afraid." Robert's lips were a thin line.

Llewellyn shook his head. Civil war, brother against brother, seemed unreal, even unnatural.

"Your flip, sir." The pub keeper returned with their glasses. "Your chowder will be right up."

To Llewellyn's surprise, Robert leaned back in his chair and shined an engaging smile on the publican. He picked up the frothy mug and took a long pull. Holding up the mug, he said, "A noble beverage."

Taking his cue from Robert, Llewellyn raised his glass, "Iechyd Da." The flip was warm, creamy, and delicious. "Lush. Like warm velvet stout."

"Very healthy, too." The pub keeper returned a satisfied smile.

When the pub keeper was out of earshot, Llewellyn asked, "Is this crisis unsalvageable?"

"We've been sitting on a powder keg since they destroyed the tea. Three weeks ago, I took the brigade on a demonstration march. The militia turned out and even manned two cannons, meaning to block a bridge."

"Zounds!" Llewellyn put down his mug harder than he expected, spilling some of the warm drink on his hand. "Attack his majesty's troops? Have they gone mad?"

"The militia fled the moment they saw us, but we found the cannon fully loaded."

"That is my experience with militia," nodded Llewellyn. During the French coast expedition in the last war, he remembered the French militia firing a ragged volley too far out for good effect, then running behind the walls of their fort. "Unless they have a stonewall or a proper parapet, they flee on the first volley."

The pub keeper returned with bowls. "Your chowder, gentlemen. The pigeons will be right up." To Llewellyn, it smelled and tasted heavenly.

"Capital," said Robert. "This soup is lovely."

"My pleasure." The pub keeper smiled. "I couldn't help but overhear you gentlemen talk about the war. Did you serve in North America? I was a captain in the 60th foot."

"Ah! You're an officer," said Robert.

"A pub keeper?" Llewellyn raised his head from the soup. The American had the likable smile and proud belly of a prosperous tavern owner—but not an officer and hardly the figure of a fighting man.

"I am a Lieutenant Colonel in the militia and a proud member of the Ancient and Honorable Artillery Company," said the pub keeper.

"Oh." For Llewellyn, 'militia' qualified the rank.

To Llewellyn's surprise, Robert raised his glass and asked, "May we have a drink with you? I am Robert Dandridge, and my friend Llewellyn Caradoc. We served together in Minden during the last war."

"With pleasure. Jason Green." He shook their hands. "I will pour myself a mug and be right with you."

While Jason filled his glass, Robert pulled over another chair. Llewellyn had hoped for a private meal. He stroked the list still in his pocket. Now Robert was inviting strangers into their conversation. To what purpose?

"So, Colonel Green, you served with the Royal Americans?" Robert asked the American when he rejoined them.

"Please call me Jason. I can't say that I was a hero, but I fought in Quebec and did my part to defeat the king's enemies."

"Ah, the capture of Quebec City was a brilliant victory." Robert reached out for Llewellyn's shoulder and shook it. "Llewellyn and I fought in the Battle of Minden in the same *Annus Mirabilis*."

Llewellyn smelled another savory dish and saw Jason's wife bringing out their pigeons. His mouth watered with anticipation. The conversation slowed while Jason and Robert watched Llewellyn reduce his birds to a small pile of bones.

"Excellent fowl." Llewellyn pushed back his plate and picked up his glass. He hadn't enjoyed the taste of food since Elizabeth died.

"It's the walnut catsup," said Jason. "Mary makes it herself."

"Perhaps we could get some brandy," suggested Robert.

When Mary had brought them three glasses and a bottle, Robert nodded toward Llewellyn and said, "Llewellyn asked me a question earlier that perhaps you can aid me to answer. He asked if war between Great Britain and her American colonies was inevitable."

Were they going to talk about politics? As a line officer, Llewellyn felt that voicing opinions about politics was improper. Certainly, no good could come of it.

Jason smiled and spread his hands in front of him as if to push away the question, "Gentlemen, I would not stay in business if I ventured opinions on religion or politics, particularly in light of the difficulties you mention."

"Wise counsel." Llewellyn glanced at Robert, hoping he would take the hint.

"Indeed, but I feel that our leaders are talking past each other," said Robert. "Perhaps it would help us to better navigate these dangerous waters if we improved our understanding."

"These are terrible times," agreed Jason. "I remember our happiness in sixty-three on hearing the news of our victory over the French. We were all united. Loyal and happy subjects of His Majesty. I would never have believed it could go so wrong in such a short time."

"It is a sad state, but as a keeper of a public house, you must have customers of different political stripes. Without betraying any confidences, could you share some of the streams of thought?"

"Yes, both Whigs and Tories drink here, but I am an Englishman and a loyal subject of King George."

"You were born on the Isle?" To Llewellyn, Jason had the twangy accent of a Yank.

"No, I was born here, but I'm still English, same as you."

"I'm Welsh, I am." It always bothered Llewellyn when he was mistaken for English. He couldn't understand why Americans wouldn't feel the same. "Is America not your country?"

"Of course, but I am still an Englishman. Or is there some new Act of Parliament that deprives us of our nationality?"

"Certainly not," said Robert. "But as a loyal subject, what is so burdensome about paying taxes that you risk angering your sovereign?"

"Most people are still loyal. They blame parliament for closing the port—not the king."

"The port was closed in direct response to destroying the tea," said Robert. "Why, I cannot understand. The Company's tea was cheaper than smuggled tea—even after the tax."

Jason crossed his arms and leaned back. "To play the devil's advocate, the tea was less expensive, but the East India Company has a monopoly. They can raise the price any time after they ruin the business of honest merchants."

"Honest merchants?" Robert leaned forward. "Most of them are smugglers, are they not?"

"It was acts of Parliament that made them smugglers, not a change in business. Parliament's distortion of trade for the sake of the Company's profits is the real villainy," Jason pointed a finger away, "Some say that limited monopolies are the first step to unlimited monopolies."

"That is alarmist speculation, is it not?" said Robert.

"After what the Company did in India, why would any colony submit to their forbearance?" Jason put a hand on the table. "I read that fifteen hundred thousand people perished in the famine," he smacked the table with each number, "not because there was no food, but because the Company took all the food and set a price so high none could afford it."

"Now you exaggerate," Llewellyn could feel his voice rise as he defended Great Britain, "What happened in India was a tragedy, sure, but Parliament would never allow a famine like that again."

"Deeds speak louder than words. Massachusetts was not the only colony that objected to paying the tax or the Company's monopoly, but parliament singled out Boston for punishment."

"Boston destroyed the Company's tea," said Robert, now sitting ramrod straight.

"Some people in Boston, but not all." Jason wagged a finger, "Do you flog your whole regiment for one man's transgression?" Jason still leaned back in his chair, but his head thrust forward. "Closing the port has broken the livings of many people, loyal or no."

"Now, just a moment," Robert held up his hands, palms out, in a peacemaking gesture. "Llewellyn, the bottle stands by you." Llewellyn picked it up, hoping that drink might break the tension. The brandy's sweet, sharp notes teased his nose as he poured. "I was posted to London after the war," Robert continued. "The government was near bankrupt. The colonies weren't carrying their share of the burden."

"I agree." Jason took his refilled glass, "As subjects of the crown, we should all bear the same loads—and enjoy the same rights."

"Oh, Fie! Not the consent dodge." Llewellyn waved his hand as if to swat away the irritating idea. Despite his short time in Boston, he was already fed up with listening to Yanks prating about their rights.

"Llewellyn," Robert still sat straight, his hands wrapped around his glass, his voice patient, "no taxation without representation is an ancient principle of English law—since Edward the First."

For a moment, Llewellyn's face felt hot. He knew the first name of every man in his regiment, he knew every drill in the British Army Manual of Exercise, read the Articles of War more often than the Bible, but he didn't know anything about English law. As a good Welshman, he wasn't an ardent admirer of King Edward either. It was obvious, however, that Robert had come prepared for this interview. What Robert's motivations were, he didn't know. Llewellyn resolved to keep his opinions to himself and let Robert lead the conversation.

"We are out on the frontier extending his majesty's realm and adding to his treasury," Jason was saying with open arms. Nodding at Llewellyn, "Wales has representation in Parliament, why not us?"

"Wales is on the Isle. We are as British as the English. Massachusetts is an ocean away, on another continent," Llewellyn said, regretting breaking his resolution seconds after he made it.

"The Sons of Liberty make the same argument." Jason pointed at Llewellyn, "Parliament serves the interest of the British, not Englishmen living in America. Our taxes go to London to pay for policies we have no say in making and awards that don't benefit us."

"Your taxes pay for the Massachusetts governor and government," said Robert.

"A military governor we didn't elect," responded Jason. "The Sons of Liberty argue that we are burdened with taxes to pay for parliament's oppression."

"The colonies are an ongoing expense. The king has made treaties with the Indian, but the colonists invade his territories and then demand protection when the Indian responds." Robert tapped the table with his finger.

"Protection?" Jason's eyes widened with indignation. He leaned forward and tapped the table—mimicking Robert. "The soldiers are quartered in coastal towns, protecting parliament's interests," raising his right arm and pointing westward, "not out on the frontier protecting American interests."

Llewellyn studied both men. Robert breathed heavily through his nose, his lips pursed, and brow knitted. He spoke with the usual self-assurance of his class, but Jason had not yielded. Instead, the deferential pub keeper had transformed. Jason looked both men in the eye and boldly stated his opinions with confidence beyond his station. There was more to this tale than Llewellyn knew. He wondered again why Robert was pursuing the conversation.

"I must beg your pardon. I have put myself badly." Robert placed his open hands on the table. "I was attending my seat in Parliament when William Pitt spoke so eloquently on the Stamp Act. Pitt reminded us that the colonies are not enslaved, and Americans are our countrymen. He said Parliament should be ashamed for taxing without consent."

"God Bless William Pitt." Jason leaned back in his chair with arms wide. "If only we could find a compromise with Parliament. We are sensible of our debt to the mother country. England planted us here, protected our commerce from foreign powers, and opened markets to our goods. In return, we have supplied immense wealth to the crown and soldiers and seamen for our wars. If the king would restore our rights as Englishmen and give us our place in the kingdom, we could rule the world." Jason tilted forward, "But if London continues to treat us like livestock, without ambition or ideals, good only for milking and shearing, then I fear—"

BANG!

The tavern door flew open, hitting the wall with a loud crash, "Lord Dandridge, Colonel Caradoc, I have found you at last!" shouted a young, red-faced subaltern bursting into the room. "Governor Gage sends his compliments and requests your presence at a secret meeting—if you please!" The last part squeaked out.

"Ensign, you bellowed 'secret meeting' across a public house," growled Llewellyn. His words recalled the secret letter in his pocket.

"There is little wonder that all our movements are known," said Robert.

They stood up from the table while the ensign blathered, "But sir, it's dark—I couldn't find you . . ."

"Thank you very much for your patience and views," Robert shook Jason's hand. "I hope we can continue our discussion another night."

"Of course," said Jason. "I apologize if I was too insistent."

"Not at all," said Robert. "Exactly what I hoped for."

"Gentlemen, the king." Llewellyn raised his brandy, hoping to end the conversation on a high note.

"The king, God bless him," said Robert.

"King and country," responded Jason. Both King's officers raised their brows at Jason's response, but Jason drained his glass without comment. Moments later, Robert and Llewellyn had settled their bill and, with the chastened Ensign beside them, were out the door.

When the door closed behind the three officers, Mary said, "Did you hear that, Jason? A secret meeting."

"Shush, Mary, they're probably still outside." Jason put his hands on top of his head and studied the ceiling. He wanted time to think and did not want to argue with Mary.

"I saw Margaret at the market this morning. She said the regulars were planning another powder raid," Mary said over her shoulder as she locked the door.

"That Jezebel." Jason rubbed his eyes and then returned to the table.

"For shame, Jason," Mary walked around the room as she locked the shutters and closed windows. "You should be more sympathetic. You and she share the wish that this crisis doesn't escalate to blows."

"We agree on that." Noticing what she was doing, Jason asked, "Are we closing up so early?"

"The sun is down; no one else will come tonight," Mary blew out all the candles, leaving only the lamp at the bar and the fireplace. "She said they're going to Concord,"

"Why would they go there? The powder is moved, and the guns are dispersed. There is nothing there for them." He picked up the bottle of brandy from the table, the three empty glasses with a finger in each one, and took them to the bar.

"They may be trying to arrest Adams and Hancock in Lexington," Mary joined Jason at the bar.

"That's the same road." He put the bottle and glasses down on the bar and leaned against it. He was still snappy from arguing with the two officers.

"Your duty is clear." Mary leaned against the bar beside him, trying to catch Jason's eye.

"Don't talk to me about my duty," Jason stared ahead at the fire to avoid her eyes. "For forty years, my duty has been to my king."

"And country."

"Aren't they the same?" Now, looking at her.

"There are countries without kings, but without a country, a king is just another man."

"I have been loyal to you for twenty years; would you want that I leave every time we have an argument?"

"If you knew a woman whose husband beat her and their children, left them in rags while he had a new coat, and spent all his money on rum and wenches, would you not advise that she leave him?"

Mary pushed back from the bar and put her hands on Jason's shoulders. He could feel her breasts against his back, "Do you know who that was? The tall one? Lord Dandridge, a close friend of the governor. And his seat in Parliament—hah—it is one of those rotten boroughs."

"Everyone knows that, but a rotten borough does not refute his arguments."

"Jason," she rubbed his shoulders. "The whole system is set up to protect the privileged. There are no Americans in parliament, no American Lords or Dukes, no Americans at court, Americans have no connections or influence."

"Now, we are just as English—" Jason started shaking his head, but Mary talked over his objection.

"We have no access to royal patronage, so why should we pay for it?"

"Your father is probably turning in his grave to hear you speak so disloyal."

"What about your brothers?"

Jason's shoulders slumped. Solomon, the middle brother and the most radical, captained one of John Hancock's ships. Solomon regularly cursed the Boston Port Act, denounced customs officials as villains, and declared the Royal Navy worse than pirates. Bill, the youngest, was more moderate, but he had recently been elected to command a minute company. If the regulars marched out, Bill and his minutemen would muster to oppose them. The militia would call up not only his brothers but cousins, friends, and neighbors. Jason didn't agree with all of them, but he couldn't stand aside if they fought.

Jason lowered his head to the bar, "You got what you want, Mary."

"Don't be angry, Jason; this is not what I want." Mary leaned on Jason, resting her head on his back. "Our business is near ruin, and my husband is going off to war—again."

Jason lifted his head. "I'm not angry with you. I'm angry at fate." Jason thought of the war-torn towns he had seen in the last war. In Quebec, he witnessed starving people eating rats and dogs, disease running unchecked and wrecked and burned homes. The naval fleet riding at anchor in the harbor could set Boston ablaze in minutes. "We could lose everything."

"Not me," said Mary. "You won't lose me. I'll always be yours."

"Thank God for that." He turned around and held her close to him.

"You're going to Westford?" asked Mary, hugging him tight.

"No, if the alarm goes out, the regiments are supposed to gather in Concord." Still holding her shoulders, Jason leaned back so he could see her face. They had been married forever, but he couldn't remember the last time he looked into her eyes. When would he see her again? "I'll meet them there."

"Now?" her eyes locked on his.

"The regulars probably won't leave until first light tomorrow morning. If I leave tonight, I can get to Concord before them." Jason glanced around the bar, "Did you already finish the dishes?"

Mary rolled her eyes, "What was I doing while you were settling the world right with the king's men?"

Chapter Two

Llewellyn, Robert, and the ensign approached Province House's wrought iron gate. A woman came down the steps and walked briskly out of the gate, slipped between hitched horses, and turned to their left. She disappeared down the dark street.

"Is that . . . ?" began Robert.

"The Duchess," said the ensign. "Pardon me, sir, I meant Lady Gage. She's quite social with the Yanks. Very popular."

"Indeed." Robert's tone was suspicious, but Llewellyn's head was full of questions about their last meeting, the next secret meeting, and he barely noticed. They mounted the broad front steps of Province House without pausing. Inside, Llewellyn followed Robert into a small room already packed with officers in Army, Marine, and Navy uniforms. Blinking as he surveyed the brightly lit room, Llewellyn recognized the commanders from every regiment in Boston.

Robert leaned in close to Llewellyn's ear, "Something big is afoot." Robert joined Admiral Graves near the fireplace and chatted about the weather as they warmed their hands. Deeply in his cups, Lieutenant Colonel William Walcott, commander of the Fifth Regiment, tugged on Llewellyn's arm as he passed. "Llewellyn, there you are. Gage has called us all. A big operation tonight. Would it not have been better to give us some warning?"

"Good evening, William."

"Nothing like a war for glory and advancement," interjected an equally drunk young captain, patting Llewellyn on the back as he spoke.

"Allow me to introduce the acting commander of the 38th, Captain Luke Lillingfield." Llewelyn knew that Robert Pigot, the former commander, was recently breveted to Brigadier.

15

Luke bowed, almost falling over. "Pleasure, Llewellyn."

Llewellyn didn't know the particulars of why such a young man was the acting commander of a regiment, but he could deduce from the blue trim and lace of his scarlet coat that Lillingfield was of the Foot Guards. Guardsmen were of better birth, had loads of influence with the Court, and were wealthy enough to skip subaltern rank and purchase a captaincy. Further, by dint of court rank and etiquette of proceedings, a Guards captain was nominally the same rank as Llewellyn. Lillingfield had most likely used the status afforded a Guardsman to repress more senior officers in the regiment to ascend as acting commander.

"All mine." Llewellyn nodded to the tottering captain without begrudging the use of his given name and pat on the back from a man young enough to be his son. "What intelligence do you have?" Llewellyn asked William.

"Nothing, really. I learned of this meeting an hour ago."

The governor's adjutant, Major Kemble, appeared at the side door, "Gentlemen, if you please, the governor is waiting." He turned about and, after a short walk down the hall, mounted the side servant's staircase, followed closely by the large troop of officers rumbling their way up two flights of steps to the third-floor attic. A musty odor underlay the smokey smells of a fireplace.

The tall and portly Governor Thomas Gage stood waiting for them, his hands behind his back and lower lip protruding as he watched his commanders file in the room. He stood in front of the fireplace beside a large round table packed with chairs. A map of the Massachusetts Bay Colony lay on the table; a chandelier shined over it. The senior officers crowded in behind chairs at the table, and the remainder found places in the outer ring.

To Llewellyn's surprise, Gage motioned to him and patted the back of an empty chair to his right. Llewellyn stood behind the chair until the governor sat down. There was great squeaking and thumping of chairs as the audience took their seats. Robert sat across from him between Admiral Graves and Brigadier Pigot.

"Gentlemen, pardon the late hour and unorthodox proceedings. The Americans seem to know our every move. We are meeting in the attic to avoid listening ears on the street." Gage spoke to Kemble, "Stephen, pray give the gentlemen a picture of our situation."

Among his many and diverse duties, Kemble oversaw Gage's intelligence network. "Gentlemen, as many of you know, in defiance of his Excellency's order, the rebels established an extralegal council wholly populated by blackguards and radicals. The so-called Provincial Congress has usurped the authority to tax, regulate trade, and, most notoriously, form a provincial army. Our latest intelligence says they intend to raise an army of eighteen thousand men."

Gasps of astonishment interrupted Kemble, followed by growls of anger, "Sedition;" "How dare they challenge the King;" "Treasonous Dogs!"

"It's insufferable," agreed Gage, shaking a fist. "We have not a spark of authority outside Boston, but I have less than three thousand troops here. There are less than nine thousand in all of North America."

After nodding in agreement with the governor, Kemble resumed his brief, "The rebels are assembling weapons and stores for their army throughout the country. The principal magazine is in Worcester." Using a wooden ramrod as a pointer, Kemble showed Worcester on the map. "There is a smaller but still significant stockpile here," he moved the pointer east and tapped a mark, "Concord."

Gage spoke up, "Last week, orders arrived from London. Earl Dartmouth has authorized me to crush this evil in its infancy. Reinforcements are coming soon from Canada and Ireland. When they arrive, we will move into the countryside to return this colony to its obedience."

"Just so," harumphed Admiral Graves.

Gage nodded to him, "Until that time, we cannot sit idle; we must keep the rebels off balance and destroy as many of their arms as our resources permit."

Nods and "indeed" from the audience. Despite their consonance with the governor, Llewellyn could see frowns and furrowed brows among his peers—the dawning realization of the immensity and danger of their task.

"However, I am sensible that a wrong move could ignite a civil war. I want it to be clear that the king wishes his subjects to return peacefully to his good graces." Gage motioned for Kemble, "Carry on."

"We have good intelligence that the Provincial Congress is reluctant to escalate the present crisis and adjourned until May," Kemble thrust out his chin, held the pointer high, with his other arm behind his back. "I advised the governor that we have an opportunity to act while the rebels hesitate."

"Thank you, Stephen," Governor Gage stood up, reached across the table, and tapped Boston on the map. Running his finger along the roads. There was a creaking of chairs as officers stood and leaned over the table to see where he was pointing. "The farthest magazine in Worcester is unattainable until more troops arrive. Concord, however, is close enough to be vulnerable to a surprise stroke."

No one spoke; there was no visible movement, but Llewellyn felt a quiver of excitement ripple through the audience.

"My plan is that a corps of flankers—two battalions, one of light infantry and the other of grenadiers, proceed to Concord tonight with the utmost speed and secrecy. The corps is to reach Concord by first light tomorrow morning, destroy the arms there, and return to Boston before the militia can turn out." Turning to Llewellyn, he said, "As my most senior and able commander, Colonel Caradoc, I offer to you the honor of commanding that corps."

"I am deeply honored with Your Excellency's trust and confidence," said Llewellyn with a sitting bow toward Governor Gage. Llewellyn was too old a soldier to show surprise. His face remained calm, but his head was bursting with all the difficulties—gathering a corps from disparate units, marching in the dark of night to a distant destination he had never visited, and all before morning. The only outward sign of nerves was his unconscious fiddling with a button on his coat.

"Admiral Graves," said Gage, "to shorten the distance and retain the element of surprise, I will require your fleet to provide boats to move Colonel Caradoc's corps across the Charles River from here," Gage touched the Boston Common on the map, "to this area south of Charlestown."

"When would you like my boats collected?" asked Graves.

"Timing is critical. It will take six hours at the quick march to reach Concord. Moonrise tonight is at nine thirty-six. Begin ferrying the troops as soon as there is enough moonlight. Llewellyn's corps will be across by ten o'clock and on the march before eleven." Placing a hand on Llewellyn's back, Gage said, "That should give you ample time to reach Concord by first light at half past five tomorrow morning."

Involuntary grunts escaped from many in the audience, and everyone with a watch pulled it out of his pocket. Looking up from his watch, Admiral Graves said, "I have repaired and gathered the fleet's boats in anticipation of an operation, but I needed more warning. It will be a near-run thing."

"Indeed. We do not have much time." Gage picked up one of the papers in front of him. Reading from it, he said, "The flankers are to come from the 4th, 5th, 10th, 18th, 23rd, 38th, 43rd, 47th, 52nd, 59th regiments, and the marines." Looking up from his note, he surveyed the room, "Lieutenant Colonel Whelks, you are to command the grenadier battalion for Colonel Caradoc."

"It's an honor, sir," said Steven Whelks from behind Llewellyn. Llewellyn turned around in his seat to nod to Steven. He was the Lieutenant Colonel of the Tenth regiment, a long-serving line officer that Llewellyn had known for years. His reputation was not sterling; there was a rumor of a woman in Quebec, but Llewellyn knew Steven to be brave and dependable.

"Covering the grenadiers will be the light infantry from the same regiments commanded by Major John Pitcairn from the marines."

Sitting behind Admiral Graves, Pitcairn appeared surprised that Gage was talking to him. He blurted out, "Sir!" Llewellyn hadn't met Pitcairn, but his reputation was hard-working.

"Sir, if you please," said Captain Shea. "Our light company is still in New York."

"Quite right. Thank you. That will still make twenty-one companies. Enough, I think, for a sharp blow." Still reading from his paper, "Now, so they may march fast, the corps is to travel light. No knapsacks, only haversacks with a single day's ration and one issue of ammunition. Questions Gentlemen?—Llewellyn."

"Where are we to draw our rations and powder?"

Gage raised his eyebrows in surprise, "Yes, of course . . ." He glanced at Kemble.

"We will have wagons with rations meet you at the powder house on the common by nine o'clock," Kemble responded.

"Are there any more questions?"

"Yes, sir." Urgent needs were beginning to drip into Llewellyn's thoughts. "I am unfamiliar with roads to Concord. Is there a knowledge-able guide? Someone who has scouted the route?"

"Thank you for reminding me; I have a man for you." Gage motioned to a man standing in the corner, "Henry." A young, shy man stepped forward. "Ensign Henry De Berniere has spied out the entire route from here to Worcester. Most of this plan is based on his report. Henry will go with you." The young Ensign bowed to Llewellyn. "Additionally, mount-ed and dismounted patrols commanded by Major Edward Mitchell went out before sunset and are reconnoitering the route. They will meet you in Menotomy."

"Sir, if I may," Steven Whelks raised a hand, "It may take more than a single hour to rouse out our flankers and assemble them on the common without alarming the country people."

"Quite right, but it can't be helped. Pray order your men to move as quietly as possible. Now, are there any other questions?" Seeing no raised hands, "We all have much to accomplish and very little time, so I will keep you no longer."

Gage stood up, signaling the end of the meeting. The officers filed rapidly out of the room, clumping down the steps as they ran to alert their flankers. Gage put his hand on Llewellyn's shoulder, wishing him to stay.

When everyone had left except Kemble, Llewellyn, and Robert, Governor Gage pulled out a sheaf of papers and handed them to Llewellyn. "Llewellyn, the letter Stephen gave you earlier today is my instruction. This one," he drew out a paper with drawings on it, "is a map of Concord. It shows the houses, taverns, and other buildings where the rebels have stored their arms. Henry drew the map with the aid of loyal subjects in Concord."

"The loyal country people in Concord fear reprisals from the numer-ous rebels in the area," said Kemble. "Their assistance has been gratifying, but they will not openly aid you."

"Take a moment to read the instructions and examine the map," said Gage. Llewellyn opened the letter he had been wondering about all day. Without waiting for Llewellyn to finish reading, Gage continued, "Our intelligence says that there are fourteen cannon, ten iron and four brass. Spike the iron guns and beat the brass ones until the barrels are bent."

"Tools?" asked Llewellyn, still reading.

"I have already dispatched two chaises of artillerymen through Boston Neck with the necessary spikes, sledgehammers, and so forth to destroy the guns," said Gage. "They will meet you in Menotomy."

Kemble stood over him and showed some of the important places on the map.

"Did you note the bridges at Concord?" asked Gage.

"I did, Your Excellency." Llewellyn disliked it when superiors said the obvious. The bridges were an easily recognizable tactical feature that any self-respecting soldier would notice. The letter that had lain in his pocket all day was disappointing. It was filled with minutia and self-evident details, listing military supplies to be destroyed from tents to bags of flour—as if a twenty-year veteran line officer didn't know what military stores were—instructions on how to destroy captured arms and equipment, including a tedious sentence about disposing of lead balls—the least valuable and most easily replaced military commodity.

On the other hand, information critical to Llewellyn's success was missing. No description of road conditions or markings for other bridges or fords between Boston and Concord. There was no intelligence on the rebel militia, neither their numbers nor likely assembly locations. It appeared that the success of the operation rested on the assumption that they would achieve complete surprise and the militia incapable of resistance. Llewellyn could feel anxiety tightening his chest. He checked his watch again.

"Detach six light companies as soon as you are able," Gage was saying. "They are to speed ahead and seize the bridges. Do you hear me?"

"Sir." Llewellyn didn't want to talk anymore. He wanted to get to his troops. Only action would restore his sense of control. "The order is clear enough. I must get started."

"Very well. If this operation is done proper, we will deprive the rebels of the means to resist and end this war before it starts," Gage shook Llewellyn's hand.

"Your Excellency." Llewellyn took his leave, ran down the steps and out the door. De Berniere, Whelks, and Pitcairn waited for him in the small circle of light from the gate's lantern.

"Gentlemen, I will dash first to my own regiment to give out the necessary orders and gather my kit. I expect you must do the same. Please meet me on the Common as soon as you are able. I will light a blue lantern so that you can find me. I wish I had more to tell you, but we must fly to meet our boats."

"That may be a problem," said Pitcairn. "The boats, I mean. Admiral Graves has repaired and gathered the boats as he said, but he did not expect an operation tonight. He gave shore leave to most of the crews. They'll be scattered to every tavern and brothel in Boston."

They heard a distant gun from the harbor—a ship's signal gun. Admiral Graves was summoning his sailors.

Llewellyn could only nod in response to Pitcairn's news. The boats were the Navy's problem to solve; he had plenty of his own. "We will sort out order-of-march at the boat landing, but the light-bobs will lead, so ferry them as soon as boats are available." Whelks and Pitcairn saluted. "We haven't a moment to lose."

After the room had cleared except for Robert, Governor Gage said, "I wanted you to know that I selected Llewellyn because of your endorsement."

"He was my mentor when I was newly commissioned. There is no better line officer."

"I'm glad to hear you affirm his abilities. This will be our most dangerous raid so far. A skillful touch is essential to avoid starting a war before we have more troops."

They stood over the table with the map. Moving his finger along the long route from Boston toward Concord just out of the reach of his arm, Robert gestured toward Concord, "I was curious about your choice of a marine officer to command the light-bobs. I am not disparaging the marines, but I did not know they are accustomed to this type of operation."

22

"I have a dearth of infantry. I moved heaven and earth to get the marines put under my command. Admiral Graves, for good reasons of his own, resisted. I cannot now, in good conscience, launch a major operation without including them."

"Indeed," said Robert with his thumb on his chin.

"I wouldn't worry about Pitcairn. He has done wonders with the marines since he arrived on station. They were a sodden lot, but they are quite respectable now." Gage motioned to two chairs closest to the fire, sat down and asked, "How was your meeting with Mister Green? Did he say where Hancock has flown?"

"I couldn't ask him directly, and I was unable to steer the conversation to Hancock." Recalling the encounter, Robert was embarrassed that Jason had so dominated it.

"Never mind. Hancock is his patron. Green would never play the informer," Gage raised his head expectantly, "But the other question is more pertinent: are the Yanks as indecisive as Kemble believes?"

Robert looked down as he spoke, his hands on his knees, "The interview did not go well. I'm afraid I managed it badly."

"Zounds," said Gage. His voice filled with exasperation. "Are they ready for war?"

"Well, I would say that Mister Green has misgivings . . ."

"Misgivings?! Misgivings, you say! Of course, they have misgivings, Robert!" Gage put his hands over his eyes, "I have written quite bluntly to North and Dartmouth about their goddammed misgivings." He put down his hands and looked into Robert's face, "I need to know if they lack resolution or are they prepared for open hostilities?"

Surprised at Gage's outburst, Robert thought about the nuance of Jason's words. "They loathe parliament, but I don't believe they will attack the king's troops." After a moment, Robert added, "At least not intentionally. One cannot discount an accident or miscalculation."

Gage frowned, his lower lip in full pout.

Robert said, "Whitehall agreed to send more troops?"

"Let me show you the letter from Dartmouth. London is completely out of touch." Gage pulled the letter out of his coat and handed it to Robert.

Reading the letter, Robert was alarmed at Dartmouth's ignorance of the looming crisis. "Rude rabble," he muttered aloud while still reading and snorted a half-laugh. "Dartmouth dangerously underrates the Americans."

"And overrates our abilities," said Gage. "He writes as if I already have all the troops he promised. I could not have been more clear—doubling the troops is not enough. And see here." Gage beat a section of the letter with his finger. "Arrest the rebel leaders? Absurd."

"You did not pass on that order tonight."

"Of course not," said Gage. "Hancock and the other rebel principals fled Boston before the dispatches arrived. Only Warren and Church are still here, and we can't find Warren. Likely whoring about somewhere."

"What about Church?"

"We have reason to leave him in place," said Gage. "In any case, there's no advantage burdening Llewellyn with impossible tasks. Getting to Concord and destroying the cannon is quite enough."

It was obvious to Robert that the rebel leaders had informers, perhaps even in London, but Robert suspected at least one spy was in Province House. Otherwise, how had they known to flee before the arrival of the *Nautilus*?

"And what of my plan? Do you believe it will succeed?" asked Gage. The chill of New England's Spring was beginning to penetrate the room. Gage picked up his chair and turned toward the fire. Robert did the same, and they both gazed into the dancing flames.

"I thought it good. No matter the resolve of the Americans, if we achieve surprise, then your plan will succeed."

"I'm glad to hear you say that. I remember the Scottish rebellion in forty-five. I fought at Culloden." He picked up a poker and stabbed at the waning fire. "Afterward, bodies of brave Highlanders carpeted the moor. One could walk across on corpses without touching ground." Gage shook his head. "Margaret, God love her, has made it quite plain that she doesn't want me to be the instrument of that kind of slaughter in the New World."

"Just so." Robert's nostrils flared. Gage's reminiscence of Culloden evoked the stink of gore and violent emotions from his own battles—both the paralyzing dread and the intoxicating thrill.

"In many ways, this crisis reminds me of the Scottish rebellion," said Gage.

"How so, Thomas?" Robert remembered his parents' worry and hushed discussions at night, his father reading out news to the servants, but the war hadn't directly touched them.

"Of course—I suppose you were a child in forty-five," Gage still poked the fire. "But last year, when the Yanks founded their Continental Congress, it reminded me of Charles raising his banner at Glenfinnan." Rolling his hand for emphasis, he said, "There was no turning back then. War was certain."

"I see." War felt tangible and imminent.

A log in the fire popped. A spark flew onto the hearth rug. They watched it grow for a heartbeat then Gage stamped on the glowing cinder. "But there is a lesson here." He faced Robert. "The battle of Culloden was dreadful butchery, but we've heard no more of Scottish insurrection. No more pretenders." Pointing a finger at Robert, "If war is thrust upon us, then we must beat the Yanks like we did the Scots. Smash them to atoms and let better men than us pick up the pieces."

His mind was shaken with conflicting emotions; Robert took his leave. Stepping out of Province House, he turned west on Marlbrough Street for home. The Moon had not yet risen, and the streets were dark as a tomb, but Robert had walked home from Province House many times, and his feet found their way without effort.

Alone with his thoughts, the prospect of another war filled Robert's mind. As the last war receded into history, Robert's professional life became unchanging years of drudgery, serving in various undistinguishing posts in London, while his marriage became a mortifying debacle. He feared he was wasting his best years. When Gage offered him the opportunity to go with him to America, Robert seized the chance to escape his life and find adventure in a new land. Maybe the glory of war was again at hand. He did not miss war's exertions, privation, and horror—but the fame of a hard-won victory and chance for advancement—he did miss that.

He looked forward to sharing a brandy with his adjutant, Major Matthew Lane, and discussing the possibilities of a new war. His house was at the corner of Winter and Treamount streets on the verge of the common. On Winter Street, he fell in behind two men ambling toward the common. In no hurry, Robert was content to follow a few paces behind.

The two men in front of him had been fussing with their pipes. Once they got them lit, they resumed their conversation.

"I heard them rousting out their men," said the man on the right.

"Yeah, it was quite a racket. Woke the children," said the man on the left.

"I guess the rumors were true."

"Another powder raid."

"A big one this time."

Startled, Robert interrupted their conversation. "Pardon." Both men jumped aside. "Forgive me; I didn't mean to alarm you."

"Sneaking up on a man in the dark," huffed the man on the right.

"Pray accept my apology; I couldn't help but overhear. You were saying something about the soldiers?"

"Yes, the regulars are being called up all over Boston," said Left man.

"A big raid this time," said Right.

Even though he was in uniform, it was evident that in the dark, the two men could not see the color of his coat. "You know the army, soldiers could be marching about for any number of reasons," suggested Robert.

"Ha-ha! True, but there are lots of rumors about another powder raid," said Left.

"They'll miss their mark," said Right.

"What mark?" asked Robert.

"The cannons at Concord, they're already hidden," said Right.

"Pardon me, I have urgent business; I must be on my way. Good night." Without waiting for their response, Robert turned and ran back the way he had come. At the corner of Winter and Marlbrough, Robert ran full tilt into a party of grenadiers turning on to Winter Street.

"Git you bloody barmpot," shouted an officer.

"Lord Dandridge. Make way!" Robert shouted. The startled grenadiers fell back; Robert untangled himself from a fallen grenadier and ran down Marlbrough. Behind him, he heard someone mutter, "Drunk as a Lord."

He heard another company of soldiers marching toward the common as he ran past Summer Street. He arrived at the front gate of Province House out of breath. In the lamp light of the gate, the soldiers recognized him and let him pass. He found Gage's adjutant at his desk. Panting from his run, Robert said, "Stephen, I must see Governor Gage; it's most urgent."

Kemble jumped up, "M'Lord, of course. Right away." He disappeared into the next room and came back out just as Governor Gage's raised voice came from the room, "Come in, Robert. Don't stand on ceremony." Robert stepped into the room without waiting for another invitation. Gage was sitting with his wife on a couch. They were sharing brandy.

"Margaret," he removed his hat and made his leg.

"Robert, it's delightful to see you again," said Margaret in her nasal American twang.

"You are lovely as ever." Moving his eyes to Governor Gage. "I don't mean to sound impatient, but I have some urgent news about tonight's—um—activities."

"Yes, it's no bother; you can speak in front of Margaret."

"Of course, but if your excellency would indulge me, I would prefer to speak privately. I don't want to bore Lady Gage."

"Oh, Robert, I love to hear about military affairs. I often wish I were born a man so I could have been a soldier."

"Indeed . . . of course—" Robert balked, not sure how to continue.

"Oh, no need to stumble, Robert. I'll leave you two alone. I have some urgent business of my own."

"That's not necessary, Meg—" began Governor Gage, but Margaret got up, curtsied politely to Robert, and her skirts swished out of the room, closing the door behind her.

"Yes, Robert? You've made your point. What is so urgent?"

Still standing, Robert briefly recounted the conversation he had overheard on the way to the Common.

"Bloody hell, is nothing secret in Boston?" Gage stood up and crossed his arms, his lower lip full out. "How could they know? I kept my plan a profound secret. I told only one—uh," he looked at the closed door, "two people before tonight."

"It is a mystery; there must be a spy among us, but no matter, I urge you to recall Llewellyn and delay this raid."

Gage shook his head. "I have my orders from Dartmouth. An overheard rumor in the street is insufficient excuse to delay. Besides, we are not likely to be favored again soon by good weather and a full moon."

"Your Excellency, by your own words, the success of this operation depends on surprise. It is clear that surprise is lost." Robert emphasized lost with a hand-chopping motion.

"We don't know that. They said Concord because that's where they gathered the arms. Many people could know that." But Gage was wringing his hands, his brow furrowed. "Anyway, I sent out patrols to stop communication between Boston and the rest of the colony."

"Your Excellency, it is likely that you are right, but no matter how swift or quiet Llewellyn's corps moves, a body of men that size cannot march undetected. They will sow dragon's teeth behind, and militia will rise out of the ground to fight them. They may reach Concord but be trapped and overwhelmed miles from succor from our forces."

"Robert!" Gage wagged a finger at Robert as if he was the source of the bad news. "The militia, even if they are forewarned, which is still not certain, they cannot assemble quickly enough to block a corps the size of Llewellyn's."

Robert put his hands on a chair back. An empty pit had formed in his stomach. "Perhaps we could delay a day to allow Llewellyn to properly assemble his force."

"The rumor you heard tonight will spread to the entire colony by the morrow. If we delay one day, that will give the militia time to gather, and your fears will become reality."

"Then let's delay until the next full moon and let the rumor pass unverified."

Gage started pacing. He stopped and stared at the spray of pistols mounted over the fireplace, "The rebel congress will meet again next month," Gage still stared at the decoration, but Robert could see his gaze pass through it. "If the current crisis worsens, we could have a rebel army outside Boston Neck by the next full moon." Gage put his fist to his chin, "I am sensible to the risks, but Caradoc is our best commander; the cream of this army is marching under his command. I believe they can succeed whether the rebels turn out or not."

"Your Excellency, if we must go tonight, then may I suggest that I ready my brigade to sally out? If the rebels turn out, I can cover Llewellyn's withdrawal."

"That is a welcome suggestion, Robert," Governor Gage nodded. "What do you believe is necessary?"

"Three battalions and a battery of artillery should be sufficient." The prospect of commanding his brigade in battle excited Robert's ambition. He could feel the hairs prickling on his neck.

"Take your brigade, and I will add the balance of the marines for good measure."

"Thank you, sir. By your leave, I will go and prepare." Robert could barely restrain a giddy smile. Four battalions and artillery under his command—it was practically an army! Even his father would be impressed, and likely, the king would hear of his operation. Robert opened the door, startling Margaret Gage, who was standing just outside.

"Oh, you gave me a fright," Margaret put her hand to her breast. "I was just passing by when you flung open the door."

"Forgive me, Meg," Robert's exhilaration evaporated as he watched her hurry away. She was born in America and too friendly, in Robert's estimation, with many of the most prominent rebel leaders. Margaret was the only person in a position to know both the plans of the British Army and have well-placed friends among the rebel leaders. However, not only was she the governor's wife, but she was also Major Stephen Kemble's older sister. Robert feared that Gage and Kemble allowed their relationship with her to cloud their judgment and were unable or unwilling to acknowledge evidence of treachery.

Chapter Three

Jason's coat, hat, and bag were on the stool next to him. Jason regarded the tavern, wondering when he would see it again. Despite the political troubles, the years since the war had been the happiest of his life.

"Why are you taking that old coat?" asked Mary.

"It's still good. A little faded. Can hardly see the patches."

Mary picked up the coat and examined it closely. "I suppose the seams are still good."

"The buttons are all there."

"Can you fasten them all?" she asked, giving him a playful poke in his belly.

"Yes!" He turned on his stool so she wouldn't poke his tummy again.

"Are you riding Fleet?" Mary set Jason's coat on her lap.

"No. The regulars have probably shut the gate at the Neck; even if it was open, that old horse would give out before Roxbury."

"He's still strong."

"I'd have to hire an ox cart to get him to the knacker's yard."

"So, how will you cross the river?"

"I'll ask Carney Stewart to row me across. He has a dory."

"I thought you hadn't talked since they destroyed the tea?"

"No, we haven't, but we didn't part on bad terms."

"You'll walk to Concord from there?"

"I'll stop at Uncle Adam's house and borrow one of his horses."

Laying the coat on the stool, she stood up and walked behind the bar, "You need another flip. You'll catch your death in the night air and falling damps."

Jason nodded. Mary mixed the beer, rum, cream, and spices and plunged a hot poker into the pitcher. Once it had frothed, she poured

30

the flips into featherweight glasses she saved just for them. Jason loved to watch her quick, expert movements. Mary set the glasses between them.

"I don't know when I'll see you again." Mary picked up her glass.

"The regulars have gone out before." Jason shrugged. "People get alarmed, but nothing ever happens." Jason picked up his own and touched Mary's glass. "Cheers."

"Even so, how will you get back? They'll shut the gate for sure."

"You are the one that insisted I go. Are you getting cold feet?" He took a deep drink, savoring the creamy elixir.

"I didn't say I wouldn't miss you or worry." Mary sipped her drink.

"If the regulars want food with their dinners, they must open the gate and trade with the rest of the country. And they're hardly doing the king's bidding locked up in Boston."

"I hope you're right." Mary looked at his empty glass, "Another flip?"

"I am getting full, and I'll need my wits about me. It's time to go if I want to get to Concord by morning."

Jason stood up. Mary's face turned beet red and contorted with fear and grief of parting. Jason reached out and hugged her, and she pushed tightly against him with her arms close to her chest, letting Jason hug her like a little girl, her face pressed hard into his chest.

"I love you, Mary."

"I love you, too," she blubbered with her head still buried in his chest. She took a deep breath and pulled back enough to show her face. "Becoming Mary Green was the happiest and proudest day of my life." She wiped her tears, "I packed you a loaf of rye 'n injun, some dry venison, and I filled your canteen with well water. It's all in the bag. Do you have some money?"

"I have enough," Now that departure was imminent, Jason was filled with foreboding. Thoughts of what might happen to his family and business crowded his mind.

"Go!" said Mary. "You need to get on the road, and I don't want to start crying again."

Jason pulled on his coat and hat and slung the haversack around his shoulder. Afraid that he might change his mind, he kissed Mary and walked out the door.

Out on King Street, the Moon was still below Boston's skyline, and the way ahead was dark, but Jason strode confidently on the familiar road. He turned right and walked past Town House toward Beacon Hill. The night was cool and damp, but he was comfortable in his coat. He was already trying to view the next few hours as an adventure. Some time away from the tavern, visit his brother near Lexington; in a few days, it would all blow over, and he'd come home. Could be fun.

In Cornhill at the corner of School Street, Jason heard the tramp of marching feet and the rattle of soldier's kit behind him. He stepped into the dark doorway of the Old Corner Bookstore and stood quiet as a company of regulars passed. *Are they moving already?* After they passed, he peered after them. He listened for more. Hearing nothing, he walked on more briskly.

On School Street there were fewer houses and moonlight shown on the road. Jason didn't believe in ghosts, but he quickened his pace as he passed the Burying Place. When he got to Beacon Street, he could see the Powder House. Horses, carts, and soldiers were all about it in great activity. He stayed in the shadows as much as he was able and redoubled his pace. He finally arrived at Carney's house out of breath and panting. Before he could knock, the door flew open. He was staring into the double barrels of Carney's scatter gun.

"What the devil do you want?" demanded Carney in a growl.

"Carney, it's me, Jason Green."

Jason didn't move a muscle as Carney's dark figure examined him on his doorstep. "Come inside then, Jason. Kat's already in bed. I'll light a candle."

"No, don't strike a light. The regulars are out."

"I know, I ain't deaf."

"I need you to row me across to Cambridge."

After a long pause, "Let me get my coat."

Carney came back wearing his coat and carrying fishing poles. "Cover" was his only explanation. They made their way down to the Charles River. Without ever saying a word, he pulled the sail cloth cover off his small rowboat. He took his shoes and stockings off and set them dry in the boat. With Jason's help, they pushed it into the water and stepped in, and only Carney's feet were a little wet. Carney set the oars and then began pulling them across the river.

"Sounds like the navy is out, too. Set those poles so they think we're fishing."

"I can't thank you enough for doing this," Jason placed a pole on each side.

"What are we doing?" asked Carney as he leaned back into a deep row.

"I'm going to join my regiment."

"I didn't know you were still in the militia. I heard you resigned from the Corps of Cadets," now, he bent forward as the oars went up and back.

"We all resigned when the governor relieved Hancock, but I renewed my commission with the minute regiment in Westford," Jason scanned across the water. "I grew up there."

"You took a commission from the Massachusetts Congress?" leaning back.

"Yes, but we still took our oath to the king."

"You aim to break that oath tonight?"

A Navy barge loomed out of the dark, packed to the gunwales with soldiers. With no room to sit, the soldiers were standing. The barge was top-heavy and deep in the water.

"Make way, you grass-combing lubbers!" shouted a sailor from the stern-sheets.

"Bugger off, mate," Carney shouted back.

"You foul our oars; I'll burn your little boat and drown both you damned filibusters!"

After turning his rowboat to run parallel with the barge, Carney called across, "Goin' to market with all them lobsters?"

"We're going to shag your mother!" yelled one of the soldiers. Laughter rippled from the soldiers in the barge.

"My mother would take the whole lot of you knock-kneed, waun-doughty, whoresons and beg for more," Carney shot back.

Jason admired Carney's gift for cursing. The soldiers did, too. They roared with laughter, rocking the barge and causing the sailor in the stern sheets to shout, "Next man which rocks the boat will swim to shore!"

Carney turned the little rowboat away from the barge, but as they rowed off, one of the soldiers started singing,

"*Yankee Doodle went to town A-riding on a pony.*"

The whole barge of soldiers joined the song.

"*Stuck a feather in his cap and called it macaroni.*"

"Goddam the king and his soldiers," Carney cursed under his breath.

"*Yankee Doodle came to town for to buy a firelock. We will tar and feather him, And so we will John Hancock.*"

The Moon was now fully up. Jason could see several big barges rowing across the river. He and Carney had been rowing right through their course, and they were lucky to have met only one. Fortunately, the barges were intent on their business and ignored the little rowboat. Across the water, they could still hear the chorus of Yankee Doodle.

"It's a damn big operation," said Carney. Beyond the barges, Jason could see the ship lights of the *HMS Somerset* and her consorts. In the dark, sitting in a tiny rowboat, the tall ships were imposing. Fear fluttered in Jason's stomach.

"I hope you know what you're getting in to," said Carney.

"So don't I."

"They're headed toward Lechmere Point, which is where I was going to land you." Carney squirmed to the right side of the bench, "Here, take an oar. We need to row farther upriver, or those regulars will pick you up as soon as you set foot on dry land." Jason crowded next to Carney on the small bench and took an oar. After a few awkward strokes, they got their rhythm and rowed in perfect tandem. Jason had strong arms from handling kegs of beer and throwing the occasional unruly drunk out of his tavern. Even against the river current, they made good time.

"I thought you were cross with me over them destroying the tea," said Carney, breaking the silence.

During the war, they had been together day and night for years, suffering cold, privation, and danger with never an angry word, but back home in Boston, they had different circles of friends. They rarely met socially. Then, during the crisis over the tea, Jason had often seen Carney standing with the Sons of Liberty during public debates.

"No. We've been through too much together."

Carney was puffing a little as they rowed. Jason asked, "If you don't mind me asking, why are you so opposed to the king? Most people blame parliament and their acts, but you blame the king?"

"I hate all the English. The king, parliament, every man, woman, and child. In Ulster, the oppression of parliament and English absentee landlords was the bane of our existence and a curse on the Irish."

"Why did you join the army then?"

"Times were tough. I had to eat." He shrugged. "The recruiters didn't ask any questions, and I didn't feel bound by an oath that I took under duress of starvation." They rowed for a few more strokes, "Since we're talking about it, why are you still loyal, Jason? Your business is in the same jeopardy as anyone else's."

"Yes, my business is hurting, but we fought the last war in Quebec—not here. If we start a war with Parliament, the navy could bombard Boston—burn it to the ground. I—we could lose everything. Is parliament's abuse worse than that?"

"That's the question, isn't it? When is it too much?" said Carney. "For me, it was when my parents had no money to feed us. I joined the army to eat and volunteered for the 60th to get passage to America. I will not brook English oppression following me here."

The boat ground up near Cambridge Bridge. Jason jumped out, still dry foot and helped pull the little boat up on the beach. Carney reached under the bench and pulled out a jug of hard cider. He pulled out the cork with his teeth and offered it to Jason. "You can stay here and drink with me until the regulars pass."

"I can't. I didn't think they were leaving until tomorrow morning, and I thought they would go out the Neck. I have to make good time to beat them to Concord."

"If a shootin' war don't start, I'll be here tomorrow night the same time if you need a ride back."

"What if a war does start?"

"I'll still be here. Maybe I'll join you. Like old times." Carney raised the jug in a farewell salute and tipped it back for a long drink. "Good luck to ya' Jason Green and God preserve Massachusetts."

Chapter Four

Nine o'clock p.m.

When he first arrived in Boston, he felt lucky that his fusiliers were posted to Fort Hill. The barracks were roomy and comfortable, with good quarters for the officers. Most other regiments were barracked in dockside warehouses and the officers in boarding houses, but tonight, a warehouse closer to Province House would have been better. Llewellyn was still unfamiliar with the winding streets of Boston, and he missed a turn in the dark. When he finally arrived at Fort Hill out of breath, red-faced, and thoroughly annoyed, he found an orderly awake, sitting by the light of a candle.

"Bleddyn?"

"Sir," Bleddyn leaped to his feet.

"Wake the Sergeant Major, Major Blunt, and both flank companies."

"Sir, the grenadiers and the light-bobs?"

"Yes. Start with the Sergeant Major and Blunt. Where's Bane?"

"Sir, most of the officers are in the Club. Bane is in his cot. Today was his birthday."

"Dew, dew!" Llewellyn exclaimed involuntarily. He knew that, like most soldiers, Bane had likely spent his birthday drinking until he blacked out. In fact, Llewellyn had contributed by giving him a shilling that morning as a birthday gift. That also meant that Bane would be of no use as his batman for tonight's operation.

"Go!" he said to Bleddyn and walked to the officer's mess. The 23rd Regiment of Foot, Royal Welch Fusiliers, was a storied regiment with an honored history but the cadre were mostly line officers who had little influence, dependent on their meager salaries and modest patronage. They could not afford to spend nights eating, drinking, and entertaining at taverns in Boston. Instead, housed in the fort's main building, the officer's mess was their social center. They observed the customary rules of the mess but sufficed with Army issued beer and rum. On Fort Hill, they called their mess the "Club" in satirical imitation of the posh London Gentlemen's Clubs.

Llewellyn opened the door and stepped into the Club. Most of the regiment's officers were present. Although he had said nothing, they all knew he was going to meet Lord Dandridge and recommend promotions. Like falling dominoes, a promotion or two would open other positions in the regiment. They were all keen to advance and had gathered to wait for his return. Just as he opened the door, the whist table burst into loud laughter. Whatever was said had drawn the attention of everyone in the room, so they did not at first notice their commander. Llewellyn waited a moment until his adjutant Lieutenant "Mack" Mackenzie saw him, jumped to his feet, and shouted, "Gentlemen, Colonel Caradoc." Immediately, the room came to attention with the sound of scraping chairs and falling objects.

Major Blunt started to speak, but, holding up a hand, Llewellyn said, "Pardon me, Henry, I must speak on Service matters. We have no time for formalities."

Llewellyn stepped up to the whist table as the center of attention. Looking into the faces of his officers, "My interview with Lord Dandridge was broken off. The Governor summoned us to a secret meeting." He paused for a moment to let their minds catch up. "I have the honor of commanding a corps of flankers that will march tonight to destroy a rebel magazine." A spontaneous cheer erupted from the assembled officers. Llewellyn smiled. He had been apprehensive. There were mixed opinions about parliament's policies in America. He was afraid some might complain or procrastinate, but his confidence was restored. "Captain Donkin and Captain Blakeney, alert your companies to prepare for an immediate march to Boston Common. We will be marching all night and probably won't return until tomorrow afternoon."

"Sir!" exclaimed both officers. Sergeant Major Gareth Sayer appeared at the door of the Club, somehow already fully dressed.

"Major Blunt," Llewellyn said, but he was looking at the Sergeant Major, "the men are to travel light. Haversacks, canteens—only water, no beer or grog—they can drink their ration when they return tomorrow. We will receive rations, powder, and shot on the Common. Questions?"

"What time are we to be at the Common?" asked Donkin.

Llewellyn pulled out his watch and frowned, "Half an hour."

"By your leave, sir . . ."

"Go, don't wait for me. Sergeant Major, I need six active men to act as runners. Don't pull them from either flank company, and I need an acting batman to meet me at the stables." Turning to Major Blunt, "Henry, provide the flankers any assistance they need to get on the march. There is no time to waste."

Blunt, Donkin, and Blakeney rushed out of the room, followed closely by their lieutenants. As soon as they were out the door, Llewellyn heard them shouting toward the barracks, followed closely by the Sergeant Major. Slipping out of the door in the wake of the growing bedlam, Llewellyn walked briskly to his quarters.

In his room, Llewellyn threw off the new coat he had worn to meet Robert and carefully placed his bearskin cap back in its box. He changed into his riding breeches and best wool stockings. Rummaging through his trunk he found an older shirt, well-worn, frayed cuffs, but comfortable. As he buttoned the shirt, he noticed the darning on the sleeve, darning done by Elizabeth. He touched the mend, recalling her fussing over the tear. A black cloud of sorrow filled his head.

The Sergeant Major knocked on the door, "Yes, come in," he recovered his composure. Many years before, beginning in Minorca, Private Gareth Sayer had been Ensign Llewellyn Caradoc's batman. Over the intervening years, as Llewellyn had advanced up the hierarchy of regimental officers, he had advanced Sayer with him.

"Sir, I assigned Bleddyn as your batman. He's getting his kit together. He will be here shortly."

"Very good," handing the Sergeant Major two canteens, "Give these to Bleddyn." Llewellyn pulled on his heavy riding boots and strained to get his feet through to the ankles. "Here, help me with these boots."

"Sit down, Colonel," the sergeant major helped pull on the boots. While Llewellyn was stomping his feet further in, Sayer picked Llewellyn's new coat off the cot and hung it in the wardrobe. "I don't know why you don't have a scarlet coat like the other officers."

"I don't have money like other officers." Llewellyn avoided the petty corruption common to other commanders, such as insisting on fopperies for uniforms or dipping into the widows' and orphans' fund. He made do with his wages. Sayer and the other soldiers esteemed his forbearance, but it won him no credit with his peers or superiors nor paid for expensive uniforms.

Sayer shook his head and asked, "What about rum, sir? It's no good for the men to go to battle without a tot."

"Make it so, a tot for each man when the company is formed."

"A tot for each man when company is formed, it is Colonel."

The Sergeant Major yelled out the door, "A tot for each man and two for the company which forms first!"

Llewellyn pulled on his older coat. The madder red had turned the color of brick from years of road dust and wood smoke, but now that he had lost weight, it fit comfortably. He grabbed his wool-felt cocked hat, and into a leather wallet, he stuffed strips of paper, pen, and ink. He also picked up his fusil and cartridge bag.

In most regiments, officers carried swords and pistols and sergeants' halberds, but it was the practice in the 23rd for officers and sergeants to carry light 'fusil' muskets. The Battle of Minden reinforced for Llewellyn the wisdom of the custom. Concentrated, synchronized, and rapid volleys from every man, private to colonel, he felt had been instrumental in defeating the massed French cavalry.

Dressed and equipped, Llewellyn headed to the stable. Bleddyn was waiting.

"Which horse, sir?" Bleddyn was nervous and appeared reluctant to act without orders.

"The gelding for me. I didn't ride him today, and I will need a strong and rested mount." Bleddyn still hesitated. "Can you ride?" Llewelyn asked.

"Yes, sir. Mostly me Dad's dray horse."

"The concept is the same. The bat horse is the brown cob. Pack my kit, I'll keep the fusil with me."

"Sir!" Together, they quickly saddled the horses and packed their kit. Llewellyn showed Bleddyn how to stow some of the kit he was unfamiliar with. They led the horses out of the stable to the barracks square.

On Fort Hill, the "square" was round, but because of their devotion to tradition, the Welshmen still called it the square. Both flank companies were formed in the grass. The sergeants were inspecting their soldier's equipment. A party of soldiers were at the well, filling canteens. Leading his horse, Llewellyn walked over to the company commanders.

"Gentlemen, I cannot tarry. Move your soldiers as expeditiously and quietly as possible." Turning to Robert Donkin, "Robert, your company will move with the light battalion under a marine, Major Pitcairn. William, your grenadiers will form under Lieutenant Colonel Whelks. If, for some reason, you cannot find your places, I've my blue lantern. You will find me there, and I'll set you right."

"Where are we going, sir?"

"Concord."

"How far is that, sir?"

"About seventeen miles west. From the common, the navy will ferry us across the river. We will march from there and return through Boston Neck. Any more questions?" Greeted with only silence, Llewellyn mounted his big gelding and rode off with Bleddyn bouncing in his saddle close behind.

The Moon was now beginning to climb into view, but in Boston, the buildings were two or more stories high, and the narrow streets were still black with night-shadows. Llewellyn rode slowly so as not to miss his turn. After a few blocks, he began to worry that he was lost again. He saw a company of grenadiers and fell behind them. They seemed to know where they were going, and after a few minutes, Llewellyn's hopes were fulfilled. Once the grenadiers marched out onto the common, Llewellyn had room to ride around. The moonlit common was dotted with pockets of companies variously standing or sitting. There was no apparent center, but Llewellyn kept riding until he saw a group of horsemen on Mount Whoredom, and he rode to them.

"Is Colonel Whelks or Major Pitcairn here?"

"Lillingfield here. I am looking for them as well as Colonel Caradoc."

"You found Colonel Caradoc," responded Llewellyn. Getting off his horse and motioning to Bleddyn. "We'll establish our headquarters here for now. Set up the desk and light the blue lantern."

"Lew, I am so glad to find you. I have decided to command my light company," said Luke. "You see, the men don't realize I haven't any battle experience. This expedition is an opportunity to show them my mettle."

"That's banging news, Captain. Where is your company now?"

"I don't know Lew. While I was saddling my horses and gathering my friends, they set off without me. I was hoping you would tell me where they were."

"The first thing one learns about command in battle is to know its location. Difficult otherwise to influence its activities."

"Of course—"

"Pardon me while I finish my thought, Captain Lillingfield. Pray, find your company, ensure that it is properly equipped and issued rations, water, shot, powder, and cartridges made. Then, with my compliments to Major Pitcairn, give your report to him."

"But—"

"Did you understand?"

"Yes, Lew, but—"

"When you find Major Pitcairn, ask him to report here when he is at leisure."

Lillingfield hesitated for a moment, then wheeled his horse and rode off with his retinue of riders. In the meantime, Bleddyn had unpacked the field desk, set it up and was striking a light for the lantern. When the lantern was lit, Bleddyn said, "That captain's a calf."

"Being callow should not be confused with stupidity."

"Sir, do you want me to go look for Major Pitcairn? It might be hours before that Captain finds him."

"No, if we go riding about, no one will find us, and we will never straighten out this bloody mess." Llewellyn pointed at the blue lantern, "Now that the lantern is lit, it will attract officers like moths to a flame."

Two riders appeared, "Colonel Caradoc?"

"Yes, Steven, is that you?"

"Yes, and I have Ensign De Berniere with me. It's a Mayfair out here. The companies have come in from all quarters. Some of the regiments thought they were doing us a favor by changing commanders. So now we have commanders wandering about looking for their companies and companies without officers."

"I experienced that already. Are the boats here?"

"I don't know, but there are people at the powder house issuing powder and shot."

Sergeant Major Sayer, with six runners, appeared, and another horseman rode up, "Colonel Caradoc?"

"Ah! Major Pitcairn, good of you to join us," said Llewellyn. "Have the boats arrived?"

"Not many, sir; Admiral Graves will send more soon. I took the liberty of dispatching one of my marine companies to secure the north shore landing area."

"Very good, we are already behind schedule. We must put this operation in order. Major Pitcairn, if you please, move to the loading site and start organizing the transport. Pray, take Ensign De Berniere with you." To De Berniere, he said, "Henry, I want you to move up with the first company. Once the corps begins to march, stay with Major Pitcairn." Turning to Whelks, "Steven, if you please, move to the Powder House and put the issue in order. Each of you take two runners and keep me informed of your progress." Llewellyn tried to project both urgency and confidence, "The priority will be to the Light companies first. As for order-of-march, try to line them up in ascending order, but don't be a slave to form. It is more important to get the corps across with dispatch than to wait on precedent."

For the next thirty minutes, Llewellyn stayed at his blue lantern, directing lost companies and officers as they arrived. One of the runners appeared, "Sir, Colonel Whelks reports that there are still no ration wagons."

"Damn," Llewellyn checked his watch.

Another horseman appeared. "Llewellyn?"

"Lord Dandridge! What is amiss?"

"I am afraid very much is amiss." Robert jumped down from his horse.

"Ahh, I was hoping my question was merely rhetorical."

"Llewellyn, the rebels may already know of your operation."

"Bloody hell."

"I spoke with Governor Gage. He feels that the circumstances of a full moon and indecisive rebel congress is too favorable an opportunity to pass, and we must carry on."

"It's already started," said Llewellyn. "The first companies are crossing now."

"Just so, however, he has given me permission to ready my brigade to sally out if the militia turn out."

"That is reassuring." Despite the seriousness of Robert's news, Llewellyn was relieved he wouldn't have to make any changes to his plan. Disrupting the chain of movement that has already started would cause even more confusion.

"Llewellyn, I beg you to not underestimate the American militia. Like the publican we met tonight, many of the officers have wartime experience. I have observed their militia training, and though not skilled, neither are they incapable soldiers."

"I will bear that in mind, Robert."

"I want you to send a message if you see any sign that the militia are turning out. I will sally at once."

"I will, Robert."

"One more thing." Robert reached out to put a hand on his shoulder. "Americans are our countrymen, but they have been coarsened by the conditions on this continent. In the Pontiac War, I saw Americans commit ghastly atrocities on the Indians. I cannot bear to repeat what I witnessed. Do not allow yourself to be captured."

"Surely they will not abuse the king's men."

"Perhaps not, but even the great American hero Colonel Washington, the Virginia planter we hear so much about, he single-handedly ignited the last war on this continent by ambushing and massacring a French diplomatic mission in the Pennsylvania wilderness."

"Robert, I will do everything in my power to avoid capture. I thank you for the warning."

"Llewellyn, is there anything I can do for you before I depart?"

"It seems our rations haven't arrived yet."

"I will discover the delay and lead them here myself."

"Sir!" Llewellyn saluted. Robert mounted his horse and rode off.

After Robert was out of sight, Llewellyn called over the Sergeant Major, "Sergeant Major, when I push off from this shore, I want you to take the runners and return to the regiment to prepare them to sally out."

"Sir? I thought it was only the flankers."

"Lord Dandridge is preparing the brigade to cover my corps if we run into trouble. He is taking our Welshmen."

"I understand, sir, but my place is with you."

"Ordinarily, Sergeant Major, I would agree, but the odds are growing that this operation will go awry. Major Blunt is a good officer, but if the worst occurs, he will need your steady hand."

"Sir, you've got the right of it, but I'll give me head for breaking if you won't need me afore this raid is over."

"Sergeant Major, I am sensible to your fears, but I dread more the late arrival of Lord Dandridge than a wound. You do us both a better service staying here."

"Very well, sir. I will go prepare the regiment."

The flow of lost officers and companies slowed. Anxious about the time and wishing to prod his corps into quicker movement, Llewellyn moved his little headquarters down to the water's edge, where the troops were embarking. There was a long queue of soldiers and horses leading to the water's edge. Llewellyn found Pitcairn, "What is taking so long? The queue goes back to the powder house. We should have set all the light-bobs across by now."

"There aren't enough boats. Until we get more, I can get less than a company across in each boat." Pointing to a group of soldiers struggling to get a horse onto a navy barge, Pitcairn said, "A horse takes up as much room as a platoon."

"The company officers don't need horses. I marched across half of Europe on my own feet." Nodding at Pitcairn, he said, "Me, yourself, Whelks, De Berniere—oh—and my batman need horses to communicate and reconnoiter; the rest will do without."

"Thank you, sir; without the horses, we can cross a company in each boat."

The clatter and bang of wagons interrupted their discussion. Two wagons pulled up to the water's edge, and a major of the quartermaster corps jumped off. "I'm looking for Colonel Caradoc," he demanded without saluting.

"Yes?" said Llewellyn.

"I got your rations. Lord, somebody or the other was quite rude. Knocked me up from a sound sleep and called me a bloody dosser. I have half a mind to demand satisfaction."

"You can be court-martialed just for uttering that challenge, Major."

"Pardon, sir; I meant no disrespect. But it's the middle of the bloody night—just to bring the bloody rations here. I had to wake my company—"

"I'm sure your story is quite tragic," Llewellyn waved a hand to cut him off.

"Sir, I'll unload the rations and leave them—"

"You will load half the rations in the next boat." Llewellyn cut him off again. "Part of my corps is already across. You will victual companies on the other side as well as the ones queuing here."

"No sir, that's not my orders—"

"What's your name?" Llewellyn was livid at the man's indolence and cheekiness but kept his voice icy calm.

The quartermaster major didn't answer, standing in sullen silence. He was tall and thick, and he glowered in Llewellyn's face. Looking into his eyes, Llewellyn could almost read his mind, squirming for a means to bluster his way out.

"Your name?" Llewellyn wasn't going to let him off the hook.

"Of course, sir, we will take them across."

It was only half an answer, but it was what Llewellyn needed. He didn't have time for a thorough dressing down.

"Act according to the directions of Major Pitcairn."

"Sir."

His anger abated, Llewellyn remounted his horse and rode to the Powder House. At first glance, it seemed all asunder, people standing or sitting all about, but to Llewellyn's knowing eye, it was organized chaos. Sitting grenadiers were rolling cartridges, and there was a proper queue for the powder issue. Whelks had distribution well in hand.

"Steven, how goes the issue?"

"Very well, thank you. It was a mob when I got here, but I managed to get all ten light companies through and dispatched to the boat landing. The grenadiers have just started drawing their powder and shot, but they will be at the landing on schedule."

"Schedule?" Llewellyn grunted. "We are well past our schedule."

"What more intelligence did the governor give you?" asked Whelks.

"Not enough. A map amateurishly drawn by an ensign and his best wishes."

"I have rarely known these hastily assembled corps of flankers to perform as hoped."

Unwilling to publicly question the wisdom of his superiors, Llewellyn allowed the lightest of nods, "I don't know half these officers and no notion of how they might stand up in a fight." After a moment, he added, "I'm sure they will do all right." But he said it without conviction. When an operation starts badly, it's difficult to set it right before a crisis—and he felt that this operation was barreling toward one.

Llewellyn rode back to the landing site. He found Pitcairn loading his horse onto a boat. "Colonel, I have dispatched six companies. Keeping with your intent, the order-of-march will be the marines first because I already landed them. The young Guardsman commanding the thirty-eighth insisted that you had ordered him first across, so they are next, followed by the 4th King's Own. The remainder are lined up according to your instructions."

"There appears to be plenty of boats."

"Most of them only just arrived. We should cross passing swift now. What are your orders for me?"

Floating across the water, they could hear soldiers singing "Yankee Doodle."

"To begin, we must impose silence on the corps. Every militiaman in Massachusetts will be woke from their beds before ever we reach Concord. Pray organize the landing site and line up the companies for immediate march when the last is across."

Chapter Five

Wednesday
April 19, 1775

Twelve o'clock ante meridiem.

The windows of Buckmans' tavern glowed bright. The building was overflowing. Outside, people carrying lamps and candles circled for a place to see behind the ones already crammed against the windows. Voices inside the tavern were muffled, but Quock could make out Reverend Clarke's deep orotund. Being young in both age and rank, Quock and Isaac could not squeeze even into a window view. Instead, they stood on the green outside the pandemonium of horses and people, their elbows braced on their newly issued Committee of Safety muskets, trying to appear like they belonged there.

"Buckmans' lit up like Pope's night," said Quock.

Isaac grinned at Quock, "What did Mister Nithercott tell you?"

"He says the regulars were coming to arrest Hancock and Adams," said Quock. "What did your dad tell you?"

"He thinks it's another powder raid."

Quock, like every other able-bodied boy, had joined the militia when he turned sixteen. Mister Nithercott hadn't asked him if he wanted to enlist or offer any inducements, but rather, Quock had insisted. He wanted to be treated the same as the other boys. No one had objected. It was the custom that every man served in Lexington's training band as part of their civic duty, including Negro slaves.

Tonight, however, the bell had rung. New England's political crisis had reached Lexington. The call to fight was no longer notional. A test of bravery and devotion for freemen and enslaved alike. Quock was determined to prove that he, too, would fight for his country and his rights.

People began pouring out of the tavern; some men mounted horses and rode off. Quock heard Captain Parker barking unintelligible coughs and Mister Nithercott, the training band's senior sergeant, shouting, "Fall in!"

The band quickly took on a military likeness as they formed their ranks. Silence settled as they listened closely to Parker's rasp.

"Report!" ordered Parker in his most military bark.

Although everyone on the green could hear the order, the Lieutenants faced about and repeated the order, followed by the sergeant's ritual response, "all present and sober," despite the reek of rum and hard cider Quock could smell wafting through the ranks.

When the military rituals were complete, Parker barked, "At ease."

"Gather round," Parker beckoned everyone forward. "My consumption won't let me shout, and I want all of you to hear."

The band broke formation and gathered in a semicircle around their elected leader. Quock pushed forward as close as he was able. Outside the circle of militiamen were families and neighbors. Despite the late hour, almost everyone in the village and surrounding farms was there, moving in close to hear Parker's raspy explanation.

"Folks, as you already know, the ministerial army in Boston sent out patrols early evening. These patrols have arrested and insulted travelers up and down the Bay Road." Parker leaned on his old Brown Bess musket and paused as a murmur of assent washed the crowd. When silence returned, he continued, "We have intelligence that tonight—as I speak to you right now—the regulars are gathering a raiding party, probably more than a thousand men, to march here to arrest Misters Hancock and Adams and to destroy the guns and powder in Concord." Parker paused to cough. "The Massachusetts Congress opposes any attempt by Parliament to execute by force their intolerable acts. We have standing orders, if Gage's troops march out of Boston, the militia is to assemble an army of observation and act in our defense."

The crowd was stone silent. Quock looked around him. These were the same people that a year before had cheered speeches and sang hymns while the town's stock of the East India Company's tea burned in a bonfire, not twenty paces from where they stood. There was still a brown spot on the green where the grass had not yet grown back. The imminence of the king's violent retribution had taken away their voices.

Parker continued to speak, "Riders are already out to spread the alarm and militia all over the country are mustering, but the regulars will use this road," gesturing to the road that bordered the south side of the green, "and we are likely to meet them first—here."

Quock felt a cold spike of fear deep in his bowels. His fellow militiamen did not seem as afraid as Quock felt. He looked at Isaac; in the darkness, he could see the white teeth of Isaac's excited smile.

"What does an army of observation mean?" asked a voice in the crowd.

"I don't know Vernon," said Parker.

"Are we going to fight 'em?" asked Vernon.

"You said a thousand men. That's too many for us," said another man. Quock couldn't tell who it was.

Parker nodded, "As long as they don't molest anyone or destroy property, we will let them pass. The regulars have gone out before without any bloodshed. I think the King's troops will get nothing tonight but a long march and blisters." A few in the crowd chuckled.

Parker motioned to the Reverend Jonas Clarke, "The Reverend is leaving soon to escort Hancock and Adams to safety, but before you go, parson, would you like to say a few words?"

"Try and stop me, John," said Clarke. Laughter rippled through the crowd. Quock had never known the parson to pass up a chance to talk, especially on his favorite subject, the injustice of the king. Clarke waited for the crowd to quiet. He kept his hands clasped in front of him, his head bowed in solemn meditation. After complete silence settled on the crowd, he still waited. Quock shivered in anticipation.

"This is the hour for which we have long prepared," began Clarke with deep-throated certainty. "Here in Lexington, under the shadow of the House of God," he raised an arm toward the Meeting House, "we will cast off the tyranny of a corrupt parliament and deny an immoral tyrant that sets himself up as our true sovereign." He thundered, "No man stands between us and God!" His voice calmed, "No other village in Massachusetts is more spiritually prepared to perform the sacrament of battle and endure the hardships of patriotism than Lexington. Yea, even at the risk of our lives and fortunes, we will brave the hazard of war to win our God-given freedoms." Quock felt he was talking directly to him. Peering into his soul and seeing his true hope. "We will not be alone. God's grace will pour down on us like a river of holiness washing the entire American continent. All the colonies will unite in a holy crusade to free every man from slavery and injustice. The tyrant will struggle, but tyranny will not endure!"

Clarke scanned the faces of his parishioners, "The enemy is pressing. I cannot in good conscience talk any longer, and words alone will not express the deep wellspring of love of country that beats in my breast." He looked again into their eyes, "But the time for words is past; now is the time for deeds. We must gird ourselves for battle. Join hands. Men and women, girls and boys, let us sing *Chester* and then gratefully submit to the discipline of the army."

Everyone grasped the hand next to them. Quock took Mister Nithercott's hand and the hand of Missus Hadley, Isaac's mom, who had pushed to the front, her eyes shining with revolutionary fire. With Reverend Clarke's strong lead, the village of Lexington sang,

> *Let tyrants shake their iron rod,*
> *And Slav'ry clank her galling chains,*
> *We fear them not, we trust in God,*
> *New England's God forever reigns.*

When the psalm reached its final note, into the silence, the Reverend Clarke announced, "Captain Parker, we are ready. What are your commands?"

"Thank you, parson, for your inspiring words." Parker turned to the crowd, "I don't expect the regulars to get here for several hours, but we need to know where they are." Parker scanned the crowd, "Bob, are you here?"

"Over here, John," came a voice in the dark.

"Got your horse? I want to send scouts to find out the regulars."

"Yeah, I'll go."

"I can go too, John. My horse is here," said Thaddeus Bowman.

"Good, come talk to me after I dismiss the band. The rest of you get some sleep where you can find it, but stay within the sound of the drum."

The crowd dispersed. Mister Nithercott was still standing next to him, his Charleville musket across his shoulders. "Quock, run home and get our bed rolls and tell Missus Nithercott we won't be home tonight."

"Yes sir," Quock shouldered his firelock and started walking home.

"Wait, Quock!" Isaac was running across the green toward him, holding his firelock in his right arm and pressing his powder horn and shot bag against his side with his left. "Dad sent me home to get our bed rolls and some cider."

The boys walked steadily and were soon out of sight of the tavern's lights, but they knew the road well, and the Moon was high, lighting their way.

"Let's run," said Isaac. "I don't want to miss the battle." Running, the boys soon covered the distance to the Nithercott farm. Quock could see that Missus Nithercott had left a candle burning in the front window. Isaac's family's farm was another quarter mile down the road.

"Want me to wait for ya'?" Quock asked.

"Yeah, I'll come knock on your door. I'll be quick." Isaac ran off into the darkness, and Quock ran the rest of the way to the house—a barking fox startled him and gave wings to his feet. Quock pushed open the front door. Missus Nithercott was sitting in her rocking chair in front of the fire, a candle burning low beside her, a basket of darning sitting on her lap, but she was fast asleep.

Quock decided to let her sleep and tell her they were staying on the green on his way out. She would fuss, and he didn't want to be late. Walking as quietly as he could, Quock picked up the candle from the window, then navigated through the kitchen to the washroom where he and Mister Nithercott had left their bedrolls and knapsacks. He picked up the whole awkward pile, hanging the equipment across both shoulders. He tried to be quiet, but he kept banging the musket stock against the wash tub, making a hollow thump sound each time. Finally getting the load arranged he picked up the candle, maneuvering around chairs through the kitchen. He could smell fresh baking. Holding out his candle, he saw dozens of jumbles cooling on the kitchen table.

He stopped and leaned his musket against the table and carefully set his candle. He put one cookie in his mouth and shoveled a half dozen more into his haversack. A piercing shriek startled him. He dropped all his bags and fell backward on the floor with the cookie still in his mouth. In the candlelight, he saw Missus Nithercott standing over him with a frying pan in her hands.

"Quock!" she shrieked. "You scared the living daylights out of me. I thought you were a marauding redcoat."

"No, ma'am," he said after pulling the cookie from his mouth. "Mister Nithercott sent me to pick up our bags. We're to spend the night on the green. They're expecting the regulars anytime."

"Are you hurt? Is Mister Nithercott all right?" she asked while helping him up from the floor. Quock saw Faith. She had come down the steps in her nightshift and stood in the kitchen doorway at the edge of the candlelight.

"Yes, ma'am. Nothing's happened yet."

"But the redcoats are coming?"

"Yes, ma'am, I have to get back. We're supposed to stay in the sound of the drum."

"Do you need more jumbles?" she wrapped cookies in a dish towel and stuffed them into his haversack. There was a light knock at the door.

"I'll get it!" shouted Faith, running for the door.

"Not dressed like that!" yelled Missus Nithercott after her, but it was too late as Faith yanked open the front door.

A startled Isaac stood at the door loaded with bags, bedrolls, two cider jugs tied together with twine hanging around his neck, and his musket. "Hello, Faith!" squeaked Isaac, staring bug-eyed at Faith and her shift. "Didn't expect everyone up."

"Faith, don't you have any shame?" scolded Missus Nithercott, pushing Faith behind her and blocking the door so Isaac could not get by.

Quock pulled all his bags back on, grabbed his musket and ran for the door. "We have to go." He squeezed by Missus Nithercott and Faith.

"You boys be careful," called Missus Nithercott as the boys lugged their burdens across the yard.

"Wait!" cried Faith. Quock stopped, and Isaac turned around. Like a deer, Faith sprang out the door barefoot, dodging Missus Nithercott, still with nothing covering her shift. She clutched a bundle to her breasts. She handed it to Isaac. "I made these jumbles for you," she stepped back and smiled at Isaac.

Quock rolled his eyes. Isaac wore his stupidest moonstruck grin, the cookies that Faith had pressed against her breasts gripped in both hands. He stood silent for a seeming eternity and finally squeaked out, "Thank."

"C'mon." Quock pulled Isaac's arm as Missus Nithercott was striding purposefully across the yard toward them. "We're going to be late."

"Quock, you take care of Mister Nithercott," called Missus Nithercott as the boys walked into the darkness. "He's too old for all this foolishness."

Back on the road, the boys couldn't run because of the heavy, awkward bags and bundles. They shared Faith's jumbles and passed a cider jug back and forth. Someone approached them on the road from the direction of Lexington.

"Where you goin', Elijah?" asked Isaac. Elijah Tidd was two years older than Isaac and Quock and an annoying know-it-all. They usually avoided his company, but he always insisted on inflicting himself on them, especially when Faith was around.

"Corporal Tidd," Elijah corrected Isaac. "We're on active service."

"We're supposed to stay in the sound of the drum, Elijah," said Isaac drawing out *Elijah* as disrespectfully as he could.

"There's nothing happening, and I can hear the drum from my house." Looking at Quock, Elijah asked, "Why are you out here anyway? Can they make Negroes fight? It's not your country."

"I was born here, too. I have the same rights as you," Quock's face was instantly hot. He balled a fist, but he was holding a cider jug in his right hand, and his awkward bundles checked his urge to push Elijah.

"Ha! Slaves don't have rights," said Elijah. "You boys do what your daddies told ya. Except you, Quock, you don't have a daddy."

"Quock," Isaac grabbed Quock's arm pulling him back, "Just ignore him."

Elijah sneered at them, then turned down the road disappearing in the dark. Quock was too angry and humiliated to speak.

"We'd be the ones in trouble if you punched him," said Isaac.

"He was right anyways," said Quock, slowing his pace. "Slaves don't have rights."

"Quock," pleaded Isaac as he took Quock's elbow and gently pulled him toward Lexington. "You're my best friend. I never asked about you being a slave an' all—I didn't want you to think it's anything between us."

"I know." Quock swallowed a swig from the jug. "You're my best friend, too."

"And you know Mister Nithercott going to free you."

"I don't know what Mister Nithercott is going to do."

"I heard that he was going to free you at your eighteenth birthday."

"I heard that, but not from him."

"When we joined the militia, my dad heard him tell Reverend Clarke that if we fight, he will free you."

"I heard that, too. Mister Nithercott told everyone in the county but me."

"Why hasn't he told you?"

"I don't know." Quock shook his head. "Mister Nithercott is a good man, but I'd be lying if I said it doesn't drive me mad that he won't tell me nothing."

"But you're gonna fight—right?"

"I thought about that a lot." Quock took another swig of cider. "I decided that instead of worrying about what a slave will do, I asked myself, what would I do if I was free." He looked at Isaac. "And fighting with you for our country and our rights is what I would do. Free or enslaved."

Isaac smiled and slapped him on the back. "Like you said, Mister Nithercott is a good man. He'll free you, and we'll whip those redcoats together."

Quock picked up the pace toward Lexington, "Amen to that."

They arrived in darkened Lexington. Quock could make out Buckman's Tavern, but the lamp-carrying crowds were gone, and only candlelight showed through Buckman's dirty windows. A dozen or so people were sleeping on the green with their muskets close by. After all the noise and excitement less than an hour ago, the quiet was unsettling. *Had the whole thing been called off?*

Isaac pushed open the tavern door and walking in behind him, Quock saw Mister Nithercott sitting at a table in the taproom with the other leadership of the training band. Mister Nithercott had been commander of Lexington's militia until six months ago, when the Massachusetts Provincial Congress had ordered all militia officers to resign and to hold elections for new officers, ostensibly to allow younger officers in senior positions. Mister Nithercott complained to Quock and the rest of the family that Congress was purging Loyalists and Tories and declined to run. The band elected John Parker, also a veteran of the last war but ten years younger than Mister Nithercott. Parker refused to serve, however, unless Nithercott consented to stay on, too. Mister Nithercott agreed, but he did not want a commission from the "faithless Whigs" in Congress and instead chose the position of senior sergeant. Thereafter, Lexington's training band continued to serve its community as it had for generations with the same mix of Whigs and Tories as before the purge. After Congress forced Mister Nithercott to resign, Quock remembered an exasperated Missus Nithercott asking her husband why he still served; Mister Nithercott replied, "It won't get done if I don't do it."

Quock carried his burdens to the table where the men were in a loud, beery conversation. "Woah there, Vern," Nithercott was saying. "I didn't say nothing about independence. I'm an Englishman, a loyal subject of King George, and I ain't no damn Whig."

"Ebenezer!" hushed his companions, nodding to the Reverend Clarke sitting with them at the same table.

"Let 'em be." Clarke raised his beer to Nithercott.

"I've known Jonas Clarke my whole life. He knows my politics," said Mister Nithercott.

"What if we shoot up a troop of the King's men? What will the King think of your loyalty then?" asked Parker.

"They're acting under the order of the ministers. If the King knew what was going on here, none of this would happen." Several men around the table nodded or grunted in agreement.

"Those lordly ministers are so drunk they couldn't find their arses using both hands," said Vernon. The table burst into a roar of drunken laughter.

Quock had heard these arguments circulate many times before. Slipping up behind Nithercott and trying to avoid interrupting, Quock whispered, "Sir, here's your bedroll and haversack."

"Thank you, Quock," he patted him on the shoulder. "Take a can of beer and you and Isaac get some sleep outside. I'll be out in a bit."

"Yes sir.—Thank you, Mister Buckman," to the Tavern owner and fellow militiaman who handed Quock and Isaac each a tankard of beer.

"You boys sleep good so you can wake us old farts in the morning." Buckman's joke earned another burst of laughter.

"Yes sir," Quock took the tankard and headed for the door.

"And don't forget to bring back those cans!" shouted Buckman as Isaac and Quock skidded out the door.

Back outside, Quock and Isaac looked for a dry place to sleep. On the green snoring, militiamen had already taken the few dry mounds and under the eaves of Buckman's was head to foot with more.

"Let's try the Meeting House," suggested Isaac. They walked across the green and found they were the first to choose the north side. They rested their muskets against the church, spread out their ground cloths and sat shoulder to shoulder, drinking their beer and gazing out over the peaceful moonlit village.

"Do you think we're ready to fight the regulars?" asked Quock.

"Course we are. We've been training nearly every week all winter." Isaac's warm breath came out in vapors. New England's spring chill nipped their faces.

"Yeah, but the regulars train every day for years. Some of 'em been in the army their whole lives."

"They might be wicked good at marching, but how much training do you need to aim and shoot a firelock? We've done that twice already, and I've been practicing a lot on my own."

"I suppose." Quock couldn't shake the feeling of impending doom. He recalled the frequent horseplay, laughter, and lighthearted spirit of musters. How would his fellow militiamen act when faced with trained and ready regulars?

"Their fancy red coats ain't bullet proof neither. Remember the fire drill?"

"Yeah." When the Committee of Safety muskets arrived, the older men spent a day teaching the previously musket-less militiamen to load and shoot. At the end of the day, they used the remaining powder and shot for the whole band to fire a volley at a line of barrels. The noise, fire, and smoke of a hundred guns going off simultaneously was thrilling. Afterward, the many bullet holes and splintered barrels impressed Quock and Isaac.

"But sometimes muster days were more like picnics than training. Maybe we had too much fun," shrugged Quock.

Isaac snorted, "Remember that muster day in Lincoln? You was wicked pissah."

"Hah! I didn't vomit on Deacon Parker's shoes."

"Yeah, Mister Nithercott whipped our asses all the way home." Both boys laughed at the memory.

"I finished my beer."

"Me too."

"I'll take the cans back to Mister Buckman."

"Thanks, Quock. I'll stay here and watch our stuff."

Quock got up, swinging the tankards in one hand he trotted back to Buckman's Tavern. When he opened the door, the tap room was dark. The drinking party had broken up. Mister Nithercott and the others must have gone outside or were perhaps among the people snoring along the walls of the tavern. One person remained at their table reading by candlelight. Quock set the cans down on the bar and turned to leave.

"Quock, is that you?" asked Reverend Clarke.

"Yes, sir, I was just bringing the cans back. I didn't mean to disturb you."

"Can you walk with me back to my house? Hancock will be waiting. My eyes aren't as good in the dark anymore."

"Course."

Clarke closed his Bible, put it under his arm, stood up and snuffed out the candle. Taking the Reverend's arm in the now pitch-dark room, Quock led him out the door. Out on the moonlit green, the parson walked with more assurance but in silence. As they neared the house, Quock could see lights in the windows. People and horses moved about the yard.

"Reverend, are you riding tonight?"

"I'm taking the cart, but yes, we must leave now before the regulars get here."

"What about the patrols?"

"I suppose there is some danger, but better to die a martyr and gain my reward in heaven than live as a slave."

"Yes sir," Quock wondered if the parson had forgotten who he was talking to.

"Quock, God has not forgotten you," Clarke held his arm, "The table is set. The banquet of freedom is ready. All are welcome. You must be bold and step up to take your place."

"Yes, sir."

"Neither has Ebenezer Nithercott forgotten his promise." Clarke wagged his finger.

"Yes, sir," The reverend opened the door and entered his house, leaving Quock standing on the step. Quock walked back to the meeting house, thinking about the parson's words. He found Isaac sound asleep and sat down next to him.

Quock had mixed feelings about the church. Although Clarke preached that all people were equal before God, in church Quock learned what it meant to be black in New England. Despite attending with the Nithercotts, Quock sat on the balcony with the other blacks. The whites called the meeting house's balcony Negro Heaven, but the blacks all knew its real purpose was to remind them of their place at the bottom of New England society.

The division of black and white was without regard to wealth or social position. Samuel Gibson, a free black man making a good living as a joiner, sat in Negro Heaven. While Patrick Duffy, the Hadley's penniless and illiterate Irish indentured servant, was on the ground floor with the whites.

His feelings were equally mixed about Mister Nithercott's promises. Since Mister Nithercott made the covenant with Reverend Clarke, he had kept his other promises. He sent Quock to school like his other children, taught him to farm, and treated him like a member of the family. As Quock got older, however, he wondered about his place in the Nithercott's affections. Mister Nithercott also took good care of his animals. Sometimes, laying on his bed at night, Quock wondered if he was only a well-cared-for two-legged livestock. Loved like a dog, but not a full person.

Quock's doubts drove his impatience to know when Mister Nithercott would keep his last promise. Quock thought of many reasons Mister Nithercott might not give him an answer on his freedom. Mister Nithercott was a New Englander through and through—stubborn and tightfisted; he was reluctant to pay a debt until he got his full value. Admitting to the covenant to free Quock was also an admission that keeping him enslaved was a moral failing. Perhaps he was afraid that Quock would leave the moment he was freed. Worse, maybe Nithercott would renege on the promise. Quock would have no recourse, no court to appeal the injustice. He had thought about this subject so often it could no longer hold his attention. Lying next to his best friend, leaning against the Church, with his hand on the cold stock of his musket, Quock finally fell asleep.

Chapter Six

The barge ground up on the North side of the Charles River. The big navy barge was several yards from shore, but it had already bottomed and could get no closer. "There's nothing for it, sir. You'll have to wade," said the midshipman from the stern-sheets.

Llewellyn was more worried about the horse than getting wet himself. The big gelding was an Army horse, used to unusual situations; nevertheless, it whinnied nervously and was moving about, nearly stepping on the wary oarsmen. The problem was getting it on shore without trampling the crew or upsetting the boat. The horse solved the problem by leaping the gunwale the moment Llewellyn removed the cloth from his eyes. Followed closely by the bat horse. Llewellyn jumped in the water up to his waist—icy cold on his balls—grabbed the horse's reins with his right hand, holding musket and cartridge box above his head with the left, and splashed to shore. When Llewellyn turned around to wave the barge off, it was already backing and turning toward Boston.

All up and down the muddy riverbank, grenadiers were jumping out of their barges and wading waist-deep, holding their firelocks, cartridge bags, and other accouterments above their heads. Whistles blew to gather the companies.

"Put a stopper in the whistling!" shouted Llewellyn.

"Sir," Pitcairn and De Bernicre appeared at his side.

"Major Pitcairn, must I repeat myself? This is to be a secret march. Absolute quiet is the watchword. Pray order all your companies to stop whistling, drums, fifes, and any other confounded noise." It wasn't the noise that worried Llewellyn so much as the lack of discipline. If small orders were ignored now, how would the troops respond in a crisis?

"I quite agree," said Pitcairn. The noise had already subsided. "May I report on the condition of my command?"

"If you please."

"All ten companies are across. We total three hundred and twenty-six men. We have almost completed the ration issue, and I have a small detachment of marines here to lead the grenadiers to their places as they arrive."

"Very good," said Llewellyn. "What is the condition of the road?"

"With your permission, I was hoping to reconnoiter and find it."

"There's no road?"

"There is nothing but marsh in every direction. For now, I am placing the companies along the riverbank."

Llewellyn checked his watch, holding it out so he could read the face in the moonlight, "Damn! Look at the time. Yes, proceed at once, but be back here before one o'clock."

Llewellyn rode along the muddy riverbank with Pitcairn and De Berniere to the front of the column, passing companies of soldiers mostly sitting or lying on any dry spot or driftwood they could find, smoking pipes and waiting for orders to move. At the head of the column, he stopped and waved on Pitcairn and De Berniere, who cantered off into the dark. Llewellyn dismounted, and, holding the reins of his horse, he walked a few yards along the bank until it was quiet and still. He heard the usual night noises of small animals rustling in the leaves and an owl call, but no church bells or drums that might signal the militia. Satisfied, he returned to his horse and rode back to the landing site.

More companies had arrived, and the marines guided them to their places. Llewellyn stood on the shore next to his field desk and the blue lantern when Whelks and his big mare landed.

"The last company is debarking behind me." Whelks sat down on a large driftwood log and took off his riding boots one at a time, pouring out the water.

"Your report, Steven," said Llewellyn.

"All eleven companies will be across in minutes." Whelks pulled his boots back on. "Because of the wait on the common, I completed victualing and set up the order-of-march as you suggested. I made a complete count; I have three hundred and ninety men."

"Thank you, Steven. The quartermaster is issuing rations to the last of the light-bobs. I expect Pitcairn shortly."

A few minutes later, Pitcairn and De Berniere rode up. "Sir, I found a road west. It's fifty rods up the riverbank."

"No road?" asked Whelks.

"We are fortunate that the governor selected a secluded spot to disembark us," said Llewellyn, trying to put the best face on the mounting illustrations of poor planning.

"I could manage with less wealth of the governor's concern," griped Whelks.

Llewellyn ignored him and asked Pitcairn, "Any sign of alarm?"

"No, sir. However, the noise of our horses crossing a bridge was quite loud, thunderous, really. To reduce noise, we avoided crossing the bridge on the return and instead forded the creek. I suggest that we employ similar measures on the march to mask our presence."

Llewellyn nodded, "The soldiers are already wet to the waste. They won't melt with another ford or two."

"Sir, if I may," said Whelks. "Fording creeks will slow the march."

"Thank you, Steven. You are quite right, but for now, secrecy trumps speed. We will only ford until dawn. If we lose too much time or we find that the militia are alerted, we will discontinue fording." Llewellyn pulled out his watch and frowned. "Gentlemen, it is past one o'clock. Move to the front of your commands. We will set off as soon as the ration issue is complete."

The brush by the river was thick and wet with dew, wetting his stockings. When Jason got close to the road, he stopped and listened. No sound. He looked both ways at the moonlit road. No one. He turned northwest and started walking. Although Jason's upper body was strong, he had short legs, he had gained more than a few pounds over the years, and he was unaccustomed to long walks. His legs were tired, but he pushed himself to walk fast. He saw a crooked stone wall he knew was only a half mile from his uncle's farm.

A few minutes later, Jason could see the gate. As he walked across the well-kept yard, Jason recalled Mary's frequent lament that it was a shame that such a handsome man had never married. Uncle Adam was over seventy years old and now lived in semi-retirement, alone but for an equally aged and unwed farmhand who had been with him for years. Uncle Adam rented out most of his land for neighbors to farm. The two bachelors kept only a garden for kitchen vegetables and a pasture with a couple of horses for pulling a cart. When Jason got to the door, he found it locked. He knocked on the door, but no answer. He pounded louder, but still no answer. Finally, he bellowed loudly toward the upper floor bedrooms, but no one answered, and no one came to the door.

"Goddam it! Is anything going to be easy tonight?" Jason walked around the house trying to open the windows and the back door, all locked. He continued to yell loudly to wake his uncle. He finally decided he was going to take a horse and leave a note. "Deaf old man," he muttered to himself.

He turned around the corner to the front of the house and stepped right up to the point of a bayonet, three, in fact, mounted on the muskets of three King's soldiers. A fourth soldier said, "Who thee' calling for Yank?"

"This is private land. What are you doing here?"

"I'm on the king's business watching out for rebels. People wandering about late at night bellowing all around is enough suspicion for me."

"This is my uncle's house. I was just trying to wake him to let me in."

"That's a Banbury tale if I ever heard one." The soldier's accent was thick, barely understandable.

"All we have to do is wake my uncle. He'll tell you who I am."

"Thee already did enough bawling to wake the dead. Thine uncle, if this is his house, is probably off with his rebel mates plotting treason against the king."

Jason glanced around with the notion of running. "Go ahead and run, Yank," said the sergeant. "Me boys need some bayonet drill."

"You'd start a civil war killing an unarmed man on his uncle's doorstep."

"P'raps mate, but that wouldn't be thy concern anymore, would it?" Speaking to one of his soldiers, "Stimson, search him. We'll know if he's armed or no, then bind him."

One of the soldiers leaned his musket against the house, then taking rope out of his knapsack, he bound Jason's hand and put another around his neck, handing the end to the sergeant. Then he searched Jason's coat and haversack pulling out his wallet and showing the sergeant the food Mary had packed for him.

"Why thankee, mate. We ain't had nothing all day but brown George and bog oranges. This will keep us till morning." In Jason's purse, he fingered the money and smiled. "He's got some shiners."

"Water," said Stimson with undisguised disgust after taking a swig from Jason's canteen.

"Oh bother," said the only one still holding his gun on Jason.

The sergeant put the wallet in his coat pocket, took out a knife to slice up Jason's bread and meat and distributed it evenly among the four of them. They wolfed it down, hardly pausing to chew.

"What's your name, sergeant?" demanded Jason.

"Sergeant Milo Thurston, the King's Own fourth regiment of foot, Captain Cochrane's company."

"Well, Sergeant Thurston, I saw you pocket my wallet. I know how much money was in there. I want to speak to your commanding officer."

"Thee will, Yank. We're on our way to meet him. I'll keep thy wallet safe and return it if they don't hang thee for treason."

"I am a loyal subject of His Majesty, and I strongly object to being waylaid by highwaymen disguised as King's soldiers."

Sergeant Thurston gave Jason a vicious blow across his back with the rope's end. "Shut it! Thee art a seditious militiaman caught trying to organize a rebellion. I'm looking forward to lashing thee to a triangle and beating the hide off thy back."

Sergeant Thurston picked up his halberd and shoved Jason on the back with it. "Move, Yank, we're marching to Menotomy. Don't want to be late to thine own hanging."

Llewellyn led his corps along the muddy riverbank until they struck the road. Once they had climbed out of the marsh, the road was reasonably dry for springtime. A rough and uneven rock wall lined the road. The wall was a good guide, reducing accidental missteps in the dark. At the first bridge, the column backed up as those in front picked their way down to the stream bank. Once at the water, the soldiers waded in manfully and then scrambled up the other side, but the damage was done—the column was moving slower. Steven crossed, still mounted, his horse splashing soldiers all around. Llewellyn dismounted and waded in beside a company of grenadiers. He didn't splash them, nevertheless, Llewellyn had to pretend not to hear their muttering about mud and cold water.

Back on the dry road, they passed several houses, all of which were dark and silent, a good sign that the militia was not yet alerted to their raid. Holding it out to catch maximum moonlight, Llewellyn examined the map Gage had given him; the road didn't fork until Menotomy. He began to relax in the saddle. Despite the inauspicious start, perhaps this raid would be a doddle after all.

In the distance, just above silence, Llewellyn heard a church bell. At first, his conscious mind resisted, but with each ring, the bell forced its warning onto him. A minute later, he heard the clatter of galloping hoofs, and Pitcairn appeared. "Sir, we can hear church bells."

"They know we're coming. We'll have to leg it now," said Llewellyn. "John, take your first six companies and march with all dispatch to seize the north and south bridges around Concord. We'll suspend fording around bridges."

Pulling the lead around Jason's neck, the small party was walking at a brisk pace. Sergeant Thurston did not pull on the lead viciously nor with any plain ill intent, but with his hands tied, Jason's walking rhythm was disturbed and awkward. Further, the rough rope chafed his neck. Sweat rolled down into the agitated skin and stung.

They walked steadily for more than an hour. There was little conversation. To Jason, the four soldiers seemed tired and afraid. The reason for their fear was obvious enough. They could hear church bells ringing. The occasional sound of a far-off gunshot would cause them to turn their heads and listen. Once, they saw a signal fire in the distance. The sights and sounds of the Massachusetts militia being called out. It was apparent to them all that someone had sent out the alarm.

Jason feared he would see his regiment fight while he sat on the sidelines as a captive. Stimson had done a poor job tying the ropes. Working his hands back and forth, Jason soon had to grip the bindings so they wouldn't drop off. He waited for an opportunity to run.

Sergeant Thurston fell back with Jason and asked companionably, "Thee can hear thy mates turning out."

"I can hear the same thing you hear, the bells, but I wasn't raising the alarm."

"P'raps, we're a bit gallied, but our patrols are on these roads. Thy militia will not save thee."

"I am a loyal subject of King George; you are supposed to be my protection."

Thurston just grinned, "Know what's wrong with Yanks?"

"We find it awkward to walk with our hands tied and ropes around our necks?"

"Art no character in thy speech."

Jason remained silent, but sergeant Thurston continued lecturing.

"At home in Wigan, even if I were blindfolded, I'd know a man's county and his station just by the manner of his speech. Here in the colonies, ye all sound alike. Even Negroes sound like topping men. It turns my stomach to listen to Yanks speaking the King's English like gentlemen."

"People I've met from Virginia have accents."

"P'raps to thine ears. To me, it's all the same. Yanks all flash the gentlemen, but ye naught but a nation of dandies. I believe that lack of character in thy speech reflects the lack of character in thy society."

"Thank you for your opinion. I will keep it safe in the jakes," said Jason. Sergeant Thurston's response was a sharp blow across Jason's back with the rope's end.

They had marched steadily without a break and the soldiers were lagging. Sergeant Thurston stopped at a house with a well in the front yard. "Take a rest. Stimson and Blackwell fill the canteens. Johnson, guard the prisoner while I bleed me lizard." Stimson and Blackwell gathered the canteens and headed to the well while Thurston jumped the low wall that bordered the road and disappeared in the dark.

Jason sat on the ground. His legs were tired, and he was glad for the relief. Johnson held Jason's lead slack. Jason looked around, wondering if this was his opportunity to escape.

"Sir," whispered Johnson when the others were out of earshot.

"Yeah?" said Jason in a normal voice, trying to appear interested.

"Sir, I want to desert."

"What?" Jason stretched his legs.

"I want to desert. Sergeant Thurston beats us like dogs. The officers steal our pay, and if we object, they lash the hides off our backs. The Yanks in Boston call us bloody backs for good reason."

"I'm not in a position to free myself, much less a King's man."

"But you know the militia. You can tell them I'm a real deserter."

"Why should I do that?" When Jason served next to the regulars in Quebec, the officers had a chronic fear of desertion. The poor pay, bad food, and harsh discipline taken together, Jason wondered more didn't desert. Nevertheless, on principle, he didn't approve of desertion.

"The recruitment officer bought me a pint, told me a tale of honored service, warm barracks, and promised five guineas, but the moment the money was in my hands. I found all the rest was lies."

"You're hardly the first man that recruiters lied to. That story's been around since Christ was a corporal."

"It's not the lies; it's the life. I was a mechanic. I can make anything you want. I would make a good colonist. I would have to live on the frontier, but I have something to offer—"

"Stop talking to the prisoner, Johnson," said the returning Thurston, buttoning up his breeches. He did not say anything else, so he apparently had not overheard Johnson's plea.

"Five pints o' beer a day, that's our ration. We ain't had naught but water." Stimson whined as he returned with the canteens.

"Shut it," said Thurston.

"We could a' carried a gill or two o' rum."

Thurston swung at him with his halberd. Stimson ducked the blow, but he stopped complaining for the moment.

"Good night, gentlemen," said a man walking up behind them. "The road is busy tonight."

The startled soldiers recovered their wits and aimed their muskets at the traveler. "What art thee about, mate?" demanded Sergeant Thurston.

With his eyes wide, he held up his arms as if to ward off a blow, "Well I didn't, well."

"Spit it out, mate."

"I was just returning home from courting my intended."

The soldiers laughed. "Well, now thee art in the tender embrace of the King's Own fourth regiment of foot," said Thurston. "Perhaps not as comely as thy lass, but I guarantee we will keep thy attention. Tie him up, Stimson." The unfortunate man was quickly bound, and the lead around his neck was handed to Thurston.

"Where art thee bound?"

"Menotomy, just a quarter mile up the road. I was going to be home soon."

"Ye will be home soon," said Thurston.

Just as the new captive predicted, a few minutes later, Thurston's squad and prisoners entered Menotomy. In the town square was a small party of mostly regulars on horseback, but one was a civilian. A redcoat had the reins of his horse. He, too, was a prisoner. With a shock, Jason recognized the mounted prisoner, a choir singer at Jason's church, a radical Whig, a Freemason, an active Son of Liberty, and, in Jason's opinion, a vainglorious bunghole—Paul Revere.

During the political crisis leading to the destruction of the East India Company's tea, Jason and Revere had argued over how to address colonist's objections to the tax. Jason wanted a reasoned and respectful approach, but Revere assigned evil intent to every Parliamentary action and questioned Jason's patriotism—a charge Jason resented.

On Election Day, a few weeks before the tea was destroyed, the Corps of Cadets was standing in an honor guard, all in their best red coats, presenting arms as Royal Custom Commissioners passed to attend Governor Hutchinson's annual dinner. Revere and his crowd of riffraff were jeering the Commissioners and throwing mud balls. Revere threw one that hit Jason accidentally on purpose. Although Jason did not react, others in the corps did, and the formal ceremony dissolved into a brawl. John Hancock, the elected Colonel of the Corps of Cadets, was furious, and two members of the Corps resigned.

That marked a turning point in the Corp's relationship with the governor. Less than a year later, Governor Hutchinson dismissed John Hancock as commander. Since the Corps had elected Hancock, they could not ignore the governor's affront to their authority. Jason and the rest of the company resigned their commissions in protest. The Corps of Cadets was no more, and, at least in Jason's mind, Paul Revere and his hooligans were in part to blame.

Thurston led them to the horsemen. "Sir, Captain Cochrane?" asked Thurston to the officer holding Revere's reins.

"Over here," said one of the horsemen.

"Sergeant Thurston reporting, sir. With two prisoners."

"Good to see you safe, Sergeant." Captain Cochrane gestured toward Jason and his fellow prisoner. "Militiamen?"

"One for certain, he was trying to rouse out his fellows when we captured him. The other one has a story, but he's still on the road late at night."

"Major Mitchell, my foot patrol captured two prisoners," said Captain Cochrane to one of the other mounted officers.

"Arms?" asked Mitchell.

"Neither of them had weapons, sir," said Thurston.

"Not very famous militiamen without arms," said Mitchell. "Keep them anyway; perhaps Colonel Caradoc will want to question them when we reach Concord."

Caradoc! The man Jason had supped with only a few hours before. It would be difficult to offer a plausible explanation of why he was out on this night. Sergeant Thurston's threats of hanging or flogging for sedition were approaching reality. Jason lowered his head to keep his face in shadow while eyeballing for Caradoc. For his part, if Revere recognized Jason, he did not show it. Out of the darkness appeared a fast-marching column of regulars.

"What regiment?" asked Mitchell.

"Royal Marines, sir," replied the lieutenant marching in front.

"Marines?"

"Yes, sir. We're the sharp end of an entire corps. Mostly Army." An officer appeared on horseback. Mitchell and the other officers conferred for a few moments.

While they talked, Captain Cochrane rode back to Sergeant Thurston. "Sergeant Thurston, 4th regiment's light-bobs are next after the marines. Fall in with them."

"What about my prisoners?"

"We'll sort them out in Concord." Then Mitchell and his party rode on with Revere in tow.

Sergeant Thurston and his squad ran to catch up with the passing company, towing Jason and his fellow captive. Jason watched the horsemen disappear and looked for an opportunity to escape. The morning was coming, and Caradoc would surely recognize him in the light of day.

As his corps marched into Menotomy, Llewellyn was anxious to meet with the mounted patrol and the two artillery chaises Gage had sent out. The horsemen could give him news on the road ahead, and he needed the gunners to destroy the artillery they uncovered in Concord. The sound of several galloping horses was a relief. Pitcairn appeared along with a party of mounted officers and a civilian prisoner on horseback.

"Sir, Major Mitchell, fifth regiment of foot," said a smallish but still dashing officer saluting from his horse next to Pitcairn.

"Lieutenant Colonel Caradoc. I have the honor of commanding this corps," returning the salute. "Do you have the artillery chaises with you?"

"Artillery chaises?" Mitchell looked at his fellows, who shook their heads. "No sir, I have no knowledge of chaises."

"Governor Gage dispatched two chaises with artillerymen and special equipment. We were to meet them in Menotomy."

"Sir, we've seen no chaises nor artillerymen."

"Quite all right, I'm sure they'll turn up. What news of the road?"

"Sir, I cannot say about all the way to Concord, but the militia has been alerted. We intercepted several riders near Lincoln and captured this one, Mister Revere." He held up the reins of the mounted civilian. "They were turning out the militia."

"Explain yourself, sir," Llewellyn demanded from the sneering Revere.

"We knew of your raid and have raised the alarm. By now, there are dozens of riders out warning the entire country. Militia from all over New England are descending on you. Your expedition is doomed. You will never get back to Boston alive!"

"Enough, sir!" ordered Llewellyn. "I'll brook no treasonous speech."

Revere stopped his boasting, but Llewellyn could see the damage was done. The angry faces of his officers were a warning that hot emotion would influence cool military reason. Worse, their small party was along-side the moving column of soldiers, and many of the soldiers had heard Revere's threatening rant. Angry rumors would spread.

The group of riders had now entered the Menotomy town square. Llewellyn signaled for the group to get off the road and then dismount. "Colonel Whelks, Major Pitcairn, keep the column moving if you please. Speed is our best security now."

"Sir," Whelks saluted and spurred his horse.

"Major Mitchell, pray ride to the front with Ensign De Berniere. Scout as far forward as you may with safety. Report any effort on the part of the militia to block our way."

"Sir, but what of my prisoners? We have two others on foot."

"Any intelligence value?"

"None to speak of. The two my foot patrol picked up were unarmed. I believe they were just in the wrong place at the wrong time." Nodding to Revere, "This one, however, certainly has some knowledge of rebel plans."

"Perhaps, but right now, he is a burden to our movement. Release them at your convenience. Before you go, I want to borrow one of your riders to send a message back to Governor Gage."

"Certainly, sir," said Mitchell. "Lieutenant Prescott here knows the road, and his horse is reasonably fresh."

"Thank you. Prescott, wait a moment while I draft a message." Mitchell and the rest of the party rode off, pulling the American prisoner with them. Prescott waited as Bleddyn unpacked Llewellyn's writing kit. Setting the paper on his knee and the ink pot by his side, Llewellyn quickly wrote a note explaining the situation. He believed Revere's threats were more bravado than fact, but Revere aside, there was no doubt the militia were turning out, and Llewellyn feared he was leading his corps into a trap. Summoning Robert's brigade to cover his return was the most prudent tactical move.

He wrote the basic facts and hoped that Governor Gage or Robert would act with haste and sufficient force. Finished writing, Llewellyn blew the ink dry, rolled the bit of paper, and wrapped it in a short piece of twine. He handed it to Lieutenant Prescott. "Take this to Governor

Gage's adjutant with all speed. I don't need to tell you that the lives of many men are at risk."

"Sir, I understand. I will not fail." Prescott saluted, leaped on his horse, and galloped off toward Boston.

Llewellyn pulled out his watch. It was almost four o'clock. If he were in garrison, the drummer would soon beat reveille. He wondered if the country people woke at four o'clock, too. He shook his head; they were farmers, and of course, they got up early.

As he marched out of Menotomy, Jason's fellow prisoner was visibly upset. "Let me go. We already passed my house." His response was Thurston's rope's end across his back. Major Mitchell and a party of riders passed them at a gallop. Paul Revere was still among them. The officers' faces were set in scowls.

As the regular's column moved, the signs and sounds of mustering militia could be heard and seen everywhere. Drums, gunshots, and church bells sounded in every direction. It was now common to see beacon fires and candles twinkling in the windows of houses they passed. The mood of the regulars had changed, too, from the usual grudging acceptance of soldiers engaged in an unwelcome chore, to sullen anger. When they heard a distant bugle, Sergeant Thurston said, "See 'ow 'e sounds blowin' that bugle out 'is arse." The soldiers laughed appreciatively, "Goddam Yanks, give the bastards the guts of my gun; 'ang the lot ov 'em."

The sky was getting lighter. Jason heard the crowing of roosters and birds twittering in the trees. Another half hour and the day was clearly dawning. Somewhere up ahead, the column halted. A few minutes later, they could hear running horses and shouts. Then, the column started moving again. They passed another building. Jason recognized Monroe Tavern. He had stopped there before on trips to Lexington to visit his brother. No beer this time.

Soon, the column halted again. Jason could hear some of the officers talking. The words were indistinct, ". . . in ranks on the green . . . several hundred . . ." Jason guessed they were talking about Lexington's militia. He didn't know how many men there were in the regular's column, but Jason figured it was at least two, maybe three battalions strong. Could the village of Lexington muster enough militia to resist a regiment or more of regulars? It seemed unlikely. Up ahead, a sergeant ordered, "Prime and load!" The order moved down the column company by company and soon all had loaded their muskets.

Chapter Seven

Five o'clock a.m.

Quock woke to the sound of a galloping horse. He sat up straight. In the gray light, he saw a horseman ride up to Buckmans' Tavern, leap off and run inside. His horse stood untethered, breathing hard, steam rising from its heaving sides. Quock shook Isaac, "Hey, something's happening."

Isaac sat up, rubbing his eyes and stretching, "What?"

"Mister Bowman just rode up in a hurry."

Isaac came fully awake, and both boys pulled on their half boots, fumbling with the laces. Thaddeus Bowman and Captain Parker came out of Buckmans' Tavern. In the quiet of the early dawn, Quock and Isaac could hear both men talking.

"Where?" asked Parker while pulling his suspenders over his shoulder.

"They're already at the Rocks. I would have been here earlier, but I got trapped behind and had to ride clear around," said Bowman.

"Lord, it's happening," exclaimed Parker.

"Damn," Both boys looked at each other, eyes wide. Quock's insides tightened. The Rocks were less than a half mile away.

"How many?" Parker asked Bowman.

"I couldn't count 'em, but the column is long. At least a thousand."

"Did you see any other militia?"

"No, sir. I heard Church bells and such; the alarm is out, but I didn't see nobody."

More men stumbled out of the Tavern. Finding William Diamond, the band's drummer, Parker said, "Get your drum and beat assembly." William ran back inside the Tavern. Quock was already rolling up his bed roll. Even before they had finished, they could hear the drum's long roll, and someone started ringing the Church bell. They packed quickly and then ran out onto the green. There were already twenty men forming up in front of the tavern and more running up from every direction.

"Prime and load," ordered Parker.

Nithercott looked at Parker with a raised eyebrow.

"Better to do it now. If we load in front of the regulars, they might take it as a provocation."

Mister Nithercott nodded, unslung his Charleville and started loading, but to the band, he said, "Cover your pans and half-cocked."

As Quock and the other men of the training band loaded their muskets, more men were still running to the formation, some loading as they ran. Captain Parker ordered, "Rest your firelocks!" Quock rested his butt stock on the ground and stood at ease. He glanced around at his fellows. They were more subdued than normal. A couple appeared badly hungover, and the overall feeling seemed to be of anxiety, mirroring Quock's uneasy mind. He looked for Isaac, and they exchanged nervous smiles. At the front of the formation, Nithercott and Parker were talking in low voices. Parker nodded at something Nithercott said.

Parker spoke to the training band, "We're going to let the troops pass by. We will not molest them without they fire first."

Just as Parker finished, Quock heard horses on the Bay Road. Even in the dim light of dawn, they could see the horsemen's red coats. The mounted men stopped, pointed at the Lexington training band's swelling ranks, then turned and headed back down the road toward Boston.

Before this morning Quock had seen soldiers several times and never thought too much about them. Now, they were the enemy on Lexington's doorstep. Butterflies fluttered in his stomach. Standing shoulder-to-shoulder with his fellow militiamen, Quock gripped the upper stock of his musket a little harder and promised himself that he would stand and do his duty.

The ringing bell and beating drum had an effect beyond the militia. People were coming outdoors to do their morning chores and were gathering around the green, watching the militia band prepare—for what? As many people were standing along the roads or on the green, as stood in the formation and more were coming out. It occurred to Quock that the militia were dressed the same as the bystanders. Several of the bystanders carried rakes, hoes, or other tools. In the early morning light, those tools might appear to be weapons, especially considering the variety of weapons carried by the militiamen. They were armed with everything from homemade blunderbusses to British Army muskets. Quock hoped that the regulars would think there were a lot more than the fifty or so militiamen that had answered the alarm so far.

"Quock!" said Nithercott from the front of the formation. "Run down to the road and see if you can see the regulars."

"Yes, sir."

"Fire in the air when you see 'em,"

"Yes, sir." Quock picked up his musket and trotted down the road until he could see past the Meeting House. Quock's heart leaped into his mouth. An endless column of regulars packed the road, stretching back as far as he could see. The front of the column was less than a hundred yards away and marching fast. Quock blew out a noiseless scream. He raised his musket and pulled the trigger, but it misfired and only burnt his priming. He ran back to the band's formation. "They're right behind me!"

The officer Jason knew to be Major Mitchell reappeared with the party of horsemen that had gone forward. The mounted marine officer was near enough for Jason to hear Mitchell call out, "Major Pitcairn, we could go no farther. There is a formation of militia drawn up on the village green.

"How many?"

"Five hundred!" shouted Revere, who was still riding with Mitchell. "I warned the whole country. The bell's a 'ringing! The town's alarmed, and you're all dead men!"

"Bollocks to that." Pitcairn ordered Mitchell, "Silence that madman. I'll ride to the front and try and keep the peace. Keep the column moving. We are behind schedule."

Mitchell aimed his pistol at Revere and said, "Any more from you, and I'll blow your bloody brains out."

The column started moving again. Thurston pulled Jason's rope, dragging him forward. After Revere's outburst, Jason could hear the soldiers curse the "Yanks" and their torments. He began to worry that an angry regular might take out his frustrations on the closest available Yanks—himself and his fellow prisoners.

After a few minutes, Jason could see Lexington less than a hundred yards away. The village green seemed covered in people.

"Sir," said Sergeant Thurston to Major Mitchell. "About these prisoners."

Mitchell was standing on his stirrups, trying to see what was going on. "What, sergeant?" He sounded distracted and annoyed.

"Sir, we have been marching all night, and the prisoners are a burden. Can we pass 'em off?"

"These men were unarmed, am I right?" Mitchell turned back to Thurston.

"Yes sir, but this one was hallo'n all about for his mates," Thurston pointed at Jason.

"We have half a thousand fully armed ones in front of us. Do you see?"

A shot was fired somewhere up in front of them. Every eye turned to the front.

"Let these go," said Mitchell, turning his attention back to Lexington. "The mad one on horse cut the reins and girth straps first. Then let him go, too. He can walk home."

Sergeant Thurston started to object, but before he could say anything, the prisoner from Menotomy threw off his ropes and ran back toward Menotomy. In one smooth motion, Private Stimson raised his musket, cocked it, and shot the prisoner in the back before he had run ten steps. The Menotomy man, who hours before had been courting his girl, flopped face-first into the road and lay still. Stimson started reloading as if nothing unusual had happened.

Sergeant Thurston dropped his halberd and grabbed Stimson's still-smoking musket, shouting, "Goddam thee, Stimson! We was releasing them bloody prisoners. We weren't to murder 'em."

Stimson was visibly surprised at Sergeant Thurston's words, then even more surprised when Jason hit him in the face with Thurston's halberd. Jason had shaken off the badly tied ropes when Stimson fired and picked up Thurston's dropped halberd. With a full-body swing, he hit Stimson in the face with the flat side, knocking him to the ground, then punched Thurston in the gut with the blunt end. Dropping the halberd, Jason leaped over the rock wall lining the road and ran all out across a field of new rye, a rope still tied around his neck.

Quock squeezed back into his spot in the formation.

"Load your musket," whispered Isaac.

"Oh yeah," Quock's nervous hands bumbling through the procedure but carefully repacking the barrel. The first rank of regulars appeared at the crossroads. In Quock's eyes, their red uniforms were brilliant in the early morning light. As the formation snaked onto the road, they seemed to march in time like clockwork men. Quock's heart plummeted into his boots as he compared the compact mass of professional soldiers in front of him to the bedraggled men dressed in homespun standing with him. To Quock's surprise, they turned right at the fork toward Bedford instead of following the road to the left toward Concord.

"Where are they going?" Quock said aloud.

The head of the first company of regulars passed in front of the meeting house just as a second column arrived at the fork. They turned right, following the company in front of them, but an officer on horseback galloped to the front of the column, shouting and waving. To avoid the horseman, the second company of regulars veered on to the green, heading straight toward Lexington's training band.

Without orders, Quock and others began to take up their muskets from the rest position.

The officer leading the company of regulars headed toward Bedford now passed the meeting house. The commander seemed to notice the band for the first time. He ordered, "To the Left Wheel! By Platoons March!"

The regulars on Quock's far right began to double-time. Quock knew from experience drilling on the green that in a wheeling movement, the outside men had to quicken the pace to stay online with the half-stepping inside most platoons. But a dozen bayonet-armed redcoats running toward him was startling. Someone cocked his musket. Quock held his musket at the ready, his thumb on the hammer.

The officer leading the second redcoat column onto the green shouted to his men, "To the Right Wheel! By Platoons March!" turning his company to face the training band. The two companies were now swinging like a double gate that would close on the training band. Quock's breath caught in his throat.

The officer on horseback rode toward Lexington's militia, pulled out his pistol, pointed it in the air, and shouted, "Disperse, damn you!" To his own troops, he shouted, "Don't shoot! Surround and disarm them!"

Parker did an about-face and ordered, "Disperse in an orderly fashion." Quock could hear militiamen in the back rank begin to break formation and run. He looked over his shoulder; militiamen running from the formation passed latecomers still running toward them. Some stopped in confusion, looking to Parker and Nithercott for direction. The regulars continued to advance with sure steps and ready bayonets.

"Company! Make Ready!" ordered the officer in the first company of regulars.

"Company! Make Ready!" repeated the officer in the second company.

Frozen in uncertainty, Quock heard more firelocks cocked. He cocked his musket and put his finger on the trigger. Some of the band's latecomers stopped at the rock wall bordering the green and shouted warnings, "Trying to surround you!" Two of them kneeled and fired at the regulars.

The regular officer on horseback fired his pistol in the air. As if in response, the first company of regulars fired a ragged volley. An acrid cloud filled the space between the regulars and the militia. At first, Quock thought they had fired over their heads or fired blanks, but one man fell to the grass. He didn't consciously pull the trigger, but Quock's musket fired, nearly jumping out of his nerveless grasp. He didn't even know where he was pointing it. Several other militiamen fired, too.

"Present! Fire!" shouted the officer from the second company of regulars. A more disciplined volley rolled from their guns. Several Lexington men fell to the ground. Only ten yards away now, both companies of regulars shouted "Huzzah!" and charged at the militiamen.

Quock broke and ran with the stampeding band. Behind him, he could hear the cheering regulars in front, screaming women and children scattered in panic. One militiaman beside him threw down his musket to run faster. Quock thought that was a good idea. Trying to keep a building between himself and Lexington Green, Quock ran toward home.

Running all the way, Quock passed out of Lexington and got within eyesight of his home. He stopped, breathing hard. No redcoats were chasing him. He was overcome with a wave of nausea. He sat on the rock wall that ran beside the road. Another wave of nausea, and he bent over and vomited between his legs. He sat with his head between his legs, spitting the vomit taste out of his mouth. He took a drink of water from his canteen, rinsed out his mouth, spitting it out, and then drank deeply.

He could see his house was only a quarter mile away. Looking back there was no one on the road. *What happened to everybody? Did the red-coats kill them?* He couldn't face Missus Nithercott or Faith, not knowing Mister Nithercott's fate. *Where was Isaac?* Isaac wouldn't leave Quock and run home. Standing up, Quock was surprised he still had his musket. Carrying it at the ready, he walked back toward Lexington.

Riding in the head of his column, Llewellyn fretted about the time. The sun was coming up, and they were still miles from Concord. He was riding next to a dozing Whelks. Llewellyn envied his ability to sleep in the saddle, but he was too keyed up. This raid was pregnant with dangers to his career. A simple mistake by any one of these seven hundred soldiers, a civilian killed or property damaged, could ruin the reputation he had spent a lifetime building.

Was that a shot? Llewellyn sat up in the saddle and listened. More shots, then moments later, the unmistakable sound of volley fire.

"Steven! There is volley fire to our front! Alert your men, but keep them marching. I am riding forward."

Without waiting to see Steven's response, Llewellyn spurred his horse into a gallop. The detachment of six light companies he had sent out to seize the bridges in Concord had not gotten far ahead. He caught up to them after less than a quarter mile. The column had stopped and swelled to fill the road as gawking soldiers moved to the verges to see what was happening in front of them. Many of them even stood on the rock walls, trying to see the road ahead. He rode through them, calling out, "Make way!" Bleddyn shouted, too, as he followed.

Minutes after hearing the shooting, Llewellyn had pushed his way into Lexington. A scene of confusion greeted him. The bodies of almost a dozen provincials lay on the village green, but he could see no other country people. Bands of soldiers ran through the village streets. Pitcairn was shouting for order, but no one was listening.

"Major Pitcairn!" shouted Llewellyn. Pitcairn turned his horse and galloped over, saluting. "What the bloody hell happened?" Llewellyn demanded.

"Colonel Caradoc." Pitcairn was panting from exertion and anxiety, "A party of militia about two hundred strong were assembled on the green. I ordered them to disperse and lay down their arms. They did not. Some of the militia fired their guns, and our men responded with a volley and then charged without orders."

"It was glorious, Lew!" Luke Lillingfield appeared at Llewellyn's elbow. His face glowed with boyish excitement.

With a strong one-armed backswing, Llewellyn knocked Luke off his horse. "Goddam you, Captain! The governor sent us out here to prevent a war, not start one!"

Looking at Pitcairn, he pointed at Lillingfield lying on the ground, "Why is this man mounted? There was no room in the boats for horses for company officers."

Pitcairn stared blankly at Lillingfield for an instant, "Sir, he was across before your order." Anxiety intensified Pitcairn's Scottish burr. "Colonel, the fighting was unintentional. I believe on both sides. No order to fire was given. The militia provoked the men. The militia Colonel ordered his men to disperse, but in the confusion, not all of them did. We may be able to salvage this as an accident."

"Do you see those bodies on the green?" Llewellyn's face was hot with anger. He could feel his eyes bulging. "The Yanks won't agree it was an accident. They'll call it a massacre. We have struck a spark in a powder room."

Llewellyn turned to Lillingfield, still sitting on the ground, his boyish face red and pinched with righteous anger. Llewellyn's blood was still boiling, but he regretted losing his temper, "Captain, you can purchase a King's commission, but you won't earn your flag sitting on your arse. Be so good as to get your men under control and get your company back on the road."

To Pitcairn, "Every minute that passes, more militia will gather against us. We still have a duty to complete in Concord."

Llewellyn rode back to the road. Intercepting a drummer, he ordered, "Beat assembly." Without a word, the drummer began to beat his drum. The drum had its intended effect and soldiers ran out from the village. Minutes later, both companies were standing in formation in front of him. Pitcairn joined him and ordered his company commanders to "Report."

While the company officers were receiving their respective reports, Pitcairn asked Llewellyn, "Sir, may I suggest a volley and three cheers for the morale of the men?"

With a deep frown, Llewellyn glared at Pitcairn, "Are you making game with me?"

Pitcairn pleaded, "No sir, but most of these men have never heard a shot fired in anger. A volley will perhaps make this cockup appear a victory."

"What about painting it as an accident?"

"The Yanks fired first. They cannot, in honesty, testify otherwise. The volley is to strengthen the morale of the men."

"Very well, afterward, get them directly on the road." He spurred his horse back to the road. Behind him, he heard the volley fired into the air, and as he listened to the throaty "Huzzah," Llewellyn wondered if he would regret the loss of powder and shot before they got back to Boston. Moments later, Pitcairn joined Whelks and Llewellyn on the verges of the Green.

"Your report," said Llewellyn.

"Sir, one of the 10th regiment's light-bobs wounded in the leg and my horse was shot twice."

"Can he march?"

"No, sir."

"Your horse?"

"Not so good, I'm afraid. I may be afoot soon."

"Take Lillingfield's horse; put the private on your prisoner's horse."

"Sir."

The sky was brightening a clear blue with a few puffs of clouds; Llewellyn pulled out his watch, "Bloody hell. I hope the Yanks in

Concord are late sleepers." Five minutes later, the last of the column marched out of Lexington.

As he ran, his feet slid in the wet field, and mud caked his shoes. Jason heard a volley fired from Lexington. He didn't turn around until he was at the far edge of the field. No one was following him. He pulled the rope off his neck and threw it down.

Jason could not be sure about the outcome of the shooting, nor could he do anything about it if he did know, so he trotted off toward his brother's farm with occasional glances behind. His trot was fast in the beginning, but as he saw no pursuers he slowed to a fast walk. Finally, he saw his brother's house in the distance. When they were still young men, Jason had moved to Boston to earn his fortune, but his brother Bill had married a farmer's daughter in Lexington and later inherited his wife's father's farm. As Jason got closer, he could see someone standing on the roof. When he got nearer, he saw it was his fourteen-year-old niece.

"Sarah, where is your father?" he shouted as soon as he was in hailing distance.

"Uncle Jason? What are you doing here? Was that shooting in Lexington? Did you come from there?"

"Come down here and talk to me like a Christian."

Sarah dived through the dormer window. Jason went over to the well and drew up the bucket. He ladled gulps of water and washed his face. The cold water invigorated him. Sarah burst out the front door and ran to his side.

"What's going on, Uncle Jason?"

"You answer my questions first. Where is your father?"

"They rang the bell. Dad and Jerome rode off to muster with their minute company at Concord."

Jason didn't see anyone else. "Where's your mother?"

"Negro Sally's having a baby. Mom's at the Whitacre's helping the midwife. She took Enos with her."

"What horses are left?" Jason walked toward the barn.

"Only two, Wicked and Goldie. Goldie's lame."

Arriving at the barn, Jason said, "The gray is Wicked?"

"Her name is Smoke," said Sarah. "Wicked is her temper."

"Saddles?"

"There's only Grandpa's old saddle."

"Help me saddle and bridle her."

Sarah talked a steady stream while putting bridle, reins, blanket, and saddle on the horse. "She is the meanest horse we ever had. Dad says he's gonna make sausage out of her if she don't settle down by the fall."

Jason tried to help, but Sarah was fast and efficient, so he stayed out of her way, just holding Wicked's reins. Wicked bit him.

"Ouch!" shouted Jason and swatted her nose.

"Keep tight on the reins. Don't let her have an opening to bite." When Sarah had threaded the girth strap and was tightening it, she gave the horse a strong knee in the stomach.

"What are you doing? There's no need to kick her."

"She's blowing out her stomach, so the girth strap stays loose. She wants to throw you."

Wicked looked Jason in the eye and stepped on his foot.

"Ouch! Darn! Son-of-a-gun! You blasted flea bag that hurt!"

"Told ya'," said Sarah, putting a half hitch in the girth strap and then stepping away.

"We'll see who's boss," Jason climbed up on the mare's back. Wicked bolted out of the stall, just missing the wary Sarah and tried to scrape Jason off against the stall gate. While Jason was recovering his saddle, she tried to scrape him off against the barn door. Jason kept his seat only by lifting his leg out of the stirrup, but that was the opening Wicked needed to bolt. She jumped into a run. Jason nearly fell off as Wicked ran full tilt around the house. Jason finally got firm in the saddle just as Wicked ran under the clothesline. Throwing the lines over his head, Jason pulled all the way back on the reins, bringing her to a near-sitting halt.

"Where ya' goin', Uncle Jason?"

"I'm going to Concord. You stay inside and bar the windows and doors. Don't let no one in!"

"Did the war start?" Sarah threw him a horsewhip.

"God preserve us! I hope not!" shouted Jason. He guided the horse onto a farm trail that ran parallel to the great road to Concord and whipped Wicked into a run. That seemed the right thing to do. Wicked was not friendly, but she could run. Holding his hat and letting her run seemed the best choice. Jason leaned low over Wicked's neck, feeling the wind in his face. *I'll make up some time at this pace.*

After a mile, Jason pulled in the reins a little and tried to slow her into a canter. But she didn't seem to understand what he wanted and kept alternating between a trot and a gallop. After a little experimentation, he managed to get her into a canter, but she had a cross gait that hurt his back, and he couldn't imagine it was comfortable for her either. To his right, he could see a long line of redcoats, their muskets topped with glittering bayonets, marching on the great road to Concord. He persisted in the canter and started to draw ahead of their column.

Robert woke with a start. Light streaming in through the window shined in his eyes. It was already full morning. He sat up. His coat was hung on the back of his desk chair, his boots lying beside the bed where he'd kicked them off; he was otherwise still fully dressed from the night before.

"Matthew!" he called. His adjutant rushed into the room.

"I didn't mean to wake you."

"You should have. No messages?"

"Nothing. Missus Bisacre is serving breakfast if you please."

"I'll be right down."

Robert quickly washed, shaved, and put on a fresh shirt. In the dining room, he dabbled at his bacon, eggs, and toast, but he couldn't stop worrying about what had become of Llewellyn's corps and why there were no messages.

"Robert!" said Matthew, rushing into the breakfast room. "I just found this on my desk. Someone must have delivered it while we were sleeping."

Matthew handed him a rolled-up cartridge paper. Robert unrolled it and recognized Llewellyn's blocky handwriting. It had a postscript from Gage written in the margins. After reading through it, he leaped from his chair.

"I'm off to Province House to see Governor Gage. Send for the commanders and have them report here immediately. I will explain as soon as I get back." Robert ran the whole way, arriving out of breath. Stephen Kemble was in the same room that Robert had last spoke with the governor the night before. He was talking with his sister Margaret, who was dressed to go out.

"Lord Dandridge, you got my message?" asked Kemble.

"Just now. Some idiot left it on my adjutant's desk without alerting anyone. Did His Excellency send out orders to the battalions?"

"Yes, sir, the runners just left a few minutes ago. The battalions are to gather on the Common and be ready to march at seven-thirty."

"Powder, shot, rations?"

"All covered in the order. Governor Gage has mobilized wagons to bring supplies and the powder house is alerted.

"Cannon?"

"Governor Gage advised that you use a battery of light guns."

"I have a two-gun battery of six-pounders." Robert considered taking more. Weighing the benefits of more cannon against the almost certain delay caused by readying more guns and crews. "That should be enough to scatter militia."

"Before you go, the governor would like to speak with you," said Kemble. "Please wait here while I fetch him." Kemble left the room. Margaret had waited while they talked, then nodding politely to Robert, made as if to follow her brother out. Robert took her arm.

"Pray tarry with me for a moment."

"A bit familiar, Robert. I have pressing business of my own."

"And what would that business be?"

"Oh, women stuff, I don't want to bore you, Robert," she said with a sarcastic tone and a wave of her hand.

Robert lightly pushed the door shut as she tried to walk by him. In a low, steady voice, "I know your secret."

She looked surprised for a moment, but there was no denial in her eyes; rather, her lips pursed in angry defiance, "I know your secret, Robert."

He was flustered, then horror-struck. His secret had troubled him his entire life. His shameful desire—but how could she know?

Margaret leaned toward Robert and, in an angry whisper, "I know you're buggering Matthew Lane."

Robert jerked backward. She had found his most vulnerable fault. If she made her accusations public, it would destroy his career and reputation, his family shamed, and his lover's life also ruined. He wanted to deny her charges, but there was no time.

"Margaret, whatever you think you know, you are exposing the King's troops to slaughter," he whispered for fear of being overheard. "They are British soldiers. Our countrymen."

"Both sides are my countrymen. Parliament is using the army to oppress the king's subjects." Imploring his sympathy with her eyes, "Don't you see?"

Were those footsteps in the hall? Robert side-eyed the door. Gage could walk through at any moment, "It's still treason, Margaret!" he whispered, "You are a traitor to your king!"

"You are a traitor to your sex!"

Governor Gage pushed open the door just as she hissed the last word. Gage's mouth opened both with surprise then suspicion. "What's all this?" demanded the governor.

"Oh, shut it, Thomas," said Margaret, glaring at both of them, "Robert has convinced me that in the present crisis, it is too dangerous to be strolling about Boston." She took off her hat and gloves and stalked out of the room without another word.

"My pardon, Your Excellency." Fear and anxiety clutched Robert's throat. "I did not intend such familiarity. I took liberty to warn her of the present state of high emotion among the country people." He clenched his fists to hide his shaking hands. "Lady Margaret interpreted my concern as an insult to her sex. As you know, we are old friends; we can quarrel like siblings."

"Never mind, Robert. I, too, thought her proposition to visit friends imprudent, but she is a stubborn woman," Gage scowled at the door she had just walked through. Turning back to Robert, "I'm glad I caught you. Kemble filled you in on the details of the plan."

"He did."

"Do not forget the marines. After my quarrel with Admiral Graves, I cannot leave them behind." He shook his head, "The Navy is like a woman; one cannot live with them, nor without them."

"Ha-ha. Just so," Robert knew his laugh was forced, and his voice quavered. "I am the last man to forget a woman!" Robert bowed, "By your leave."

Gage held Robert's arm, "If the Yanks have fired on the King's troops, we must hit them hard. They must regret their sedition."

"We are of the same mind, Your Excellency."

On the walk back to his house, Robert's whole body shook from the confrontation with Margaret. He could not afford to be distracted in the coming battle—*It was damnable blackmail!*—Trembling, he stopped for a moment. Clenched his fists and resumed his walk, concentrating on breathing in and out. He was angry at himself for surrendering to his shameful lusts, angry at Margaret for threatening him, and angry at the bloody Yanks for creating the crisis.

Back at his house Matthew walked into the bedroom as Robert packed his kit.

"Yes, Major Lane?" Robert was curt and formal. Matthew looked hurt, but only for an instant; then, he responded with the same formal demeanor.

"Your Lordship, Major Blunt from the 23rd of foot to see you,"

"Yes, show him in."

Henry Blunt came in, bowing his head in a nervous, deferential way.

"Henry, isn't it?" said Robert without extending his hand. Robert remembered Henry well from the last war but liked to pretend his unfamiliarity. When they were lieutenants together in the German states, Henry exercised a broad cant of slurs: molly, poofter, sodomite, that he liberally sprinkled around Robert. He never directly insulted him; Henry was a weak bully, but Robert counted him among his tormentors.

"Yes sir, your Lordship, sir," Henry said. "Did Colonel Caradoc speak about my situation last night?" Llewellyn had not spoken of Henry, but Robert already knew that Henry was ambitious for promotion and wanted Robert's influence and patronage. Robert felt no sympathy for him; rather, he enjoyed the petty torture.

"No, I'm afraid not." Before Henry could ask more awkward questions, "Your report? Is your battalion ready?"

"Oh, yes, M'Lord, the battalion is marching already. We should be at the Common in a few minutes. Have you had word from Colonel Caradoc?"

"Yes. He was well at three o'clock this morning. He sent a note. It appears the worst has happened. Despite the governor's precautions, spies warned the Yanks of his expedition," said Robert. "In any event, we are to sally out and provide Colonel Caradoc whatever assistance we can render. There may be fighting before this day is over. Ensure that your men have an issue of powder, shot, and cartridges ready."

"Sir! We kitted out the men last night and they slept on their arms."

"Very good. I will meet with all the commanders on the common at seven o'clock."

Shortly thereafter, the commanders of the 4th and 47th regiments reported in, as well as the battery commander of his cannon.

"Sir," said Captain Barker, commanding the battery. "I am short of my full complement of men. I require at least four more to operate my guns efficiently. Six would be better."

"Colonel Caradoc was to meet two chaises with some fourteen gunners and their equipment. When we link up with them, you will take those men and their equipment under your command. In the meantime, I will provide you with some infantrymen. They can at least carry shot for you."

"Sir, what about shot?" asked Captain Barker.

"We must move quickly if we mean to be of any use to Colonel Caradoc. We cannot afford to drag an ammunition train."

"I have two limbers ready; that's twenty-four shots per gun. A standard mix of case and round,"

"That's enough for militia."

"Sir!" saluted Captain Barker.

By six-thirty, even the marching band had reported, but not the marines. "Where can they be?" Robert said to Matthew.

"Perhaps they went straight to the common."

"Yes, let's not dawdle any longer."

Ten minutes later, Robert was riding on the Common past the battalions of his brigade. He swelled with pride, knowing that all these men were under his command.

"Still, the marines are missing." Robert was frustrated. Llewellyn could very well be in a fight for his life, and here he sat waiting.

"Your Lordship, may I ride to the marine barracks and discover the delay? Perhaps you could begin the march, and we will catch up," suggested Matthew.

"Yes, ride—no gallop—to the marine barracks, but I must wait. Governor Gage was insistent that the marines accompany us." Matthew galloped off back into Boston.

Robert got off his horse and walked through his three resting battalions. They were mostly sitting and smoking their pipes but would jump to attention when Robert approached. Robert put them at their ease and made small talk with the privates and sergeants. It was a practice he had learned from Llewellyn. Robert patted shoulders, asked about families, made jokes, and inspected weapons, canteens, and other kit. He was always surprised at the insight he gained into their morale and readiness. Insights that he could not get from formal reports. After thirty minutes Robert had reached his drummer at the head of the column, but the marines still had not appeared. "Pray beat commanders assemble."

Minutes later, Major Henry Blunt, Lieutenant Colonel William Nesbitt of the 47th regiment, and Lieutenant Colonel George Maddison, commander of the 4th regiment, were assembled with Lord Dandridge's small staff.

"Gentlemen," said Robert. "During our forced delay I have taken the opportunity to speak with some of your men. I commend you all on their appearance. The men show their usual good nature; their kit is serviceable, and all of them are ready for a row with the Yanks. I am a little concerned about their temperament. They are perhaps too eager for battle. Is it inexperience?"

"M'Lord, if I may venture an opinion."

"George," Robert nodded.

"Months of confinement to Boston plays a part, the men are keen for an adventure. But they also see this operation as a chance to strike back at their persecutors."

"The Yanks glare at the men and insult them. The animosity has affected their spirit, especially the youngsters," said Henry Blunt.

"Quite so," agreed Nesbitt. "The people insult and abuse them on one side, and the officers restrain them on the other. I overheard one of my sergeants describe Boston as a bear garden with themselves as the bears."

"You can assure your men that if the colony is indeed roused to armed rebellion, we will strike back." Robert felt his anger with Margaret, himself, and most of all the damned Yanks welling up in his chest, "Strike them hard."

Quock walked slowly back to Lexington. Looking left to right, he gripped his musket tight, expecting an ambush at any moment. As he neared the outskirts of the village, he heard another volley roar out. Quock jumped the wall that lined the road and ducked behind it. To his surprise, there were a dozen of his fellow militiamen, plus women and children, hiding there already.

Three huzzahs from the regulars followed the volley. To Quock, the tenor of the regular's cheers expressed a tone of insulting triumph. He saw Mister Nithercott further down. Nithercott motioned to Quock to stay low then raised up on his knees and peered over the wall.

"*Prime and load,*" he whispered.

A woman cried and grasped her children. Most of the militiamen loaded their muskets while peering over the wall. One man continued to squat, his hands on his head and musket underneath him, and made no move to reload. Following Nithercott's example, the remaining men laid their muskets across the wall and pointed toward Lexington. No regulars were in sight.

They waited.

Nothing happened.

A little girl, no more than eight years old, ran from the village. She saw the men behind the wall and waved. "They're gone!" she yelled. The militiamen stood up, grinning sheepishly, and patted each other on the back. Mister Nithercott waved over Quock and hugged him. "Glad you're safe." Mister Nithercott would often give him an affectionate pat on the back or a congratulatory handshake, but that was the first time Ebenezer Nithercott had ever hugged him.

They clambered over the wall, and together, the group walked back toward the green. Quock looked for Isaac, stopping to peer under a porch where Isaac had once hidden when they were kids playing hide-and-seek. Another boy and his sister were hiding there.

A Negro woman, Cleo Estabrook, ran past him toward the green, her mouth open, her eyes wide with fear and apprehension. Before Quock could see the green, he heard a woman's loud shriek and then crying. He started to run toward the sound as another woman screamed. By the time they got to the green, there was a chorus of wailing. Quock could see almost a dozen bodies lying on the grass. Some already attended by a cluster of people.

From every direction, a torrent of people poured onto the green. A babble of crying out, "Tom! Tom! . . ."—"Have you seen . . . ?"—"I can't find . . . !" Families ran and hugged their man when they found him or dashed from cluster to cluster shouting the names of the missing loved one. When a new arrival recognized a body, more voices joined the loud and horrifying wailing. Mister Nithercott and Quock stood together, speechless. Everything was noise and confusion.

"Chase!" shouted Mister Nithercott to Missus Nithercott and Faith, who had just appeared on the edge of the green. Their heads swung from side to side, their eyes wide, and they held each other's hands. Quock waved his hands over his head to get her attention. Missus Nithercott saw him; relief washed over her face. She and Faith ran to them. They both hugged Mister Nithercott, their words falling over each other. Quock was beginning to feel left out when they both turned to Quock and repeated the performance. Quock had never felt so much like part of the family. Finally, Faith and Missus Nithercott relaxed their embrace.

"I was so worried! What would Faith and I do without our men?" said Missus Nithercott, still hugging Quock and reaching out to her husband. "Oh, dear God," she interrupted herself. "That's Louise." She was looking at Louise Hadley, Isaac's mother who was kneeling with one of the bodies on the green, cradling the head in her lap and crying to heaven. Quock knew that tousled blonde hair and the faded blue, too-big-for-him coat. His best friend Isaac, his lifeless head in his mother's lap.

In rapid succession, waves of denial, shame, and grief swept through Quock. "No!"

He ran toward Isaac. As he got closer, he could see the blood on the ground, Missus Hadley's dress and the deep, ugly wound in Isaac's chest. Isaac's lifeless eyes, one lid half closed, stared unseeing. Isaac was gone.

As if he had been hit with a physical blow, Quock bent over, fell to the ground, and howled with pain. He felt Faith hugging and crying on his back, but his anguish was too much, and he could not move to console her. After an eternity, immeasurable time in a world of sorrow and guilt, Quock forced himself to sit up. He hugged Faith, who was still rocking and crying.

"Faith, stand up," said Missus Nithercott. "We have to help Louise."

Faith and Chastity Nithercott moved arm-in-arm to Louise's side. Already, a crowd of family bunched around the distraught mother and fallen son. Quock stood up, unsure of what to do. He started to follow Faith and Missus Nithercott, but Mister Nithercott gently took Quock's arm, saying, "Louise has all the help anyone can offer her. For us, mourning will have to wait; this battle isn't over yet."

Quock glared at him. "Why not? They're gone." Mister Nithercott led him to where he had dropped his musket, picked it up and handed it to him. The unwelcome and awkward weight of the musket pulled his spirit to the ground as Quock followed Nithercott. Mister Parker, who was standing outside a knot of his family, bent over someone on the grass.

"John, they'll be coming back," said Mister Nithercott.

John Parker's face was set in grief. "They bayoneted my cousin," his voice choked with emotion. "Cold steel right through his loving heart."

"A lot of good men died," Mister Nithercott agreed. "But the regulars will be back before this day is over. Either the same bunch or new battalions from Boston. We can't wait and let them slaughter us like hogs again."

Parker nodded, wiped his eyes, and asked, "What do you think?"

"They're headed for Concord. They'll do whatever business they're set to then they'll go back to Boston," Mister Nithercott gestured to the road bordering the green, "This is the shortest way." He paused, then pointed west. "I say we move away from Lexington, so they don't know who done it, and ambush the sons-of-bitches on their way back."

"Good idea, Eb, but we gotta let these families take care of their own. Do you think an hour is long enough before we call them back?"

Mister Nithercott paused, considering the problem, "It will take the regulars at least an hour and a half to get to Concord. Maybe an hour or so to search for guns that aren't there."

"Yeah," said Parker, his voice clearer. He wiped his nose with the sleeve of his coat. "Even if they're stubborn they won't stay in Concord more than a couple hours. Then another hour plus to get back here."

"We can spare two hours for the families to care for their dead and treat their wounded, but we need to say something to them now before they skaddle home."

"Eb, my consumption. I can't call out loud enough to get their attention."

"Drummer?"

Parker pointed to Bill Diamond with the wounded Prince Estabrook, Cleo and the extended Estabrook clan were helping Prince to walk home. Quock often sat with Prince on Sundays in Negro Heaven. Quock was worried about his wound, but Prince was already walking without aid. Bill Diamond still had the drum around his neck, pushed behind him so it didn't get in the way. Not knowing what else to do, Quock followed Mister Nithercott over to the drummer.

"Bill, I need you to beat assembly," said Nithercott. Diamond stared at Nithercott as if he had said something insulting. Nithercott repeated, "Beat assembly."

Parker had joined them during Diamond's hesitation. Confronted with the leadership of the training band, both Deacons at church, Diamond pulled the drum to his front, took out his sticks, and beat assembly. The effect was not the same as it had been so many times before when battle was a distant possibility, not a shocking reality. The militiamen did not run to their places. Instead, they ignored it at first, then drifted over as the drumming continued. They did not fall into a formation but stood around Parker and Nithercott. To Quock, they appeared dazed and angry.

"Fellas," said Nithercott. "We have been dealt a sneaky and deceitful blow." Many of the men nodded. "Yeah!" one man shouted.

"They'll come back this way. We must prepare ourselves for battle."

"We done enough!" shouted Vernon. "We lost good men."

"We have not done enough," said Parker in an angry rasp. "We were going to let them pass. We didn't want it, but war's come to us anyway."

"Do you want more to die?" asked Vernon.

"Do you want to stay enslaved to parliament?"

Mister Nithercott raised his hands, interrupting the building argument, "Go and take care of your families. In two hours, Quock, Captain Parker and I will meet back here. We are going to pay back those regulars in their own coin. We welcome any men that join us."

"Of course, Quock will be here; he's a slave. He's got no choice. We're free men," said Vernon.

"Thank you, Vernon," Mister Nithercott put his hand on Quock's shoulder, "You reminded me. I told Quock that if he fights as a militia man, then I would free him."

Quock stared open-mouthed at Mister Nithercott.

"Quock fulfilled his part of the bargain this morning. I fulfill mine now. Ladies and gentlemen, meet Quock Nithercott, free man." The last two words, however, came out as one, Freeman. "Quock is now fighting of his own free will."

Parker slapped Quock on the back, shook his hand, and smiled through his still teary eyes, "Congratulations Quock Freeman. We needed some good news today."

"Thank you, sir," was all Quock could say.

Chapter Eight

Seven o'clock a.m.

As a farmer's son, Jason was reluctant to trample spring planting or disturb newly plowed grounds. He rode Wicked on a winding route using trails and farmer's footpaths around planted fields. He galloped or cantered when the trails gave enough room to spur the mare. Wicked continued to employ her vicious cross-canter and Jason's back was beginning to feel the wear. After a spate of hard riding, he finally passed to the front of the fast-moving red column to the North. When he could see the gleaming white steeple of Concord's meeting house, he turned onto a path that would take him back to the great road a couple of hundred yards in front of the regulars.

He had hoped to arrive to find his regiment already mustered, but it occurred to him that they might not even be there yet. They would have to march ten miles from Westford to reach Concord. When did they get the alarm? How long did it take to muster? The new minutemen companies were supposed to be ready in thirty minutes, but it never worked out that way. People were late, signals weren't heard, and there were always reasons to delay.

Jason saw a column of militia snaking out of Concord, heading straight toward the oncoming regulars. Were they going to blunder into a battle? Abandoning restraint, Jason spurred Wicked to a run across a plowed field, leaping a low wall. "For Christ's sake, STOP!" he shouted at the top of his lungs, knowing they couldn't hear him yet.

Llewellyn checked his watch and frowned. The sun had fully risen above the horizon. There were only a few clouds and a light breeze. By any normal measure, it was a beautiful spring morning, perfect for a ride, but he was behind schedule. Worse still were the possible consequences of the clash in Lexington. The best he could hope for was a scandal in Boston. A rise in the already high political temperature. But Llewellyn knew that word would reach London that British troops had fired on country people. Armed or not, whether they fired first or not, he would have to explain his actions. Llewellyn dreaded the thought of a court-martial, but at least the court would be fellow officers—men he might know. Explaining his action to parliament was another kettle of fish. He had no notion of politicians; lies, inflammatory speeches, and political theater were their common bread. Anything could happen if his fate were cast on their mercy.

Llewellyn pushed the fears from his mind and put his watch back in his waistcoat. He had to focus on the problem at hand. The Massachusetts militia was likely gathering around his expedition like circling wolves. Even the latest sleepers in Concord were already up and moving about their business. Did they know his corps was close? He sat up in his saddle and strained to see the spire of Concord's Church. He spied an approaching horseman.

"Sir," Mitchell saluted. "Major Pitcairn sends his compliments and wishes me to inform you that a column of militia is marching toward us."

"Very well," Llewellyn turned to Whelks riding beside him, "I will ride to the front to see if we may pass. If you hear shooting, pray incline your division to the left. Your division will be the left wing. If the opportunity presents itself, wheel to flank the militia. The light companies will act as the anvil to your hammer. Do not wait for my signal, but do not fire without it."

"Sir. Incline left and flank. Do not fire." repeated Whelks.

Llewellyn spurred his horse to the front of the column in time to see the Concord militia marching away. "What happened?" he asked Pitcairn.

"Not sure what they are about, colonel. They were marching toward us. I was getting ready to throw out skirmishers, then they counter columned and off they go," he swung an arm up in the direction of the receding militia.

"A brilliant victory, Major Pitcairn," deadpanned Llewellyn. Both Majors laughed.

"Let's keep an eye on them," said Llewellyn. Nodding toward the gleaming spires to their front, to De Berniere, he asked, "Is that Concord finally?"

"I believe so, sir," said De Berniere. "I was only here once—a few months ago, but I recognize the steeple and the Liberty Pole."

Llewellyn sat tall in his saddle, pulled out a spyglass and scanned the hills to their right. People, some of them armed, were watching the column. Too far away to worry about for the moment. On the left, a single rider in a green coat on a grey horse was galloping across the fields. He came on the road two hundred yards in front of the regulars, turned his horse toward Concord and chased after the disappearing militia column.

"What is he on about?" asked Mitchell.

"Do you suppose he is one of the riders sending out the alarm?" said Pitcairn.

"A wee late," said Llewellyn.

"The British are coming! The British are coming!" teased Mitchell, waving his left hand. All four officers laughed.

"Come now, gentlemen," Llewellyn suppressed a smile. "These people are our countrymen. Mustn't mock."

Llewellyn watched the militia disappear, "If the militia pass through Concord, then we must seize the bridges and block their return. The north bridge is particularly important. Governor Gage gave me intelligence that the local militia commander, a man named James Barrett, his house lies two miles beyond the bridge and hides a magazine. Detach companies to seize the bridge, prepare to march to the Barrett house, and search it."

"Sir," said Pitcairn.

"Once we secure the bridges, we may rest and breakfast the troops. Major Mitchell, if you please, act as my adjutant for the remainder of this operation."

"Very well, sir."

Addressing his officers, "Gentlemen, we must remember these people are His Majesty's subjects, and our soldiers are to behave accordingly. There is to be no destruction of private property and our relations with the country people correct." His small staff all nodded their understanding.

Turning around in his saddle, and spoke to the men marching behind, "Now that the operation is no longer a secret, let's hear the fife and drum. We'll make a proper show in Concord."

The drum and fife players grinned. Nodding to each other and began a familiar tune. The music spread quickly down the column. The tired soldiers stepped a little higher, straightened their kit, and a sergeant began to sing.

> *Here's fourteen shillings on the drum*
> *For those who'll volunteer to come*
> *To list and fight the foe today*
> *Over the hills and far away*

Before he had finished the first line the rest of his company had joined in the singing.

> *O'er the hills and o'er the main*
> *To Flanders, Portugal and Spain*
> *King George commands, and we obey*
> *Over the hills and far away*

By now, the entire column was singing in deep-throated manly bass. Llewellyn smiled and joined the song.

> *Through smoke and fire and shot and shell*
> *Unto the very walls of hell*
> *We shall stand, and we shall stay.*
> *Over the hills and far away*

Wicked had finally winded, and Jason let her walk up the hill toward the militia. Turning in his saddle as they climbed, he watched the regulars march into town. It was military pageantry at its best. The drum and fife were playing, soldiers singing, bayonets glittered, and the red uniforms shone in the morning sunlight. The soldiers high-stepped as if they had not spent the night marching nor fought a skirmish two hours earlier. Admiring the martial beauty of the British Army, Jason wondered where he would be now if the King had granted regular commissions to Americans.

"Jason!?" shouted his brother Bill. "How'd you get here?"

"I thought I'd warn you the regulars are coming."

"You always had a flair for the obvious."

When he got closer, Jason dismounted and told Bill the details of his adventures in Lexington and since.

"Jerome!" Bill yelled to his son. "Take Wicked here from your uncle and put her with our horses. Fetch her again if Uncle Jason needs her."

"Yes sir," Jerome gingerly gathered the reins, watching Wicked closely and leading her to a small group of horses picketed on the reverse slope.

"Come with me. We're meeting with Jim to talk about what we're going to do next."

Jason could see the people gathering around the tall and venerable Colonel James Barrett, watching the redcoat's activities. Jason had known him for years. Barrett was a local institution, serving Concord in various political jobs and the king in hard service during several campaigns in the last war. He was well known for his Patriot views, but Jason appreciated that he was no firebrand. Barrett had visibly aged since Jason had last seen him. It occurred to Jason that Barrett must be well into his sixties now.

"Jason Green!" said a surprised Barrett. "Is the Westford militia with you?"

"Not yet; I just arrived from Boston and was hoping to meet them here." Jason briefly recounted what he heard in Lexington and what he knew about the regulars.

"Did you see the fighting in Lexington?" asked a short, stocky, red-haired man his brow furrowed in righteous anger. "Reuben Brown said he saw the Redcoats fire volleys at our militia."

"Yes. There was some shooting, but I don't know who fired first," Jason held his hands up.

"Did you get any sense of their strength?" asked the red-haired man.

"No numbers, of course, but it's not a single regiment. The companies are from different regiments—marines and light infantry in the fore and grenadiers in the main."

"I was hoping to go out and discourage them, but when I saw how large the force was, I decided we didn't want an ill-considered confrontation," said Barrett.

"I agree," said Jason.

"I counted twenty-one companies as they passed. Anybody else count?" asked the red-haired man.

"I got nineteen, John, but I may have lost the thread," said another minuteman.

"All right, make it twenty companies of regulars. Maybe a thousand men," said Barrett. "And we have only two hundred."

"More militia are coming, Jim," said Bill. "We'll soon have enough to make a show."

"Our license from the Provincial Congress is to observe," responded Barrett. "We don't have the authority to act against them without provocation."

"What about what they did in Lexington?" The red-haired man asked. "We can act in our defense."

"Jason just said he did not know what happened in Lexington." Barrett frowned at the red-haired man. "They haven't done anything here, and we are badly outnumbered. We should wait until more militia arrive before we confront the king's troops." Thinking for a moment, he added, "I must consult with the selectmen and the Committee of Vigilance. We don't want to get anybody killed or property destroyed." Colonel Barrett then walked away joining a group of older men Jason recognized as local politicians taking refuge on the hill.

"We'll get no decision from them." The red-haired man gestured toward Barrett.

"John," said Bill to the red-haired man. "Have you met my brother Jason? He's the Lieutenant Colonel of the Westford minute regiment." Turning to Jason, "This is Major John Buttrick from Concord."

"Welcome," John shook Jason's hand. "You rode all the way from Boston last night?"

"Yes, it was a lot more exciting than I anticipated," said Jason.

John laughed. Seeing that the redcoats were now sitting and eating, he said, "Well, they're having their breakfasts; let's eat ours. My wife's just over here. She has a kettle of mush, and she may have brought some coffee, too. You're welcome to join us."

"Thank you! I wasn't hungry until you said breakfast; now I'm starving," Jason patted his growling belly.

The three of them walked over to a woman as short and red-haired as John with four girls. The grass on the hilltop was still flattened from the weight of winter's snow. The girls had spread out a blanket on one of the drier spots and opened the baskets and cloths they were carrying. Missus Buttrick spooned big piles of mush and handed the first plate to Jason.

"Butter or molasses with your mush?" she asked Jason.

"Both, please," he said. "If you don't mind me asking, why did you follow your husband up here? I doubt the regulars would molest you at home."

She smiled and handed him a plate of fresh butter and a small jug of molasses. "Our house is just down the hill." She pointed to a small, neat house close to where the regulars were having their breakfast.

"Ah! A little too close to the action."

"Coffee?" asked John.

"I've never had it." Jason could smell the brew in the mason jug, "but I'm willing to try. Giving up tea was the hardest part of the embargo."

"Too true," said John. "For Abby and me, coffee has the same stimulating and healthful benefits. Now that Abby has learned to roast the beans, we don't miss tea at all."

Soon, all eight of them were eating. The girls finished quickly and ran to join their friends playing on the hillside. Abby shook her head and chuckled, "All the excitement seems a wonderful distraction from their chores."

"We hadn't met before, but I heard Bill speak of you often enough. You were in the last war?" asked John.

"Oh! The war. Are you going to talk about that?" Abby frowned.

"Seems like the time and place."

Abby didn't respond and concentrated on her food.

"I was. In the Sixtieth foot. I fought in Quebec," said Jason.

"Me too. I was in the rangers."

"You have some stories to tell. The rangers went on raids across the Lawrence River?"

"Yes, sir. We learned the Frenchies around the fort were hiding grain and livestock and supplying the garrison in secret. We were ordered to burn their homes and barns." He shrugged and looked at his own house, "They're Papists, so I didn't object on principle, but still hard to burn a man's house right in front of him. His wife and children were standing in the yard crying and wailing as their house burned."

"John Buttrick, you did no such thing!" Abby's eyes were wide.

"I had orders, Abby. It was war."

"This is why your mother destroyed all your letters." Abby stood up and crossed her arms. "No one has to do anything; people make choices, John." She made as if to go but then just stood above them, glowering in righteous indignation. "Thank God our children didn't hear you."

There was a long silence. Jason concentrated on his mush. Abby was distracted by the behavior of her girls and left.

Following her with his eyes, John said, "Hard to talk about what happened." He took a sip of his coffee. "But she's right; it was shameful business." He took another sip and shook his head, "Then the damned regulars looked down on us for doing the job they put us to."

"The officers were an arrogant bunch," agreed Jason.

"They were. I never thought of myself as an American until that war."

"That's right," Jason stuck out his chin. "The regulars never accepted us as Englishmen." Thinking about his conversation with Llewellyn and Robert, "They still don't."

"They treat us like we're a different race, like the Scotts or Irish."

"Truly." Jason sat back and looked down the hill at the regulars. "The cold, the fear, privation—I accepted all that as part of war. Being spurned by my countrymen was my biggest disappointment."

"It's the scorn. Americans are just servants to be officered by our lordly English masters," said John. Abby came back. She didn't sit but stood listening.

Jason nodded, "If there is a war, the seeds were sown in the last one."

"I hope the fruit is bitter to those that planted it," said Abby, looking down at her home.

Llewellyn and Edward Mitchell sat on gravestones atop the hill. Through their spyglasses, they watched the colonial militia gathering on the hill northeast of town that overlooked the Concord River bridge.

"Even pitchforks," said Mitchell.

"Can't have a peasant revolt without pitchforks, though most seem to have firelocks," said Llewellyn.

"Oh, three-quarters at least."

Llewellyn put down his spyglass. The epitaph of the gravestone across from him read, '*Where you stand, I once stood. Where I am, you will one day be.*' Llewellyn pondered it for a moment, "The Yanks must be a gloomy race."

"I've seen the same in English graveyards," said Mitchell. "I would prefer something different on mine."

"I don't know what I want on mine, but I do not want my epitaph to be, 'He failed at Concord.'"

Behind them, Pitcairn, Whelks, and De Berniere labored up the hill. Their faces were slack with fatigue. Llewellyn motioned for them to sit, and they slumped to the ground, leaning back on their hands to drink in the morning sun. Holding a piece of salted beef wrapped in a handkerchief in his right hand and a canteen of tepid tea in the left, Llewellyn sat on a headstone and listened to his officer's reports.

His back against the gravestone with the gloomy inscription and his legs crossed in front of him, Whelks began, "I have posted pickets at all roads in and out of Concord. We have seen no militia other than those gathering on yonder hill. My troops are otherwise enjoying their breakfasts and preparing to search for the rebel arms."

"What is the attitude of the villagers?"

"We've seen hardly any. All the doors and windows are shut. No one is outside. It's a ghost town, really."

"Very good, but we must remain vigilant. Assign a grand division as a reserve," said Llewellyn. "Major Pitcairn, your report."

Pitcairn sat up and crossed his legs Indian style, "Sir, I sent three companies to secure the south bridge. I set six companies to seize the north bridge and search the magazine at the Barrett house. Captain Parsons is commanding three companies that will search for arms. Captain Lillingfield commands the three companies guarding the north bridge."

Llewellyn looked up from the map he was unfolding when Pitcairn mentioned Lillingfield's name, but he didn't say anything.

"I kept the marine company with me to act as reserve," finished Pitcairn.

Llewellyn nodded, cut off a small bite of his salted beef and directed their attention to the map Gage had given him. He spread it out on the grass, "This draught is marked with the locations of the rebels' military stores." De Berniere stood above them, pointing out buildings and landmarks on the map and where they could see them from the hill.

"John, your men undoubtedly have the most dangerous bit. They pass directly below the gathering militia. Ensure that Lillingfield sends us a message on the first sign of trouble."

"Sir."

"Any questions?" seeing none, "Give the men ten more minutes to rest and finish their tea, then search the town, destroy the arms, and we will be back on the road in an hour. We can drink to our success in Boston this evening."

Llewellyn sat down in the grass to finish his salted beef and sip from his canteen. Across the village of Concord, the scenes of his corps were tranquil. The troops were mostly sitting or lying down smoking their pipes; some congregated at wells, getting water. A few men, including his batman, were watering the horses at the mill pond. John Pitcairn came and sat next to him.

Llewellyn studied the marine commander. It was the first time that Llewellyn had really had an opportunity to see him in full daylight when other issues were not pressing. John was older than Llewellyn had expected, probably mid-fifties. Short and stocky, but still very fit.

"I am envious of the Army," said John.

"How so?"

"I should be more exact; I am envious of your sergeants and corporals." He gestured to a squad of soldiers. "There is a sergeant inspecting the flints. Over there is another checking their shoes and kit. It is farther away, but I believe that is a corporal organizing the filling of canteens at the well. In a few minutes, this corps will be refreshed and ready to campaign, and I have not seen an officer give a single order."

"Officers direct the Army, but the good sergeants and corporals run it. I cannot fathom how we could operate without them. But the marines haven't any?"

"We have sergeants in name, but the Admiralty formed the marines Forces only twenty years ago. We have not yet built a body of custom and tradition so that the sergeant knows what to do without orders."

"The relationship between officer and sergeant is like a good marriage. Each of them has a role, and the worthy sergeant is jealous of his authority."

"Thank you, sir. I am of the same mind, and that is what the marines need. When I arrived in Boston last year, they were a riotous, drunken lot. My sergeants required perpetual minding. I drilled the men relentlessly, slept in the barracks for weeks to watch over them and—God forgive me—used the cat unmercifully." Leaning forward, John said, "The marines are much better now, but that poor show back there in Lexington causes me some concern about how they will behave in the face of the enemy."

"Poor show?" asked Llewellyn. "Do you mean we fired first?"

"No sir, the rebels fired first, but it was panicked and undisciplined. If my marines had kept their heads and not returned fire, then perhaps there would have been no bloodshed." He turned to Llewellyn and added, "I asked for the victory volley to build some sadly lacking confidence. It was not my intent to mock the country folk. I have not put any marines on that expedition to the Barrett House so that I may watch over them."

"Unfortunately, the Army has little to crow about in this expedition. I can only hope the sergeants will pull us through."

"Come now, Llewellyn, you underrate our achievements," said Steven Whelks who had just sat down next to them as they were talking. "We woke twenty-one companies from their beds, formed an ad hoc corps, crossed a major river, marched almost twenty miles, swatted away a militia force half our size, and are now about to destroy a rebel magazine. We did it without proper planning and in less than twelve hours. There are few armies in the world that could boast the same."

"Jolly good. We shan't leave the job half done. Let's rouse the men and finish it."

The three of them stood up. Llewellyn felt the soreness of hours in the saddle as he stood. Whelks and Pitcairn walked back down the burying hill—a little stiff, too, Llewellyn noticed—and addressed a group of waiting captains. Llewellyn watched as they assigned each of them a place to search. The captains swiftly returned to their companies, and Llewellyn nodded with satisfaction as platoons of soldiers fanned out through Concord, hunting rebel arms.

"There they go." Colonel Barrett, who was standing near Jason. He was watching a party of three companies of regulars through his spyglass. The regulars had crossed the bridge and were marching up the road away from Concord. "They're going to my house. They must be working with old intelligence. They won't find anything, but I hope they don't burn it." Barrett walked away, mounted his horse, and rode off toward his house.

"What the hell?!" exclaimed John, standing up.

"The regulars are going to his house," said Bill.

"Bill! What's he going to do? Serve them tea? He's leaving his regiment in the face of the enemy!"

"Are they the enemy?" asked Bill.

As they watched, Barrett rode down to the hill. On the road he galloped past marching regulars, neither paying attention to the other. Jason thought about what he had been able to see in Lexington, his treatment at the hands of Sergeant Thurston, and the murder of the man from Menotomy. However regretful, everything that had happened so far could be explained as blunders and perhaps the criminal act of an individual, but not purposeful acts of war. "I don't know," said Jason to his brother, "not yet anyway."

"We're supposed to wait until they deprive us of our arms? Murder us like they did in Lexington. You saw it!" John's face was red.

"I was too far away to see what happened. Maybe it was a mistake, or the Lexington militia provoked them." None of the men on the hill were from Jason's regiment, but with Barrett gone, he was the senior officer present. He was determined not to be pushed into an act of war. "We have authority only to observe unless we are threatened."

"You give cautious counsel," said John, frowning.

"If the regulars molest anyone or vandalize property, then we'll march down there."

"If we are an army of observation, we should at least let them know we are witnessing," said John. "We could move some companies over there just above my house." John pointed to the next, lower hill just above the bridge. "And we can get some separation between us and this milling crowd of civilians."

Jason looked around at the growing throng on the hill. It was becoming increasingly difficult to distinguish between militia units, refugees, and the curious gawkers. "That's reasonable."

An hour after dismissing his officers to search for the rebel stores, Llewellyn was still standing on Burying Hill with his spyglass. While he impatiently waited for a report, he watched the distressing growth of the militia on the opposite hill overlooking the north bridge. There were at least a thousand people on the hill. Some were women and children, but through his spyglass, most appeared to be armed men. A large detachment of militia had moved closer to the bridge but were not yet threatening to attack.

He surveyed the surrounding ground and spotted the Liberty Pole. The flag flapped in the breeze. It had nine red and white bars. The rebellious stripes of the Sons of Liberty. To Llewellyn, if not illegal, it was disloyal and a deliberate provocation.

Someone was shouting. It was a Lieutenant running up the hill. Llewellyn half ran down the hill to meet him.

"Colonel Caradoc, sir. Colonel Whelks sends his compliments and wishes me to tell you that we have found the cannon."

"Finally! Where?"

"Sir, buried behind a tavern. May I show you the way?"

"If you please."

Llewellyn walked briskly next to the puffing lieutenant. They soon came to the tavern. The door was open, the lock broken, and inside, a frowning local man sat in a chair surrounded by a small party of grenadiers.

"Just in time," Whelks said. "We are digging up twenty-four pounders planted in the garden."

Llewellyn smiled with relief. "Twenty-four?"

"No. Three cannon. They are twenty-four pounders. This man here," he pointed to the unhappy civilian sitting in the chair, "is Mister Ephraim

Jones. He had barred the door, but with a little encouragement from our grenadiers—"

"They bashed the damn door down!" shouted Mister Jones interrupting Whelks. "Someone needs to pay for that door."

"Just so." Whelks led Llewellyn out the tavern's back door and into the yard. A squad of soldiers were digging. In the bottom of three holes, he could make out the mud-caked forms of cannon. "We searched his property and found little, but we saw some fresh-turned earth in the yard and the guns underneath." Waving a hand toward a door partially beneath the tavern, "Mister Jones is also the town jailer. He had three prisoners, one of them jailed for being a loyalist. We released them all."

"Brilliant," said Llewellyn. "What else did you find?"

"I politely but firmly reminded Mister Jones of the penalties for sedition and obstructing a king's officer in his duty."

"He threatened me!" shouted Jones. Two larger grenadiers were pushing Jones to follow. "I'm an Englishman, and I demand my rights!"

"I will note in my report that Mister Jones objected to the questioning. However, he revealed that the carriages associated with these guns are stored in the town meeting house."

"All very well, good show, but weren't there any more?" Llewellyn nodded toward the cannon, "Three guns hardly constitute the armament of an army. There are supposed to be fourteen guns. Nothing else? No powder?"

"Very little." Whelks shrugged, "Mister Jones had a firkin of musket balls on his property, and there are casks about the carriages for flour and salt pork."

"It ain't against the law to eat pork, you damned bloody backed bastards!" shouted Mister Jones, still restrained by two grenadiers.

"Very well." Llewellyn ignored the outburst, "Spike the cannon, burn the carriages, stove the barrels, and throw them and the musket balls in the mill pond."

"Llewellyn." Whelks reached out to touch Llewellyn's sleeve, "I believe we very much regret that the artillerymen and their chaises never joined us." Pointing at the guns still half buried in the three-foot-deep hole, "Those guns are fifty hundredweight apiece. Just getting them out of the ground will require a team of horses. The gunners had the horses to move 'em and the tools to spike 'em proper."

"Bloody hell, where are those goddam gunners and their chaises?" Llewellyn examined the massive guns. "How does one destroy several tons of solid iron?"

"Sir," said John Pitcairn, who had walked up as Whelks explained the problem. "One of the benefits of our association with the Navy is that we know cannon. On board ship, Marines often help man them. We do not have the tools here to destroy them proper, but if we commandeer some horses, we can drag them to a blacksmith. My Marines can beat the trunnions so they cannot be mounted and hammer some nails into the touch hole. Might not be permanent damage, but it will annoy the rebels."

"Make it so," said Llewellyn to Pitcairn. To Whelks, "Destroy the rest as I ordered. Whatever companies are not engaged, have them search further. I want to assure the governor that we left no stone unturned. And pray send someone to chop down that damned Liberty Pole. Burn it and the flag with the gun carriages."

Llewellyn watched as parties of soldiers and marines set about their tasks. He strolled through the village, doors and shutters still shut tight and no people in the streets, trying to calm his anxiousness while his corps completed the tasks. As he walked, he absently toyed with a button on his coat.

"Sir." It was Mitchell walking beside him. "Is it possible that the Yanks were forewarned of our raid?"

"Of course, they were warned," Llewellyn impatiently waved a hand. "Not only have they dispersed their military stores, but they are gathering in great strength." Pointing up to the hill overlooking the North Bridge, "You see. There are more than five hundred armed men up there. They could not gather so quickly without prior knowledge of our operation. We need to be methodical; there has already been too much haste, but we must begin the return march soon."

"Do you fear for our success?" asked Mitchell, searching Llewellyn's face for reassurance.

"I do not fear for the triumph of our soldiers over militia." Llewellyn clasped his hands behind him. "Militia cannot stand against us in their ranks, but they will fight. If they gather in enough strength, there could be a scenario when the pure weight of numbers . . . well . . . it may be bloody work to fight free."

A party of marines passed, riding a team of horses already harnessed. They galloped toward the tavern, and Llewellyn turned to watch them, "Oh, bother." At the Town House, soldiers had set fire to the gun carriages and the liberty pole too close to the building. Fire had climbed the pole, and now the roof of the Town House was burning.

Llewellyn shook his head in deep regret. He had gone too far. His orders did not include liberty poles or flags. He had ordered the liberty pole burned out of spite, and now his hubris had come back to bite him.

"Pride goeth before destruction, and a haughty spirit before a fall."

"Pardon?" Mitchell looked at him.

"A biblical warning, I ignored."

Mitchell and Llewellyn walked briskly toward the fire. By the time they got to Town House, Whelks was organizing a bucket brigade to douse the flames. An angry old woman holding a bucket stood in the yard, simultaneously cursing and directing the running soldiers. Llewellyn watched the two lines of soldiers pass buckets and throw the water on the fire.

Whelks saw him and hurried to report, "We can keep this fire from spreading, but I have to call men off other duties to fight it. May I commit the reserve to continue the house-to-house searches?"

"No sir," said Llewellyn. "We must discontinue the search, but the militia is gathering outside Concord." Pointing at the billowing clouds of smoke coming off the Town House, "And this smoke will certainly draw more. Put out the fire, but keep the reserve handy; I fear we will need those men soon."

More than an hour after he departed, Barrett reappeared. "They didn't find anything. We had already hidden the guns in the cornfield," he said to Jason and the other officers. "The gentleman in command was quite polite. Very kind to my family. They did their duty and disturbed nothing. I believe that we can trust the regular officers. They are the right sort of people."

"Smoke!" shouted a minuteman. Everyone on the hill turned to Concord, where a column of black smoke was rising. "They fired the Town House," said Barrett, his eyes wide with surprise.

"That tears it." Buttrick's face was red with righteous anger. "They're burning our homes and destroying property. We must act now!"

"I agree," said one of the selectmen standing with the group of officers. "Every man in the fire brigade is up here. If we don't go down quickly, the whole town will burn."

"You are always demanding radical solutions, Thomas," said Barrett to the Selectman. "We are supposed to observe unless they attack us first."

"Look at all these men here, Jim," said Buttrick, motioning at the swelling ranks of militia behind them. "It's their homes!"

Barrett glared at Buttrick. He scanned through the group and caught Jason's eye. "What about you, Jason?"

Jason knew Barrett had asked him because Jason had a reputation as a Tory, loyal to the king. Barret hoped he would support his wish to avoid confronting the king's troops, but for Jason, the tide had turned. Whatever mistakes may have happened in Lexington, the volleys and the huzzahs were the work of the regulars. Below him in Concord, the town was burning; the regulars were responsible for that, too. Around him were the anxious faces of the Concord militiamen as they watched the smoke rise above their homes and businesses. Jason straightened his shoulders. "We cannot ignore the fire. We must act."

"I understand the urgency, but I command the Concord militia, not the minutemen." Barrett searched for someone to agree with him. "There are companies of the Concord minuteman regiment over here. John, you are not the commander. There are companies from Acton and Lincoln, and you're from Westford Jason with no troops at all. Who is supposed to command this group?" asked Barrett.

Barrett asked one of the company commanders. "What about you? Do you want to march into Concord and fight the regulars?"

"I do not suppose I do." The militia company commander was visibly surprised by the question. Barrett crossed his arms and nodded in affirmation.

Jason knew Barrett was right about the militia; they were not ready. The Massachusetts Provincial Congress had taken some steps to convert the militia into an army, but they had not finished the job. But Barret was wrong that there was no one to command. Jason was the most senior officer on the hill after Barret, and he had commanded in battle. He had spent his entire adult life serving in either the Army or the militia. He also belonged to the Ancient and Honorable Artillery Company and the Corps of Cadets. *What was the purpose, if not to serve my country?*

"Facta Non-Verba," said Jason aloud. Barrett looked at him puzzled, "Deeds, not Words. The motto of my society." Addressing the larger group, Jason said, "I'll do it. I will lead any companies that will follow me."

"I'll be your second and march with you!" Buttrick nearly jumped with excitement.

Another Captain from a Concord minute company raised his hand. "We'll go."

Barrett ignored him and instead addressed a company of minutemen that had just arrived. "Captain Davis, Lieutenant Colonel Green proposes to take the Concord militia down to confront the regulars. Your Acton men don't have to go."

"I ain't afraid to go, and I haven't a man that's afraid to go," he said.

Barrett's face fell. "Then your company can lead," he admonished him in the tone of a schoolteacher scolding a miscreant student. There was silence all around as they waited for Barrett to speak again. He frowned and said to Jason, "You and John can command if there is a fight. In the meantime, we will avoid provocation. We will march peacefully into Concord and offer to put out the fire."

To the drummer, Barrett said, "Beat assembly." Immediately, the militiamen, who had wandered about the hilltop as they waited for something to happen, started running back to their formations. The scattered militia companies formed in seconds.

"Commanders assemble on me," ordered Colonel Barrett. Jason and the company commanders assembled in front of Colonel Barrett. When all were gathered, Colonel Barrett said, "Gentlemen, the regulars appear to have *accidentally*," he held out both hands, palms out, "started a fire." He glared at Buttrick, daring him to contradict his assertion. "We will march down to Concord in a column of twos and offer our assistance in putting out the fire."

"What about skirmishers?" asked Buttrick.

"I don't want to provoke a confrontation with any battle formations."

"I agree," said a selectman who had joined the commanders' huddle unbidden. "If we get into a fight, then the whole town will burn."

"What about sending a couple of companies to block the return of the detachment that went to your house?" said Jason. "We could be caught between them."

"What don't you understand, Jason?" Barrett glared at him. "If we block the regulars, they will consider it a provocation. No tactical formations. Understood?"

Jason wanted to speak but saw it was useless. Barrett smiled reassuringly, "Don't worry, Jason, they will let us pass. We just want to help put out the fire."

"Can we at least load our muskets?" asked John.

Barrett frowned. "Yes, but don't fire unless you are fired on first." Acknowledging John's angry face, he added, "If the regulars fire first, then do what you must in defense of lives and property."

Barrett examined the faces of the officers around him. Noting their nodding acceptance of his conditions, he said, "All right, back to your formations. We will start filing from the right on my command."

Moments later, in a loud, clear voice, Barrett ordered, "Battalion!"

"Company!" came the military echo from the company commanders.

Then, in patient succession, waiting for the military echo between each command, Barrett ordered, "Shoulder your Firelock! To the right Face! File by twos from the right! To the front, march!" Jason ran to the front of the formation, filing down the hill along a narrow track that wound along the easiest gradient toward the bridge. He jumped in front of the line next to Captain Davis.

"What are you going say to the regulars at the bridge?" asked Davis.

"Hell, if I know." Jason shrugged. "Pray, may we pass?"

Davis laughed and shook his head, "Let's hope they're agreeable."

Once the track turned back toward the bridge, Jason could see the regulars. The two companies on the north side were marching back toward the bridge. They stopped on the north bank of the Concord River. The officers were talking and pointing at the oncoming militia.

Jason looked behind him. He was the head of a long column snaking down the hill. Buttrick was marching in front of the Concord minute company directly behind the Acton men. He could see Barrett astride his horse still on top of the hill, imparting a warning to each company as they passed, "Don't fire first!"

Five hundred men, two abreast, made a long column, and it was impressing the regulars. The nearest two companies of redcoats crossed the bridge, joining the third company on the opposite bank. Their combined force moved into a tightly packed street, firing formation aiming, a hundred muskets across the bridge.

Jason admired their training. It would take his regiment all morning to get in the street firing formation right. The regulars had formed in minutes, but the officers were shouting conflicting orders. Groups of a dozen soldiers each started running to the right and left. The river was only a few yards wide and the soldiers on the flanks could rake the length of the militia column. Fortunately, a very young officer—Jason was already close enough to see faces—countermanded that order, and the flanking soldiers ran back to join the formation blocking the bridge.

Jason could feel his eyes widen as they marched nearer the regular's muskets. The muzzles appeared huge, each one crowned with a bayonet. Panic gripped his chest and squeezed tighter with every step. *This is not a good idea.* His hair felt like it was standing straight up on his head and might lift his hat off. The regular's formation was unwavering. *They are not going to let us pass. Maybe I can walk forward alone and assure them of our peaceful intentions.*

Jason turned to Davis to tell him his idea, but before Jason spoke, a redcoat officer ran onto the bridge and began to pull up planks. Davis raised his arm, pointed at the officer on the bridge, and yelled out, "You! Stop!"

Turning back to the regular's phalanx of muskets, Jason recognized Sergeant Thurston in the front rank. Kneeling beneath him was Private Stimson, aiming his musket directly at Jason.

"Oh sh—"

Stimson disappeared in a cloud of fire and smoke. Jason felt a tug on his sleeve and heard the puff of the musket shot. He looked down at his sleeve, then raised his head with the whistling of dozens of lead balls past his ears and the clatter of a ragged volley. The regulars were now shrouded in a cloud of their own gun smoke. They had fired a volley! Before he could react, somebody pushed Jason from behind, and beside him, Davis leaped into the air and fell.

"FIRE! For God's sake, soldiers, fire!" shouted John Buttrick from behind him.

With no musket in his hands, Jason charged down the slope toward the bridge. He hoped to bowl over some regulars before they could reload. Jason ducked as an excited militiaman fired his musket directly over his head. Behind him, the two abreast column dissolved into a mob. People seemed to be running and shooting in every direction.

For a moment, Jason couldn't see the bridge for all the gun smoke and nearly ran into the Concord River. He changed course and ran up onto the bridge. For the few seconds he was delayed, a dozen militia men ran across the bridge in front of him. Jason ran across, wondering what he was going to do when he got there. On the other side of the bridge, a fallen redcoat trying to get off his knees jabbed at a militiaman with his bayonet. The militiaman parried the blow and smashed his tomahawk into the soldier's head. When he pulled the ax out, part of the man's scalp and skull cap came with it, and the regular fell back to the ground.

Jason ran out of the smoke on the south side of the bridge. The regulars were gone. To his right, he saw them running toward Concord, leaving their dead on the ground, their wounded hobbling behind. There were bodies strewn on both sides of the bridge. Militia dead and wounded mostly lay on the north side of the river; he stood on the south side among red-coated bodies.

Jason felt dizzy. His eyes wouldn't focus. He looked around again, but he didn't know what he was looking for. In the last few moments, the social order he had known all his life had been dashed to pieces. Last night, he shared food and drink with the king's officers; this morning, he fought a battle against them. Last night, they were his countrymen; this morning, they were the enemy. Jason's stomach and emotions were both in free fall. *What do I do now?*

"We came to put out the fire," shouted a militiaman at the backs of the retreating redcoats.

"We can forget marching peacefully to town," said John, standing beside Jason.

Jason's heart beat rapidly; he was out of breath and panting. He shook his head to clear the growing fog of indecision. There were only a few dozen men on the south side of the Concord River. Looking back from where they had come, they could see the remaining hundreds of militiamen running back up the hill.

"What the hell?" John gave a frustrated gesture toward the backs of the running militiamen, "What are they running from?"

"We can't fight our way into town to put out that fire." Jason talked aloud to gather his thoughts. "And the regulars will come back to secure the bridge."

"What?" asked John. "Why?"

"Their detachment at Barrett's farm." He found some focus for his thoughts. They needed to organize the remaining militia, or the regulars would massacre them when they returned. Some of the men were sitting, some even laid down as if they were exhausted from the short run, and others were pulling at the regulars on the ground, searching their bodies for souvenirs. Two militiamen were arguing over possession of a regular's musket. Jason shouted, "Fall in!"

"Oh yeah. They have to cross back," agreed John, looking across the bridge and up the road for signs of the returning regulars.

"Fall in!" Jason yelled again louder. This time, John Buttrick shouted, too and pushed the Massachusetts soldiers into a formation. After a few minutes, they restored order and some military semblance.

"Luther, you're a sergeant; get in your place," said John to a man in the back row.

"Oh yeah." Luther moved down to the right end of the formation. Another minuteman moved, taking the sergeant's position.

With order restored, Jason's sense of purpose returned, too. "Count off," ordered Jason, pointing to the first man in the first rank. They counted off to forty-nine.

"That makes fifty-one of us and a thousand redcoats about a half mile away," said John. "We can't defend this bridge without reinforcement."

"I need a runner to take a message up to Colonel Barrett," said Jason. Several militiamen raised their hands. Jason picked one carrying a pitchfork rather than a musket.

"Tell Colonel Barrett that we hold the bridge," Jason told the man. "We need reinforcements to keep it. Also, tell him I recommend he send a blocking force toward his house. I will wait here for his orders. Do you understand?"

"Yes, sir."

"Good, run now." The volunteer ran back across the bridge toward the militia on the hilltop.

"How do we defend this bridge?" John asked Jason.

Jason looked at the bridge and the ground around them, turning a complete circle, "We could go back across and try and defend it with the river between us, but there's no cover. We don't have time to dig parapets, and we don't have enough people. We'd be caught between two fires when that detachment returns."

"If Barrett brings them down, we'd have enough."

Jason looked up the hill at the churning crowd of militia and frowned. There was no sign yet of order. He could see Barrett on his horse shouting at the disorganized mass of men, but one company seemed to be marching away.

"Here they come," John pointed down the road toward Concord. A large party of regulars was marching toward them.

"We're not going to get reinforcements in time." Jason searched the ground for a place to stand. "Let's move over there behind that stone wall. We can't cover the bridge, but we can defend from there and threaten the bridge—force them to divide their force until . . ."

"Until what?"

"We get more soldiers, I guess—I don't have a plan, John."

Llewellyn was sitting in a comfortable chair provided by the same woman who had so cursed the soldiers that had started the fire. The fire was all but out. Grenadiers threw buckets of water on the still smoldering bits. Llewellyn saw a young ensign running toward him from the direction of the north bridge.

"Oh, bother." He stood up and walked to meet the running man.

Mitchell started to follow him, but Llewellyn waved him off, "Bring up the reserve if you please." The ensign was waving his arms making jerky excited movements. Seeing Colonel Caradoc coming forward, he stopped running. Breathing hard, he saluted as Llewellyn approached, "Sir, Captain Lillingfield says-uhm-that-uhm-sends his best compliments—"

A distant crackling of musketry distracted the runner. He looked back down the road, then back to Llewellyn and shouted in round-eyed hysteria, "The militia are coming down the hill! Thousands of them, sir!"

Llewellyn turned around. He could see Mitchell with two companies of grenadiers. He waved them forward, and they broke into a double-quick march. To the ensign, "Lead on." The ensign hesitated. Llewellyn pushed the young man in front of him. They had not trotted more than a hundred yards when Llewellyn saw a panicked mob of soldiers running toward him. Llewellyn stopped, stood in the middle of the road, and grabbed the first man who tried to run past him.

"Hold here," firmly shaking him. Next, he grabbed the strap of a drummer who tried to dodge him; he said to him calmly, "Beat assembly."

"They're right behind us!" the wild-eyed drummer struggled in Llewellyn's grip.

"Beat assembly," Llewellyn firmly but quietly ordered. The drummer saw the two companies of grenadiers hard behind Llewellyn, which seemed to restore his sense of duty, and he stopped pulling.

"Drummer beat assembly. Must I say it again?" Finally, the drummer obeyed. Responding to years of discipline, the panicked mob stopped running and began to form their ranks.

"Officers assemble on me!" He raised his voice over the drum but restrained it to a parade ground tone. He didn't want to sound panicked or angry, just stern. A group of young ensigns, lieutenants, and Captain Lillingfield stepped forward. Their faces were white, eyes round, and mouths open with fear.

Mitchell and the reserve of grenadiers arrived. "Major Mitchell, please take command of this detachment. Keep about a hundred yards behind. These young gentlemen and I are going forward to reconnoiter the bridge."

"Sir," saluted Major Mitchell.

"Follow me," said Llewellyn without looking at his gaggle of young charges. He could hear their heavy breathing as they followed behind him toward the bridge and the battle they had just fled. Llewellyn strode briskly, trying to present a calm, confident, yet still very severe countenance. When he was out of Mitchells' earshot, Llewellyn glared back at them, "Gentlemen, that was a shameful exhibition. Running before the enemy. Men have been shot for less."

"But sir—" began one of the older Lieutenants.

"There is no excuse; please do not insult us both by offering one." Llewellyn cut him off. They quailed away from him.

"It is not a crime to be afraid," said Llewellyn. "Some say it is a sign of intelligence. But acting on your fear is cowardice." Now Llewellyn could see the bridge, the scattered bodies, the lingering smell of gunpowder, and two scores of militiamen crouching behind a stone wall a hundred yards to the right.

He continued forward. "I was so afraid at the Battle of Minden that I did a wee in my breeches. Didn't even know it until later that night. I washed out my linen myself rather than let my batman know what I'd done."

Some of the young officers smiled, but Llewellyn kept a forbidding frown, "Our soldiers benefit little from army life. Most of them took the king's shilling because they had nothing better. Their pay is low, rations short, and discipline is harsh." The small party arrived at the bridge.

Llewellyn stopped walking and turned a stern eye on his young charges. "They fight for comradeship, regimental pride, and brave leadership." He clasped his hands behind him. "Officers provide that leadership. It is your duty to your class, your country, and your king to master yourself to take a bullet rather than run."

Across the Concord River, he could see hundreds of armed men on the hill, but they were a formless mass and did not appear to be a threat to the bridge or the road. At least not yet. "Captain Lillingfield, you were in command. Please tell me what transpired, sir."

"Sir," said the puffy, red-faced captain. He appeared even younger in the daylight, almost a boy. "The militia came down the hill. There were hundreds—"

"What kind of formation were they in?"

"It was a column." He shook his head. "Uh—two abreast."

"In column? Not ranks? No bloody skirmishers?" Llewellyn's eyes were wide, and he could feel his face redden. He gritted his teeth to restrain himself from shouting at them.

"No, sir." Luke's voice quavered. "Then Lieutenant Sutherland tried to pull up the planks. The Yanks shouted at him, and then one of our soldiers fired. It started a volley. I didn't order it. It just happened. Then the Yanks started firing, and Private Pendrick was hit in the head, and his brains were blown all over me." He held up an expensively tailored sleeve; the blood stained his scarlet coat black. "Then I—I lost my head, really. I tried to help Pendrick, but his brain fell out onto the ground . . ." Luke Lillingfield wiped tears and snot on his other sleeve.

"Sir, we were in the street firing formation." Ensign Lister interrupted Luke's shaky explanation. He was in better shape emotionally and spoke more clearly as he tried to control his breathing. "When the fourth regiment fired, they moved back to let the next rank fire, but the country people fired, hitting some, and in the confusion, some of my men thought the King's Own were running. Then everybody started running."

"You should have stopped them," said Llewellyn. "It was your sacred duty to stop them." Llewellyn scowled at them, speechless with anger. He turned his head away to keep his temper. He saw the rock wall where a militia band was taking cover.

"Come on." He led them within fifty yards of the wall. "Captain Lillingfield, do you see those militiamen over there?"

"Yes sir," Lillingfield's voice was calm and clear.

"Count their muskets if you please. You can see them plainly. They are aimed directly at us."

While Luke counted, the small party stood silent. The young gentlemen were unable to look away from the musket muzzles. Llewellyn motioned for Mitchell, who walked up alone.

"Major Mitchell, please have a detail stack arms and recover our dead and wounded. Do nothing to provoke a reaction from this lot behind the wall."

"Sir," Mitchell saluted and ran back. Soon a platoon of twelve men were stacking arms in triangles and moving to the bridge unarmed. After several very long minutes, Luke said. "Sir, I count fifty militiamen. I counted twice to be sure."

"Just so. Now, up on top of that hill. What do you see?"

"Several hundred militiamen. Maybe a thousand; it's hard to count from here."

Llewellyn started to reply but stopped because a countryman was walking up to them with a jug of cider and a tray of small tumblers.

"Extraordinary," said Llewellyn.

"Can I interest you gentlemen in a cup o' cider?" The grinning provincial waved his jug.

To Llewellyn, the man seemed a bit gwallgof. He smiled oddly and appeared unaware that a battle had raged here minutes before or that fifty nervous militiamen aimed muskets at him. Llewellyn was already committed to standing in front of a firing squad of rebel militia. A nip of cider seemed in order. "Yes. A tot for each of us."

"Sir. He's barking mad," whispered Ensign Lister.

"I'm sure that speaks well for his cider."

When each of them was holding a tumbler, Llewellyn toasted the king. The young gentlemen raised their cups and downed their drinks.

"The king!" said the provincial, taking a drink straight from his jug.

"Thank you. Good sir, would you please offer a cider to the officer commanding the militia?" Llewellyn handed him some coins and pointed to the militia behind the wall.

"My pleasure." The provincial trotted off toward the stone wall with his jug and tray.

"Why aren't they shooting?" asked Luke.

"Because Major Mitchell behind us would attack and destroy them."

"Why don't we attack them?" asked Ensign Lister.

"The militia are ensconced behind a stone wall. Our men would prevail, but the militia would fire a volley before they run and may injure some of our grenadiers. I will not risk more men for a position that is of no consequence to us."

"Sir, if I may, why are we here then?" asked Luke.

"Because I need to keep that bridge open until our detachment at Barrett's farm returns. We and the militia there," he nodded to the militia positions, "are at an impasse. As long as we stand here, they will not move against the bridge. When our detachment returns, we will no longer require it and can leave the bridge to them."

Llewellyn let them reflect on that, then resumed his lecture. "Gentlemen, as you can see, of the hundreds of militia that came down that hill, only fifty crossed the bridge. The rest ran—as is the custom among the militia." He held up a finger. "If you had kept your heads and fired another volley, the militia would be driven off, and we would have undisputed possession of the bridge." Clasping his hands behind him, "Therefore, we will stand here until our detachment returns or . . ." he nodded to the militia behind the wall, "the militia shoot us down."

Captain Parsons' detachment appeared as Major Mitchell's recovery detail was carrying the last body off the bridge. As he heard the expedition safely clap across the wooden bridge, Llewellyn turned to the militia behind the wall. A man, his belly straining the buttons on his faded green coat, stood up. He held a tumbler of cider in his right hand and raised it in salute. Llewellyn touched his hat in response. He looked familiar. *Could it be the pub keeper from last night?*

To his small party of officers, he said, "Gentlemen, let us not try the patience of the militia any longer. We will retire to Concord."

"Sir. Are we going to be court-martialed?" asked Lillingfield, struggling to keep a brave face.

Llewellyn pointed at a well, "Wash your faces, straighten your uniforms, return to your commands, and provide your soldiers with the bold leadership the king expects of his officers. Nothing more will be said."

Relief swept across their faces. They smiled at each other. Lillingfield said, "Thank you, sir. I was praying the Yanks would shoot me."

"The day is still young."

They walked back to Mitchell's companies stopping at a well for the officers to clean up and drink. Afterward, they dispersed to their companies. "Leave a picket to screen our flank and march the rest back," said Llewellyn to Mitchell.

"Sir. Look at this." Mitchell motioned Llewellyn over to a line of soldier's bodies being loaded onto a commandeered wagon. Mitchell pointed at the first body, "He was scalped."

The dead soldier had an ugly head wound. What remained of his scalp and skull cap hung over the side of his head. Across the field, the militiamen, maybe the man that had scalped him, had relaxed; most were standing or sitting on their wall but still watching the regulars with muskets in hand. Had Mister Green and his men scalped a king's soldier? The seeming mutilation evoked Robert's warning about American atrocities.

"Thank you for showing me," Llewellyn said to Mitchell. "We must not leave our wounded. Requisition more wagons for the wounded and these bodies."

"Sir."

"Get more wagons than we need; there will be more casualties before this day is done."

Chapter Nine

Eleven-thirty o'clock a.m.

Whelks, Pitcairn, Mitchell, and De Berniere assembled on Llewellyn as he sat on a headstone in the cemetery of Burying Hill. Llewellyn noted that Whelk's men had extinguished the Town House fire, and the smoke was dissipating. From where he sat, Llewellyn could also see parties of regulars scattered around Concord, breaking barrels with axes. A group of marines were dragging one of the three big cannon into the mill pond and otherwise finishing their business of destroying rebel arms. A very meager haul of armament, to be sure.

"Colonel Caradoc, my pickets report large formations of militia are gathering," said Whelks. "I believe that the Yanks surrounding Concord now outnumber us."

"Thank you for that report. How goes the destruction of the military stores?"

"Slowly," said Whelks. "The little powder and shot we found was easy enough to dispose of, but destroying the foodstuffs following the governor's exact instructions is time-consuming and demands many men."

Llewellyn nodded to Pitcairn.

"Sir, we've bent the trunnions on the cannon and pounded nails into the touch holes," said Pitcairn, pointing to the mill pond where his marines guided the horses dragging the damaged cannon. "Most of my companies are forming pickets all around the town. After the attack on the north bridge, I sent another company to reinforce the division at the south bridge. We are ready to march, but I beg that we rest Captain Parsons' detachment. Except for a brief respite for breakfast, they've been on their feet since last night."

"Quite right," said Llewellyn. "Steven, I am sensible of the forces building against us, but briefly, I must rest the light-bobs. My intent

125

is that Pitcairn's battalion will lead again on our return march. I expect to use flanking movements as we encounter militia. The grenadiers will guard the rear and will be called up to disperse any stubborn resistance."

"I understand, sir," said Whelks. "What would you have me do?"

"Relieve the light-bobs from all fatigue duties, pickets, and so forth," said Llewellyn. "Major Pitcairn, recall your companies and assemble them along this road with the head of the column near where the Liberty Pole stood. Get them off their feet and let them eat their dinners."

Llewellyn picked up his spyglass and examined the militia on the north bridge and surrounding hills. "Sir," asked Major Mitchell, "may I ask what you are looking for?"

"Cannon. According to Governor Gage's intelligence, there were to be fourteen guns. We found only three. I fear we may discover those missing guns on the road to Boston, manned, loaded, and aimed at us."

He put down his spyglass and took out his watch. "I wish to start the return march no later than twelve-thirty. Steven, when the march begins, pray collapse your pickets as we withdraw with the last division covering the road between us and the north bridge."

"Sir, what about the stores?" asked Whelks.

"Throw them in the mill pond."

"Unbroken? What about the governor's instruction?"

"Given the choice between another broken barrel of pork and getting his flankers back, I believe the governor would choose his flankers." Llewellyn felt they didn't fully grasp the situation. "Gentlemen, our mission to Concord is finished. Despite our efforts, a civil war has begun. The rebels are assembling an army four times the size of His Majesty's forces. Governor Gage will require every musket and corporal to defend Boston. It is our clear duty to return this corps intact."

"Sir, the men are keenly aware that a soldier was scalped at the north bridge," said Mitchell. "How will we respond to that outrage?"

"We will not respond. However barbaric, it is not the misdeeds of an untrained militiaman at issue, but the correct and lawful behavior of his Majesty's troops and, by extension, the king." Whelks and Pitcairn were frowning. Llewellyn continued, "We took an oath to do right by His Majesty's subjects. Militia are by nature undisciplined, and some will yield to savage impulses, but they are still our countrymen. If we respond with equal or worse atrocities, then to whom do the loyal subjects turn for aid? As my mother always said, two wrongs don't make a right. You must exercise the utmost restraint on your soldiers."

"No justice then?" asked Mitchell.

"Justice will have to wait until we restore the king's peace."

From the bridge, Jason could see a picket of grenadiers about a quarter mile down the road toward Concord. Jason walked with John Buttrick out onto the bridge. A column of militia four abreast was marching down the hill toward them.

"Let's pick up the wounded and lay them at my house until their families can get them," said Buttrick, pointing to his house, which was only a hundred yards up the hill.

"Good, also send a small picket down the road so that we're not surprised if they move toward us."

John quickly gathered four volunteers with muskets under a sergeant, whose only weapon was a homemade halberd, the blade beaten from a pruning hook. They walked in a skirmish line toward Concord. The rest of the men crossed the bridge and began recovering the wounded. Among the first of the casualties Jason found was the body of Isaac Davis, the commander of the Acton minute company, lying face down. Buttrick helped lift Isaac's body. Although Isaac hadn't been a big man, his body was heavy to carry, even for two men. They laid him down with the other dead.

"This is just the first day, John," said Jason, looking at the sad line of corpses. "How many more brave men will this war take?"

"Massachusetts will need a lot more."

There were already several people walking among the dead and wounded, trying to help or look for loved ones. One woman screamed when she recognized her husband and cried as she hugged the body, unnerving Jason. The wounded, some moaning, others cursing, were helped onto Buttrick's porch.

"What do we do now?" asked John.

Butterflies danced in his stomach as Jason thought about his response, but he strode purposefully back across the north bridge toward

Concord. "Taking this bridge shows that we aren't hopeless provincials. Maybe we can hurt them bad enough to make them stop these raids. We have to gather everyone that will follow us."

"Sure, we took this bridge," John waved at the bridge, "but do you think we can stand against them in battle?"

"No, we can't do that with militia." Jason shook his head, "but if we could ambush them somewhere."

"I know just the place. The bridge over Mill Brook at Meriam's Corner. The stream is not as wide as the Concord, but it is deep and swollen with spring runoff. The regulars will have to cross on the bridge and won't be able to flank us."

"How far away is that?"

"About a mile, but the regulars will go by the great road. I know a trail. If we march fast, we can cut them off."

As they spoke, minuteman companies tramped loudly across the wooden bridge. Soon, the small plain on the south side of the Concord River had become a parade ground. Jason called for officers to join him and Major Buttrick.

"What orders did you get from Colonel Barrett?" Jason asked his brother.

"None. He rode off home when he saw the regulars leave the bridge. Some other boys did the same. Whole companies just marched away. I guess everyone's their own General 'round here."

Jason saw his nephew Jerome riding down the hill, leading two horses. Wicked was stubbornly pulling on her lead.

"We still got plenty of men ready to fight," said Bill.

Turning to the bigger group, Jason stepped out to where he could address the whole crowd, "For those of you that don't know me, I am Lieutenant Colonel Jason Green; this man here is Major John Buttrick. We expect that the regulars will march back to Boston when they are done in Concord, and we intend to march ahead and ambush them," Jason was interrupted by a fierce cheer. "We will take whatever companies choose to join us." Another cheer. Despite himself, Jason smiled at their enthusiasm.

A man rode up from the direction of Concord in a great hurry. "The lobsters are forming up on Lexington Road," he shouted, waving his arms and pointing,

"If we want to catch them at Meriam's Corner, we gotta go now," said John to Jason. "We will have to march around the outside of the circle if you understand what I mean."

"I don't, but let's not delay. Lead the way, John."

"We can take horses, and I'll show you the lay of the land. We'll have positions selected for these companies by the time they get there."

Bill held up his hand, "Wait, John, if we don't pursue them from behind, they might get wind of our ambush. We need to send a few companies to follow tight behind and distract them—I can do that."

"We'll catch them going and coming," said Jason. "They won't know what hit them."

Jason and John conferred briefly with the other captains and split the companies into a pursuit battalion led by Bill and a blocking battalion that John and Jason would take to Meriam's Corner.

Jason mounted his horse and followed John onto a track that led east and south around the hill where they had just waited out the regulars. Buttrick was riding at a canter, but Wicked kept up her cross canter all the way to Meriam's Corner. Jason was never so glad to dismount.

Leading their horses, John led Jason as he stepped out onto a bridge. Jason peered up and down the road—it was empty. The creek was just as John had described it to him: narrow but deep, swollen, and spilling its banks. A ridge on the north side of the road raised steep banks, making it difficult to cross anywhere but at the bridge.

Buttrick stomped his foot on the road, "This is Lexington Road. That's Meriam's farm over there." Pointing east, "that way is Boston;" pointing west, "and less than a mile up there around that bend to the right are the regulars."

A militia company came marching up the road from the east.

"Where are you from?" Jason asked the leading man.

"We're from Reading. I'm Captain Matthew Daley. The company behind us is from Chelmsford. We heard the regulars are in Concord."

"If you keep marching up that road, you will run right smack into 'em. We're setting up an ambush here. You're welcome to join us."

"Has the war started?" asked Daley.

"The regulars attacked and killed men in Lexington and here in Concord," said Jason.

"It's no rumor? You saw it for yourself?"

"I did. The regulars fired on us when we had our muskets shouldered. They killed the man marching next to me."

"Then we'll fight. Where do you want us?"

"The regulars are coming down this road." Jason gestured toward Concord. "We need cover somewhere we can shoot at the bridge."

"Over there in Meriam's farm," said Buttrick, "and along that rock wall. We need to get the men undercover before the regulars get here."

The distant sound of drums and fifes silenced them.

"They're coming," said Jason. "I'll stay here and position these companies."

"I'll ride back and bring up our militiamen," said John.

Buttrick mounted his horse and spurred it into a gallop. Pulling Wicked by the reins, Jason ran the new militia companies to positions in the barns and other outbuildings of Meriam's farm. He tied up Wicked at a fence post out of sight behind the house. The militia companies were barely in place when Jason saw the leading regulars around the bend marching toward the bridge. Peering through the kitchen window, Jason still had no musket. He looked around the kitchen but could see no weapons.

Llewellyn was on his horse at the front of the column when Pitcairn rode up, "Sir, I believe we are ready."

"Very well, send two companies up on that ridge if you please." Llewellyn pointed to the ridge line that ran parallel to the left side of the road. "We can wait until they are in place. I would prefer to have our flank covered as we march."

Two companies of light-bobs climbed up the ridge. They used the short-mown grass of the old burial ground as egress, formed a skirmish line, and began to work east through the trees and brush along the ridge.

When the flankers had passed the front of the column, Llewellyn ordered the drummer to beat March. At the front of the column, a light company moved forward, keeping parallel with the flankers on the ridge, followed at about forty yards by the main body of troops.

They had marched only half a mile when Llewellyn saw Pitcairn spur his horse and gallop forward, disappearing around a bend in the road. A few minutes later, he reappeared and rode directly to Llewellyn.

"Sir. There is a bridge. The stream is flowing fast with steep banks; it is not fordable. We will have to bring our flankers back in to cross it. I recommend that the column halt until the flankers can secure the far side."

"Pray, recall the flankers and proceed as you recommended, but I am not going to halt the corps. We will invite trouble if we are too timid."

"Sir."

In response to Pitcairn's signals, the two companies on the ridge trickled out onto the road. By then, Llewellyn could see the bridge and caught up with Pitcairn who was directing his light companies across the bridge.

"Sir, the flankers could see a large body of militia on the other side of the ridge marching parallel to us, but they didn't offer to fight," said Pitcairn.

"Very well." Llewellyn scanned the top of the ridge on his left. "We may encounter them on the other side of the stream. Send the first two companies that cross to the north directly. Perhaps we can intercept them before they hinder our march."

Minutes later, the first two companies crossed the bridge and formed up facing north. When the next company of light-bobs were midway across, a single fountain of fire and smoke erupted from the window of a farmhouse on the far bank of the stream on the right-hand side, followed a moment later by the 'pop' of a musket. A ragged and unexpectedly large musket volley gushed from the windows and doors of the farm's house, barn, and outbuildings.

Despite the robust volley, Llewellyn noted that the ambushers were more than a hundred fifty yards away. Their shot went wide or fell short, knocking up puffs of dirt. One ball smacked his saddle but fell to the ground, spent. They had fired too soon and spoiled their own ambush. An amateur mistake by a militia army.

Unfortunately, the light company crossing stopped mid-bridge to make ready to return fire. For a chilling moment, Llewellyn feared they would block the whole corps. Before Llewellyn could react, Lillingfield, whose company was next in the queue to cross, raised his sword, shouted 'Huzzah!' and charged through the standing company. Both companies followed him toward the farm buildings, cheering as they ran. The intrepid Lillingfield led them all the way into the smoke-wreathed farmstead.

Llewellyn spurred his horse into a gallop. By the time he reached the bridge, the rest of the light infantry had crossed at a run. Llewellyn rode across as a remarkable number of militiamen burst in every direction from the farm, prodded by British bayonets.

A rattle of musket fire from Llewellyn's left. The militia that had been moving parallel to the corps on the other side of the ridge were coming out of the woods. The trail was narrow, and the trailside brush cramped them as they tried to exit the wooded path. Before they could come out in large numbers, Major Mitchell, who had crossed directly behind Llewellyn, raised his sword and shouted, "Come on!" He charged the militia still crowded together on the narrow trail. The two light companies that had been facing left charged into the wood behind Mitchell and even some of the grenadiers ran across the bridge to join the battle. The militia scattered in front of Mitchell as he rode them down.

Llewellyn swiveled in his saddle to see the two mini-battles.

"Now that was a proper battle." Pitcairn rode up grinning. He looked ten years younger. "Did you see Lillingfield charge? The bloody yanks just poured out of every window and door. Some of them jumped from the second floor. They were in such a rush to flee."

"We have gone less than a mile from Concord, and we are already fighting pitched battles," said Llewellyn. "What does that say for the next fifteen miles?"

The crackle of musketry made Llewellyn turnabout. The bridge was packed with grenadiers moving to the east side. Beyond the bridge, a line of grenadiers faced rearward, shrouded in their own gun smoke. Another hundred yards beyond was a group of about fifty militiamen running away, some turning to shout and taunt the grenadiers.

"Oh bother," Llewellyn spurred his horse. He waited impatiently, allowing most of the remaining grenadiers to pass by before he re-crossed the bridge. He met Whelks with his rearmost company.

"I'll need wagons for the dead and wounded Colonel," Whelks spoke gruffly, his face beet red.

"What happened?"

"We were being followed by a couple of hundred militia, but they were staying well out of range. When the grenadiers were distracted by the action at the bridge, a treacherous lot dashed forward and fired into our backs. They ran off under the cover of their smoke." Motioning to his men, "The grenadiers fired back more from frustration than affect."

Two grenadiers were lying motionless, and several more wounded, staggering from their formation or sitting on the ground holding their wounds. The ambush from behind had caused more casualties than the much larger battle with the militia to their front.

"Steven, you must keep the rearguard alert. I recommend that you detach three companies and appoint a good captain as rearguard commander." Steven Whelks was only a year junior to Llewellyn, and he hated giving him orders like a subaltern, but time was more precious than hurt feelings.

"Of course—sir," Whelks nodded; his tight-lipped face was red with shame and anger.

"Recover your casualties, then move the rest of your men across. We mustn't dawdle." Llewellyn unconsciously fiddled with a button on his coat. The number of militia was growing by the minute; he could feel the noose tightening around his corps. He had to keep the momentum forward before the growing militia tide blocked their way.

Llewellyn crossed the bridge again and galloped to his forwardmost light company. He found Pitcairn talking to Lillingfield. The young captain's face was slack with fatigue, glistening with sweat, and far more serious than any young man should. He listened intently to Major Pitcairn, who was speaking to him from his horse.

Llewellyn sat up tall in the saddle and examined the ground in front of them. Although they had passed down this road the night before, it was different in the daylight. The stonewall that lined the road was not a uniform product of a commercial or government project but rather an organic assembly of farmers gathering rocks from their stony fields and stacking them along the road. It ranged in height from knee to chest high. In some places, it was neat and firm; in others, it was little more than a linear pile of stones, but it did offer limited protection for soldiers marching on the road.

The road passed through gently rolling hills surfaced with crops and pastureland, with patches of trees and orchards. Houses, barns, and taverns dotted the terrain. The trees and buildings offered concealment for the rebel bands, but Llewellyn thought his flankers could use the cover, too. Pitcairn and Lillingfield concluded their discussion, and Llewellyn urged his horse forward.

"Sir, we sent the rebels packing," said Pitcairn. "The only disappointment is they appear to have rallied somewhat, and Lillingfield's forward platoon report more militia on the road in front of us."

Nodding to Lillingfield, "Captain Lillingfield, your actions at the bridge are commendable."

Luke saluted with a short, grim smile. "Thank you, sir. I am trying to do better."

"Major Pitcairn, divide your battalion into two wings," Llewellyn ordered. "One on each side of the road. They are to be the beaters. We'll flush the rebels out of their ambushes. Use Major Mitchell to command one of the wings. I will bring up the grenadiers to be the guns in the center. Not pheasant hunting perhaps, but I hope that we can take the initiative from the rebels."

Jason rode together with John. Behind them, they could not see the regulars anymore. With them marched a ragged band of militia gathered from the flotsam of the last battle.

"Damn that farmer," cursed John. "The regulars were more than a hundred yards away. Spoiled the whole ambush."

"We have to get some fire discipline and find a way to get the militia to stand and fire a second volley," said Jason.

"You saw how they charged," John waved a hand. "A regular can run fifty yards faster than our men can reload. We got no defense against the bayonet."

"If we could get them to stand in formation and fire by rank like they've been trained, we would blunt the charge."

"Your Westford regiment could do that?"

"Well—" Jason shook his head. "We practiced it once just before Christmas." He shrugged, "We learned a lot." Jason was able to ignore John's dismissive grunt because a long column of militia marching toward Concord interrupted their conversation.

"The regulars are right behind us. We are going to try and form an ambush," said Jason to the commander of the leading formation. "How many companies are with you?"

"I know we look like a big army, but it's just happenstance." said the leading commander. "We're from Billerica; the company behind is from Sudbury. The rest just kinda' fell in behind us as we marched. I don't know where they are from."

Jason stood tall in his stirrups to look down the column and count the companies. Then he turned to see how many stragglers from the Meriam's Corner battle had stayed with them.

"There's a lot here, John," Jason said to Buttrick. "More than five hundred men altogether."

"We could really do some damage if we get them organized before the regulars get here."

"I'm Lieutenant Colonel Jason Green, and this is Major John Buttrick," Jason told the leading men. "We have already had two battles with the regulars. Are your men ready to fight?" Jason said the last part loudly enough for the men behind to hear. A cheer that rose in volume as it moved down the column answered his question.

"I'll take the last five companies to the south side of the road. John, you take the rest and our stragglers and take the north side. We'll sandwich them between us."

"Good, but let's be careful not to shoot at each other."

"We can stagger the line. I'll stay to the east about a hundred yards."

Jason led the first companies out into the fields to the south of the road. They trampled newly plowed fields as they moved into positions. He found a good stone wall and placed four companies behind it, facing the road. The remaining company he placed on the left, guarding the approaches from the west.

"Do you really think they'll come from that direction?" asked the militia commander from Framingham, frowning at the orchard from which Jason's imagined flankers would appear. It was too early for the trees to bloom, and except for buds, the branches were naked, permitting a view deep into the apple orchard.

"They have light infantry flankers with them." Jason tried not to sound condescending, "It's possible they'll just march down the road and let us shoot them down, but it's more likely they'll send flankers to push us away from our ambush. The flankers would come from the vicinity of that orchard. It's the only covered approach." The Framingham militia commander shrugged his shoulders, "I guess. My fellas don't want to miss the fighting."

Llewellyn waved Whelks forward.

"Colonel Caradoc, I appointed a rearguard commander. He has three companies that he will rotate to keep the rebel militia back."

"Very well. I expect the road in front of us will hot up as we move forward," said Llewellyn. "I divided the light-bobs into two wings to cover the north and south flanks. Form your battalion into parallel columns."

"We'll be six abreast . . ." Whelks surveyed the narrow road in front of them.

"I can sum, too," said Llewellyn.

"You can be a boor sometimes, Llewellyn."

Llewellyn was embarrassed. He had been patronizing with Steven. A man he had known for years. "I beg your pardon, Steven. It was rude of me to be so curt," Llewellyn touched Steven's sleeve.

"Never mind. I understand your intent; you want me to have the flexibility to fight both sides of the road or to quickly form a battalion front."

"Just so."

"However, I was contemplating the narrowness of the road. In parallel, six abreast, as you ordered, I would like to march the columns in open ranks. That will give the men sufficient space to fire in their ranks while still moving forward."

"Brilliant, that is very near an innovation, Steven."

Steven shook his head, "None of that now. Nothing progressive, just applying the manual of exercise to the conditions."

"Very well. Would you care to hear the rest of my plan?"

"If you please."

"Pray march your grenadiers briskly, but don't get ahead of the light-bobs. When you hear firing on either flank, beat double-time. You must get your men out in front of the light-bobs so that you can hit the rebels in their flanks as they flee the light-bobs. We will snare them in their own ambush."

"Ah, get under their knickers, eh? But what if they don't run?" For a brief awkward moment, Steven's leer about knickers reminded Llewellyn of the rumor of a woman in Quebec. He brushed the thought aside.

"Militia won't stand. They will fire in haste and run."

"What of the rebel militia in our rear?" said Steven. "They continue to press, and they grow in number."

"Pray ask your rear commander to break contact when you begin to double-time. I expect that the rebel militia lacks the organization to reform their column fast enough to overtake us if we move swiftly."

It was a complex operation. The air was filled with shouted commands, drums, and sergeants' curses, but the various units of Llewellyn's corps moved confidently into their positions as smoothly as dancers found their places in a waltz, and the corps never lost its forward momentum. Llewellyn smiled to himself, pleased at the efficiency of the British Army and spurred his horse forward, keeping an eye on his flanks.

Despite the coming bloodshed and carnage, Llewellyn eagerly awaited the coming action. He hoped a sharp blow would scatter the militia and ease the road home. But his eagerness was more than a reflection on tactical success. Llewellyn was relishing the excitement of battle. Elizabeth's death had sapped his life of purpose. Despite his best efforts to renew his pride in his children or happiness with his friends, sorrow clung to him like black tar. Regardless—or perhaps because of—the danger of imminent death or mutilation, this struggle with the Yanks filled his thoughts and was a welcome respite from his chronic grief.

Jason had no sooner tied Wicked to an outhouse a hundred yards from the road than he heard a distant musket volley. He ran forward to his companies facing the road. Crouching down behind the wall, Jason removed his hat and peered over.

He couldn't see any regulars, but the firing from the northwest was so rapid that for a moment, it became a continuous roar, then faded away just as quickly. Jason heard the rapid stomping of a man running behind him. He turned in time to see a militiaman from the Framingham minute company run past. A moment later, he heard a volley from the direction of the Framingham company. Even before the firing had died away, two more militiamen ran by.

Jason grabbed the nearest company commander by his sleeve and yelled, "Follow me!" The entire militia company stood up with their commander and ran toward the sound of guns.

The Framingham militia ran past them as Jason and his followers rushed toward their vacated post. When Jason saw the redcoats, they were charging from the apple orchard less than a hundred yards away. At the sight of their gleaming bayonets, Jason felt an electric shock of fear. He stopped and raised an arm; the militia company lined up on his right and left. The regulars gained the western rock wall that the Framingham militia had abandoned, vaulting over it in their hurry to close the gap.

Jason raised both arms above his head and shouted, "Present!" Those that had them raised their muskets, aiming at the charging regulars. The red tide was less than fifty yards away and closing fast, but fleeing Framingham militiamen blocked a clear shot.

Some of the faster redcoats were now only thirty yards away. Their eyes were round and fearful, yet they continued to charge as fast as their legs could carry them.

The last militiaman passed Jason's line. "Fire!" yelled Jason, his arms swinging down to point at the charging regulars. Fifty muskets erupted with fire and smoke. When the smoke cleared the regulars were running away. The militia company cheered in surprise, relief, and exultation.

"Hold that wall," Jason shouted at the company commander he didn't know, leading a militia company he knew not where they were from.

Jason turned around and ran back to the north-facing companies. He arrived in time to see his militia force scatter in every direction, followed closely by charging grenadiers. The miter-hatted regulars caught a slower militiaman and bayoneted him. He fell, and several more grenadiers joined the first, repeatedly stabbing the unfortunate man, now dying in the grass.

"Damn you!"

One nearby squad of grenadiers heard then saw Jason and gave chase. Jason ran. After about twenty yards, he looked behind; he saw only the backs of the redcoats. They had already given up their pursuit and turned back to the road. He stopped, panting heavily, and watched them. The redcoats were walking slowly, practically plodding, their weapons lugged over their shoulders rather than carried at the ready. Jason circled back toward the spot where he had tethered Wicked.

Shaking his head, Jason could kick himself as he thought about the last action. Since the last war, his tactical instincts had withered. It was plain as day that the regulars would try and skirt his line, but he had sent only one company to defend the flank. When the light infantry had forced him to shift out of position, the grenadiers hit his exposed flank. A clever maneuver that made it clear to Jason that Caradoc's tactical skills were sharp, and the technical competence of his units was first-rate. The realization depressed Jason. Militia, however enthusiastic, could not hope to defeat such opponents.

Now that the excitement of the fight was over, Jason's feet grew heavier with each step. Walking slowly, plodding as much as the redcoats were, he saw Wicked grazing, still tied to the outhouse. Even from a distance, he could see a musket through the intervening naked tree branches. It was leaning against the outhouse wall next to the door. It had not been there before. As he got closer, Jason recognized it as a British army issue musket, a Brown Bess. The bayonet was still fixed. A regular must be in the outhouse.

His hands were shaking with reaction from the fear and fatigue, and his stomach churned. In his mind's eye, he saw himself forced to wrestle for control of the musket. He heard someone moving inside the crudely planked outhouse. In a near panic, Jason ran forward, grabbed the musket, leaped back a few feet, cocked the hammer as quietly as he could, and raised it to eye level. A moment later, out stepped a regular buttoning his breeches. His eyes down, he didn't notice Jason, only a few feet away. Finished buttoning, the soldier reached for Wicked's reins. Wicked bit him. The soldier howled and jumped back, holding his hand. Jumping and cursing, he turned around, putting his hand under his arm and looked up into the mouth of his musket.

"Private Johnson?" asked Jason.

"Mister Green? Don't shoot!" Johnson put his hands in the air.

"What are you doing here?" asked Jason with the musket still leveled at Johnson's face.

"I deserted. I hid in this—uh—shed until me mates had gone back. The Yanks—pardon sir, I didn't mean to insult—are shooting at us without relief. I am ready to surrender. I want no more of this fight or the army."

"What were you going to do with my horse?" Jason lowered the gun.

"I didn't know it was your horse, sir. I was going to surrender to the farm yonder," Johnson pointed at some rooftops down the hill. "I wanted to return the horse, maybe sell Bess," nodding to his musket that Jason was pointing at him, "and find work."

"The horse is mine, and now so is the musket."

"But sir, it's my musket. I need the money."

"This gun was the property of King George, and now it belongs to the Massachusetts militia. It's not yours to sell." Holding out his hand, "Give me the cartridges, too."

"I had to buy these from me own wages." Johnson took off the cartridge bag.

"Send a receipt to the Massachusetts Congress." Jason took the cartridge box. While Jason armed himself, Johnson sat down under an apple tree.

"Go on down to that house." Jason nodded toward it. "Farmers are always looking for hands. They may give you a meal for work."

"I will, sir, but I am just going to sit here for a moment. I am so tired. We marched all night." Johnson began to nod even as he was speaking.

"Are you hurt?" asked Jason. In the last war, he had seen a man bleed to death without anybody knowing he was wounded. He appeared to have just fallen asleep. No one realized what had happened until they tried to wake him.

"No sir, I am fine, just very tired." Johnson closed his eyes and lay still. Jason feared the worst and went to shake him, but then Johnson snored.

Jason envied the sleeping soldier. The accumulation of the continuous exertion and fear of the last few hours brought drowsiness on him like a blow.

Jason's eyelids drooped. *I could nap, too. I did my part. The battle will get on fine without me.*

"What about your regiment?" he asked aloud. *You don't know where they're at. They could be anywhere.*

He braced himself on the musket.

"I need to catch up to the fight; my country needs me." *You'll be killed for sure. Look at the hole in your sleeve; the ball barely missed you. You won't be so lucky next time. What good are you to your country dead?*

Jason tried to raise his arm to see the hole in his sleeve, but the reward didn't seem worth the effort. His knees were about to buckle. He crossed his arms on the musket muzzle and rested his chin.

"What will Mary say?" Jason raised his chin and rubbed his eyes. *Mary won't know if I don't tell her.*

Wicked bit Jason's arse.

"Ow! Son-of-a-bitch!" Jason jerked wide awake, grabbing at his backside with one hand and swatting at Wicked with the other. Wicked went back to grazing. "Damned horse." Jason rubbed his butt. He took a canteen off the saddle, slapped at Wicked's nose when she turned her head toward him, and took a deep drink.

Jason took the reins tight under the mare's chin so she wouldn't bite him, "I'm spent, but Mary's labor with little Jay was longer than this." He washed his face from the water in the canteen and took a refreshing gulp. Still talking to the horse, "She has expectations of me; I can't disappoint her. My only consolation is that you may die with me." Jason swung up in the saddle, spurred Wicked, and headed east, leaving Johnson snoring under the apple tree.

Jason directed Wicked back to the road. The great road was littered with debris from fleeing regulars, mostly cartridge papers and a dropped canteen, but no sign of the owners. He knew Caradoc wouldn't wait for the militia to gather and overwhelm him. To get ahead of him, Jason would have to move faster.

Both ways on the road he could see militia men in small groups moving east toward Boston, but no sign of John Buttrick. He couldn't catch them, just chasing in their wake. He knew a faster way. He crossed the Great Road going north. He remembered an old Indian trail that Bill had shown him—*There it is.* He turned east on the narrow trail and spurred

Wicked to a gallop. Before he had ridden a mile, he saw two armed men walking, one limping, in the same direction.

"Where are you from?" Jason asked as he passed the two men.

"Concord, we're chasing the regulars, but I twisted an ankle," said one, leaning on his comrade. As Jason suspected, they were march casualties from militia companies marching ahead.

"Who is your commander?"

"Bill Green. They're not too far up there. We'll catch 'em soon."

To his right, through the trees, he heard the regular's drums beating a Quick March. The beat was fast. He spurred Wicked into a gallop. After another quarter mile, the drums were to his rear. Ahead, he could see militia moving into ambush positions. Standing in the middle of the trail, he saw his brother pointing into the woods.

"Jason! How did you find me?"

"The trail. Remember that time? You were courting the girl with the bodice."

"Elizabeth Graham," Bill flashed an embarrassed grin. "Listen, Jason. I put my company into these woods overlooking the road. There are militia companies on both sides. It'll be a turkey shoot here in a few minutes."

"A lobster shoot," said one of Bill's men with a grin.

"How can I help?"

"Can you cross the road and give the militia commander on the other side a notion of our position?"

"On my way!"

"Did you see?" Mitchell asked Llewellyn, pointing up the road.

"What?"

"Remember that rider? The one that crossed the road just before Concord. I believe I just saw him again, crossing the road in front of us from north to south."

"Grey horse? Green coat?"

"The same."

"How far away?"

"A quarter mile. In that wood, where the road rises."

Llewellyn stood in his stirrups, considering the lay of the land. The road rose slowly to a causeway that passed into a large wood with low ground on both sides. The road appeared to curve right in the forest, but it was hard to see much else for the trees.

"Beat Commanders Assemble," Llewellyn ordered his drummer. A few minutes later Whelks and Pitcairn had joined him.

"Sir," said Pitcairn, "My forward company is reporting movement in the wood to our front."

"Just so," said Llewellyn. "I fear another ambush. The wood is too large for us to bypass." To De Bernie, he asked, "Is there another way?"

"Sir, I am not familiar enough with the country. I was only on this road once."

Llewellyn nodded to Pitcairn, "Pray send a grand division on wide flanking maneuver to the south of the road." To Whelks, he said, "Bring the rearguard closer. We must tighten up and turn this column into a hedgehog of fire."

The roadbed was built up so it would still be passable in the spring, but the south side of the wood was wet with spring run-off. Wicked splashed through puddles yards across.

"Where is your commander?" Jason asked a small knot of men.

"Are the regulars coming?"

"You can see them if you walk a couple of rods that way. They will be here shortly and there are militia on the other side of the road. You'll be shooting each other if we're not careful. I need to speak to your commander."

"Loammi!" shouted the man.

"Keep your voice down!" hissed another militiaman.

"Are you the commander?" asked Jason.

"Yes, sir, Major Loammi Baldwin from Woburn. Who are you?"

"Lieutenant Colonel Jason Green from the Westford regiment. There's a battalion of Concord militia on the other side of the road, and soon, you will both be shooting at the regulars between you."

Loammi raised his arm toward the road, "The road rises above this low ground. We and the Concord militia will both be shooting up," he gestured skyward. Jason nodded in understanding; the regulars would be marching on a road raised at its high point almost five feet above the marshy ground. The militia firing at the regulars would be firing over the heads of the militia on the other side.

"There's the drums. Where can I be of service?"

"The road curves sharp south about a hundred or so yards that way," Loammi raised his chin toward the east. "We plan to shoot at them here, then move about fifty yards east and shoot them some more," Loammi whispered and ducked down behind a tree.

As quietly as possible, Jason dismounted into an ankle-deep puddle. The cold water seeped into his shoes as he tied Wicked's reins to a branch and crept behind a tree. Silence settled on the wood except for the loud trills and gunks of the woodland frogs earnestly courting in the puddles around him. But soon, the tramp of marching feet and beating drums drowned out the amphibian love songs. Jason leaned up against the tree.

"There's a saddled horse on the right side! About seventy-five yards into the woods." He heard a British-accented voice shout out.

Damn! Jason realized that the regulars could see Wicked. Why hadn't he thought of that? There was nothing to do about it now.

"Graham! Take your platoon and flush 'em out!" ordered another voice.

Moments later Jason heard the clatter of regulars' kit and splashes as a platoon left the dry road and scrambled down into the woods. A musket shot, followed by more, then a rising rattle of muskets. Jason turned around the tree to aim his newly acquired musket. At a farther distance than he expected, Jason saw a dozen regulars splashing back to the road. He could see an occasional flash of red uniform but no clear targets. The regulars he could see were too far away for a good shot. He ran forward but hidden under the puddle's black water were holes and submerged branches. He hadn't taken more than a couple of steps when he tripped and fell full length. He fell on his left side, keeping the musket up with his right arm to keep from wetting the powder. As he got back to his knees, a crash of musketry assaulted his ears, and the road had become invisible, enveloped in gun smoke. Out of pure frustration, Jason fired through the smoke in the direction of the road.

"Battalion!" a hoarse shout from the road.

"Company!" echoed a chorus.

"By platoons, fire!" The volleys from the regulars were now smaller but very rapid. From the militia side, there was just an irregular banging of musketry as the militiamen loaded and fired of their own accord.

Jason stepped behind a tree to reload. The great noise of shooting grew until it merged into a single roar. A thick, acrid fog of gun smoke filled the forest. Leaves and twigs rained down as musket balls whipped through the treetops. Reloaded, Jason peered around the trunk to find a target. He couldn't see very much through the smoke, but he heard hoarse shouting east of his position. Remembering Loammi's plan, Jason cautiously splashed eastward.

Normally calm, Llewellyn's gelding wrestled with him to get away. His poor horse had very nearly consumed his allotment of bravery. Fortunately, the grenadiers showed greater courage and discipline than his horse. Despite the smoke, fire, and confusion, they were moving admirably. Each company fired by platoon ranks. The front-ranked platoon fired a volley and then stopped to reload. The rank behind passed through their open left flank so as not to disturb the first platoon's reloading and became the front rank. The new front platoon fired in their turn. Sergeants and officers shouted orchestrated commands to keep the near-perfect harmony. Whelks appeared out of the smoke.

"Magnificent performance, Steven; your men have upset the Yank's ambush." Llewellyn had to shout over the roar of musketry. He felt dangerously exposed, but he dared not show it.

"We are using shot and powder at a prodigious rate, and the march has slowed to a crawl."

Pfsh- the unmistakable sound of a musket ball passed between them.

"Keep them moving. Listen for my command. There will be a change shortly. I want to avoid getting quagswagged at the corner."

Jason struggled through the muddy puddles. He passed a motionless man lying doubled over, his head completely submerged in the puddle he was lying in. Five yards farther, another man sat with his back to the tree.

He was equally motionless, staring sightlessly to his front. Jason couldn't tell if he was dead, wounded, or paralyzed with fright. Neither did he take time to find out as he sloshed past the grim harvest of militiamen. Since he had started his journey from Boston, he had not yet fired an aimed shot at the enemy. Jason was intent on contributing to the battle. Behind a thick tree trunk, he found a relatively dry spot, propped up his musket, and took aim at the road. He cocked his firelock. Through the smoke, he could see the leading redcoats coming into his range.

Thunk!

Jason flinched and nearly dropped his musket. A ball had hit the tree inches in front of his eyes, accompanied by the roar of a musket volley. To his right, Jason saw regulars charging in his direction. He had been flanked again. He turned his musket from the road to the new menace and fired, but he knew as soon as the powder ignited that his shot was high. Dozens of other militiamen around him fired, too. The gap between them and the regulars filled with smoke. Jason ducked behind his tree and reloaded again.

The grenadiers were doing good work, but the militia had all the advantages of firing from behind trees at the exposed regulars. The casualties were mounting in Jason's corps.

"Leave him!" A corporal shouted at a grenadier who stopped to help a tumbled mate. Llewellyn was ashamed as the column left behind the fallen, but stopping to carry dead and wounded would slow their movement and allow the rebels to inflict even more casualties. Finally, above the uneven banging of militia muskets, Llewellyn heard a disciplined volley. The light-bobs had descended on his ambushers. Now that the light-infantry flankers were distracting the militia fire, this was the opportunity to break free of this bloody wood.

"Battalion!" he shouted as loud as he could, his voice cracking at the strain.

"Company!" came the military echo.

"At the double time! March!" The latter order of execution was premature and swallowed by the military echo of his companies, but they heard, and the entire corps broke into a trot. At the double-time, they could no longer fire back, but the militia had turned away from the column of grenadiers and were now firing at the light infantry that he had sent to flank them. After only a few minutes of double-timing, the column cleared the entangling wood and came out into more open country.

Primed and loaded for the third time, Jason peeked cautiously around his tree. He couldn't see any regulars. He crept slowly toward the road. The smoke began to lift, and by the time he got to the road, a light breeze had blown it aside. He could see the retreating column of redcoats now over a hundred yards away.

"We whooped their arses," shouted a militiaman emerging from the forest.

"Did ya' see 'em run?" said another, watching the redcoats march away.

Jason was both disappointed he hadn't fired yet and relieved that the redcoats were gone. He turned around and walked up the causeway. The tree-shaded road was littered with dead and wounded regulars. At the road's corner, a group of ten militiamen surrounded a smaller party of prisoners. It was a kind of victory. They had shot a lot of regulars, but it wasn't decisive. The main body had gotten away. Jason was certain that casualties would make the king and parliament angry, not dissuading them from their course.

Standing among the militiamen guarding the prisoners, Jason could see his brother. Jason waved. Bill was fishing a ball out of the barrel of his musket, frustration written on his face, but he briefly lifted a hand to wave back. By the time Jason reached Bill, he had worked the ball out.

To the west, Jason saw a horseman ride up and address a small party of militiamen at the bottom of the road. They raised their arms, pointing toward Jason and Bill.

"Glad to see you safe, Bill."

"Same. That was a hell of a fight."

"Like a meat grinder. What's your butcher's bill?"

"Remember Tom Watts? Sparks set off his musket before he could bring it up, and he shot his cousin James. He's our only death. Two wounded. I don't know about the other companies, but we got the better of them."

"Are you Jason Green?" asked the rider who had now arrived.

"You found him. I don't know you."

"Captain Ortigal Butts. General Heath sent me to find you."

"General Heath? William Heath?"

"Yes, sir, the Committee of Safety promoted him to general this morning and made him commander of the militia for this battle."

"Thank God somebody's in charge of this mess. How did you find me?"

"General Heath told me to follow the sound of guns and look for a man in a green coat—and here you are." Marveling at Jason with wide eyes, "Just like he said."

"Where is Heath?"

"He wants you to meet him in Lexington."

Turning to his brother Bill, "I'm ordered off. What are your plans?"

"We're paid for the whole day," shrugged Bill. "So, we will continue to pursue them as best we can."

"We snookered 'em," exclaimed Edward Mitchell. "They'll take a while to untangle after that thrashing."

"It didn't all go our way. We're arse over tit," said Steven. "I've not been through such a battle since the last war, and we left some men in that bloody wood."

While they talked, Llewellyn surveyed the road ahead, trying to divine his next plan. To the south, he could see a group of about fifty militiamen moving parallel to them, but they were at least a quarter mile away and making no move to interfere in the corps' march. Behind him he could see dozens of militiamen on the road, but no organized pursuit.

"Maybe we've gotten ahead of them at last," ventured Pitcairn.

Llewellyn nodded, hoping that Pitcairn was right, but the wooded ridgeline to the north of the road could hide plenty of militia. He wondered how many more ambushes they would endure before they got home.

Chapter Ten

Twelve o'clock p.m.

They buried Isaac in the apple orchard between their homes. The same apple orchard where Isaac and Quock had met and spent long days playing, talking, and laughing in the shade of the trees. For Quock, every tree and rock held a memory of Isaac. Now, in the center of the orchard was a never-imagined ending to their friendship.

The Hadleys had wanted to lay Isaac's body in the house, but their servant Patrick Duffy objected, "You must bury him quickly; the king's troops will be back."

"What do I care of the king's revenge?" Missus Hadley glared at Duffy. "What more can he do to us?"

"Do you think they'll forget what happened here? Just like Ireland, they'll be back with their triangles to beat confessions out of us—and they'll build gallows on the green to hang traitors. If they think you are part of the rebellion, his troops may drag your other sons and husband away in chains. If you're lucky, they'll just burn your house," said Duffy. "We must bury him quickly, in secret, and hope that your loyalist neighbors don't sell you out."

Quock and Mister Nithercott helped Isaac's father and brothers dig the grave hidden in the center of the orchard. Missus Nithercott helped wash and dress the stiffening body and covered his death wound with Isaac's Sunday clothes. He was buried in a rough coffin they had pieced together, wrapped in the blanket that he had shared with Quock the night before. The Hadley family stayed at the graveside when Mister Nithercott took Quock's arm and led him back to the house. Faith and Missus Nithercott followed close behind, walking arm-in-arm.

When they got back to the house, Mister Nithercott and Quock picked up their firelocks and kit. Mister Nithercott hugged Missus Nithercott and Faith. Quock hugged them as well.

"Must you go?" asked Missus Nithercott. "Haven't you done enough?"

"Chase, it won't get done if we don't do it," said Mister Nithercott.

She didn't respond. Her face was red, and tears ran down her cheeks. She hugged Faith close to her.

"Come back, Quock," pleaded Faith.

"I will." He knew that he had made a promise he only wished he could keep.

Quock and Mister Nithercott walked back to Lexington. Walking down the familiar road, Quock pondered his much longed-for, but still surprising, freedom. He had always imagined the announcement of his manumission as a joyous event. In his daydreams, he pictured a party and feast, maybe with potted pigeon and a great cake like Christmas. Instead, the urgency of the crisis had overwhelmed his good news. When they found out, Faith and Missus Nithercott had been happy for him, smiling through their tears. Isaac, the person Quock most wanted to share the news with, lay cold and dead in his grave.

The Lexington Green was empty when Quock and Sergeant Nithercott arrived. All the people and debris of the skirmish had disappeared. The only sign of the conflict was the scattered dark blood stains on the grass.

"Eb!" coughed John Parker, arriving on the green with the drummer.

"Not a big showing yet," said Mister Nithercott.

Quock wondered if the four of them would attack the regulars alone. He was ready.

"Let's beat assembly and see what happens," said Parker.

William started beating loudly and forcefully. Seconds later, armed men began to pour out of Buckmans' Tavern and the Meeting House. Within a few minutes, the ranks were filled. There were nearly twice as many men now than during the early morning's skirmish. Even Vernon was there. The men of Lexington's Training Band were grim-faced. There was no obvious drunkenness, no boisterous joking or calling out that normally went with muster day formations. They stood steady in silent ranks. Quock took his place, as did Parker and Nithercott.

Captain Parker called for the report and the Lexington Training Band resumed the military routine. Once Captain Parker had received the report that all were present and sober, he put the band at ease, and the drummer beat Officers Assemble. Mister Nithercott joined the officers; although he was a sergeant there was never any question that he wouldn't, and the leadership of the band huddled to discuss what to do next.

Quock sat down, as did most of the men. Normally, during breaks he and Isaac would talk or horseplay. Now, even though Quock knew every man and boy in the formation, he felt alone, untethered to the world he had known. His fellow militiamen looked equally lost; they all resided in their own worlds of disbelief, sorrow, and regret. No one disturbed the silent gloom.

The officer huddle broke up, and they came back to the formation. Quock and the rest of the men started to get up, but Captain Parker motioned for them to stay seated.

"Men-*cough*-we-*cough-cough* . . ." Parker stopped trying to talk and, holding his throat, motioned to Mister Nithercott.

"We still don't have any word from our regiment, but people have seen other militia companies heading for the great road to Boston. Our plan is to move to the ridge to the west of here near Fiske Hill. It overlooks the road, and if the Redcoats come back this way, we will ambush them from behind the rocks and trees," said Sergeant Nithercott. "Any questions?"

There were none. Only nods of agreement. Sergeant Nithercott turned to Captain Parker. He nodded, and Sergeant Nithercott threw his shoulders back.

"Company!" Nithercott bawled out. "Stand to attention!"

The Lexington Training Band leaped to their feet.

"Shoulder your firelocks! To the left face! March!" Lexington's training band marched off the green and onto the road.

Marching at the front, Parker motioned to the drummer and fife player, "White Cockade." The cheerful yet martial notes of the song of Scottish rebellion pierced the gloom. The militiamen stepped to the beat. Quock felt his spirits lift just a little. They marched less than a mile until they came to a lumber yard on the backside of the patch of wood and large stones that overtopped the great road. Sergeant Nithercott halted the formation.

"To the left face!" The militiamen faced to the left. Captain Parker stood in front of them. He signaled for them to crowd forward.

"Men, we are going to take up positions here," Parker rasped. "The trees and rocks should slow and break up a bayonet charge. Take positions that are far enough away to stay hidden but close enough so that your ball will reach the redcoats."

"How do we know the regulars are coming back this way," asked Vernon.

"We don't, but they don't come out this far very often so I can't think they know many other ways back." Parker stopped talking for a second to clear his throat. "Sergeant Nithercott will be on the west side. I will be on the east. The idea is for the redcoats to march past our company until they reach my position before we fire. That way, everyone will get a chance to shoot a redcoat before they can react. My shot, on your far left, will be the signal for the first volley."

Parker turned and pointed into the woods. "Go on now. Find a spot. We will come around and check your positions."

Parker led the band in a wide skirmish line into the wood. Moving through the trees and rocks, Quock came across three women and two boys hiding in some bushes. One of the boys was Peter, the Nelsons' slave. The childless Nelsons had bought Peter when he was only two years old. Quock often sat with Peter and his birth parents in Negro Heaven at Church on Sundays. Missus Nelson was sitting with him. She clutched Peter to her side and shrunk away when Quock approached her.

"Missus Nelson, we're from Lexington."

Missus Nelson put one hand to her chest and the other at her mouth. "Oh! Quock, is that you? What's going on?"

Quock recognized the other refugees as Missus Nelson's niece and nephew and her sister-in-law, the spinster Tabitha Nelson. Tabitha was known as a sharp-tongued woman unafraid to speak her mind, but now she was quiet, owl-eyed, and her hands were trembling.

"We aim to ambush the regulars," he responded. "You should get far from this road."

"Can I stay with you?" asked Peter. "I want to fight, too." Missus Nelson hugged Peter closer and shook her head.

Mister Nithercott appeared, "No, Peter. You need to take care of Missus Nelson."

"Where can I go, Ebenezer?" asked Missus Nelson. "The regulars took Josiah last night. Our house is by the road. I'm afraid to go back, and I don't know where else to go."

"Elizabeth, go to my house. Take the north trail. Chase is there. You can stay until the regulars are gone."

"Thank you, Ebenezer. We are so frightened."

"I ain't afraid," Peter said to Quock.

Quock nodded, putting his hand on Peter's shoulder, "Get her to safety."

After watching them leave, Quock continued down the hill until he could see the road. He wanted a big rock to hide behind, but the militiamen in front of him had already filled the best spots. After nosing around, he found a tree that was thick enough for good cover. It was closer to the road than he liked, but he thought if he lay down, the redcoats couldn't see him.

Sitting behind his tree, Quock watched Captain Parker and Sergeant Nithercott move up and down the road, studying the band's position from the enemy's point of view. They adjusted individual positions, "You're too close" to one, "Move up you can't see the road," to another. Waving his hand back and forth, Mister Nithercott ordered, "All you fellas are wrong. I can see you clear as day."

Quock's platoon leader, Lieutenant Lee Munroe, visited Quock, "Quock, this is a good spot. I can't see you from the road when you lie down. Are you primed and loaded?"

"Yes, Mister Monroe." Monroe was thirty years old and deserving of a "Mister" to the teenage Quock.

"I'm sorry about Isaac Hadley. I know you two were close."

Quock could only nod.

Munroe reached out and touched Quock's shoulder, "Do you know what you're supposed to do?"

"Yes, sir. Stay hidden until Captain Parker fires, then jump up and shoot the nearest redcoat."

"That's the plan." Munroe smiled

"What do we do after the first volley?"

"I hadn't thought of that. You're the first to ask," He paused to think for a second, "For the time being, reload and fire until someone tells you to stop. I'll ask Captain Parker." Lieutenant Munroe patted him on the shoulder again. "There's been a lot of bad news today, but I don't want to forget to congratulate you on your manumission."

"Thank you, sir." Quock smiled. "I hope I get the chance to celebrate." Despite his grief and fear, he felt a warm spot in his heart for Mister Munroe.

"Hopefully, someday, we will all be celebrating our liberty."

Soon after Munroe left, Elijah Tidd appeared. "Hello, private. I'm checking my troops." Elijah also patted Quock on the back, but he made the gesture feel condescending.

"I missed this morning's fight. I didn't hear the drum."

"It seemed like forever, but I guess the whole thing lasted only a few minutes," Quock remembered his shock, fear, and panicked running.

"I was sorry to hear about Isaac. He was a good man."

"Yes, he was, Elijah. Isaac was brave and didn't run."

"Corporal Tidd!" screeched Tidd. Several militiamen shushed him, fearful that the approaching redcoats would hear him. In a hoarse whisper, Tidd said, "Are you saying I'm afraid? I wanted to be there. The drummer was too quiet. By the time I got to Lexington, the regulars were gone. They would have run from me." Tidd's face was beet red, "You need to keep your place. You might be a free man now, but you're still a Negro."

Tidd's words were like a bucket of cold water on his head. Tidd sneered at him and walked away. Quock brooded on Elijah's words. Were his dreams of freedom just delusions? Free at last, but not equal. How could the color of his skin make him less of a man than Elijah Tidd?

There was no one for Quock to share his frustration. Of his two best friends, Isaac was dead, and Faith was miles away at the farm. With no one to talk to, Quock pushed aside fears and tried to focus on the coming fight, but there was nothing to do but wait. At first, Quock lay down hidden, but as time passed, he sat up and then stood to see if he could see the enemy coming.

Time passed slowly.

The rest of Lexington's training band sat quietly and craned their necks west for signs of the enemy. Quock moved sticks and forest duff to make his seat more comfortable, but all he did was expose roots and stones that were even more uncomfortable.

Was that a shot? Quock sat up and peered down the road. Maybe not, just the sound of a branch falling or someone chopping wood. *There it is again.*

Some others had heard the faint pop noise and were looking down the road while others were still talking. Another sound of multiple puffs, louder this time.

Tidd ran by crouched double. "That's volley fire," he whispered loudly.

Quock ducked down as if the redcoats could already see him. Hunkering down, the whole training band listened to the growing sounds of conflict. There were many individual shots punctuated by throatier volleys. Quock still couldn't see any redcoats. After a few minutes Quock got back to his knees, then stood up and looked down the road. Nothing. Other militiamen were standing, too. Mister Munroe stepped out onto the road.

Far down the road, Quock saw a flash of red and fell to the ground on his stomach. The regulars were still half a mile away, but he didn't want to give away his position. Then, to his surprise, about twenty militiamen came running down the road from the west. One of them was holding his arm. Another held his musket as they ran.

"What news, Josiah?" asked Mister Nithercott in a loud whisper.

"They're right behind us and angry as hornets," shouted back Josiah Nelson. They disappeared around the bend in the road.

The sound of shooting stopped. Quock lay on his stomach, his face pressed to the ground, and the musky-sweet smell of rotting leaves filled his nostrils. For many long minutes, Quock heard nothing and was tempted to peek but was too afraid to raise his head. Then the faint tramp of marching feet, the tin clatter of soldier's kit, hoarse voices, and muttered curses came to his ears. Minutes later, the noises sounded like they were right next to him.

"Picket guard! To the left, form a squad!" shouted a British accented voice. Quock understood the meaning of the order. The regulars were watching the woods in which Lexington's training band was hiding. Quock pressed his body closer to the ground and pulled his musket against his side. In his mind, he rehearsed his next moves.

A root dug into his stomach, and his cheek was pressed against a stone. Moving his head slowly, he couldn't see any of his fellows. He wondered if he was alone. Would Captain Parker ever shoot? The tramp of marching regulars continued as if they weren't moving at all—or an endless centipede . . . Maybe if he sat quietly, they would pass—*BANG!*

"FIRE!" shouted Parker in his loudest rasp.

Following the movements of his mental rehearsal, Quock pushed himself to a kneeling position, pulling his musket upwards. His left hand was on the forestock; his right grasped the firelock cocking the hammer back. Redcoats packed the road as far as Quock could see in both directions. Around him, the forest had come alive with militia. The regulars saw their movement, too, and were already raising their muskets. Quock leveled his gun, but trees blocked his aim. Aiming through a gap at bobbing heads, he pulled the trigger. Snap! Flash! POW! His target disappeared in fire and smoke. A loud and soul-satisfying volley roared out from Lexington's training band, almost simultaneous with Quock's shot.

"Fire at your mark!" yelled a British-accented command. Seconds later, a bigger volley roared out from the King's muskets, ripping through the tree branches and pranging off rocks. Quock had already ducked behind his tree, reloading as fast as his trembling fingers allowed. All around him, Quock could hear men screaming in pain, shouts of command, and running men crashing through the woods.

"Battalion, to tree!" came the same British voice penetrating the racket.

"Huzzah!" came a multi-throated cheer.

Reloaded, Quock looked for another target. Gunsmoke and trees obscured the scene, but a regular on horseback, holding a small musket, shouted to draw the regulars'—and therefore Quock's—attention. Quock fired, and the redcoat fell off his horse.

"Quock!"

Quock looked up the hill toward the voice that penetrated the pandemonium. Mister Nithercott was waving for him to follow. Behind him, he could hear the regulars scrambling up the slope toward him. Running as fast as he could, Quock caught up with Mister Nithercott and they both ran until they reached the woodlot. Captain Parker and Vernon were there. They stopped and reloaded. Kneeling behind a pile of planks, Vernon, Parker, Nithercott, and Quock aimed their guns to the edge of the woods. Quock trembled when he heard the tramping and snapping of branches getting closer, but the regulars didn't follow them out of the woods. A few minutes later, all was silent.

"They ran," said Mister Nithercott to Captain Parker. "I tried to stop them, but they ran like rabbits."

"Most of 'em ran the second they fired. I wouldn't be surprised if some of them aren't shot in the back," agreed Vernon.

"We can't win this war if we don't stand for a second volley," said Parker.

"Quock fired a second time." Mister Nithercott patted Quock proudly on the shoulder.

Llewellyn lay in the dirt of the road. He couldn't feel the wound other than a vast numbness in his left buttock. He still held the reins of his horse. He pulled it to him and inspected the big gelding for wounds. Nothing. Bleddyn appeared out of the smoke and dust.

"Sir." Bleddyn grabbed hold of him and tried helping him up. "Are you shot?"

"Yes, I'm shot!" Llewellyn was annoyed at the stupid question.

"I'll get a wagon—"

"No, help me on my horse. If I don't get up there now, I won't be able to do it later."

Painfully, Llewellyn regained his saddle with Bleddyn pushing on his rear. A wave of pain washed over him as he put his weight on the saddle. He took out a handkerchief and pressed it to the wound. Doing so, he unintentionally saw the black and bloody entry wound, and a wave of nausea made his eyes swim. Using Llewellyn's sash, Bleddyn helped bind the wound tight. Major Mitchell rode up.

"Sir, you've been shot."

"Thank you for that observation. What of the militia?" Llewellyn gestured up the slope.

"Dispersed. We found two bodies. The chaps say they shot more, and there are blood trails."

"Our casualties?"

"Roughly the same, I'm afraid."

"We cannot afford to trade casualties with them one for one."

Having dispersed the militia, the infantry were stumbling back out of the woods onto the road. They were visibly exhausted. Despite the mild spring weather, their dirt and powder-stained faces were streaked with sweat. The pride of the light infantryman's uniform, the whiteness of his breeches, waistcoat, and gaiters were now as stained and dark as their faces.

"We must change our tactics if we want to get our corps back to Boston," said Llewellyn. To Major Mitchell, "Pray pass Colonel Whelks my compliments and ask if he is at leisure to join us for a council." Even as he said the words, it sounded odd to Llewellyn that he should use formalities in such a desperate situation. But he knew that if he deviated from the time-honored form and allowed his anxiety creep into his speech, then like a plague, doubt would spread from him to his officers to his men. They must believe that he was the master of their situation.

Mitchell saluted, "Sir," and turned his horse back down the road.

Turning to Pitcairn, "Is there a house or barn by the road where we can meet." He almost slipped and said he wanted a safe place to meet, but that wouldn't do.

"Not a house, but I believe I saw a rock face a few rods up the road. It might provide a place of limited observation from the enemy."

"Very well, let's ride up there immediately."

A few minutes later Llewellyn and his small command staff had assembled. Llewellyn got off his horse, careful of his now painful wound and sat on a camp chair Bleddyn unfolded for him. Looking at the cliff face, Steven said, "At least they can only shoot us from the South."

"That's enough, Gentlemen; we don't have time for idle talk." Llewellyn was feeling his wound and in no mood to banter. "Give your report if you please."

"Sir, we are being sorely pressed from the rear," said Whelks. "I have divided my command into three, three company divisions. They are rotating, and the rearmost is firing almost constantly. I have one two company grand division in reserve. We have expended most of our powder and shot."

"Your casualties?"

"I can confirm six killed and twelve wounded. I'm afraid that there are more missing, but I do not have a good count. The wagons we requisitioned in Concord are now packed with dead and wounded. Some of the wounded are riding the cart horses."

"Sir," said Pitcairn. "The situation of my division is similar. My casualties are mounting, particularly among officers. Tenth regiment's company no longer has unwounded officers. The powder and shot are equally depleted."

"Sir," blurted out De Berniere. "I very much regret my advice to Governor Gage. When I gave him my report, I said that Worcester was too far. Ten thousand men could not march to Worcester and back. I should have said Concord."

"Enough!" barked Llewellyn. "I'll brook no more talk like that."

"Llewellyn," said Whelks. "We cannot deny that our position is grave. The men have the will to fight, but soon, through ammunition expenditure alone, we will be deprived of our means."

"Sir," added Pitcairn, "our circumstances are no reflection on you. Anyone can see the entire operation was badly conceived. If Governor Gage had given us time to develop a proper plan, then the boats would have been on time, and the soldiers victualed before we ever set out. We'd be back in Boston now instead of fighting for our lives short of Lexington."

"Perhaps we can negotiate a safe passage with honor," suggested Mitchell.

"Yes, you were at Minorca, Llewellyn," agreed Steven. "Blakeney negotiated an honorable surrender and was absolved of blame for the loss of the fort."

"What of Admiral Byng?" Pitcairn asked Whelks.

"Bing?" asked De Bernie.

"Admiral Byng was the commander of a hastily assembled fleet rushed to Minorca to relieve the garrison. He was defeated by superior French forces, then court-martialed for not doing his utmost, and shot by firing squad," said Pitcairn.

"Oh," said De Berniere. Every eye turned, avoiding Llewellyn's eyes. But Llewellyn was not thinking of Byng. Instead, he recalled the scalped corpse at the Concord Bridge and Robert's warning of American barbarity. *If I surrender my soldiers to the militia mob, can their officers restrain them? Bloody hell, who would I even negotiate with? There doesn't appear to be any commander.*

"Gentlemen, get hold of yourselves," demanded Llewellyn. "I did not invite you here to discuss the terms of surrender. You are experienced enough in war to know that battles never go as planned." Llewellyn held their eyes. "The casualties are regrettable but not unprecedented. His Majesty's armies have suffered far higher casualties and yet prevailed. We will do no less today," Llewellyn glared at his officers, daring them to disagree. They nodded their heads in bleak agreement, but Llewellyn feared their despair more than the enemy. He needed to restore their spirit if they were going to fight free of the rebel masses.

Llewellyn quashed his anger, "Last night Lord Dandridge told me that he was charged to assemble his brigade to sally out of Boston if the rebels threatened. Early this morning, I sent him a message, and he is likely already marching to reinforce our corps and aid in our safe return."

"I value Lord Dandridge's many shining parts, but you cannot assume that your dispatch got through. The militia was already turning out when you sent the messenger. It is better than even odds that he was intercepted," said Steven.

"Even without my message, Lord Dandridge must know by now that the rebels contest our return."

"I do not know Lord Dandridge as you do, but we are all line officers here, and we know that the promises of the high-born are no more valuable than the man that gives them," said Pitcairn.

"Then be assured, John, Lord Dandridge will not fail. He values merit in battle more than his fortune or title. The only man I hold in the same esteem is Sergeant Major Sayer and he is marching with Lord Dandridge."

"High-born or no, he faces the same obstacle that we face, thousands of heavily armed Yanks," said Steven. "If he sallied from Boston Neck, then the rebels certainly destroyed the Cambridge Bridge. It may take him hours to cross."

"Heaven helps those that help themselves," said Llewellyn. "I am re-assured that the Yanks are fighting like militia. They do not stand in open combat instead, they rely on ambush and greater numbers to overwhelm. We must stop reacting to their tactics. We will go on the offensive and drive them before us like cattle."

"All the way to Boston?" asked Whelks.

"If we must, but I am sensible about the physical limits of our men, I propose that we assault from here into Lexington, which I believe is little more than a mile to our front." He glanced at De Berniere, who nodded in response. "Lexington is modestly defensible and likely keeps some stores. If we are fortunate, they may have some powder. We can rest, water, and regroup there."

"What is your design?" asked Pitcairn.

"We are no longer restricted by marshlands. The terrain here is to our advantage. It is rocky and reasonably dry, not unlike northern England. We will divide into wings. John, I believe there are more wooded hills to our north between us and Lexington. I want your battalion to form a skirmish line and drive the rebels from those hills. Do not neglect your reserve, but do not commit them against stubborn militia positions. Flank and bypass, there is no terrain we wish to take or hold."

Turning to Whelks, "Steven, detach three companies to act as the rearguard. Form the remainder in a line of two ranks to the south of the Great Road, move east, and assault any rebel resistance. We will put the wagons and walking wounded in the center on the road. Major Mitchell, assume command of the trains and rearguard."

"The numbers of militia behind us are greater than those in front," said Whelks.

"We must accept some risk. I am counting on militia disorganization. So far, they have been slow to reform their ranks and slow to resume the march. If our rearguard is lively, I do not believe they can overtake us,"

"When do we start?" asked Mitchell.

"There is no time to lose," said Llewellyn. "I will ride to the center of the road a few rods forward. Form your wings on me."

"Sir," saluted the gathered officers, and they turned their horses and rode off.

Llewellyn remounted his horse and, with a considerable amount of effort, did not grimace with pain. As he, Bleddyn and De Berniere sat alone on the road, Llewellyn saw a small party of three militiamen sneaking forward, unsuccessfully using a haystack as cover. Llewellyn raised his fusil and fired. He saw his ball kick up dirt to their right, but the militiamen ran anyway. With drums beating, the grenadiers, led by their officers, moved to form a two-rank line on his right.

The grenadiers were visibly exhausted. Despite the beating of the drum, they walked—or plodded rather—into position. Llewellyn could not help but regret that his Welshmen were not here instead of the grenadiers. To be fair, any soldiers would be tired, but Llewellyn felt his familiarity with his men, and in turn their trust in him, could help overcome the evident growing despondency among the grenadiers. Normally, Llewellyn would have dismounted and marched with the soldiers to rejuvenate their spirits with his example, but his wound prevented any demonstration. Fortunately, Steven rode up to some malingerers and chased them on with the flat of his sword. Seeing Whelks, the sergeants rallied and pushed the grenadiers into a respectable line.

Thinking about his regiment, he recalled Pitcairn's words. With little doubt, the excessive secrecy, even from Gage's officers, was the undoing of this expedition. It was ironic that the only people unaware of the raid were the men who were supposed to execute the plan. He thought of Captain Lillingfield. He was certain that Lillingfield's breakdown in Concord was not a lack of moral fiber but fatigue. A situation that could have been avoided if Lillingfield had not drunk himself stupid on the eve of the expedition. How many other soldiers and officers, in their ignorance of an impending operation, overindulged? This was indeed a poorly prepared operation. Llewellyn shook those thoughts from his head. No time for regrets.

Turning around, he saw the motley collection of horses, wagons, and walking wounded had caught up to him. Further behind, he could see a mass of American militia pressing his rearguard. The popping of musket fire to his left signaled that the light infantry had begun their assault. Llewellyn spurred his horse to a walk and the assault to Lexington began.

Llewellyn watched as Pitcairn, waving his sword, led his men across an open woodlot. The hills were rocky and uncultivated. The country people had chopped down most of the trees and a thick new growth of brush provided abundant cover for the thronging militia. This dense landscape forced Pitcairn's men into small groups, usually moving Indian file, winkling out the American militiamen and driving them off the hill.

To Llewellyn's right, the more open-plowed fields and pastures allowed the grenadiers to maneuver as they had trained. Stone walls, small copses, and other obstacles broke the perfect line, but these impediments were natural to any battlefield and did not hinder the grenadiers. The rebel militia could do nothing to slow the red tide sweeping all before it.

With cautious gratification, Llewellyn watched the militiamen run, then turned his horse and moved to the rear. He passed the wretched train of walking wounded and wagons filled with the disabled and corpses. He soon reached the three grenadier companies fending off the American militia. Here, the officers and sergeants filled the air with commands as the grenadiers maneuvered their men.

"Prime and Load!"

"'Bout!"

"Company, make Ready!"

"Present!"

The company would hold their fire until the Americans either pressed too close on the march or stopped to form a line of battle. Then, "Fire!" The volley caused the Americans in the front of their formation to scatter. After the grenadiers fired, fresh orders came,

"Shoulder firelocks!"

"To the right wheel, march!"

Then, they would march briskly past the next waiting grenadier company, and the process would begin anew. The American hosts were too muddled, and the road too congested for the rebels to use their superior numbers to overwhelm the line.

Sitting on his horse, one of the grenadier companies passed near him. "Tidy work!" he shouted to the young lieutenant.

The lieutenant commanding the company ran over to Llewellyn and saluted, "Sir, we could carry on all day, but we are dreadfully short powder and shot."

Llewellyn returned the salute. "I'll see what I can do." He turned his horse and rode back to Mitchell.

"Edward, with Henry and Bleddyn, gather the cartridges from the dead and any of the wounded too injured to use their arms. Take what you gather back to the rear guard."

To De Berniere, "Henry, I believe I overheard you say that you were a gunsmith?"

"Yes, sir. A bit. That was my cover as I spied out these roads."

"Good; when you take back the powder and shot, also take some flints and a couple of muskets for spares. Give my sincere compliments to the company commanders and offer your services as gunsmith. Those men and their muskets are all that stand between us and ruin."

To Llewellyn's satisfaction, Bleddyn leaped onto a wagon filled with wounded and corpses and began stripping the bodies of their powder bags and cartridge belts. He handed them out to Mitchell. De Berniere seized a firelock, the forestock slick with blood, examining it for serviceability. Satisfied with their efforts, Llewellyn spurred his horse back into the lead.

At the front of the formation, Llewellyn could tell from the sound of the musket fire in the hills that the light infantry was moving slower than the grenadiers. The difference was due in part to the hilly brush-covered terrain, but there was also far more of the enemy. Even from below, he could see militiamen hiding behind every rock and bush. *There must be a thousand Yanks up there.* The grenadiers, on the other hand, faced only scattered bands, no more than fifty together. Whelks had to constantly shift his ranks to keep the enemy in front of him and prevent flanking.

Most particularly, the light-bobs were spent. Because of the constant requirement for flanking movements, they had put many more miles on their legs than had the grenadiers. Llewellyn signaled to Whelks to slow his advance. When they got closer to Lexington, he intended to release the grenadiers to clear the village. He could already see the spire of Lexington's meeting house in the distance, but he couldn't divide his command just yet.

While he slowed the advance, Bleddyn returned. "Sir, we delivered all the powder and shot we could find. Ensign De Berniere and Major Mitchell are staying—" Bleddyn looked east, "Did you hear that?"

"No, what did you hear?"

"I thought I heard cannon."

Llewellyn's spirits plunged. He thought of the cannon not found in Concord.

"God help us if they have finally brought up their cannon," said Bleddyn, perfectly echoing Llewellyn's thoughts. His wound had become painful he could feel his leg swelling. He wondered how he would defeat a battery or several batteries of cannon. "From what direction?"

"Sir, I'm not—there it is again. To our front."

Llewellyn wanted to rise in his saddle, but his wound kept him from standing on his stirrups. Apparently, the grenadiers had heard it, too, because they were searching the rolling hills in front of them. A man on a knoll shouted and waved. Then a "Huzzah!" from the grenadiers around him. Llewellyn rode forward, and after only a few steps, he saw the cause of their celebration. In the distance, south and east of Lexington, flags and glittering bayonets adorned the crimson ranks of British soldiers. Lord Robert Dandridge had arrived at last.

Muskets on their shoulders, Quock, Vernon, Nithercott, and Parker walked toward Lexington on a trail that meandered north of the Great Road. They picked up a few more Lexington men along the way. Corporal Tidd, and Lieutenant Munroe among them.

"Why did you run?" asked Nithercott.

"I didn't run," said Tidd.

"You did a fair imitation," said Vernon.

"I wasn't going to stand there and let the redcoats shoot at me while I reloaded," retorted Tidd. "I was reconnoitering for a better fighting position."

"Way back here?" asked Vernon.

"We can't beat the regulars unless we can stand and fire repeated volleys like them," responded Parker.

"And they got bayonets," said Munroe. "We can't stop a bayonet charge with just musket butts and tomahawks. And we need bigger formations. Real regiments, not a bunch of militia bands that never train together."

"And uniforms," said Tidd, "and flags like a real army."

The rapid popping of muskets interrupted the conversation. Orienting himself, Quock figured they were just north of Fiske Hill. The group stopped and scanned the hill. Quock couldn't see anything at first, then a group of men bounded off the hill.

"They're from Lincoln. Same bunch as was running up the road before our ambush," said Nithercott. "Hey! Thomas!"

One of the Lincoln men stopped running, turned their way, waved, and walked over to Nithercott. The other minutemen stopped running and stood uncertainly.

"Ebenezer! What brings you to these parts?" he said with a laugh but still panting from running.

"What's going on up there?"

"We came here planning to ambush the regulars, but they attacked us first. Several hundred of them are running riot up there, shooting and bayoneting."

Farther east, Quock saw another band of men come streaming off the hill.

"There's militia from all over Massachusetts up there, but the regulars are tough."

"Where are they going?" asked Parker.

"The regulars? I don't know for sure, but they're going in the direction of Lexington," said Thomas.

A shock of fear struck Quock. Missus Nithercott and Faith were home unprotected.

"We better move," said Parker, "and get our families out of harm's way."

The remnants of the Lexington's training band broke into a trot.

Chapter Eleven

Two thirty p.m.

Robert stood with Sergeant Major Sayer, a spyglass pressed to his eye, watching the progress of Llewellyn's corps as it joined Robert's brigade. It was evident that discipline was fraying—some soldiers were running, others were still walking, and the grenadier's lines were dissolving—unmistakable signs of panic.

"Something must have happened to Colonel Caradoc," said Sayer. "He never would have permitted such disorder." Sayer pointed at one grenadier running far in front of his companions and waving madly, "Look at that fellow acting the fool. The colonel would have the hide off his back."

Robert was worried, too. Llewellyn was more than a friend and mentor; Llewellyn was the father he wished he'd had. His father was disapproving, emotionally distant, and throughout his boyhood, had upbraided Robert for "acting the pouffe." During the last war, Robert had joined the Army, demanding a line regiment going to Hanover, in a vain effort to impress his father.

In the army, Robert failed to convince his peers of his manliness. A few days before the Battle of Minden, he was charged with escorting a deserter to prison. On his return, a friend told him that while he was gone, some of the younger officers, led by Henry Blunt, had jested about "Dandy-ridge" and "Lord Molly." Llewellyn had cut them short, berating them as gossips and blatherskites unfitting of the officer's mess. Robert was mortified to learn that he was an object of derision but equally touched that Llewellyn had defended his reputation. Llewellyn never mentioned the incident, but thereafter, Robert adapted his behavior so as not to invite more mockery. Llewellyn became his model of honorable masculinity.

As he fruitlessly searched the intervening ground, Robert's fear for Llewellyn's safety boiled into anger. Beside Robert rested a two-gun battery of cannon. He pointed to a concentration of militiamen that threatened the grenadier's flanks and ordered the artillery captain standing ready, "Fire a ball at that band of rebels if you please."

Seconds later, the cannon spoke, and a ball hurdled at the militiamen. They scattered in panic even before the ball reached them. The ball caused no casualties but dispersed the group.

Perhaps from either pride or shame, Llewellyn's officers and sergeants began restoring discipline. One officer jumped in front of a running group of grenadiers with a drawn sword, and a sergeant's halberd knocked another shouting private flat. The grenadiers restored their line and merged with Robert's brigade with some credit. Robert recognized Lieutenant Colonel Whelks and waved him over. Before he could ask about Llewellyn, Whelks said, "M'Lord, beyond my rear detachment, there is a large party of Yanks that have harried us from Concord."

As Whelks was speaking, a nearly formless mass of rebels poured down the road behind the farthest grenadiers.

"Look how far back that column goes; there must be a thousand men." Robert was astonished.

"M'Lord, they are pressing us close."

"Pray fire on that great rebel concentration, Captain Barker," Robert ordered his battery commander. "Both guns this time." The greater distance caused the gunners to elevate the cannon, but a few moments later, both cannon bucked and roared. Two balls soared toward the rebel congregation, scattering them into the fields and forest.

"Your Lordship, please do not judge the performance of the men by the last few minutes," Whelks wrung his hands. "Until they saw your brigade, the men had fought bravely against overwhelming odds."

"It is evident that His Majesty's troops behaved with their usual intrepidity and discipline. I admire the spirit of your men."

"Thank you, M'Lord." Gratitude and relief were written on Whelk's face as he nodded his thanks.

"Is Colonel Caradoc with you?"

"There he is," interrupted Sayer. He walked briskly out to a man on horseback. As he got closer, Robert was relieved to see Llewellyn on his horse, but he slumped to his right, barely able to keep in the saddle, a bloody sash wrapped around his waist. His face was set in a grim mask. His normally immaculate uniform was as dirty as his face. He had never seen Llewellyn so done up. Robert feared the worst.

"Matthew!" he shouted. "Fetch my surgeon."

"Sir!" Matthew ran off.

Robert took the reins of Llewellyn's horse from Sayer. "How are you, old friend?"

Caradoc looked him in the face, "Bleeding awful. Me trains are loaded with dead and wounded, there are thousands of blood thirsty Yanks after me head, and I've been shot in the arse." After a pause to examine his arse, Llewellyn added, "Thank you for asking M'Lord."

Robert smiled, "Llewellyn, I must beg you to pardon my tardiness. I am so happy to see you. Let me help you." Sayer helped Robert get him off his horse, and they carried Llewellyn to two tables pushed together inside a Tavern Robert was using as a headquarters. The surgeon came over, and Robert said, "I will be with you in a moment."

Walking back outside to Steven Whelks, who was gathering his officers, Robert said, "Colonel Whelks, we have secured a perimeter. Pray form your battalion in that pasture and let them rest, redistribute shot and powder, and let the men have their dinners. We will have a meeting in half an hour to plan our next move." Whelks saluted and departed to pass on the orders. Robert went back to the Tavern and found Llewellyn lying belly down on a table with the surgeon working one end while the Sergeant Major spoke to the other.

"I told you!" Sayer was saying to Llewellyn. "I told you if you went without me, you'd catch a ball."

"I shan't forget you next time."

"And look where you got yourself shot such a shameful wound. Serves you right."

"Treat my men first," said Llewellyn to Robert. "I am fine; it's lack of sleep, really."

Robert lifted his chin toward Llewellyn's other end. "Does that often happen when you're knackered?"

Llewellyn grunted but said nothing.

"No heroics, Llewellyn. I brought half the army surgeons in Boston along with their orderlies and wagons. Your men are being well looked after. MacDonald is my surgeon, and I remain unwounded."

"Ye've got too much lead in your arse," said the surgeon in a thick Scottish burr. "It would be best if I removed it."

"I pray that you are speaking of the lead and not the arse. I still require the latter, and former has already overstayed its welcome."

MacDonald signaled for his orderlies. Taking Llewellyn's arms and legs, they braced him against the table. "These laddies will keep ye heid while I poke the wound."

"I sincerely apologize for my late arrival." Robert moved out of the way of the orderlies. "We had a bit of confusion with the Marines; they didn't get the word until late. When we sallied out, we discovered that the damned rebels pulled up the planks on Cambridge Bridge. We crossed on the stringers and re-laid the planks to cross the cannon and horses. Then, we nearly lost our way. Fortunately, a loyal subject pointed us on the right road."

"Sod's law."

"Just so. Pray tell me about the Americans. What may I expect?" Robert winced and turned away as MacDonald poked deep into Llewellyn's wound. Sergeant Major Sayer helped hold the leg.

"Have you not already encountered many?" Llewellyn grunted. Beads of sweat formed on his forehead.

"None a'tall. All the homes were locked and shuttered, and few people on the road."

"Did you gather the two artillery chaises? We never met them."

"I did not find any artillery chaises," Robert relaxed as MacDonald straightened up and pulled his tools from Llewellyn's wound.

"As for the militia," said Llewellyn, "they are keen but cannot stand against a proper attack. There are thousands of them, though, aren't there?"

"Quite so. Are they centrally directed? Is there a corps commander?"

"Not that I could attest, or at least not often. Mostly, it appears to be corraded battalions. We are often being shot at from both sides of the road. They must be shooting each other as often as they harm us." Llewellyn paused, then added, "However, I did see our jollux publican from last night. He was in Concord."

"Mister Jason Green? Are you sure?"

"No, I am not sure, but I was within fifty yards of a man that looked very like him in Concord. He is wearing a green coat and riding a grey. I thought I saw him two other times. In each case, there was some credible performance from the militia."

"By Jove, the fox."

Llewellyn cried out with an involuntary convulsion as the surgeon resumed work.

"Keep ye heid," said the surgeon, "I almost have the peccant piece."

"Cannon?" asked Robert, slightly ducking his head and putting a hand next to his eye to avoid seeing the surgeon's deep probing into Llewellyn's wound.

"None used against us, but we found only three in Concord." Llewellyn's face was deep red and set in a grimace.

"If Gage's intelligence was correct, then we may find the remainder on the road." The door opened, Matthew poked his head in and signaled Robert. Nodding to Matthew but speaking to Llewellyn, "I must leave you in the good doctor's care. I will visit again before we depart."

After Robert left, the surgeon and his staff continued to work on Llewellyn.

"Me father was in the Army," said the surgeon amicably.

"I come from an Army family, I do," grunted Llewellyn as he flinched.

"Be still. I have a grip on the ball, but it's near the femoral artery. A bad prick, and you would bleed out before you could stand up."

Llewellyn snorted in acknowledgment.

"He was in Bonnie Prince Charlie's Army."

"Is that so?"

"Killed by an English ball on Drumossie moor."

"I'm Welsh," said Llewellyn through gritted teeth.

"That's why I'm going to save your life," said the surgeon.

Outside the Tavern, Robert pointed his spyglass toward the hills west of Lexington. "M'Lord, if I may have a moment of your time," interrupted Sergeant Major Sayer.

"Of course." Robert put down his spyglass.

"Sir, it's not Colonel Caradoc's fault; he had no sergeant to advise him, although I begged him to let me come along—"

"Yes, Sergeant Major, what is it?"

"Sir, it's the wagons. It's no good. The dead and wounded are mixed together. Some wounded men may see it as a sign of their future if you understand my meaning."

"Indeed, I do."

"By your leave, I'll move the dead to different wagons from the wounded."

"Make it so, Sergeant Major," nodded Dandridge. Sergeant Major Sayer saluted and strode off to rectify the wagon problem.

Robert went back to watching the last of Llewellyn's light infantry come down from a ridge and make their way to the brigades' lines. An officer of the marines was walking toward Robert, holding his left arm.

"Oh! Major Pitcairn, my horse!" shouted a young Captain. Robert recognized Lord Lillingfield's son.

"Luke, I beg your pardon," said Pitcairn. "She was alive when I saw her last. She was surprised by a rebel volley and threw me off. In her confusion, she ran into the rebel lines. I could not recover her."

"I had a brace of pistols in holsters on the saddle. They had my family crest."

"The pistols were still safely holstered last I saw your horse."

The young captain turned away, frowning and unhappy.

"M'Lord," Pitcairn saluted, "Major John Pitcairn, Royal Marines. I have the honor of commanding the detachment of light infantry. My battalion is safely in your lines."

Robert returned his salute. "Are you wounded?"

"No, M'Lord, I banged my arm a bit falling off the horse, but I'm still fit."

"Very well. Your marines are with us. They are currently guarding our south flank. Please resume command of your battalion."

"What will become of the balance of my light-bobs?"

"Lieutenant Colonel Whelks will assume command and form a reserve."

Quock, Mister Nithercott, Captain Parker, and twenty others from the Lexington Training Band walked back into Lexington. They were coming in from the north, and the road took Quock and Mister Nithercott past their farm. Although Quock gazed longingly at their home, he and Mister Nithercott stayed with the band until they reached Lexington's green.

The village green had transformed into a military parade ground. A company of minute men, all of them strangers to Quock, was on parade near the road. They were in open ranks, and militia officers were inspecting their equipment. A guard stood at the door of Buckmans' tavern. There were horses picketed all around it and men running in and out.

"Buckmans' got a lot of business," said Nithercott.

A tall, thin man with a big nose and concave chest stood with a drummer and fife player in the center of the green.

"That's Abel Jeffries," said Parker. "He's the regimental adjutant." Turning to Nithercott, "We should go and see what he wants."

"Company halt!" ordered Nithercott. The entire training band had already come to a voluntary stop as they gaped around them.

Nithercott and Parker walked over to Jeffries, followed closely by Quock and the rest of the training band, who gathered around the trio as they talked.

"Abel, what's going on?" asked Nithercott.

"Hi Eb, glad to see you safe. We're assembling the whole regiment. I am to instruct you and John that Lexington is to form a fifty-man-minute company. Only the most able-bodied."

"The Committee of Safety told us to do that months ago, but we voted against it," said Parker.

"There's a war on now, John."

"I know there's a war, Abel; we've been fighting it. What's different?"

"The Committee of Safety is trying to assemble an army, not just a militia and fifty men is the quota for Lexington."

"Where are we going?"

"To fight the regulars and drive them out of Massachusetts."

Quock listened to them talk and wondered what was going to happen next. Was there going to be more fighting? The redcoats are gone. Isn't it over?

"What are they to bring with them?"

"Four day's food, enough powder and shot for sixty rounds, bedrolls, a change of clothes if they got one."

"Not all the band is here. We got scattered after the last fight."

"John, I'll be here until the regiment marches. I'll tell the stragglers as they come in."

"Not all of them will come here. Many will just go home," said Nithercott.

"Orders are for the Lexington minute company to form here at four o'clock to join the regiment."

Parker took out his watch and then pulled Nithercott and Lee Munroe together for a private discussion. After a few minutes, Parker patted Lee on the back and walked back over to the training band.

"Lexington Training Band, fall in!"

Surprised, Quock and the other members of the band hurriedly found their places.

"At ease. You heard what Major Jeffries said. I got consumption, and I ain't able-bodied enough to go campaigning. I am turning over command of the minute company to Lieutenant Lee Munroe until you can organize regular elections. May God save New England and speed your safe return." Parker nodded to Lee Munroe, "Lee, it's your turn."

"I ain't got a speech," Lee said. "All that's going, meet back here in an hour. Don't forget, four days of food, sixty rounds, and sleeping rolls. Dismissed!"

Stunned, Quock watched Lexington's training band dissolve. The men shouldered their muskets, and each of them headed toward his own home. Quock saw Mister Nithercott talking with Obadiah Kendall. They shook hands, and Mister Nithercott shouldered his Charleville musket. Unsure of what he should do or where to go, Quock walked with Mister Nithercott back to the farm.

"You have a decision to make," said Nithercott. "Are you going to join the minute company or stay on the farm? You're a free man now, and I can't decide for you."

"If you're going, I'm going too."

"I'm not going. I'm too old. I have already fought in two wars. My campaigning days are over. Obadiah will take my place."

Despite the months of political activity in Lexington and training with the band, war had been an abstract concept. He and Isaac had talked about it as a great boyish adventure, not the lonely, frightening, bloody chaos of his recent experience. He had dreamt of his future someday as a free man, but whether or not to march off to war was not among the choices he had considered.

"I don't want to influence you either way." Mister Nithercott wasn't looking at Quock but at the road ahead. "But you've done your piece more than most, and I sure could use you here."

"Do you think we've done enough?"

"We've done as much as anyone." They walked in silence for a moment then Nithercott said, "The army is not the place for a smart young man. The officers are self-serving, neglectful, and greedy; the sergeants are cruel. They'll beat the hide off your back for little reason." Patting Quock on the back, "We can stay in the militia. That way, if the King's men come back, we can go out and fight 'em together. We don't have to leave our home to serve Massachusetts."

When Quock didn't respond, Mister Nithercott continued, "You got until we get home to make up your mind because we got to tell your—uh—Chase. If you decide to go, then we got to gather your things."

I have done a lot today. Risked my life twice. Would I survive another battle?

Quock and Mister Nithercott were nearing their farm, and behind it, he could see the apple orchard. The apple orchard where they had buried Isaac only a few hours ago. *What about avenging Isaac?* Quock had fired four times. The first shot was a misfire. The second was fired into space. The trees, smoke, and excitement had concealed the result of his third, but his fourth shot, he knew he had hit a man. He saw him go down. How many more men do I have to kill to avenge Isaac? Another one? Three? Would there ever be enough? Isaac was still dead, and nothing Quock did could bring him back or soothe the grief of his family. The blood debt was paid, and boundless revenge was not a good reason to go to war.

Without Quock even noticing they had arrived at the front door of the house. The familiar sights and the smell of boiled dinner on the stove brought a rush of love for his home.

There is a lot to do on the farm. Spring planting was just starting. Mister Nithercott is too old to do it all on his own. "I'll stay for now. If the redcoats come back, I can go out again." He said it aloud rather than to Mister Nithercott, but he smiled at Quock and opened the door.

Gasps and shrieks greeted them. Quock was surprised by the large gathering in the living room. Missus Nelson, her slave Peter, the spinster Miss Tabitha Nelson, and Missus Nelson's teenage niece and nephew Elizabeth and Johnathon leaped up from their places. Quock had forgotten Mister Nithercott had offered the Nelsons the safety and hospitality of their home.

Missus Nithercott's face was already flush from cooking. When she saw Ebenezer and Quock, she burst into tears of happiness. Faith and Missus Nithercott raced to embrace them.

"Oh! Thank the Lord, you made it home!" said Missus Nithercott.

"Have you seen Josiah? Is he with you? Did he go home? Is it safe to go home?" the Nelson women and children crowding the questions into a cacophony of noise.

"Wait!" shouted Mister Nithercott, holding his hands over his head. "I did see Josiah and Thomas briefly. They were safe last I saw 'em, but it is not safe for you to go home yet. The redcoats are just south of Lexington. Now we're hungry and want our dinner. We'll tell our tale at the dinner table."

"Oh my God. Dinner is going to burn. We were just getting ready to serve it," said Missus Nithercott.

In a flurry of skirts, excited relief, and nervous laughter, the women ran to set more places on the table and bring out the food. They set everything on the formal dining table in the main room. Normally, the Nithercotts ate their dinners in the kitchen. It was more convenient, and in winter, it was warm. Quock ate the formal table even less often than the rest of the family. They relegated the Negro slave to the kitchen when guests were present, but today, Mister Nithercott took Quock by the arm and sat him to his right. Faith sat on Quock's right, and Missus Nithercott sat in her customary place at the foot of the table nearest the kitchen door so she could run in and gather food, utensils, or dishes as needed. The Nelson family filled the rest of the seats.

Mister Nithercott mumbled grace; they filled their plates, and as they ate, Mister Nithercott told the rapt audience of their adventures since they had marched off that morning. After he had eaten his fill, Quock pushed back his plate and sat mostly silent, only speaking when Mister Nithercott asked him to verify or elaborate. Mister Nithercott was telling how Quock had stayed behind and fired another shot, ". . . most of 'em scattered like chickens, but not Quock . . ." Faith smiled at him. ". . . almost for sure got an officer. He was on a horse, and only officers ride . . ." Quock was luxuriating in the rediscovered warmth of family when he noticed one was missing from the table.

Quock looked past Missus Nithercott into the kitchen. The door was propped open so it would be easy for her to go back and forth. Peter, the enslaved boy, sat alone at the kitchen table eating his dinner and listening closely to the table conversation. Quock watched Peter remembering his lonely meals. Quock got up from the table, went into the kitchen and picked up Peter's plate and cup. "Come with me," he said softly so as not to interrupt Mister Nithercott and led him out to the dining room table. Quock placed Peter's plate and cup to the right of his own.

". . . and then we saw your husband coming down off Fiske Hill . . ."

Faith jumped up from her place, "He can have my chair; I'll get another." She whispered so as not to interrupt her father. She slipped into the kitchen, bringing back a stool that she set at her place and sat back down.

Mister Nithercott kept talking, nodding a welcome as if bringing Peter to the table was normal and even expected. Red-faced, Chastity Nithercott and Elizabeth Nelson stared down at their plates. Tabitha stared wide eyed, and mouth open at Quock, Peter, and Faith.

"We don't feed the servants at the dinner table at our house," said Jonathon Nelson.

"Jonathon!" admonished Elizabeth, her face even more red.

"Why are you scolding him, Liz?" Tabitha pointed at Jonathon. "The boy is only speaking the hypocrisy he sees at home every day. His father and uncle talk for hours about the king violating their natural rights while keeping a slave and never once mentioning women's rights. Peter is your adopted son in all but name. Why do we treat him different?"

"Everyone is welcome at my table," said Ebenezer Nithercott.

And there it was—exposed. For eleven years Quock had lived with the Nithercotts without receiving an invitation to sit at the big table when guests were present. He had lived with unequal treatment his whole life, and it had become so familiar he no longer noticed. The onset of war broke the sense-numbing daily routine, and now the disparity was there for all to see.

"She's right." Quock nodded to Tabitha. "The war isn't over for me." There was a silent pause at the table. Quock looked at the Nithercotts. "Reverend Clarke told us this war was about freedom."

"You are free now, Quock," said Missus Nithercott, her eyes big and eyebrows arched with worry.

"It's not just freedom." Quock placed his hand on the table in front of him, "it's a place at the table. When the regulars came to Lexington, I stood in the ranks just like everyone else. I took the same risks, and I earned the same rights."

Silence. The Nithercotts stared at Quock. He wondered if they were angry with him.

"You're right," said Mister Nithercott just above a hoarse whisper, speaking slow and sure. "The rights of man are as natural to you as to them—to us." Gesturing to the tureen of boiled dinner on the table, "It's not right, but sometimes folks see their rights like dinner; they're afraid that the more they share, the less there is for themselves."

"That's right!" Tabitha pointed a finger at Mister Nithercott in angry defiance. "And those that decide who gets a serving are the ones which already got theirs."

"But it's like the parable of the laborers," said Missus Nithercott. "Jesus says that everyone gets an equal reward."

Quock was surprised at the Nithercotts' until now unspoken liberal views. Although there were occasional glimmers of abolitionist ideas, they would notice Quock and change the subject. They usually only talked about local politics, like whether pigs should run loose in Lexington's dirt streets. Perhaps the unintended result of freeing Quock was also the emancipation of thoughts they had long hidden from themselves and each other.

Quock felt emboldened to say new things, too, "My Mama said I should live a life of consequence. Maybe fighting for the liberty of my country and winning my natural rights is what she meant."

"Huzzah!" shouted Tabitha, both fists in the air and a triumphant grin on her face. "Now, this war is about something I can believe in!"

They heard a distant rumble like thunder.

Mister Nithercott cocked his head to listen. "Cannons. It's begun." To the rest of the table, he said, "The regulars are moving." To Quock, he asked, "What are you going to do?"

Quock was momentarily frozen with indecision. *Must action follow understanding?* He looked at Mister Nithercott and said, "It won't get done if I don't do it."

Mister Nithercott nodded ascent, "I'll help you gather your things." Looking at Missus Nithercott, "He needs four days of food."

Missus Nithercott started to protest, then nodded and smiled bravely at Quock. The Nelsons cleared the dishes and stayed in the kitchen. Quock and Mister Nithercott went to the next room and started repacking Quock's knapsack. After they laid everything out on the living room floor, Mister Nithercott said, "You'll need to bring some extra clothes, especially stockings. And put on your gaiters. You'll be marching across a lot of broken country."

Quock ran to his room upstairs. They had moved him into one of the bedrooms upstairs when the older girls married and moved out. He had a small wardrobe of clothes. There wasn't much to choose from, so he grabbed all his stockings and most of the rest of his clothes. He dug into his trunk, the same one he had brought from Boston all those years before and pulled out a small bag of coins. It was the money he and Isaac had earned over the winter gathering and selling deadfall. Then he fastened on his gaiters and rolled down the steps to the great room.

Mister Nithercott held a book. "Before you close your pack, I want to give you this." At first, Quock thought it was a Bible, but printed on the cover was *Manual of Exercise*.

"I bought this the same day I bought—uh . . . I brought you home— so I would know drill commands for muster. You will need it more than me."

"Thank you, sir," said Quock surprised at Mister Nithercott's generosity and admiring the elaborate drawings on the cover.

"And I want you to take my musket," said Mister Nithercott. "That Committee of Safety gun is good, but the French make better muskets," It was the Charleville musket Mister Nithercott had brought back from the last war. It was an elegant and sturdy weapon. Quock had rarely been allowed to touch it. He was speechless as Mister Nithercott placed it in his hands.

Missus Nithercott returned with his haversack packed with food and another book. "I put in some more jumbles," she said. "I wanted to show you this." She held out the Nithercott family Bible. She opened it up to the back pages, where there was a list of Nithercotts dating back to England. All the births, weddings, and deaths. She pointed to an entry above Hope and Charity's weddings and right below the recorded birth of Faith Nithercott. There in Missus Nithercott's artful writing was "*Quock. Adopted July 4 in the Year of Our Lord 1764.*" Tears welled up in his eyes. Missus Nithercott hugged him, "I wrote that a few weeks after you came to live with us. You are part of this family, and I love you like my own son. Now you are leaving." She finally let him go. Holding him by the shoulders at arm's length, she said, "You will always have a home here."

Behind her came Faith, also bearing gifts. She gave Quock a small package of writing materials, paper, a bottle of ink, and quills. "I want you to write every week," she said. "I will," she added with tears in her eyes.

After carefully packing every item, Quock dragged all his equipment and weapons out into the yard in front of the house. It made an imposing pile. Musket, shot bag, powder horn, cartridge box, bullet mold, lead bar, a small ax, knife, haversack crammed with four days of food, canteen, and knapsack packed with his spare clothes, bedroll and other necessities. Quock pulled it all on and, with help from Mister Nithercott, stood up.

"It weighs a ton," said Quock.

"Good Lord," said Missus Nithercott, "Is he carrying too much?"

"It will get lighter soon enough," assured Mister Nithercott. "I'll help you carry it as far as Lexington." He took the haversack and musket. Chaste and Faith gave him more tearful hugs. Peter ran out the door and hugged Quock, too. "Come back and take me with you."

"I will. When you're bigger."

"Don't forget the Ladies!" Quock turned around and saw Tabitha Nelson at the side of the house. She must have gone out the back door and come around to the front to shout to Quock. "While you're fighting for Negro rights, don't forget the ladies' rights! If I were a man, I'd join you, but the men are afraid to arm women."

Quock was unsure of what to say. He waved back then he and Mister Nithercott set off down the road toward Lexington.

"Tabitha Nelson," said Mister Nithercott, shaking his head.

"Do you think women would fight?" asked Quock.

"I don't know about all of 'em, but I believe Tabitha would blow our fool heads off if she thought she had a reason."

Quock grinned.

"Quock, I was being selfish earlier. I wanted you to stay on the farm. The army isn't as bad as I painted it. Lots of people think they can't bear army life, but any man with a brain between his ears will do fine."

"Yes, sir,"

"I fought in two wars, and there were many hard times, little food, freezing cold, fever, but day-to-day, the army's no more work than a farm."

"I don't want to be flogged."

"Do what you're told, and you won't get flogged. Some men can't figure that out. They think they're smarter or know more than the men what's over 'em. They end up with a bloody back."

"I guess."

"Officers and sergeants are no smarter than anybody else, but they still know things a private don't. If it ain't illegal or immoral, the best course is just do what you're told."

"What about getting killed in battle?"

"You know that's possible, but more soldiers die of fever than from the enemy. Dirty camps bring camp fever. Watch for lice, and wash your clothes and yourself regularly. Most importantly, dig good jakes."

Quock glanced up to see if Mister Nithercott was serious or joking.

"Another thing." He shook a finger. "When you do get into a battle, they will tell you to shoot at the officers. That's worthless advice. Officers got an exaggerated sense of their importance, and they assign the same importance to enemy officers. But I never heard of a battle lost because an officer got killed. But I have heard of battles where most of the officers are killed, and it's still won."

Mister Nithercott raised the musket he was carrying and aimed down the barrel, "Your enemy is the man in front of you. Shoot him before he shoots you, and you'll live longer." For an instant, as he aimed down the barrel, Quock could see the young soldier Ebenezer Nithercott.

"Is that what it was like for you?"

Mister Nithercott lowered the musket. "Yeah, but fighting for my king, not against him." Mister Nithercott shook his head. "I hope I'm not sending you off to . . . Anyway, everyone else is going. They can't hang us all."

As he walked, Quock realized that each step was taking him farther from the only home he could remember and closer to a new life of danger and privation. His feelings were a cruel mixture of homesickness, boyish anticipation of adventure, and sadness that Isaac wasn't going with him.

Riding around the perimeter of his brigade, the ferocity of the Americans troubled Robert. From every direction, militiamen were sneaking up to his pickets to take long potshots. He got off his horse and laid his spyglass atop a wall to train it on Lexington. He flinched when a musket ball smacked into the stone inches away, splattering him with dust and tiny pebbles. Equally disheartening was the numbers gathering around his brigade. He saw militia bands forming in every direction. A road cut allowed him a view of more than a mile. At the farthest distances, he could see more rebel columns marching toward them. Gage's intelligence about an army of eighteen thousand men was prescient. He would have to disregard his recent experience of marching through deserted countryside. Instead, he had to prepare to fight his way back to Boston, and they would have to leave soon, or the gathering minutemen would overwhelm his brigade.

He visited Caradoc's wounded, moaning in wagons. He shook hands for those that could shake, asked how they were, and promised to have them safely in Boston soon. Sergeant Major Sayer showed him the wagons he had filled with corpses. The corpses were stacked in the bed, but the arms, legs, and clothing were akimbo—their modesty shot away with their lives. The day had warmed and already flies flitted about the corpses. Confronted again with the terrible costs of his chosen profession, Robert's insides squirmed. The smell of blood and offal was overpowering. Robert restrained an urge to pinch his nose.

"The man here's been scalped," said Sayer, pointing to one bloody-headed body. The man's head was black with dried blood. The visible part of the brain dried to leather hardness and loose edges of the scalp had curled. During the Pontiac War, Robert had seen several scalped men—both red and white. Although the wound was horrific, there was a lot of damage to the skull, unnecessary during scalp taking, and too much remaining scalp. It couldn't be a scalping, not even a badly botched one.

"The men are saying that the dead are being mutilated and ears cut off," added Sayer. Robert surveyed the bodies in the wagon, but there were no obvious signs of mutilation. Sayer was passing along rumors and fears, not first-hand knowledge. "M'Lord, what are we going to do about this savagery?"

Rumors of Yankee atrocities could serve a purpose. Desertion was a chronic problem in the British Army, and it would be too easy for footsore, frightened, or disaffected soldiers to rationalize surrender or desertion to a Christian, English-speaking enemy. He needed his men to fear and loathe the rebels. Tales of scalping and mutilation would give them second thoughts about Yankee mercy.

To Sayer, he said, "We will mind Governor Gage's caution to avoid unnecessary civilian casualties, but the kid gloves are coming off. The Yanks will regret their barbarity and disloyalty." Sayer would pass along Robert's passive confirmation and word would spread through the sergeants' informal network.

Minutes later, at his makeshift headquarters in the tavern, the commanders of Robert's five battalions and battery of artillery gathered for a council of war. He relished the moment. This was his main chance. A desperate battle against overwhelming odds, and he was the commander and central figure of the drama. If he did this right, he would be a hero. His name would be in all the news sheets. His reputation solidified and maybe a promotion to Major General. But first, he had to break out of the closing rebel encirclement.

"Colonel Whelks, I acknowledge your men have gotten less than an hour of rest, but I cannot afford to offer more," said Robert. "I intend to keep your battalion in the center of the formation. I will not commit them to battle as long as circumstances allow."

"The men will do whatever is asked of them, but we have very little shot or powder remaining."

"Shot and powder will be dear before this day is done," said Robert. "The rebels are forming a cordon around us. The silver lining is that they lack the discipline to withstand a determined assault. Bearing that in mind, my design is to feint toward Lexington to confuse the enemy, followed by a determined frontal assault eastward. Once we breach the cordon, we will use flanking movements to keep our motion. Robert turned to Blunt, "Major Blunt, I want the 23rd to be the vanguard of our assault."

"Thank you, sir."

"My plan also requires a skilled rearguard to keep the Yanks off our backsides. Major Pitcairn, may I ask your marines to form the rearguard?" asked Dandridge.

"M'Lord, my position is awkward. I must confess a weakness. I am not confident that my marines can execute the complicated movements required of the rearguard. Their mettle is keen, but marines are usually shipbound, and large formation maneuvers are not our custom."

"Thank you for that admission. Can your marines execute an offense in concert with cannon?"

"We are very accustomed to fighting with cannon, M'Lord, and my marines are very offensive."

"We all know the marines are offensive, Hah-hah!" Pitcairn and the other officers laughed, too. Robert knew that it was a long military custom that the senior officer was the cleverest man in the room, but he still enjoyed his witticisms even if the laughter was louder than the small humor would normally arouse.

"Very well, the marines will lead; the Welshmen will conduct the rearguard."

Pitcairn nodded his agreement, but Robert wasn't finished yet, "When you attack, I want two volleys, no more; the third volley is from the cannon. Then, charge through the smoke. Understood?"

"Sir, two volleys, third volley cannon, charge through the smoke."

"Good." Robert pointed to Colonel Nesbitt, "Bill, your battalion will form the left flank and will lead the feint to Lexington." Nodding to his battery commander, "Captain Barker, you are to fire at Lexington for the feint, then shift your fire to support the marines on my command. Colonel Maddison, you are on the right. Colonel Whelks, your men are in reserve. Move behind the marines and keep the wounded with you." Robert picked up a map and drew with a piece of charcoal how he expected each battalion to advance.

"M'Lord," said Whelks. "Lone country people have taken to shooting at our men from houses and barns."

"Thank you, Steven, a useful observation." To the greater group, "If a Yank abjures fighting with the regulated militia, then he is a brigand, and the honors of war do not apply. Instruct your men that they are to burn the house or barn from whence the shot came. If there is a family inside, chase them out first. The king would not want news of us burning women and children alive in their homes."

"Sir, if I may," said Colonel Nesbitt.

"Of course."

"There are several buildings to my front from which country people are already taking shots at my men."

"Burn them when you execute the feint toward Lexington." Looking into their eyes, Robert said, "Let me be clear. The Yanks have chosen armed rebellion over the king's peace. We must show them the error of their way. We are not to violate the rules of war, but this is no longer a raid but a punitive campaign." Robert's commanders nodded their understanding. Robert pulled out his watch. "Gentlemen, it is now three o'clock we will commence our return movement in thirty minutes. Good hunting."

Jason tied up Wicked outside of the tavern where a minuteman told him 'General' William Heath had set up headquarters. Fortunately, the hitching post had a water trough for horses and there was grass on the green. Several other horses were already there. He looked down at his feet. He was wet up to his breeches; his dirty stockings sagged over his equally dirty shoes. He pulled them up, but he couldn't get the wet left stocking to stay up. He stood up and brushed off his coat. As he walked up to the door, he heard Doctor Joseph Warren's voice, "Why did you call for Green? He's a notorious Tory."

Jason hesitated at the door.

"I've known Jason for years. Whatever his politics, he loves his country," answered a voice Jason knew to be Heath's.

"I cannot trust a Tory," said Warren. Jason was surprised. He knew Warren mostly from his many speeches for the patriot cause, particularly on the anniversaries of the Boston Massacre, but they rarely met socially. Jason didn't know that Warren knew him well enough to form an opinion of his character.

"I trust him, and more importantly, Hancock trusts him," responded Heath.

William Heath, like John Hancock, and Jason were all members of the Ancient and Honorable Artillery Company and the Corps of Cadets.

The tall and handsome Doctor Joseph Warren, on the other hand, was a fire-breathing Son of Liberty and ambitious politician, but with no military experience. He served with Heath, however, on the Committee of Safety, which oversaw Massachusetts' military policies and resources.

Joseph Warren had never given Jason cause to dislike him, but Paul Revere was his disciple. An association with Revere was excuse enough for Jason to distrust him. Mary rarely agreed with Jason on the character of various Whigs, but she trusted Warren even less than Jason but for different reasons. Joseph was a widower with children. It was commonly thought that he was informally engaged to Mercy Scollay, one of Mary's many friends, but a marriage date was never announced, and Warren's intentions were uncertain. Mary felt that Joseph didn't respect Mercy's devotion to him and his children. She also thought Joseph was too friendly with several of Boston's eligible—and in some cases ineligible—ladies.

Rather than listening in on a private conversation any longer, Jason knocked on the front door. Even before he had finished knocking, a man opened the door and ran out, leaving the door ajar. Jason strode in and found Heath and Warren sitting at a table to the right of the door.

"Jason!" Heath said with warm enthusiasm. "I am so glad you got my message. I heard that you had snuck out of Boston and led a charge in Concord."

"William, it's good to see you." Jason shook both their hands. "Joseph, always a pleasure." Nodding to Heath, "I have been in a running fight with the regulars, starting here in Lexington, but I don't know the big picture."

"We've just come from a meeting of the Committee of Safety in Menotomy. They believe we have an opportunity to turn this sow's ear into a silk purse." Heath leaned back in his chair. "If we can defeat and capture this corps, we can stop these confounded powder raids and maybe use the prisoners as leverage to get the rest of the ministerial troops out of Massachusetts."

"Like hostages?" Jason nodded his agreement. The same plan had occurred to him.

"More like an exchange." Heath put out his hand. "Jason, sit down. You look done up. Have you had your dinner?"

"I haven't."

"Mister Buckman, pray bring something for Colonel Green!" shouted Heath.

"Everything's gone," said Buckman from behind the bar. "I've had a busy day myself. I'll check in the kitchen, but don't hold out no hope."

"Sit down, Jason, and join us, and we can plan our campaign," said Heath.

Jason took off his hat and sat down.

"Good God, man, you're bleeding." Warren stood up and pressed his handkerchief to the right side of Jason's neck.

"I am?"

"Is that from a musket ball?"

"Probably, I guess. There's been enough flying around."

"It's just a scratch, but two inches to the left and you'd be a dead man." Joseph's eyes were round in admiration.

"Thank you." Jason pressed Warren's handkerchief to his neck, pulled it away, and noticed blood on his collar.

Heath pulled a twig from the top of Jason's hat. "And your coat. Is that a hole?"

"I've ruined a collar and my coat. Mary will be angry."

Heath and Warren laughed. Heath slapped the table.

"She'll be thankful to have her husband back alive," said Heath.

"Have you come to organize this battle?" asked Jason.

"I'm going to try." Heath frowned. He nodded to Joseph, "The committee was gracious enough to appoint me an acting brigadier and command of the operation to resist the regulars, but I need your experienced advice." Jason had to suppress a twinge of jealousy. He was older and senior to Heath. Neither had Heath fought in the last war. Instead, his reputation was as an excellent administrator. William's ample figure, which exceeded Jason's immoderate waistline, was a tribute to Heath's devotion to the social side of militia service. Jason wondered if he had been more political and a Whig, would he have been at the meeting and perhaps gotten the promotion to brigadier?

"Thank God," said Jason. "We need a commander."

"What has been the stratagem so far?" asked Joseph.

"Stratagem?" Jason laughed. "The column is moving too fast for us to concentrate against them. We've fought with whatever militia was at hand." He leaned forward, "But I have seen the full column, and there is less than a thousand men and no cannon. There are considerably more than a thousand militia in pursuit. If the regulars have stopped to rest, I believe we can assemble sufficient forces to overpower them."

"There are more than a thousand now," said Warren. Jason raised his eyebrows and sat back in his chair.

"A brigade of four battalions sallied from Boston," said Heath. "I counted them myself, including a battery of cannons. They have merged with the original raiding party and lie just south of here."

Jason frowned and slumped in his chair, "That's probably more than two thousand men."

"I have sent out runners to assemble the regimental commanders," continued Heath. "I believe there is most of three regiments and a mix of various companies from all over Massachusetts. I am forming a cordon around the regulars. If they wait here long enough, we may have our artillery by the morning."

"Here you go," interrupted Mister Buckman, laying a plate of beans and a can of beer on the table.

"I have no money," said Jason. "I was stopped, and the regulars took it."

Buckman, his eyes and his temper both bloodshot, gave Jason an inflamed glare and reached to lift the plate and can off the table.

"Here." Warren pulled out his wallet. He handed Buckman some coins. Buckman left the plate and stomped off back to the bar.

"Thank you very much," said Jason to Joseph.

"It is the price for your tale. We must know how to beat the regulars."

Jason took a bite of the beans. Half the beans were burnt and scraped from the bottom and sides of the kettle; the rest were cooked to mush, but to Jason, it was the best plate of Boston beans he'd ever eaten. Pushing back the empty plate he picked up the can of beer and took a long drink.

"I can't thank you enough," said Jason. "I didn't know how hungry I was."

Joseph bowed to Jason.

"What can we expect of the regulars?" asked Heath.

"I believe that this is just a raid. They were carrying only haversacks. No knapsacks or shovels, axes, or any heavy equipment—and no trains. They've been commandeering wagons for their dead and wounded. So, unless this new brigade brought a resupply with them, they will run out of food, shot, and powder before the day is out."

Heath put his hand to his chin, "We were able to see the entire brigade quite close. They marched past our meeting at the Black Horse Tavern."

"If they had known, they could have captured the entire Committee of Safety right there," said Warren.

"We locked the doors and watched them through the shutters," said Heath with a tense laugh. "I saw two field pieces, but no wagons, and just haversacks on the troops."

"Then we should attack the regulars directly. Surely our regiments and moral superiority can break their line," declared Joseph. Seeing Heath frown, he added, "Or form ranks astride the road and offer battle."

"The militia is not ready for a great battle." Jason shook his head, "We have outnumbered the regulars since Concord, but they push through like a hot knife through butter."

"Are you suggesting that our men want courage?" demanded Warren, his chin out and brow knitted.

"No. I have seen numerous acts of courage," said Jason. "Too much courage but not enough soldiering. Our men lack the discipline to stand under fire, training on firing in ranks, and the hundred other abilities commonplace to the regulars."

"We ain't got cannons, drums, nor flags for signaling. An army without communications is just a mob," added Heath. "A pitched battle on their terms would be a disaster and set back our cause."

"Have they no weaknesses?" asked Joseph.

Despite the food and a chance to sit Jason was spent. He could not get his mind around the problem. Thinking out loud, he said, "They must be worn out, too."

"There's an idea." Heath pointed to Jason, "If we just let them march down the road, they will be in Boston before sunset. We can force the regulars to fight all the way." Holding his hands with the thumbs and forefingers touching and moving the illustrative circle across the table. "Threaten them from all directions and compel them to flank and keep skirmishers out."

"I don't understand," Warren was frowning. "How will forcing them to fight be any different than marching? The distance to Boston is the same."

"As the crow flies, yes," said Jason. "Forcing the regulars to fight— deploy flankers, wheeling, countermarch, forming a front, reforming the column, etcetera, etcetera," he waved a hand, "will put two or three times as many miles on their legs. It is far more tiring if they must fight all the way."

"Still, we would need some way to stop them altogether once they are worn out." Heath frowned. "Or they will just keep pushing until they regain Boston."

"The bridge at Cambridge?" suggested Joseph.

"The relief column came out Boston Neck. They will likely return the same way." Heath held out his hand toward Jason. "We can use the

Charles River as a barrier. I already sent an order to tear up the planks from the Cambridge Bridge and gather militia on the other side to prevent them from crossing."

"Yes. that might work." Jason nodded.

"If we keep up the pursuit behind them and they see the bridge to Boston is blocked—perhaps they will despair," said Heath.

"And then they must surrender!" Warren grinned, holding up a fist.

"But we must force them to choose Boston Neck and not turn north to Charlestown." Heath turned to Jason.

"That's right," agreed Jason. "They still have the navy, and that's how the first group left Boston."

"If we form a blocking force north of Watson's Corner. They cannot see the bridge yet from there." Heath was visibly warming to the plan and rubbed his hands. "If they see a big corps ready to offer battle, they may choose the path of least resistance and turn south to Boston Neck."

"You just said that we can't risk a conventional battle," said Joseph. "Isn't that what you mean by a blocking force?"

"We can bluff. If we can assemble a force large enough—or at least appears large." Heath was still looking at Jason.

Jason groaned mentally, fearing the next words. Despite his mild jealousy, he had been thankful to find Heath in command. He'd hoped he could stop fighting and stand aside in good conscience, but he could see Heath was forming other plans.

"It's not grand, but it is a way that matches our means to our ends," said Heath. "Jason, go to Watson's corner. Gather all the militia you can find along the way and arrange your forces as we discussed."

"I will." Jason tried to sound more enthusiastic than he was.

"Timothy Pickering's regiment is marching from Salem," said Heath. "They will probably already be there. They can strengthen your line."

Warren started to say something, but two booms from distant cannon interrupted him. All three men stood up and ran to the door. They got outside in time to see two cannon balls pass through the steeple of Lexington's meeting house. Falling boards and splinters scattered people on the green.

"They're moving," said Heath. The three men could see the regulars on the nearby hill. Two thousand men marched in a great dance. Several hundred regulars were advancing toward Lexington. Two farmhouses were already on fire.

To Jason's eyes, there was considerably more pageantry in this new larger group. There were many more horses, each of the regiments carried their colors, there was a drum major mounted on a huge black and white piebald draft horse and a marching band. As the three men watched, the band struck up a tune.

"I can barely hear it from here," said Heath. "What are they playing?"

"Yankee Doodle," Warren spoke between pursed lips.

"They mean to provoke us," said Jason.

"We'll play that tune when they surrender," growled Heath.

"General Heath." The martial display before them caused Jason to feel that military formality was needed. "You must delay the regulars as long as possible. It may take a while for me to gather enough militia for a display."

"Dread, not Colonel Green; I will stall them here as long as I can. Then follow with all of New England's militia." Turning to Warren, he said, "Doctor Warren, may I beg you to proceed to Menotomy and organize the defenses there? Force the regulars to fight house-to-house. That should slow them."

"You have my word! These fellows say we won't fight! By Heaven, I hope I shall die up to my knees in blood!" declared Warren.

Jason felt Joseph's declaration a bit melodramatic, reminiscent of Revere's earlier effusions, but it certainly committed him to the fight. The sound of distant musketry spurred Jason and his companions to run to their horses.

Quock and Mister Nithercott could see clouds of smoke rising from behind Lexington.

"Good Lord," exclaimed Nithercott. "They're burning farms."

When they arrived at Lexington Green, they gazed wide-eyed at the war-wrought changes to their little village. Smoke from burning farmhouses billowed over the sky. An endless column of militia marched down the great road—the same road the redcoats had used that morning—toward Boston.

"There's a hole in the meeting house," said Quock.

"Lucky, it didn't catch fire. All our powder was up there in Negro Heaven," said Lee Monroe. They hadn't noticed him even though he was standing near them.

Munroe asked Quock, "Ready?"

"Yes, sir,"

"Good. Go draw some shot and powder and make some cartridges. We're marching in a few minutes."

Quock nodded and ran off to a group of Lexington militia with kegs of powder. He filled his powder horn, then sat down to roll cartridges. The shot was sized for the Brown Bess musket that most militia carried, not his new Charleville. Fortunately, he had plenty of lead balls from Mister Nithercott.

Mister Nithercott sat next to him and helped with the cartridges, showing him the best way to use the dowel to roll the paper and tie off the bottom of the paper tube. Accustomed to working side-by-side, they spoke in one- or two-word sentences. Quock's stomach was aflutter, and keeping his hands busy helped cover his growing homesickness. They were done too quickly, and Quock looked around for something else to do but the men were heading to the formation.

"Here's the rest of your stuff. You'll be leaving soon." He helped Quock strap on his equipment.

"Quock," said Mister Nithercott. Quock met his gaze.

"I'm not very good at goodbyes."

"Goodbye, sir. Thank you for everything you've done for me. I know I wasn't always the best servant—"

"No. Stop. It's me that owes an apology. You were more than a servant. You are part of our family." Mister Nithercott stared at his shoes, then at Quock. "You're like a son to me and Chase. It's to my everlasting shame that I never told you before now. I am very proud of you." Mister Nithercott shook with suppressed crying. He croaked, "I can never get that time back. You're a man now and will make your own choices, but I hope you come back and visit me and Chase when the battle is won."

Mister Nithercott awkwardly hugged Quock, and Quock hugged him back, squeezing him tight. Quock closed his eyes to keep his tears back. He wanted to tell him he loved them like family and that he would return, but he was too choked up to speak. "They're calling for you." Mister Nithercott wiped a tear from his eye.

Quock nodded and turned his back on Mister Nithercott, and walked to join his company.

"You'll always have a home with us," called Mister Nithercott. "I am very proud of you!"

He turned and waved to Mister Nithercott. Minutes later, the re-formed Lexington minute company marched onto their place onto the great road. Quock turned and waved again. Mister Nithercott, standing alone on the green, waved back.

Chapter Twelve

Four o'clock p.m.

Jason Green and Joseph Warren galloped along the great road to Boston, trying to get distance between them and the regulars. After gaining a good mile on the redcoat brigade, Jason slowed his horse to a cantor.

"That's a wicked cross cantor," Warren noted the awkward gait of Jason's horse.

"It's a wicked animal."

"Shall we slow to a trot to save our mounts and your back?" asked Warren.

"That would be appreciated."

"Turnabout!" shouted Jason to a militia company marching toward them.

"We heard the regulars are that way," shouted the commander, pointing west.

"That's right. There are two thousand regulars right behind us. We're going to concentrate the militia in Menotomy." They were close enough now for Warren to speak rather than shout.

"There's already hundreds there now."

"That's not enough," responded Jason. After reiterating his order and his reasons to the reluctant militia commander—who apparently thought attacking two thousand regulars with his fifty-man minute company was the height of tactical genius—the two men rode on.

Half an hour later, they arrived on the outskirts of Menotomy. Just as the militia company commander had described, there were already minutemen all around the town. Some were sitting by the road resting, others forming in ranks behind stone walls, and others were rolling barrels and turning over wagons to form barricades. There was no clear plan, just disconnected companies, each doing what they thought best.

"God preserve us; we are an army of laymen." Jason surveyed the activity with a frown.

"How will I control these people?" asked Warren.

"The regulars are too close; you don't have time to establish any authority. Urge them to fortify each house. You won't have to maneuver. Just shoot the regulars as they pass."

"I can do that. You go on, Jason. Your blocking force is our best hope for defeating our majestic British masters."

Jason saluted and spurred his horse, but Warren grabbed Jason's reins to hold him for a moment.

"Don't count on Timothy Pickering, Jason," warned Warren. "He believes in our cause, but he is officious and will probably demand Congress endorsement before he will commit to fight the regulars."

Robert sat astride his horse as he watched the marines and cannon fire scatter the American militia. "Like a broom to dust," said Mitchell. Most of Mitchell's patrol had reverted to their respective regiments. Robert was the honorary Colonel to Mitchell's regiment and since the 5th regiment wasn't present, he offered his service to Robert for the remainder of the battle.

Robert turned to look behind. "Their numbers are astonishing." There was a horde of militia pressing the brigade's rear. "I wish I could adequately describe the scene to Parliament. If they could see the number of angry country people mobilized in opposition to our policies, they might reconsider their coercive acts."

"Politicians are fortuitously absent from the battles they create."

"Well said."

"M'Lord, we are nearing Menotomy." Mitchell waved east. The afternoon sun caused Menotomy's church steeples to cast ominous claw-like shadows on the rooftops. "The town is considerably larger than other villages, and the buildings are closely spaced for at least a half mile."

Robert turned in his saddle to watch their rear, "The Welshmen are not practicing good fire discipline and expending shot and powder too quickly." He said to Mitchell, "I am going to visit Major Blunt and curb his enthusiasm. Pray tell Major Pitcairn what you told me. Forewarned is forearmed."

"M'Lord." Mitchell saluted and rode off. Robert gently spurred his horse and rode to join Henry Blunt.

Robert couldn't help but recall the infamous incident sixteen years ago when Henry led a pack of young officers spouting slurs about him at the officer's mess. Robert wasn't present, and he reminded himself that it was nearly ancient history. The officers involved were mostly teenage youths—probably drunk—and were now mature, responsible officers. Further, Henry had never repeated his affronts either publicly or in private. Robert never acknowledged the incident. Instead, he took the moral high ground and forgave Henry. So, finding fault with Blunt's handling of the regiment now wasn't petty revenge, he told himself, but fully justified by the occasion.

Henry and the regiment's adjutant were standing to the left of the 23rd's line. The Welshmen were in three ranks, firing by platoon at a sprinkle of American militia hiding behind a wall.

"Major Blunt," said Robert, "your men are shooting far too much."

The adjutant, Frederick Mackenzie—he was called Mack, Robert remembered from the last war—now an elderly lieutenant in his forties, nodded in agreement.

Blunt was startled by the unannounced appearance of his brigade commander and blurted out, "But sir, this is how Colonel Caradoc drilled the regiment. The standard is five volleys a minute."

"Just so, and for good reason. Caradoc's company ruined a regiment of French cavalry at Minden with the heat of their volleys, but one must not be rigid on tactics." Pointing at the militia, "This is not Minden, and those people are not French Dragoons."

Mack smiled but covered his mouth with his hand.

"What do you suggest, M'Lord?" Henry's brow was furrowed as if he couldn't understand the problem.

"Hold your fire until they are ready to attack. Divide your companies into divisions and fall back in stages. Force the Yanks to deploy and slow their pursuit."

"Thank you, sir. I also need more shot and powder."

"My point exactly," replied Robert. "There is no more shot or powder until we reach Boston. Pray instruct your companies to fire only when the enemy presses too near."

197

"Yes, M'Lord. Thank you for that wise counsel . . ."

Robert didn't wait to hear the last obsequious inanity. Turning about, he spurred his horse until he was close behind the marines as they advanced in ranks on Menotomy. The Yanks greeted the marines with a volley from the nearest house. Every door, window, and rock wall in front of the house hid militiamen. The marines responded with a volley from each of their two ranks, followed by the cannon as the third volley. The grape-sized balls from the case shot blasted wood chips off the walls, broke windows, and knocked shingles off the roof. With a loud "Huzzah!" the marines charged through their own smoke.

"Brilliant!" cried Robert.

The surviving militiamen ran out the shattered door or fell out through the broken windows, running to save their lives. Robert turned his attention to the south flank. Another group of militiamen fired a volley at the marines from a low stone wall, but they were inattentive to their rear. Flanking companies from the 47th regiment bayoneted many of them and drove the rest away.

To the north, Robert could see soldiers with the blue facings of the King's Own entering Menotomy. There, the militia seemed equally unprepared for a flanking movement, and many were caught between the charging marines and regulars. Robert rode to Major Pitcairn and said, "Brilliant assault! Check for wounded and anybody hiding inside, then burn the house."

The battle was not won, however. Both the 4th and the 47th regiments were already hotly engaged with other militia formations defending other buildings in the densely built-up Menotomy. Robert saw Colonel Maddison riding toward him.

"M'Lord," saluted Maddison. "The town is infested with rebels like fleas on a dog. Every building and stone wall hides a new band. They are mostly running before us, but we are using an extraordinary amount of shot and powder." William Nesbitt, who had ridden up as Maddison was speaking, nodded in emphatic agreement.

"Don't spare the bayonet," said Robert. "It's just as effective as shot at close quarters."

"M'Lord, the militia are defending houses with their women and children inside," said Nesbitt. "It is a despicable and cowardly tactic to keep us from burning their homes."

"They are a loathsome lot; nevertheless, we are invading their homes. Likely, they were not able to evacuate their innocents. Pray continue to restrain your men." Robert held up his hand for emphasis. "The object you must keep uppermost in your minds is to move quickly through this town and on to Boston. We cannot afford to become delayed in house-to-house fighting. Time is a commodity even dearer than shot and powder."

Robert rode to the house the Marines had just cleared. A squad was striking a light near a pile of furniture they intended to burn. More marines streamed by Robert, intent on assaulting the next house. To his alarm, ten yards away, a man leaped out of the house's cellar and aimed his musket at Robert. Before he could react, the rebel fired.

Llewellyn sat uncomfortably with his weight on his right butt cheek in the back of a chaise commandeered for the wounded. Across from him lay Steven Whelks in considerable pain from a wound to his upper thigh. The surgeon couldn't operate because they were moving, so he staunched the wound, immobilized the leg with a splint using a broomstick and Whelk's sash, then administered a stout dose of laudanum. Steven was drifting in and out of consciousness.

The sounds of gunfire were continuous, often punctuated by the boom of cannon. Smoke hung in great clouds over the town, casting an ominous shade. As Llewellyn watched a house burn, he frowned. The battle had become pitiless. He wondered how they would make peace with the Americans after this frenzy of violence.

Lieutenant Mackenzie rode up to the chaise. "Colonel Caradoc! Major Blunt gave me leave to visit you."

"Mack! I'm so glad to see you."

"How are you feeling, sir?"

"In good spirits. I am. I was beginning to feel a bit sorry for myself, but then the surgeon brought poor Colonel Whelks here. We have nearly identical wounds, but in his case, the ball hit bone, and he's in a bad way."

"Makes one appreciate the little mercies."

"Just so. And the battle? When the chaise is not moving, I can stand, but I cannot see much."

"No worries, I suppose; we are scattering the rebels and should be out of Menotomy soon."

"It appears that the battle has turned decidedly fierce," observed Llewellyn.

Mack nodded, "Lord Dandridge ordered us to burn houses and buildings the rebels were using to fire on us." Mack coughed from the smoke, "Did you notice in the last war that burning German houses and French houses had their own peculiar odor?"

"I did. And now I know that American homes smell different when they burn."

"We are in an awful business."

"Indeed. What else, Mack? You don't sound entirely confident."

"There's always good and bad . . ."

"Give me the good."

"After a shaky start, Major Blunt has the regiment in hand. We are holding off a horde of Yankee militia."

"What's the bad?"

Mackenzie hesitated, then blurted out, "Looting."

Llewellyn scowled, "Go on."

"It started when the men were told to burn houses. Some would grab spoons or trinkets they could stuff in their pockets—only if they were burning the house under orders, you understand—they thought it was going to be destroyed at any rate," Mackenzie shrugged, "but once it started, the looting got out of control."

"It always does. Ignoring a sin is as good as endorsing it."

"It's the house-to-house fighting. We cannot oversee their actions. The men have lost all restraint and are looting every house and even churches." In a lower voice, he added, "I'm afraid some of the officers are encouraging it."

Llewellyn was disheartened but not surprised. There was constant tension between good discipline and a soldier's efforts to supplement his meager pay and rations. But Llewellyn believed that the British Army system of buying and selling commissions was more insidious than petty theft. His officers aspired to more senior rank; Henry Blunt was particularly ambitious, but poor in both money and influence. The temptation to augment their finances from the enemy was evidently too much for some. Llewellyn knew he had cut short this vile weed.

"Pray return to Major Blunt, assure him of my good health, and in the presence of the Sergeant Major, tell him that I saw some of the King's Own looting. I would be terribly disappointed if I discovered any Fusiliers partook in such criminal activity. It would be a pity to hang a man for the sake of a spoon."

"Sir!" Mackenzie saluted smartly and rode back to the regiment.

Behind him, Jason could hear the low thunder of cannon. He turned about and saw several columns of smoke rising above Menotomy. *They must be burning every house.* He worried about Mary and their tavern. *Would the regulars burn it in retribution? Would they let Mary leave Boston?* The more he thought about the consequences of the erupting civil war the more he was convinced that he must win the day. If they could capture the expedition, they could force Governor Gage to bargain.

In front of him, he couldn't see any militia. Almost the first time since dawn, the road was empty. Wicked was tired but didn't offer too much resistance to a steady ground-eating trot. After an hour of uneventful travel, he saw a column of regulars with two wagons a quarter mile to his front. The soldiers marching behind the wagons wore blue coats with red facings of the artillery. There were two columns of ununiformed armed riders flanking them.

Loyalists aiding the King's troops. Did Gage send out more artillery?

In this stretch of road, there were no nearby woods or homes. Jason couldn't see any easy way to avoid passing the column unless he got off the road and rode all the way around. It would be obvious to the loyalists that he was trying to escape. He reached down and patted Wicked's neck. It was wet with sweat, and her mouth foamed around the bit. There were at least a dozen mounted men in the column beside the horses pulling the chaises. He knew there wasn't enough vigor left in his horse for a running fight. Bluffing seemed like the only alternative.

He let Wicked slow to a walk and tried to appear unconcerned about their presence on the road. He needed a good cover story. Saying he was out hunting seemed too obvious a lie. However weak the storyline, pleading ignorance of the fighting seemed like the only choice. The Loyalists riding on the outside of the column would soon force him off the road.

It occurred to Jason he might know some of the Loyalists. Many Boston Loyalists were friends and customers at his tavern. Would they stop him? The column was very close now, and Jason pulled on Wicked's reins to force her to the right as they passed. He covered the royal stamp on the musket with his hand as casually as he could. He slightly hunched over with his head down like a tired traveler. His hat covered much of his face. He prepared to spur Wicked to a run if he was recognized.

"Jason! Is that you?"

The voice was familiar. Jason brought his hand to the tip of his cap to partially hide his face and still see who was calling his name. "Uncle Adam?"

"What are you doing here?"

Jason dropped his hand in relief.

"David, this is my nephew, Lieutenant Colonel Jason Green," Uncle Adam gestured to the old Indian driving the wagon.

Jason looked at the column closely for the first time. The regulars were unarmed and had all slumped to the ground when the wagon stopped. They were tied together, and the lead of the rope was tied to the back of the last chaise.

David raised his right hand in a salute. "We're damned glad to find you. We want to turn in these prisoners to the proper authorities."

"Jason, this is Captain David Lamson, our company commander," introduced Uncle Adam.

Jason recalled his uncle speaking of David Lamson over the years, but Jason had never met him. Uncle Adam had described his militia commander as a half-Indian who had fought with the Rangers against the French. By the look of David's long black hair (streaked with white), Roman nose, the feather in his cocked hat, and moccasins, he appeared full-blooded Indian. Jason noticed the gray heads of Uncle Adam's other companions, "This is your alarm company."

"Yes, sir, but we're still spry enough to capture these regulars," said Lamson.

"They ambushed us!" shouted an indignant and wounded British officer from the back of the chaise.

"I told you to shut the hell up!" Lamson raised a hand to the officer, who cringed away from the blow.

"What happened?" asked Jason.

"We ambushed 'em," said Uncle Adam.

"We got the alarm last night. We mustered at Jacob's Tavern. Nobody told us what we were supposed to do, so after a few beers, we went down to the road out of Boston and set up an ambuscade. Like we used to do on the French," said Lamson.

"It's the King's Road, and we are the King's troops. You have no—"

"Shut the hell up!" Lamson raised his fist and threatened to punch the officer. The officer grabbed his wounded arm and flinched away.

"We warned 'em to stop," said Uncle Adam.

"That's right," agreed Lamson, "but they didn't. So, I ordered the company to fire. We killed two, wounded this one, and we had to chase the rest of them down. Took all morning to get 'em all. Fortunately, Bob over there brought his dogs." A mounted, portly, white-haired man at the back of the column with a small pack of dogs lolling on the ground next to him waved and smiled.

"To be fair now," said Bob, "Mother Broderick caught six of 'em." The alarm company laughed.

"Missus Broderick's over seventy," said Uncle Adam. "She was out digging dandelions when six of them surrendered to her."

"That's a hell of a story." Jason climbed off his horse and looked down inside the chaise. "What's in there?"

"Nothing really," said Uncle Adam.

"Yeah," agreed Lamson. "No powder, lead, or not even much food. Just a bunch of tools. The only arms they had were muskets and they threw those in a pond. We got a pack of boys fishing them out."

Jason climbed inside the chaise. There were no powder casks but some sledgehammers, spikes, and bars of all sizes. "This is artillery equipment. There's no cannons?"

"Nope," said Lamson. Jason turned around to speak to the British prisoner, but Lamson said, "He won't talk except to complain. So, Colonel, can we turn these prisoners over to ya'?"

"No, sir, and we need to get them outta here. The regulars have a brigade in Menotomy and are heading this way. General Heath ordered me to gather all the militia I can find and form a blocking position north of Watson's corner. You gentlemen are the first company of my new command."

Lamson gave him a sour frown. "We been up all night."

"Me too. If we wait any longer, the regulars will come along and relieve you of your prisoners and your freedom."

Lamson gave a lopsided smile. "In that light, lead on Colonel Green."

Jason climbed off the wagon, took Wicked's reins, tied them to the back of the chaise, and sat back down next to Captain Lamson.

"Need to rest my horse a bit." Pointing behind them, he said, "Take us back to Watson's Corner, turn north, and we'll gather up an army."

"Halleluiah," said Lamson with no enthusiasm.

Turning around, Jason addressed the prisoner, "So what were you going to do with those tools?"

"I was not keeping secret my activities," said the artillery officer. "I do not know our purpose. Yesterday afternoon, I was ordered to gather two chaises and fill them with tools for spiking cannon and meet a column in Menotomy. We got lost in the dark. When these gentlemen—these high-waymen—screeched at us to stop, I ignored them," he waved a dismissive hand at David Lamson. "As I tried to say before, I am a King's officer on the King's Road. I am not required to explain my actions to the country people. Now, two men are dead, and these brigands have obstructed a King's officer in the performance of his duty. I will put in a good word for you at your trial if you release us now."

"You are prisoners of Massachusetts. If you behave according to the customs of war, you will likely be exchanged when we negotiate a truce," said Jason.

"You speak as if we are at war."

"We are."

"Hoo-ee, that's good," said Lamson, "Cuz this whole ambush thing could've gone real bad if the war hadn't started."

East of Menotomy, Robert rode beside the moving column of soldiers. A memory of the Battle of Minden had forcefully returned. For years after the war, he relived the terrifying moment in his dreams. He stood again on the plain before Minden after the French Calvary's second charge. He stared wide-eyed at the carnage around him. The biting smell of gunpowder mixed with the odors of blood, guts, and earth plowed up by the hooves of thousands of horses filled his nostrils. The sounds of screaming horses, pleading wounded, and shouted orders created a cacophonic assault on his ears. To his front and flanks, dead and wounded Frenchmen and their mounts lay in heaps. Rider-less horses galloped madly about the field, trampling the dead and wounded alike. Next to him lay his batman George Jones, his lower jaw a mass of gore, teeth, and broken bone. His mangled body was trampled by horses, but his eyes looked at Robert and blinked.

Sergeant Sayer's hoarse voice ordered the shattered ranks to "Dress right; prime and load." Then he heard Llewellyn's gruff but calm announcement, "They're forming for another go." The ghastly scene around him fell away as he focused his entire being on the French lines. Thousands of cavalry were massing for another charge, blowing their bugles—God, the bugles. The entire Minden plain seemed to grow a forest of lances. He usually woke from the dream, bathed in sweat, sometimes shouting out commands. The memory was so vivid that it made him nauseous. He clenched his teeth to keep down his gorge. Llewellyn's chaise was nearby. He rode toward it, shaking his head, trying to clear his mind.

"Llewellyn," said Robert, riding alongside the chaise as it bounced down the road. Llewellyn was on his knees, leaning over the driver's seat, holding the reins. Fretfulness gripped Robert's chest and throat. He had to say something, or he wouldn't be able to talk at all. "How are you, friend?" he croaked.

"Well enough. Frustrated by my confinement while my men were fighting. Driving the chaise to put another man in the fight. But Robert, I heard you were nearly shot."

"Quite so, from little more than ten paces. Fortunately, in his excitement, the rascal missed me entirely." Robert shook his head and stared at the horses pulling the chaise as if they interested him, "What disturbs me is the man shot when he was surrounded by my troops. It was morally certain he would be instantly cut down."

Two marines had bayoneted the rebel, who screamed in rage as he fell. As Robert watched the man die, he realized with terrible conviction that the rebels would fight every step of the way. No matter how hard he hit them, the rebels would not slink away like beaten dogs. The righteous anger that had stoked his resolve in Boston evaporated.

"I dread the enthusiasts. They cannot be influenced by clear reason," Llewellyn shook his head in sympathy.

"I came to seek your counsel."

"Of course, Robert."

"Remember Minden?"

"How could I forget?"

"It was completely mad," Robert's memories crowded the words out of his mouth. "Thousands of French cavalry in their ranks bearing down on us. The very ground was trembling under their hooves. I had read descriptions of cavalry charges before, but no words can prepare one for such an experience." Robert took a deep breath.

"It was fearful," Llewellyn nodded his head.

"Just so. I was terrified throughout, but the cruelest bit was the third charge." Robert hesitated to admit his fear, even to a friend who shared his experience.

"The whole force came out for a last go," said Llewellyn. "I feared we'd be swept away."

"It was so unfair. We had twice beat them. It felt improper. They should not come back, but they did." Robert glanced around to see if anyone was listening. The wounded Whelks in the back was unconscious. "I feel the same sense of outrageous fortune now."

"How so?" asked Llewellyn.

Robert struggled to find the words to name his fear.

"After we finally fought free of Menotomy, I found it heartening that there is so little sign of the rebels," said Robert. "I hoped that we were finally rid of them or that they were cowed into submission. But after further reflection—I fear that the militia has been gathered up so they may concentrate against us elsewhere. There are at least three settlements before we reach Boston Neck. Will they all be like Menotomy?" Naming his fear seemed to dissipate its power. He could already feel his chest loosening.

Llewellyn was silent for a long moment, "Was Menotomy that bad?" He looked into Robert's face.

"Not like Minden, but it had its difficulties," Robert stared at the ground. "The jumble of houses broke up our formations. The Yanks turned every building into a fort. We don't have the shot and powder to fight three more battles like that."

"It's never as bad as you think," Llewellyn adjusted his seat. "Undoubtedly, the Yanks are having problems of their own. If you carry on, their faults will show out."

For Robert, talking with Llewellyn was a magic incantation. He could feel his composure returning. He could think again. "Thank you, Llewellyn. I envy your strength and deplore my failings."

"Bah! You are one of the most brilliant officers of this age," Llewellyn waved a hand. "The Yanks will have another go, but we've been through worse."

"Yes, we have." Like a tea kettle removed from the fire, Robert's boiling spirits calmed. He pointed at a group of horsemen in the distance. "Ah! There is Major Mitchell. I sent him forward with De Berniere to investigate the Cambridge bridge." Robert raised his hand in salute, "Thank you for your wise counsel. *Ich Dein.*"

Llewellyn smiled and returned the salute, also saying the 23rd's motto, "*Ich Dein.*"

Raising his hand, Robert shouted, "Drum Major, beat Commanders Assemble!"

Shortly thereafter, in a pasture by the road, the surviving commanders assembled on Robert. "My best compliments to you and your men for their performance in Menotomy, but we still must reach Boston. Report the condition of your men and arms." To Captain Barker, Robert asked, "Your cannon, sir?"

"M'Lord, I have enough powder and ball for two shots."

"Two per gun?"

Barker held up the index finger on each hand, "No, M'Lord, one shot per gun." Then he dropped his fingers forward one at a time, "Boom, boom. Done."

"Bloody Hell," said Nesbitt, echoing Robert's thoughts. Without cannon, their advantage over the rebels was not as certain. He felt the anxiety creep back into his gut. With effort, he kept his face calm.

"Colonel Nesbitt, your report," said Robert.

"We are still counting the casualties, but they are comparatively light considering the intensity of the fighting. Unfortunately, I probably have only two to three cartridges per man remaining."

"I am the same," offered Maddison. Pitcairn nodded in agreement.

"Major Blunt, how goes the defense of our rear?" asked Robert.

"M'Lord, the enemy is pressing us hard. I have implemented strict conservation on shot and powder; nevertheless, our ammunition is nearly exhausted."

"Quite right. Rotate with the 4th regiment and take their place on the flank."

"Thank you, sir."

"M'Lord, I have compiled our casualties from the entire brigade," said Matthew, who, in the absence of the wounded Caradoc and Whelks, was now commanding the remainder of the original expedition but retained his duties as brigade adjutant. "I estimate that we lost almost fifty dead and more than a hundred wounded. Perhaps another half hundred missing."

With a little flourish and champing of horses, Major Mitchell and Ensign De Berniere arrived.

"I pray that your report is favorable," said Robert to Mitchell.

"M'Lord, the rebels have removed the planks from Cambridge Bridge. They are using them to construct barricades on the far side. There is a battalion manning the rampart they are digging."

"How many men?" asked Robert.

"Maybe two to three hundred with more coming."

"We can cross on the stringers," said Pitcairn. "If we have sufficient covering fire."

"That's what we did coming out, but the rebels had neglected to defend it. A lapse they appear to have remedied," Robert shook his head. "The river is too wide for musketry; only cannon have the range to keep the rascals' heads down while we cross." Robert put his fist to his chin. "What about boats?"

"The rebels have them."

"And other roads?"

"Sir, there is a road that leads north, but a rebel army lies astride it."

"Army?" said Nesbitt, his brows knit in anger and disbelief. "Army?"

"More than a thousand men. They were deploying in ranks as if they intend to offer battle."

"Gentlemen, you have been grumbling that the Yanks won't meet us in open battle. "Now your wish is fulfilled," Robert tried to sound casually amused.

"Not at the end of a bloody day with weary soldiers and empty cartridge boxes," said Maddison, his lips pursed in a pouting frown.

For a moment Robert watched the long column of his brigade passing by. They weren't marching but route stepping. Many were evidently footsore. Only discipline and fear of capture kept them moving, but for how long? A decision had to be made, but he needed a moment to think and more information. "I will assess the situation for myself." To his commanders, he said, "In the meantime, march as fast as you can without blowing the legs of our men. Make maximum use of the bayonet, and do not fire your muskets unless necessary." He pointed at Captain Barker, "The cannon are not to fire at all except on my express order."

Robert cantered to the head of the column with Major Mitchell and Ensign De Berniere. The noise of almost continual gunfire that had haunted them since Concord was gone. The silence was broken only by musketry from the rear, where the mass of American militia continued to pursue.

An hour later, Major Mitchell said, "M'Lord, you can see the crossroad from here."

Robert pulled out his spyglass and surveyed the scene, "We need to ride a bit closer." Moments later, at a better vantage, Robert again raised his spyglass and examined the terrain. To the south he could see the spires of Cambridge, but not yet the bridge. Robert knew that beyond the Cambridge Bridge were the towns of Brookline, then Roxbury—and their militia probably reinforced with refugees from Boston—before finally reaching Boston Neck. This route promised a river crossing opposed by a strong militia force and two more Menotomy-like battles against swarming rebel irregulars. Robert took a deep breath.

He turned his spyglass to the north. The road north crossed an open plain of planted fields and pastures with scattered farmhouses and barns but no towns or villages in sight. Overhead, scudding clouds were beginning to pile up, portending rain later, but the sun still shone scattered rays on the rebel army lying a mile up the road.

"Where does this road go?" Robert asked De Berniere.

"M'Lord, the country people call it Charlestown Road."

Robert didn't respond. Instead, he continued studying the rebel ranks. "Their general has put his men close to the trees, so the slanting shadows make it difficult to get a good count," Robert explained aloud. "The line is almost a half mile long—maybe a thousand men in the front rank alone."

"Did you want to investigate the bridge?" asked Mitchell.

"Just a moment." Robert carefully studied the ground. The rebel general had chosen his position well. The rebel line was along a slight rise, fifty yards behind a rail fence. The rails were no great obstacle, but attacking infantry would have to dismantle or climb over them, slowing their advance well inside the range of the rebel muskets. If the rebels stood their ground, they might get off a second volley before the infantry was ready to charge. Worse, Robert knew that his soldiers might stop and fire back, further stalling the advance.

A man sitting astride a grey horse rode in front of the militia. Robert examined him closer for a moment. He was dressed in the same fashion as a typical countryman, nothing remarkable. Robert was moving his spyglass away when he noticed the green coat. *Could it be?* Robert eyed the rebel ranks again. The front rank was unevenly spaced. Men stood or sat, smoking pipes and talking, their informal countenance breaking the discipline of their line. The trees and shadows cast by the setting sun, together with the sloppiness of the line, obscured the scene, but searching closely, he could find no sign of a second rank. None were hiding in the trees behind them either. The line was long but only one rank deep—there were no cannon.

"Tally ho," said Robert almost to himself. He shut his spyglass and put it away. "I have found the line."

"What did you see?" asked Mitchell.

"The fox. The rebel general, I believe I know him."

"He is not capable?"

"If it is Mister Green, then he has already shown he is capable. An experienced and wily opponent." Turning to De Berniere, he asked, "So why is he there? You said Charlestown Road?"

"Sir, I've not traveled it, but that's what the Yanks call it."

"Are there any other settlements between here and Charlestown?"

"Not that I know of."

"Charlestown is just across Back Bay from Boston. We could return the same way Caradoc crossed." Robert examined the line again. It could well be a bloody battle. On the other hand, it would be only one battle. The kind of battle at which the British Army excelled. "We have twice his numbers and cannon. He does not know that we are low on shot and powder. I will call his bluff."

From his place in front of the militia formation, Jason looked northward up the road toward Charlestown. In the distance, he could see a lone horseman. Even at a distance, he recognized Uncle Adam. His alarm company had left with the prisoners, but at Jason's request, Uncle Adam had gone searching for the missing Colonel Timothy Pickering and the Essex militia regiment. There was no militia marching behind him. As Uncle Adam got close enough to speak, Jason took a deep breath to calm his nerves.

"Your father would be very proud of you," said Uncle Adam. "When you told me what you were doing, I thought it was impossible, but look at that line." Adam leaned over in the saddle to admire the long line of militia companies. "There are nearly twenty companies here."

"Thank you, Uncle Adam. It helped that most of the Watertown, Cambridge, and Brookline minutemen were already here." With no authority other than his instructions from Heath and Warren, Jason had gathered every militiaman and company that marched up the road and set them in the line. Twice, he had to move the line of militia as it grew, and he got more familiar with the terrain. He spread them in a single rank to lengthen the line. It was imposingly long, but it needed a second rank to carry off the ruse.

"It sure would help if the Essex regiment would come. Did you find them?"

"They're up on Winter Hill." Adam pointed to the bigger hill to their North. "That's the best-equipped militia regiment I ever saw. They all got good firelocks, bayonets, all their kit, and they even wore brown coats like a uniform. If they marched fast, they would be here in no time."

Jason's heart leaped. *Finally, something is going right!* "Are they marching?"

"I doubt it."

Jason clenched his fist. His lips were tightly pressed together. It took every ounce of Jason's self-control not to scream. "Did you tell Colonel Pickering the regulars are coming this way and that I need him?"

"I did, and he said lieutenant colonels don't give orders to colonels."

Jason gritted his teeth and closed his eyes for a moment. "Did you tell him that General Heath had ordered this stand?"

"Of course I did; Jason and I mentioned Warren too. He didn't know nothing about Heath's promotion. He thinks you and Heath are acting beyond your authority. He says he won't let radical hot-heads push him into rash—"

"Radical hot heads!" shouted Jason. Wicked became restless and tossed her head. "I've done everything humanly possible to avoid this war!"

"I know that," Uncle Adam held out a hand toward Jason, "but he says he had no word from the Committee of Safety and would not oblige his militia to fight the regulars without the blessing of Congress."

"His militia? It's the Massachusetts militia!" shouted Jason. His outbursts were making Wicked nervous. Jason had to hold tight to her reins.

Uncle Adam waved his hand in dismissal, "There was no turning that man's heart. He won't come down from that hill unless the Provincial Congress orders him to."

"Damn! God damn him to Hell!" shouted Jason. Anxiety squeezed his chest so he could barely breathe. His line was too thin. The regulars would sweep them aside. The plan would fail.

With a slight side nod to the militia line, Uncle Adam said. "Jason, this is what we got, and you're making 'em nervous." Jason saw that the militiamen had noticed his outburst. He smiled and waved, trying to appear confident.

"Here they come," said Uncle Adam.

South of them toward Watson's Corner, Jason saw a couple of regulars on horseback, spyglasses out, sizing them up. A half mile behind them was a long red column of regulars. Jason glanced at his own line.

"Butchers and bakers and candle stick makers," said Uncle Adam, "Against all the king's men."

"They only have to hold just long enough." Jason held up two fingers. "Two volleys. Until Heath hits the regulars from the rear." The militiamen were all standing up now, shouting and pointing at the advancing redcoats. If he didn't do something they would run before the regulars even got here. Maybe bring together the commanders to try and stiffen their resolve, but he had no drummer to beat assembly, nor a bugler, no signal flags.

"Uncle Adam, please ride to the far side and ask all the commanders to assemble in the center. Then come back, and I'll join you shortly." Jason rode off in the opposite direction.

"Commanders!" Jason shouted while riding down the line. "Assemble on me!"

After riding down the whole line shouting his request, he rode back to the front center. Slowly, a heterogenous collection of men, some on horseback and some afoot, gathered around him.

"Gentlemen, the regulars are coming this way." That was a stupid observation. Every one of them could see the long column of redcoats marching toward them. "General Heath hoped they would see us and turn toward Boston, but they didn't. The battle is coming here." Jason tried to hold their eyes. He knew few of them and wondered how he could convince them to fight a battle they were unprepared to fight. "In front of us is a brigade of regulars, but they are tired from marching all night and short of shot and powder. Behind them is the bulk of the Massachusetts militia in hot pursuit. If we can hold them in place, they'll be caught between our anvil and General Heath's hammer. We will crush them between us and end this war before it gets started."

They stared past Jason at the advancing scarlet column with big round eyes, like moonstruck deer.

"But you said they weren't coming."

"I know, but—"

"They got more than us," said another.

"On this side," Jason was feeling desperate, "but General Heath has at least two thousand militia right behind them." Jason didn't know how many men Heath had, but two thousand sounded good. "If we can hold them for just two volleys, then we will outnumber them."

"What about the Essex regiment? Are they coming?"

"No, they aren't. We'll have to fight without them."

They looked at the column of regulars, then at their own line. Without any dismissal, they started to drift back to their militia companies. "Hold your fire until they get to that rail fence, then let them have it. Keep firing until they retreat!" Jason shouted to their retreating backs. Not one acknowledged Jason's orders.

"Gentlemen," said Robert to his assembled commanders. "We are going to show these country people the grandeur of the British Army. We will march in column up to that plain" he pointed to a flat pasture about two hundred yards in front of the rebels. "Then incline left until we are on a line parallel to the rebel line. Speed must give way to precision and appearance. Belay route step, the men are to march in step, knees high as on parade, and I want the colors flying. Pray place the cannon in the center with my color guard.

"What of the rearguard? The enemy is still pursuing," said Nesbitt.

"When I begin moving the brigade from column to line, move your regiment into a line of three ranks facing to the rear. Keep at least a hundred yards between your line and the back of the front line. The Yanks will leave their column and form a line too. That should slow them. Don't shoot until they force an engagement. Charge them with the bayonet, if you must, to keep them back. I intend that we will strike the rebel army in front of us before we are pressed too hard by our pursuers." To the bandmaster Robert said, "It would please me if the band would play 'O'er the Hills and Far Away' as we march into position, then on my signal play 'God Save the King'."

"M'Lord, you want us to discontinue 'Yankee Doodle'?" asked the bandmaster.

"Yes. I do not want to provoke the Yanks but impart an appreciation that they are standing against their king and the might of the British Empire."

"I thought I was too old to get scared," said Uncle Adam, watching the regulars' parade in front of their line. "My butthole's tighter than a frog's arse."

Jason and Adam were both mounted in the middle of the militia line. Normally Jason would have laughed at his uncle's irreverence, but he could feel anxiety tightening his chest. His heartbeat was so fast that he wondered if he was going to die of apoplexy before a British bullet killed him.

Watching them approach, Jason saw little sign the regulars were as tired as he hoped they were. They stepped high, marching in near-perfect lockstep and assured pace. In only a few minutes, they were a little more than a hundred yards away, just out of musket range, arrayed parallel to Jason's line. The regular's line was not as wide as the Yankee militia, but three ranks deep with cannon in the center.

Jason marveled at their martial beauty. Each regiment carried its standard, and a color guard carried the Kingdom's flags to the center, and the cannon unlimbered next to them. A chance ray from the setting sun glistened on polished bayonets like wet saliva on the shredding teeth of a gruesome monster.

"This must be how a dragon's mouth looks just before it eats you," said Uncle Adam.

The regular's band marched to the center next to the Kingdom's flags. They faced right, and on a signal from the commander, the band struck up "God Save the King." The entire array of men on both sides of the plain came to attention. The regulars started singing.

> *God save great George our king,*
> *God save our noble king,*
> *God save the king!*

Jason heard the men in his ranks singing the familiar lyrics. Not all of them, but many more than he had expected.

Send him victorious
Happy and glorious
Long to reign over us
God save the king!

In a flash of understanding, it occurred to Jason that a lifetime of loyalty to the king would not vanish in a day. He remembered singing to the same anthem as the French surrendered at Quebec. A year later, after the defeat at the Battle of Sainte-Foy, the same music was played as Jason stood at attention over the mass grave of many Royal Americans, including his father-in-law.

Looking at his wavy line of motley-dressed militia farmers and tradesmen, a stab of guilt pierced Jason's conscience. *This is treason. The king would see it no other way.* In the regular's line, however, every red-coated soldier enjoyed the king's warrant. Their flags and banners were emblazoned with symbols of his kingdom. The might of the British Empire backed their deeds. *What authority do I have? A commission from a Provincial Congress.* The entire idea of Massachusetts sovereignty equal to the king sounded foolish.

When the last note played, Jason heard the regular's Brigade Commander roar out, "Brigade!" He was at once answered with "Battalion!" in perfect military echo. "Forward! March!" The drums began to beat in perfect unison, and two thousand regulars surged toward Jason's hundreds.

"They're getting skittish," said Uncle Adam.

As Jason watched, several men broke ranks and started running. He spurred Wicked and rode along the front of his wavering line. Wicked could feel his tension and reared up. "Hold!" shouted Jason, one hand tightly on the reins, the other holding his musket in the air. There was no military echo of his command.

Fire and smoke belched from the regulars' cannons. Jason flinched as he felt the wash of the passing missiles, followed by the boom of the cannon. He turned around and saw the cannon balls scatter the nearest militia company. Then, as he stared in horror, the entire American line dissolved, and the militiamen ran into the woods behind them, disappearing in moments. Seconds later, Jason and Uncle Adam were all that remained of his faux army.

"Christ on a stick," said Uncle Adam. Jason stared at him round-eyed. To his front, the regulars were still marching toward him.

"Time to get the hell out of here," said Uncle Adam and the two men spurred their horses and galloped off the plain.

Robert pulled out his watch, "Less than five-minute delay." He closed the watch and put it back into his pocket. Majors Lane and Mitchell were staring at him in unabashed admiration.

"M'Lord, two cannon shot and an army destroyed," said Matthew in near worshipful wonder.

Robert nodded, "Don't mistake this success as a victory. The war has only started. Quickly put the brigade back in a column so we may escape. If we push the men, we may cross the Charlestown Neck before dark."

Chapter Thirteen

Five o'clock p.m.

Quock marched behind Corporal Tidd amid a seemingly endless column of militia. Of the enemy, there was little sign. Occasionally, they would see a piece of abandoned equipment, a hat, bayonet or belt. When these articles appeared, a militiaman would run off the road to snatch it up as a souvenir, but most often, the bayonet was bent or broken, or the hat torn and useless. If the regulars were abandoning good equipment some lucky militiamen ahead of them in the column had already picked it up.

The marching would often stop, only for minutes sometimes, other times longer, and then resume without notice. Other times, they would have to run to keep their place in the column. Just outside Menotomy, the column stopped for so long that the Lexington men sat down, pulled out their pipes, and smoked until the marching resumed. There was never an explanation for the sudden stopping and starting, and after a while, they stopped asking their officers.

If the enemy were absent, their works were everywhere. Outside Menotomy, Quock and his fellow militiamen saw thick columns of smoke rising above the town. When they entered the town, they passed the residue of battle. Burning buildings everywhere. Sometimes, they would see where a house had stood, and nothing was left but smoldering wood and the blackened chimney. Other houses were riddled with musket shot or large gaping holes from cannon fire. Quock had never seen such devastation.

At first, the battles were fresh, and the scenes of families carrying off their dead and wounded were frequent. Crying and wailing women, mournful church bells, and the absence of children playing near the road all made Quock's spirits low. The other men had grown quiet, too.

As they neared the center of Menotomy, the column passed a relatively untouched home. A woman came to the window carrying a small boy. The boy waved at Quock. Quock smiled and waved back. The mother pointed at the long column, waved, and smiled, too.

Further down the road, another family was standing in front of their house near the road and waving at the ceaseless stream of militiamen passing by. A hundred yards later a cluster of children were running back and forth with sloshing buckets drawn from a nearby well, offering drinks of water from ladles to the passing rebel soldiers. Quock wasn't thirsty, but he took a drink from an enthusiastic young girl.

They came to a crossroads, and a small crowd of people gathered, cheering the militiamen as they passed.

"Where are you from?" a woman called out as they passed.

"Lexington," answered Lee Munroe.

The small crowd cheered. "Give 'em hell, Lexington!" shouted an old man.

The Lexington minute company spontaneously cheered in response, raising their muskets in the air in an informal salute.

"God save King Hancock!" shouted Tidd. Hancock was Lexington's most famous son, and the Lexington militia cheered again.

Speaking over his shoulder to Quock, Tidd said, "Hancock's my cousin. If they make him King, I'll be a duke or a Lord."

Quock rolled his eyes and said a little prayer against the ascension of Hancock.

Through the rest of Menotomy and following villages, the column of militiamen was hailed as victorious liberators. Quock felt like he was in a parade. The men started to laugh and joke. Quock's spirits lifted, too; his pack didn't seem so heavy, and the miles were not so long. It occurred to him that if the regulars had intended to beat them into submission, they had done the opposite. The whole people of Massachusetts were in rebellion.

Outside of Menotomy, the column began to march more briskly. When they reached Watson's Corner, Quock could see that the militia column had split. Part was heading south, and the Lexington Minute Company turned north with their regiment. The sun was setting, but the pace did not slow. Soon, they neared a water view.

"I think that's Boston's Back Bay," Corporal Tidd gestured at the water.

"Where are we going?" asked Quock. Tidd shrugged.

A few minutes later, they could see the Mystic River on their left and the bay on their right. Tidd said, "We must be headed to Charlestown. My Uncle Ben lives there. I hope the redcoats don't burn his house."

They marched through the gathering darkness of twilight. Burning buildings cast jumping satanic shadows. On the hills beyond the Charlestown Neck, Quock could see the occasional flash of musket fire against the black of hills. Without warning, a giant flash of fire lit the entire Back Bay. The roar of cannon rolled across the advancing militia.

"A broadside from a ship-of-the-line!" shouted Lee Munroe.

Quock couldn't see the fall of the balls in the dark hills. They waited for renewed firing, but apparently, the Royal Navy felt it had made its presence known and didn't fire again. The militia never stopped marching. After crossing the Neck, somebody directed them off the road and the Lexington minute company was led up a slope. After another fifteen minutes of struggling up muddy pastures, they came to the top of a hill, and the column halted. Black darkness settled on the land.

Lieutenant Lee Munroe called the men together, "Fellas, we are to make camp on this hill. The redcoats are down there somewhere toward Charlestown," he pointed down the far side of the hill into the darkness. "We are to hold this position until morning. We will send out pickets to guard against a sneak attack or the redcoats trying to break out. The rest of us can sup, but we must sleep on our arms. Sergeant Kendall will name the guard and the rotations."

After almost an hour of sitting in the dark nibbling food from his knapsack and waiting for fresh orders, Corporal Tidd came to tell Quock that he would be standing guard with Vernon.

"It took an hour to figure out who was going to stand guard first?" Quock asked.

Corporal Tidd shook his head, "Everyone thought he had something to say."

Tidd led them out to their guard post. The curmudgeonly Vernon complained the entire way. "The idgits elected over us couldn't organize a ladies' tea party; if it were up to me, we would know where we were and what we were about; there would be no damn pickets; a good tavern would be handy instead of sitting in a pasture carpeted with cow dung."

After a while, Corporal Tidd stopped, said, "Here," and then left them. Vern made no pretense of standing guard. Carping all the while, he took out his sleeping roll, laid out the ground cloth, rolled himself in his blanket and after a few minutes of low grumbling, commenced to snore.

Quock stood alone in the dark. The emotions of the day churned through his worn-out mind. One thought chased the next as tears flowed down his cheeks. He grieved for Isaac and felt desperately homesick for the Nithercott farm. He had dreamed his whole life about the day he won his freedom, but he never imagined that day would be like this one. Nearby, in the darkness, he could hear the enemy moving.

Jason dismounted from Wicked outside Heath's headquarters in Cambridge. He stretched his legs and his back and walked about a little, but he was still stiff and sore from head to foot. He patted Wicked's neck and stroked her nose without fear of reprisal. Wicked put her head down and drank from the trough at the hitching post. There was no guard at the door. A man Jason recognized walked out with his head down, not seeing Jason as he passed. Jason was too tired to call out to him. Inside, Heath was sitting by the fire, speaking to a weary but excited militia officer. Heath saw Jason and waved him in without interrupting the officer.

"They were asked to bring four days of food, but you know how they are. It won't last two days before we need to find more victuals," said the man.

"I quite agree Abijah. I have already sent messages to the Committee of Safety asking for provisions and, above all, money so that we may affect a siege," Heath waved to Jason, "Jason, come in. Are you done up? Can I beg one more service from you?"

"Of course."

"Please go up to Charlestown Peninsula and inspect the line up there. We are not sure who owns what or where the line runs. Do you know where that is?"

"Of course, I've been there many times," Jason stood with hat in hand. He didn't move to leave. "I want to explain what happened at Watson's corner."

Heath waved his hand, "Jason, there is no need. After Menotomy, my force dissolved as we marched. I had less than a thousand men by the time we got to Watson's Corner. If the regulars had known, they could have defeated us piecemeal."

"My blocking force dissolved on the first shot," said Jason.

"We are not ready for this war." Heath leaned back in his chair and shook his head.

"What about Warren?"

"He was shot in the head in Menotomy."

Shocked—Jason's head dropped in defeat.

"Oh, not that bad," said Heath, waving a hand. "Destroyed his wig, gave him a bit of a headache, but he will be alright. He's at his mother's house."

Jason was too tired to feel relief, but his sense of duty drove him on, "Do we have enough militia to lay siege?"

"Plenty, I think. The Massachusetts Congress has ordered a full mobilization, and other New England colonies are sending troops. A Colonel from Connecticut was in here a few minutes ago."

"We will have to stitch this army together like a rag quilt."

"We must begin tonight. That's why I need you to find out the front line. The fighting stopped; for now, I need someone with wartime experience to inspect the positions. Then tell me what needs to be done in the morning."

"Of course," Jason put on his hat to leave.

"Spending the night with your regiment?" asked Heath.

"I was thinking so, but I don't know where they are, and I have no tent or blanket."

"The Westford regiment is south of here outside Boston Neck. I'm sending you up further north. Come back here when you're done and spend the night. I need the advice of a man with your experience and whose politics do not confuse his judgment. We can talk over our next move in the morning."

"Thank you, William. I will be back in a couple of hours."

"Here, Jason, Abijah Pierce can escort you up. It is his regiment outside Charlestown," Heath introduced the man he was talking to.

The two men barely spoke as they rode across the Charlestown Neck. Jason was bone tired and welcomed the silence. He reminisced on the times he and Mary had picnicked with the kids on the hills above Charlestown. Even before that, they visited Charlestown when he and Mary were still courting. Atop Breeds Hill, on a moonlit summer night, as they gazed down on Boston, he had asked her to marry him. He wondered if she was safe. He ached to be home.

The night was pitch dark. Clouds blocked the moon and stars. The air felt damp, ready to rain. Fortunately, they could make out the militia line by the hundreds of cookfires twinkling in the hills. They finally came to a guard post. Abijah Pierce got down off his horse and disappeared in the dark. He reappeared a few moments later, "This is Lieutenant Lee Munroe. He can show you our most forward position."

Lieutenant Munroe was equally uncommunicative. Jason followed him up a hill through a line of sleeping militiamen. Finally, he stopped and called out in a loud whisper, "Vernon!"

"Vernon's asleep," came the response.

"Good, you should be rotating. Quock, this is Colonel Green. He's here to see our forward positions."

"Yes, sir."

Lee left Jason with Quock and the snoring Vernon. Jason wasn't exactly sure what Heath had wanted him to inspect, but he thought asking a picket what he knew about his duties and his awareness of a situation was a start. If the guard didn't know what he was doing or why, it would be an indicator of the readiness of the militia.

"Quock? Am I saying that right?" asked Jason. Jason walked over next to Quock.

"Yes sir, Quock—Freeman."

"All right, Private Freeman, what are your duties?"

"I'm guarding against a sneak attack."

"Where are we?"

"I don't know the name of the hill, but that down there is Boston." Quock pointed down the hill to glimmering lights. A cold wind blew from the sea.

"You're on Bunker Hill, and that is Charlestown. Boston is the lights over there across Back Bay. Can you see it now?" Jason pointed to Boston's distant lights.

"Yes, sir, I've never been here before."

"That's all right. We all have a lot to learn. Do you know where the enemy is?"

"Yes sir, it's too dark to see 'em, but I can hear 'em."

From down the hill, they heard a distant call, "Number four—All's well!"

"There they go. They call out like that every while."

"That's because they are a well-trained army. You can hear the other guard posts responding. That tells everyone the sentries are awake and alert, and the enemy's not about."

"Yes, sir, should I be doing that?"

"Did they tell you to call out?"

"No, sir."

"Is anyone else calling out?"

"Just the regulars."

"Then don't for now. Wait for them to change your orders. I don't want to get shot by a nervous minuteman."

"Yes, sir. Over there, I can hear them building something," Quock pointed toward the northeast. They listened for a moment. Jason could hear the scrape of picks and shovels on New England's rocky ground.

"They are already fortifying their positions. They expect a siege."

"Yes, sir."

They stood and listened to the sounds of the British Army. Jason gazed across Back Bay into Boston and tried to find a light at his home. From this distance, he could not be sure. *How will all this end?*

"Sir, you been in the army before?"

"Yes, I was in the last war."

"Is every day in the army like today?"

"Ha-ha!" Jason laughed for the first time since he had left his tavern. "Fortunately, no. It wasn't a good day for you?"

"Yes sir—well, it was both. It was the best day and the worst day of my life."

"That's war, as I remember it."

They stood quiet for a moment. "Sir?"

"Huh? Yes?"

"Are we going to win this war?"

Jason shook his head, "I don't know. Maybe win is not the right word," Jason stared into the darkness where the British army lay. "The

British Empire is the mightiest military power since the Roman Empire. I don't think we can beat them in a straight-up fight."

"What about the other colonies? What if they help?"

"The New England colonies are already sending troops. I don't know if the others will risk it, but even if all of them join us, it's not enough."

"What about the French? They don't like the British. What if they helped us?"

Jason was surprised. *Were people already thinking about conspiring with the French? More treason. How would they ever reconcile with the king?* "I wouldn't count on that. The Bourbons are tyrants. They won't fight King George to win us rights they won't give their own subjects. Besides, you can't trust papists."

"What can we do?"

"Well, maybe we don't have to win—just not lose." He shrugged his shoulders. "I don't believe our differences with the Crown are that far apart. If we can convince the King to restore our charter and recognize our rights, then there's no reason for a war."

Vernon's snoring stopped. They could hear him getting up, grumbling. He walked away from them, then the sound of urinating.

"Rights for Negroes too?"

Jason wondered who he was talking to, but the clouds blocked even the starlight; the darkness was impenetrable. He crossed his arms. "Why not? I hadn't thought of that, but yes. Anything else would be hypocritical." They stood side-by-side, silent, staring down at the lights of Boston.

"Do you have family down there?" asked Quock.

"Yes, my wife and youngest daughter live near the center of town."

"How are you going to get them out of there?"

"I don't know," Jason frowned. "How can I get them out safely—or get the regulars to leave without burning Boston behind 'em? I fear calamity for my family and my living."

The wind picked up, and Jason felt a raindrop on his face. He looked up to the black sky just as a cold rain poured down.

"Great," growled Vernon from the darkness. "The perfect end to a goddam perfect day."

Llewellyn sat on a camp stool beside a fire near the riverbank. He had a horse blanket over his shoulders for cover against the rain. His wound ached. Neither the blanket nor the fire could restore the warmth to his body. He shivered. Robert threw more wood on the sputtering fire to keep it blazing against the steady shower.

"May I join you?" asked a Lieutenant Colonel walking into the fire's light.

"Please, Alex," Robert stood up from throwing a small log on the fire. "Have you two met?"

"I'm afraid not," said Llewellyn, pushing back the blanket on his shoulders and starting to stand up.

"Good God, Llewellyn, don't stand up," Robert motioned him back down. To Alex, "Llewellyn was shot outside Lexington."

"More accurately, I was shot in the arse," said Llewellyn. All three men laughed.

"It's not serious then?"

"No. The surgeon said the bullet was almost spent. I believe the rascal had loaded his musket in haste and hadn't set the ball proper. God willing, I shall recover completely."

"Alexander Leslie is the commander of your relief, the 64th Black Knots," Robert held out a hand toward the newcomer.

"The same M'Lord," Leslie made a leg with a deep bow.

Motioning to Llewellyn, "Llewellyn Caradoc is the commander of the Welsh Fusiliers and my mentor for many years."

Leslie stepped over to Llewellyn's seat and shook his proffered hand, "Very glad to meet you. My Major is walking the lines with your Major Blunt. I hope we can relieve you shortly."

"Thank you," said Llewellyn. "My wounded and the flankers have already crossed back to Boston. I hope to have the remainder of my regiment in their beds before they are soaked."

"I can't do anything about the rain, but we should have your men off soon enough," said Leslie. "My men are just glad to be off Castle William, no matter the circumstances." He pulled his cloak up a bit higher on his shoulders. "If I may trouble you for news of our opponents, I understand there was quite a punch-up."

"I was just contemplating the action; I was," Llewellyn stared into the fire. "I regret not exercising more control of my people. Perhaps if I had moved with my leading companies into Lexington, I could have better restrained them and avoided bloodshed."

"You are being too hard on yourself," Robert waved a hand. "Your regrets are after-battle remorse. Civil war was inevitable."

"I agree with Lord Dandridge," Leslie gestured toward Robert. "Just February, Tommy sent my regiment to Salem to retrieve some cannon. If it were not for a drawbridge this war would have started in Salem."

"How so?" asked Llewellyn.

"The country people were forewarned and raised a drawbridge to where they kept the cannon," Leslie raised his hands. "By the time I forced them to lower the bridge, their rebel companions had spirited the guns away. If the bridge had been down and we seized those cannon, I have no doubt the country people would have fiercely resisted. We narrowly averted violence even without the cannon."

"So, if the governor knew all this, was our expedition a fool's errand or a deliberate provocation?" asked Llewellyn.

"Certainly not," said Robert. "The governor knew that war was coming, but he was hoping to destroy the provincial's means to resist before it started."

"The Americans cannot hope to win a war against the most powerful military on the planet," said Leslie. "I heard they are cowards. Running at the mere sound of cannon."

"Do not judge them by the first day of fighting," said Robert. "We narrowly escaped. Had we not turned north and instead tried to fight our way to Boston Neck, it could have been much worse." The rain subsided for a moment. Robert stabbed the ground in front of the fire with the stick. "It is true they could not stand in ranks against us, but they have men who know very well what they are about."

"Militia cannot hope to defeat regulars," said Leslie.

Robert pointed the stick at Leslie, "True today, but they demonstrated great perseverance and resolution. We must finish this war quickly before they can forge the mass of raw militia into an army."

"Will London send the troops we need?" asked Llewellyn, thinking about the thousands of militia he had seen. "It will take an army the size of the one we had in the last war to restore the king's peace."

"Thucydides said the three causes of war are honor, profit, and fear." Robert stood up. "Rebellion is an affront to the king's honor and a challenge to parliament's authority. As for profit, the Americans will certainly not pay their taxes now. Nor will the king meekly surrender the wealth of an entire continent." Robert threw his stick in the fire, "And as for fear, American rhetoric on establishing a republic—that will quake the knees of the British peerage." Pointing to Llewellyn, "There are no worries there. The king will commit whatever troops he must to return the colonies to their obedience, and parliament will find the money to pay for it."

"God bless America!" Leslie threw both arms in the air, "Promotion and patronage for us all."

"You're both cynics," Llewellyn admonished. Robert and Leslie chuckled.

"Ah, here they are," Robert nodded toward two figures moving into the firelight.

"Lord Dandridge," Major Blunt saluted. Blunt had no cloak; his uniform coat was soddened, rainwater dripped from his fingers, and he shivered in the cold, blowing clouds of steam with each breath. "Edward and I have walked the line. The Black Knots are at their posts, and our men are moving to the landing for transport back to Boston."

"Very good," Leslie saluted Robert, then Llewellyn.

Llewellyn returned the salute, "Colonel Leslie, you are a good relief."

Excerpt from next book in the series:

The Redoubt

The redcoats were engaged in a parade. The bulk of them marched to Quock's left, but a big section stayed directly in front. The British soldiers found the positions they wanted, stopped, and turned to face the rambling American earthworks. The drums and fifes stopped. The entire British line, seemingly thousands of soldiers, stretched across the peninsula. Their lines ruler straight.

"Quock I'm scared," whispered Jacob.

"You boys thirsty?" Vernon brandished a wooden bottle. Quock had forgotten his burning thirst. "Spruce beer. I been saving it for a special occasion. I guess this is as good any." Vernon took a deep drink and passed it to Jacob. Jacob drank and passed it to Quock.

Quock had never liked the piney taste of spruce beer, but it was sweet going down his parched throat. He handed the bottle to Warren. Warren looked at the mouth of the bottle, at Quock, and balked. Quock's face went hot with anger and humiliation. He had seen Whites hesitate like that before. Warren had qualms about drinking after a Negro. After only a second's hesitation, however, Warren grasped the bottle, tipped it up and finished it, squinting like he was drinking medicine.

Passing back the empty bottle Warren asked, "Do you practice this ritual before every battle?"

Quock shook his head, too angry to speak. "I never been in a battle," said Jacob. Vernon laughed and put the bottle back in his pack.

The drums began to beat. The long ranks of regulars marched toward them, stepping in time to the drums. They carried their muskets pointing to the sky. The tattoo of the drums competed with the whooshing and crackling sounds of the burning Charlestown. Smoke from the giant blaze darkened the sky and cinders rained down from the smoke's black clouds.

"This must be what hell is like," said Jacob.

"Some of us will find out soon enough," said Vernon.

"Prime and Load!" ordered Colonel Prescott walking along the top of the berm, stepping over their muskets, his eyes on the approaching enemy.

Quock was still seething with humiliation and anger, his fear forgotten. He was going to show Warren that he could fight as well as any white man. He had already loaded, but he checked his frizzen, pan, and flint, there would be no misfire.

"Aim low," said Prescott. He was loud without shouting. "At their waists." He looked calm as he paced.

Leaning on the berm to steady his musket Quock smelled the freshly turned dirt. He could feel the hairs prickling on his neck as he aimed at the redcoats. The unmown grass was so long it appeared that the regulars were wading in it. When they were still two hundred yards out Quock heard some men cocking their locks.

"Steady," Prescott spoke in a conversational tone and kicked up the barrel of one over eager militiaman.

When the phalanx of redcoats got a hundred yards out Prescott stopped pacing. "Wait until we can see their gaiters!"

"Why aren't they shooting?" asked Quock.

Prescott jumped down to stand on the other side of Warren and looked across at Quock. Speaking almost casually he said, "If they keep their drill, they will wait for us to shoot first, each rank will volley in quick succession, then they'll charge us through the smoke." Quock remembered from his first battles that bayonet armed regulars could run across the distance between them faster than he could reload.

"When will we fire?" asked Warren peeking over the berm. "They're awfully close."

"I'm going to let them march close enough that we can't miss, then blow them all to hell," said Prescott. Louder he shouted, "Wait for me to fire!"

The redcoats were close enough now for Quock to see sweat glistening on their red faces and hear the swish-swish of their steps as they strode through the deep grass. Quock's hands trembled. His sweaty palms slickened the smooth wood of his stock. He fought to control his breathing as he aimed at the waist of the regular directly in front of him. A rail fence blocked their progress. The front rank stopped, pushing it down. The second rank crowded behind them.

"FIRE!" shouted Prescott.

Quock squeezed his trigger. The lock snapped, the pan flashed, the stock leaped against his cheek. Around him his fellow Patriots roared out their defiance in fire and smoke.

Glossary

Military terms are not familiar to many people, and even for those with military experience, there has been an evolution in the use of common terms since the 18th century. Much of the information on ranks is derived from Don M. Hagist's excellent article "Untangling British Army ranks."

Private	Private	Lowest ranking soldier
Ranker	No American equivalent	An informal term referring to a "gentleman" serving as a private because he could not afford to buy a commission.
Corporal	Corporal	Junior noncommissioned officers (NCO)
Sergeant	Sergeant	Noncommissioned officer
Sergeant Major	Sergeant Major	Not a formal rank in the 18th century, but a designation for a unit senior NCO
Subaltern	No American equivalent	An informal term for a commissioned officer below the rank of captain
Ensign	Second Lieutenant	Junior commissioned officer. In the cavalry, ensigns were coronets.
Lieutenant	First Lieutenant	Company officers. Often commanded companies when captains were not available.
Captain-Lieutenant	No American equivalent	Commander of the Colonel's company.
Captain	Captain	Commanded companies or held staff positions
Major	Major	Staff officers

Lieutenant Colonel	Lieutenant Colonel	In the British Army, they were the tactical day-to-day commanders of a regiment. In the American militia, lieutenant colonels were usually the second in command.
Colonel	Colonel	In the British Army, colonels commanded regiments but were usually absent, serving in higher military or political positions. In the American militia, the soldiers elected their colonels, often local gentry, and they actively commanded their regiment.
Brigadier	Brigadier General (One Star)	In the British Army, Brigadiers commanded brigades of two or more regiments.
Major General	Major General (Two Star)	In the 18th century, Major Generals were, in most cases, the highest-ranking officers, commanding at a range of levels.
Lieutenant General	Lieutenant General (Three Star)	The military governor of Massachusetts, Thomas Gage, was a Lieutenant General.

Ancient and Honorable Artillery Company: Chartered in 1638 to train young officers for service in the Massachusetts militias. Membership in the company was traditionally selected from the middle and upper classes of Boston.

Annus Mirabilis: Wonderful Year in Latin. The British public dubbed 1759 Annus Mirabilis after a string of victories, including the Battle of Minden in Germany and the Battle of Quebec in North America. The victories of 1759 were considered a turning point in the Seven Years War.

Bat horse: The batman's horse.

Batman: A soldier assigned to a commissioned officer as a personal servant.

Battalion: Applied to an assemblage of two or more companies but less than a regiment. When a regiment was deprived of its flank companies, it was often called a battalion.

Boston Tea Party: In 1773, a group of the Sons of Liberty destroyed a boatload of British tea by throwing it into Boston Harbor. This action set off a series of escalating responses that led to the Revolutionary War. The moniker Boston Tea Party did not appear until 1834.

Brown Bess: The British soldier's nickname for the standard Land Pattern Musket.

Cavalry: Horse-mounted army formations that performed a variety of battlefield missions, including reconnaissance, screening movements, and raids behind enemy lines.

Charleville Musket: The French Army's standard musket.

Cob: A large stout-built pony native to England and Wales used to pull plows or carts or carry a farmer to market.

Company: A British infantry company was formally organized with 47 men, including a captain commanding, two lieutenants, two sergeants, three corporals, a drummer, and 38 privates. British army line companies were chronically under strength and usually numbered only thirty-plus.

Corps: In the 18th century "corps" was a flexible term applied to a variety of organizations. The 700 men, two battalion force that raided Concord was at various times called a corps while Lewis and Clark's Corps of Discovery was only 42 men.

Corps of Cadets: Formed in 1741 with a dual mission of providing trained officers to the Massachusetts militia and an honor guard to the governor.

Division: The meaning for the 18th century British Army was to divide—each company divided into two subdivisions—sometimes called platoons—each led by a lieutenant. Two companies formed a grand division.

Dragoon: Mounted infantry. Dragoons used horses to move about the theater during a campaign but dismounted and formed in ranks as infantry in battle. Not to be confused with cavalry.

Firelock: A musket is made up of three components: stock, barrel, and lock. The lock or firelock was the trigger mechanism. Firelock was a colloquial word for musket.

Flankers: Each British regiment had two flank companies. One light infantry and one grenadier.

Flip: Beverage usually made with beer, rum, sugar, cream, and eggs heated with a hot poker. Flips were popular in taverns in Britain and colonial North America. Most taverns had their variation on the recipe. The forerunner of eggnog.

French and Indian War: The name Americans gave to the war against the French and their Indian allies, fought from 1754 to 1763. Europeans called it the Seven Years War.

Fusil: A shorter and lighter version of the British Army's Land Pattern Musket.

Fusilier: A soldier that carried a fusil.

Grenadiers: Flank companies intended to be manned with the tallest and strongest men in the regiment. They wore special tall hats called miters to make them appear taller and more intimidating to the enemy.

Lexington Training Band: The term training band dates to King Edward the First in the 13th century. Parliament reformed the training bands into militia in the 17th century. The people of Lexington, however, were a conservative and independent-minded bunch and stuck with training band when they founded their militia. Retaining their stubborn streak into the 18th century, when the Massachusetts Provincial Congress ordered the formation of minutemen companies in 1774, Lexington stayed as a training band. (https://www.lexingtonminutemen.com/the-lexington-training-band.html)

Light-bobs: Nickname for a light infantry company.

Light Infantry: Flank company manned with "active" men, used for flanking movements, particularly in rough or wooded terrain. They wore modified uniforms to allow greater freedom of movement.

Militia: A military force raised from the civil population. In colonial Massachusetts, all able-bodied men between the ages of 16 to 60 were eligible and required to serve. Militiamen generally did not have uniforms and brought their weapons and equipment.

Minutemen: The minutemen were companies formed from volunteers from Massachusetts' regular militia. The volunteers were supposed to be younger, more active, and more politically reliable than the regular militia. The goal was for minutemen to receive better equipment, training, and pay and to be ready in a minute. The war broke out before the system was refined.

Patronage: The British royal patronage system was the support, encouragement, privilege, or financial aid that the king and the aristocracy bestowed on British subjects. The king could provide direct financial aid, land, or offices that provided financial benefit. For example, colonelcies were a form of patronage. The colonels of British Army regiments did not exercise tactical command but instead benefitted financially from selling uniforms and equipment to the members of the regiment. During the French and Indian War, Americans were promised land as patronage to encourage enlistment. After the war, the Royal Proclamation of 1763 forbade land grants west of the Allegheny Mountains. This proclamation outraged many American veterans, including George Washington, and convinced many Americans that royal patronage did not benefit them.

Platoon: In the 18th century, companies were subdivided into two platoons as firing units rather than formal units. Platoons were used to orchestrate volley firing, with one platoon firing while the other was loading.

Pope's Night: In the 18th century Protestant dominated Massachusetts, Pope's Night was an anti-Catholic holiday. It was adopted from the British Guy Fawkes Night and celebrated on November 5. The celebrations involved drinking and riotous behavior, particularly in the working-class neighborhoods of Boston. By 1775, Pope's Night activities had become anti-British.

Regiment: A foundational military unit commanded by a colonel. In 1775, a British Army infantry regiment consisted of 10 companies: one light infantry, one grenadier and eight infantry companies. Including the regimental commander and staff, a regiment at full strength was approximately 500 men.

Regulars: A moniker Americans applied to British soldiers. Also called: King's men, King's troops, Ministry army, lobsters, redcoats, and bloody backs.

Seven Years War: A global conflict involving the major European powers led by the French and British, respectively. The war began in 1754 in North America between French and British colonial militias and their corresponding Indian allies. France and Britain declared war on each other two years later. The war ended with the signing of the Treaty of Paris in 1763, with the French surrendering their North American colonies to the British Empire.

Sons of Liberty: Appearing in all thirteen colonies, the Sons of Liberty were an informally organized, underground, sometimes violent, political organization that resisted Parliament's "Intolerable Acts." Their flag had nine vertical bars, four white and five red. The Sons of Liberty skirted the definition of terrorists. They were not an organized military nor represented a government, but their violence was infrequent, usually spontaneous, and directed at political enemies rather than a policy of murdering innocent people to terrorize the population.

Tory: In England the Tories were an off-and-on-again political party ideologically mostly conservative on the political spectrum and often represented landowners and rural interests. In the 18th century, being a Tory was more of an expression of sentiment rather than membership in an organized political movement. In the American colonies, loyalists, people opposed to independence and republics were often labeled Tories.

Whigs: Like the Tories, for most of the 18th century, there was no organized Whig political party. King George III ruled through a collection of "Kings Friends" of all political stripes, leveraging royal patronage and influence. The Whig label was usually applied to the more progressive politicians and often represented industrialists and urban interests. In the American colonies the Whig label was usually associated with people seeking confrontation with the British Parliament and were suspicious of the king's motives to his colonies.

—— Dana's Chocolate Chip Cookies ——

1   cup salted butter, softened
1   cup sugar *(I use Turbinado sugar. Same calories, but the taste is subtly different.)*
1   cup light brown sugar packed
2   tsp. vanilla extract *(I always fill the teaspoon until it overflows into the spoon bowl.)*
2   large eggs
3   cups all-purpose flour
1   tsp. baking soda
½   tsp. baking powder
1   tsp. sea salt
2   cups chocolate chips (whole bag). *(I use dark chocolate.)*

Instructions
1. Preheat oven to 375°F.
2. Line a baking pan with parchment paper and set aside.
3. In a separate bowl mix flour, baking soda, salt, baking powder. Set aside.
4. Cream together butter and sugars until combined.
5. Beat in eggs and vanilla until fluffy.
6. Mix in the dry ingredients until combined.
7. Add 12 oz package of chocolate chips and mix well. Chill dough for at least two hours if you don't want your cookies to spread. I often do not chill – still works and tastes great.
8. Roll 2-3 TBS (depending on how large you like your cookies) of dough at a time into balls and place them evenly spaced on cookie sheets. (or, use a small ice cream scoop).
9. Bake in preheated oven for approximately 8-10 minutes. Take them out when they are just **BARELY** starting to turn brown.
10. They will be soft, so let them sit on the baking pan for 2 minutes or move the whole parchment with cookies still on before removing to cooling rack.

Acknowledgments

Deep gratitude to Sunbury Press for taking a chance on my novel. Great appreciation to Sunbury's founder Lawrence Knorr who personally edited the draft while working on his PhD. A good map is indispensable to historical military writing, so praise to Monica Tucker-Harley for creating the map. Enormously grateful to Joanne Elder who created my author's website, led my marketing plan, and provided wise counsel on all of the former. Thanks and praise to my Beta readers, most particularly Paul Molholm and Tiffany Graham. Their insightful reviews were invaluable.

While writing this novel I conferred with a mountain of sources including Nathaniel Philbrick's Revolutionary War series, particularly "Bunker Hill," which was an eminent authority. I relied heavily on Mark Urban's "Fusiliers" for details of the 23rd regiment of foot, (the famous Welch Fusiliers) and the workings of the British Army. Numerous other books aided my efforts to breathe life into the characters, D. Michael Ryan, *Concord at the Dawn of the Revolution*; *Prelude to Revolution*, Peter Charles Hoffer; *The British Are Coming*, Rick Atkinson; *The Men Who Lost America* Andrew Jackson O'Shaughnessy; and *An Empire on the Edge*, Nick Bunker to name just a few of the many excellent sources I consulted. *The Journal of the American Revolution* and Wikipedia also aided me to provide context or illuminate everyday life in the 18th Century.

For articulating Quock's life and times Joyce Lee Malcom's *Peter's War* was vital. For understanding his world view I relied on more contemporary sources including the gritty narratives of Ta-Nehisi Coates *Between the World and Me*, James Baldwin *Another Country*, and Spike Lee movies, particularly *Da Five Bloods* were huge influences. Lastly, I was inspired to write this novel while standing on the North Bridge in Concord Massachusetts and walking the well-preserved trails and buildings of the Minute Man National Historic Park.

I worked hard to write a plausible novel with an authentic voice set at the dawn of the American revolution. Nevertheless, many historians will disagree with my views of those long-ago events. Despite all the outstanding and well researched references noted above, the historical record is chock-full of contradictions, contending contemporary eyewitness accounts, and plugged with huge knowledge gaps. The gaps and differing views provide the novelist with plenty of room to create a narrative. On the other hand, unlike the nonfiction historian who is duty bound to spell out diverging evidence and a range of possible motivations, the novelist must choose the characters' actions and consequently disregard other well-founded options. All factual errors, mischaracterizations, and affronts to historians' theses are solely mine and I beg your forgiveness.

About the Author

Dana R. Dillon served twenty years in the Army as an Infantry and Foreign Area officer. Dana led an infantry platoon, commanded a company, and served on battalion, brigade, and division staffs. After eight very rewarding years, Dana transferred into the Foreign Area Officer program where he studied international relations and worked with foreign militaries. When Dana retired from the Army, he went to work as a national security and international policy analyst at the Heritage Foundation a Washington DC Think Tank where he published over 100 articles

and a book *The China Challenge: Standing Strong Against the Military, Economic and Political Threats that Imperil America*. Additionally, he appeared many times on national news programs on CNN, MSNBC, FOX, NPR, VOA, and local TV and radio shows. After 9/11 he went back to work for the Army at the Pentagon where he currently serves as an intelligence analyst. In his profession, Dana studied the background and roots of many wars and revolutions noting the similarities in origins and goals across wide cultural gaps—knowledge he found relevant when studying the American Revolution. Dana has many fond memories of the Infantry and is sympathetic with his historical predecessors. Despite the warlike nature of his profession, Dana lives peaceably in Fairfax, Virginia with his true love, their children, and dogs.

Follow Dana on his website at **https://danadillonwriter.com**.

www.ingramcontent.com/pod-product-compliance
Lightning Source LLC
Chambersburg PA
CBHW011347010726
47493CB00011B/2990